"I love a book that makes me laugh out loud on one page and gasp on the next."

"You are helping keep the tradition of being literate alive."

"If Indiana Jones can get away with it, I guess you can."

"…a look into the dark hearts of human beings…"

"…characters we care about, plus comic relief…"

"A conclusion I bet Agatha Christie would envy."

"…Are you getting the idea I loved this story?"

"Are all of Tom's books mysteries? I would like to buy more of his books, if you have more."

"The truth is rarely pure, and never simple."
—*Oscar Wilde*

Other books by Tom Bender

Run For It!
Cemetery Plot

Avenging Allison

By Tom Bender

Copyright © 2017 Tom Bender

Book Production: Jessica Friend
www.jessicafriendphotodesign.com

Cover painting: Jim Zatlukal
(from a photo by Jennifer Sherwood)

Cover design: Jessica Friend

First edition: January 2018
ISBN: 978-0-9996583-0-7

Printed in the United States of America

DEDICATION

This book is for my wife, Beth

—and—

for *all* of our children, and *their* children, and *theirs* as well (including some sweet kids we picked up in player trades) *and* spouses, too (so help me!)

(This book is also for all my wonderful manuscript readers)

(Special thanks to Jane Ellen Freeman, author of Jeremiah Lucky and the Guardian Angel *and other works. For an introduction to Jane's books, go to JaneEllenFreeman.com)*

(Special thanks to cover artist Jim Zatlukal, emeritus professor of art, State University of New York at Buffalo)

DEAR READER,

This is a work of fiction. All the characters in this novel come straight from my brain; they have no real-life counterparts. Furthermore, all of the *settings* are fictional too. That is, although there *is* a southern Illinois, and there *is* a Shawnee National Forest, *my* southern Illinois and *my* Shawnee National Forest are not real. Nor is my city of Stanton, nor any other town or place in the story, even if they have the same names as real places. I made up these places, just like I made up the characters. So if you are from southern Illinois, or you have the same name as one of my characters, or you just think everything in life should be real, go ahead and be amused. But don't you believe it: *nothing* in this story is real.

As my Cambridge Dictionary says, what you have here is "the type of book or story that is written about imaginary characters and events and does not describe real people, or deal with facts."

You also will find as you read the story that my fictional people are living in my imagined version of 1987. Thus they have no access to cell phones, the Internet, or other high-tech equipment. Why? I like it that way. It allows them to go about their lives free of encumbrances to actual life that I see in the present time. Hey, it's my story. But, I wrote it for you. That's the one thing about it you can believe. I hope you have fun reading it.

Tom Bender, the author

THANK YOU, THANK YOU!

Readers of the manuscript for this book included my wife Beth, my friend Jane Ellen Freeman, and a number of my children and grandchildren and other relatives and good friends, including Sarah Bender, Jim Bender, Betsy Slone, Jim Downey, Ned Jenison, Natalie Lavengood, Ann Perdew, Will and Jen Sherwood, Amy Dunlea, and Jeremy Reynolds. (And me, of course; I was forever rewriting and fixing it.)

Beth read the story often as it evolved. Jane Ellen Freeman read not one but two drafts.

The painting on the cover is by our friend Jim Zatlukal. (The painting represents two characters in the story: Allison Morrison is giving her sister Mallory a piggyback ride.)

Several people critiqued particular aspects of the text. Among these experts were a private pilot (Jim Downey), a family physician (Will Sherwood), and a southern Illinois newspaper publisher (Ned Jenison).

The book design and production are by Jessica Friend. Jessica produced my last book, *Cemetery Plot*, too.

My thanks to all, and to anyone I—heaven forbid!—accidentally left out of these kudos.

If you find any mistakes in this book they are my fault.

PEOPLE YOU'LL MEET IN THE STORY

Barber, Caitlin, a high school girl
Beaulieu, Helen, society editor
Beets, Hamilton, Illinois State
  Senator
Beets, Sugar, a country singer
Billingsley, Carla, a neighbor child
Biro, Antony, a thug
Buford, Francis, a secessionist
Bush, Hattie, a high school teacher
Chen, Lincoln (Link), a lobbyist
Chen Chuntao (Joy), Link's wife
Dudley, Leonard (Lenny), editor in
  chief
Foltz, Madelaine, housekeeper
Harris, Franklin, city editor
Hirsch, Otto, a thug
Holman, Harrison (Harry), a
  headhunter
Hutmier, Mike, the new city editor
Kimball, Mr., a high school principal
Long, Bert, chauffeur
Lockhart, Henry, a private eye
Marx, FBI agent
Meyer, Melissa, campus reporter
Morrison, Brian, state desk reporter
Morrison, Cindy, a country singer

Morrison, Allison, a daughter
Morrison, Mallory, a daughter
North, Abi, state desk reporter
North, Fred, Abi's husband
Perkins, Mr., a father
Perkins, Dougie, a 10-year-old
Pickens, Thomas, an attorney
Ritchie, Gradison, publisher
Rivers, Stone Mt., a country singer
Roper, Louis, a reporter
Smart, Ed, a forest ranger
Smart, Betsy, his wife
Smart, Daniel, a stringer
Soto, Arturo, Caitlin's boyfriend
Stevens, Garland, a professor
Sutter, Eric, minister/policeman
Thomas, Lee Ann, a reporter
Three Mexican boys
Tully, Jake, Eagle County sheriff
Walker, FBI agent
Wright, Jeff, a lobbyist
Wright, Olivia, his wife
Wright, Julie, a daughter
Wright, Justin, a son
Wright Nathan, a son

ONE

On a warm and sunny Saturday afternoon in April of 1987 I went to an art show at the Stanton University Art Center in southern Illinois. The exhibit was of erotic photographs by Robert Mapplethorpe. There'd been a big flap about it. In fact, County Commissioners had tried to shut it down for what they called "a pornographic assault on community values." But it hadn't closed. Seven of the photos got cordoned off, and visitors were warned that these seven were particularly offensive, and that several others were also of "flagrant sexual impropriety."

Mapplethorpe's work, while interesting to some art enthusiasts, was offensive to a lot of southern Illinois people. Otherwise there wouldn't have been such a flap. And two of the offending photos were of children. But at any rate, bottom line, the commissioners' fury didn't prevail, and people who wished to do so got to see what most would consider perversions. So, for some people it was like a girlie show at a carnival, with bold men, and women as well, peeping in. Titillating, I think the word is.

Lee Ann Thomas, my boss on the state desk at the Stanton Post-Times, was with me at the show. Like me, she was curious to see what the excitement was all about. It was the final weekend for the show, so if you wanted to see it, it was that day, or Sunday, or never.

Lee Ann and I got separated, of course; when you go to an art exhibit it's to each his own. But at one point I spotted her and watched as she paused in front of one of the photographs. She cocked her head at it, sort of like a sparrow, then scrutinized the identification placard. I got close to her and asked her what she made of the shot. The photograph she was looking at, she finally said, was "homoerotic and sadomasochistic."

I considered the picture. It showed—well, I'm not going to say what it showed. "Is that your considered opinion?" I said.

"No. I read it on the card there."

"Are you aroused?"

I got her New York City smile. Although we were working for a newspaper in flyover country—near the Shawnee National Forest in southern Illinois—she kept her New York City attitude close at hand.

"What do you think this is about?" she said.

"1 don't know," I said. "Besides sex, you mean? Rebellion? I mean, this guy isn't going along with the crowd."

"I would agree, yes," she said. "A different perspective, whether we want to consider it or not. Integrity."

"Integrity?"

"I think so," she said. "Art has to be honest, ethical, don't you think? Otherwise it's just wallpaper. Or worse—trying to sell you something, even deceiving you. Think about Nazi art, Soviet art—propaganda, getting people with the program. On the other hand, this stuff tells the truth, at least as this artist sees it. You might not like what interests him, but he isn't lying to you about it."

"Art's usually ahead of me," I said.

"That's the point, isn't it? There's a new mood in this country, don't you think? We're going to a new place and we don't know where it is. Art is one of the road signs."

I glanced sidelong at her. We were just having a peek at some stuff at a show in the art center, and here she was, giving me a larger perspective. The downside was that sometimes when she got intense about things it signaled the onset of one of her depressive episodes. I always watched for those. It seemed to me she might be getting into one now.

"I never got a lot out of the soup cans," I said.

She smiled at that, and I relaxed a little.

We chose not to walk through the cordoned-off exhibit. I just wasn't ready to go there, and she wasn't, either. We strolled to the exit, her heels clicking on the parquet floor.

Bright sunshine—and one, lone picketer, who hadn't been present earlier—greeted us as we went out through the glass doors. His placard on a stick said "Repent This Abomination." He was discussing his position with another man. We overheard him saying, "No, I have certainly *not* been in there." We moved along.

We stopped further on along the walkway to take in nature's own artistic offerings. Down in the ravine to the east the redbuds were in blossom—tiny cranberry-colored beads strung along slender crooked limbs. The dogwoods were on display too—white and pink flowers that always excited me—a sign of spring. But fragile. Dogwood blossoms don't last very long.

For all the natural beauty around us, I was suddenly so focused on Lee Ann I was mute, as if I'd just seen her for the first time. Love comes upon us like that, does it not? We are caught by a turn of the head, a look in the eye, a touch. Vermeer knew this.

His people, such as the girl in the turban, her earring gleaming, surprise us. So it was with me, at this moment, with Lee Ann.

We stopped at a little café with tables on the sidewalk and got some wine. Lots of people—college kids, couples, elderly people, together and alone, people with various kinds of dogs, one guy shouldering a talkative parrot—went past our table. It was warm, maybe 65 degrees. I shifted in my chair to fit better, and also to get the light out of my eyes.

"You remember a character named Connie Rivers?" Lee Ann said.

"Huh?"

"In *The Grapes of Wrath*, they're on the road, it's hard times, and this boy, Connie Rivers, the father of Rose of Sharon's new baby, is with them. One day Connie Rivers is gone. Just gone. Steinbeck never mentions him again. Never. In the entire book. After the boy disappears Rose of Sharon is never the same."

"Steinbeck? I don't recall the scene," I said. Lee Ann had lost her husband like that, less than a year back, a deep razor cut to her heart.

"Did you find that stuff sexy?" I said.

"Did you?" she said.

"Well, maybe. But I think about sex all the time anyway."

"You do." When she smiled her look was acerbic, that slight twist to the side of her mouth. Her lips were just a tad thin, suggesting she might bite, rather than suck, your lips.

We sipped our wine.

"I'm glad we went," she said.

"Because?"

"Well," she said, drawing it out, like maybe she didn't want to tell me, "I've been trying to get a fix on where I am. The Midwest. The South. Wherever it is. Seeing all those people in there made me feel good. Whether they ultimately liked it or not, they were deciding for themselves. To my mind, that tops the community values alleged by a few powerful people." She frowned. Then she said, "I see they're doing Salvador Dalî in May. Won't that be fun?"

She was assessing life in Stanton, Illinois, a lifetime away from New York City. When she first arrived, she believed all there was west of the Hudson was sagebrush. But I had hope; there were surprises for her like the art center.

We gave the sun and mood fifteen lazy minutes, watching the passing people.

I looked around for a waitress.

"They're happy to greet you, you know," she said, "but they don't want to see you go. That's why you never get the check. It has to do with their social side."

My turn to smile.

The waitress came, a college girl, childish and cheerful, with some hope about the tip, but not too worried about it either. Part of the education provided to me by my two daughters was to tip liberally. Mallory had worked, and Allison had filled in from time to time, at a luncheon place, Chierney's. Allison was just 15, under-age, when she started, but she got away with it. "These girls don't make that much money," Mallory had said to me once. "Sometimes they have a baby at home."

The two girls were quite different from each other, Mallory diminutive, physical, strong, a field hockey player; Allison taller, less physical but self-possessed, assured. A photo I had posted on my refrigerator caught them in something of a role reversal, Mallory riding piggyback on her sister, the two of them joyful, clowning around. The image flashed through my mind.

Lee Ann and I headed back to the office, a twenty-minute walk in the cooling day, and climbed the rickety stairs to the second floor of the Post-Times building. Lee Ann went to her desk and I to mine. I started opening mail from stringers, measuring clippings.

Stringers clipped and saved their stories that we printed, and pasted their clips in a string. About once a month they sent us the strings and we paid by the column-inch. We had about forty of these people on contract, writing up social news and calling in anything that seemed important to them. One of the stringers appeared to me to have set some sort of one-month write-up record, with no less than forty-four column inches on club meetings. Occasionally we got tips on real news from stringers. Then we went after stories ourselves. Lately there hadn't been much of that.

"Should I do a column on Mapplethorpe?" I asked.

Lee Ann frowned. "It's closing. Besides, Harris wrote something."

"I missed it."

"I'm sure you did." She gave me the New York glance, meaning she thought I should lighten up about Franklin Harris. Not likely; for a while, Harris had been my boss, and I'd concluded he was a smug and self-righteous jerk.

TWO

On the first Saturday in May, about a month after Lee Ann and I went to the Mapplethorpe show, a ten-year-old boy in a town at the extreme south end of our circulation area, a little burg called Everest, saw something falling in the sky—or said he did. The boy's name was Dougie Perkins and he had a reputation for making things up. He turned to his buddy and pointed to where he'd seen it. It was gone. His buddy didn't believe him. *A story like that, well. Sort of like a flying saucer. And from Dougie Perkins.*

So the whole thing should have died right there. Except. In one of those moments when kids talk about things they've been thinking about, in bed, tucked in for the night, before falling asleep, the boy insists to his big brother that his story is true. Because his brother hears this in a sort of confessional bedtime moment, he thinks about it. Then, casually, a day or so later, the big brother tries it out on a pal. Like he doesn't believe it of course, but what does his pal think? That's the way of big brothers. They pay attention, even when they don't let on that they do.

Then they take your story to court, trying it out on a pal of their own.

That's how I got downwind of the story—not from the big brother but from a pal of *his*, a 16-year-old high school junior named Daniel Smart. Daniel was having a Coke with me in a café in a small town called Connerville. The two towns, Everest and Connerville, happen to be very close to each other on the north edge of the Shawnee National Forest—about a forty-five-minute drive south from my office in Stanton.

It was a week after the little boy had his vision. I had driven down to Connerville to interview Daniel to be our stringer in the area, replacing the present stringer, a woman fairly well connected in town but who hadn't seemed up to the job. All we got from her was Eastern Star kinds of stuff. She didn't want to dig and she certainly didn't want to ruffle feathers. The Post-Times was trying to build circulation. To build circulation you have to report interesting local news, and sometimes reporting it ruffles feathers. Lee Ann had decided to replace the woman. Thus my mission to consider Daniel.

Daniel was in line to be editor of his high school paper beginning in the fall. He'd done some sports reporting for us—calling in the scores of games, that kind of stuff—which was why I'd looked him up.

"So, Daniel, are you interested in being a stringer?"

"Sure. But I may be working at the lumber yard too. I got a job there for the summer. Part-time, mostly Saturdays."

"Good for you. It shouldn't be much of a problem, not for what I need from you. What will you be doing there?"

"I'll just sort of be in training— out in the yard."

We sipped our drinks.

"Will you feel comfortable asking people questions, checking things out?"

He thought about it. "I do that for the school paper."

"Doing it with an adult might seem a little—ah—pushy."

He shrugged. "I ask questions in class. My teachers are okay with it."

I smiled. "Good."

"I'd be replacing Mrs. Penny?" he asked. "She doesn't want the job anymore?"

"We've decided to terminate that relationship, Daniel."

"What does that mean, Mr. Morrison?

I liked his question; his interest in seeking clarification, getting to the bottom of things, suggested he'd be a pretty good stringer. "It means we let her go and she didn't take it too hard."

He appeared satisfied.

"Anything going on around here that I might not know about? Right now, I mean?"

He considered. "I don't think so, but I don't know for sure. I'm gonna figure out a kind of beat, you know? Where I check on things?"

"Good," I said. "But remember, we can only pay you for what we use." You manage a news beat like cops manage theirs—get around to see people and places and check things out. Having a beat seemed like a lot of work for what we paid. But I wasn't going to discourage Daniel at this point because I thought he was a good prospect for us.

We fooled with our drinks.

"I did hear a kind of weird story," he said. "Like maybe for your column?"

I guessed from his referring to the column that his family took the Post-Times, which was good. Not a lot of people around Connerville and Everest took the paper, which was why we were trying to find a better stringer than Mrs. Penny.

I filled my column, *Outtakes*, with stuff I picked up here and there that didn't qualify as news but that readers might enjoy. For example, I stood up for a knife thrower one time—an "impalement artist," as he called himself, although I'd hoped that wouldn't happen in my case—and wrote a column about the experience.

"What's the story?" I said.

"I have a friend, Randy Perkins? He lives over toward Everest. His little brother was down at Green Lake and saw something falling out of the sky. At least that's what he told Randy. He—his little brother, I mean—said it looked like a person."

"Huh. You're talking about a lake near here?" Several small lakes dotted the Shawnee National Forest area south of Connerville, but I'd never paid attention to exactly where they were.

"Yeah. It's a couple of miles south." Daniel smiled for the first time. "I'm not swearing to this story, you know."

"How old is Randy's little brother?"

"Ten, I guess."

"He was down there swimming? What?"

"I don't know. There's a little park in there."

"With his parents? A picnic or something?"

"No. Just this buddy of his."

"Pretty young to be going to a lake in the Shawnee without his parents," I said.

"You see kids that age. It's only a half hour or so on your bike. From Everest or from here, either. A lot of kids go down there.

I could hear Lee Ann: *Little kids alone in that forest?*

"When was this?" I said.

"Last Saturday."

"Does his brother believe the story?"

Daniel smiled. "Randy thinks his little brother is, ah—" He searched for a word.

"Fanciful?"

"Yeah, like that."

I shrugged. "Well, thanks for telling me. You never know. Sometimes the darnedest stories turn out to be true."

Daniel and I finished our drinks. I gave him a one-page contract to read, sign, get one of his parents to sign, and mail back to me.

***

As I drove back to Stanton I thought about the little boy's story. A person falling? How much trouble would it be, really, for me to go down there and check it out? As matters stood, it was just a story a kid told his brother, and his brother told Daniel. But it might reach the ears of the sheriff. Rumors and tall tales get around, especially in small towns. So I'd be wise to be quick about it.

When I got to my little rental unit, where I'd been living since my wife Cindy and I separated, I phoned Daniel to see if he and his family were going to be okay with the contract. His dad had co-signed, he said. I asked him if he could get his buddy Randy Perkins to bring his little brother down to the lake so I could get the story firsthand and then have a little help from the three of them looking around.

"You think it's a good story?" Daniel asked.

"Intriguing, I have to say."

"You want me and Randy to just go look around?"

"Nah. I'll come down." It was too early in our new relationship for me to send Daniel off on an errand like that.

"When?"

"How about tomorrow afternoon?" I said. That would be Sunday. My two daughters lived with their mother. They hung out with me every other weekend. This wasn't my weekend. So I had nothing better to do.

"I'll call you after supper," Daniel said.

"Good deal."

Daniel called at six o'clock. We were to meet Randy and his little brother Dougie around two o'clock Sunday at the lake. He told me a way to get in there.

About five minutes after Daniel hung up I got another phone call.

"Morrison," I said.

"Yes. I believe you're planning to meet my ten-year-old son tomorrow down at Green Lake?"

"To whom am I speaking?"

"Well, that would be obvious, don't you think? My name is Raymond Perkins."

Uh oh. "Yes, Mr. Perkins, that's true. I'm a reporter with the Post-Times. Our new stringer, Daniel Smart, and—ah—I guess—ah—your sons Randy and Dougie, are meeting me there at two o'clock. We're checking out Dougie's story, you know, about maybe seeing something falling—ah—around there?" Said like this, by one adult to another, it sounded stupid.

"How old are you, Morrison?"

Not too many months before, when I'd been digging into a story about a dead boy, I'd been through a similar inquisition, that time at the hands of a guy who was putting pins in a county map to keep track of people he thought were perverts. Long story. Lucky for me, I was safely out of that picture. That was another time. But now this. Abuse of children was a hot topic in America these days. When I was a kid, one summer my brother Bob and I hitchhiked out to Yellowstone Park and got jobs. My Aunt Bessie and Uncle George, with whom we lived, didn't think a thing of it. Neither did Bob and I. Lots of people gave us rides when we stuck out our thumbs. We had a great time out there and then hitchhiked home. Maybe we should have been worried; it never crossed our minds. But that was another time—a time of innocence in America, as some people said.

"I appreciate your concern, Mr. Perkins," I said, "but let me ask *you* a question. Do you believe Dougie's story or do you think he made it up?"

"What business is that of yours?"

"I'm a newspaper reporter, Mr. Perkins. "I'm just trying to find things out."

THREE

After hearing from Mr. Perkins I drove—how to say, resolutely—the four miles or so from my little rental unit to May Street in Stanton, where the Post-Times building was located, parked in the office lot, and walked about a block to a little hamburger joint, The Press Club.

The dingy, long, narrow café, redolent of frying burgers, tried to replicate the mood of newspaper hangouts long gone. To the left as you walked in was the bar, backed by a mirror doubling the number of bottles. To the right was a long row of booths, reminding me of a Disney tunnel ride. I waved at Arnold, tending bar, and he returned the salute.

Taking off my jacket, I shook off a few raindrops, tossed it before me onto a bench, and slid in across from Lee Ann. This being Saturday night, we'd agreed to meet for a bite to eat.

She smiled. That smile said she was suspicious of everything and everyone, and had no patience with people she thought to be fools. Besides the NYC attitude, she had an urban disdain for the outdoors. She was uncomfortable with nature—that is to say, anything off the pavement. She saw me as her protector against southern Illinois. Which of course is where she'd wound up.

"You're late."

"Yep."

I liked her ways as a boss, and accepted her attitude and biases as part of the package. For two months now we'd been the two-person state desk team at the Post-Times, she in charge, me the staff. Her best management attributes were her brains, her wit, and her wide gaze.

I was quite different: quickly and completely focused. Throw a stick and I'd chase it, as one of my army buddies once observed.

Our different styles, she with the wide gaze and I with the quick focus, helped explain why Lee Ann was the state editor and I worked for her. Other reasons included her relative youth, her charm, and her looks. Our publisher had a thing for her, I was certain.

"You're late."

"What have you been up to?" I said.

"Just before I came over here I had an interesting exchange with our new society editor," she said.

"Oh?"

"We were the last two people in the office. She stood up to get out of there, looked my way, and said I had 'the most interesting aura.' That's what she said, '*aura.*' Then, while I was trying to figure out what she meant, she changed the subject. 'Oh, the literacy project,' she said, like she was remembering something, or somewhere she was supposed to be. 'Would you get the lights?' With that, she gathered up her stuff, jumped up, went to the wall, swept down every switch in the panel, and ran down the stairs. There I sat in the dark, thinking how weird."

"Strange indeed," I said.

Lee Ann grinned. "Ditsy. But I don't get the aura thing." With her index finger she traced a halo in the air around her head.

"An aura is not a halo," I said.

"No?" I got the glance.

"There was a guy named Edgar Cayce," I said. "You know that name?"

She shook her head.

"He was a healer and a mystic. According to people who follow him, we have some sort of energy field around us. It glows. They claim they can see this glow—people's auras."

"People *follow* him? Where did you hear that?"

"I did some work at the naval station in Norfolk. It's about twenty miles from Virginia Beach, where the Edgar Cayce A.R.E. is located. Cayce people call it 'the Beach.' They have some sort of psychic research going on there. I've driven past the building."

"A.R.E.?"

"Association for Research and Enlightenment."

"Psychic research?"

"That's what they say."

"The Navy?"

I laughed. "No, no. Well, now you mention it, who knows? But what's this 'literacy project'?"

"I have no idea."

Given Lee Ann's wide gaze, she was perhaps wondering why I, an army guy, had been at a navy facility and knew about Edgar Cayce.

Arnold set my martini in front of me and I took a sip. Icy cold. "What do we know about this new society editor?" I said.

"Her name is Helen Beaulieu. The story is, her husband is the new manager at the bottling plant. Maybe they came here and she needed a job and applied to be the society editor. And maybe she's gotten in with those faculty wives."

Stanton society revolved around university people, as I knew.

Our new society editor and her husband had come to us from Toronto just a few weeks back. I'd heard that much. She looked like a petite runway model, if there is such a thing. What would mystify Lee Ann was *why* a farmland newspaper such as ours would have a society editor.

Skipping Lee Ann's aura—I didn't get that stuff—I told her about the falling man in the Shawnee Forest, and reported my plan to go down there. Then I told her Mr. Perkins' reaction to me inviting his son Dougie to join me.

"Ten years old? I'd consider your proposal a little strange myself. You're not still thinking of going?"

I shrugged. "I don't need the boy to come. Our new stringer, Daniel, will be there, and maybe his buddy Randy, the kid's older brother. The three of us can go in and look around."

She sipped her wine. "Tell me about this new stringer."

"He's a nice kid. A quick study. Not afraid to ask questions. He's the one who suggested the falling man might make a column."

She nodded absently. "Let's say the boy did see something falling in the forest. How would you get in there? Isn't it pretty much a swamp?"

"It's a forest, not a swamp. Well, I guess there's some cypress swamps in there. It's all mixed up. There's farms in there, too. Private land. Anyway, it's huge—farms, forest, swamp— all mixed up. And it covers most of the bottom quarter of the state."

"It seems unlikely to me that you'll find anything," she said. To Lee Ann, the south end of our circulation area, which bordered the Shawnee, was even more primitive than Stanton proper, full of snakes and southern preachers. Yet, she wanted to bolster our circulation down there—precisely in the territory where I'd be going.

"If you believe the child," she said, "there had to be an airplane, right?"

This widening of her gaze suggested she was at least considering possibilities.

"First," I said, "I need to find a body—or something, anyway. Otherwise, no story."

"Okay," she said, leaning back.

Her jacket had slipped slightly, baring her shoulders, and in the dim light she looked younger—and far too New York for Stanton, Illinois.

"But you still have to ask yourself, falling from what?" she said. "It wouldn't have been an airliner, right? You don't just open an airliner door and jump. Well, I guess a guy did that once, with a parachute and a rucksack full of money. But I never heard of it happening again. And if somebody jumped from an airliner, or some part of an airliner fell off, we'd have seen something on the wire." She paused, recalling something else. "I remember an engine blade came loose from one of those big airliners once. I think it broke a window and sucked a guy out. Over Albuquerque, I think." Her face registered that horrific vision. "Always keep your seat belt fastened," she said. "But, again, that's the only time I heard of anything like that. So you'd have to think it's local—one of those little private planes. Maybe we can find out if a plane like that lost something or other—or maybe one of its occupants. I don't know. Do people fall out of those little private planes?"

I shook my head. "That would take a lot of checking. That's why I'm going down."

She narrowed her gaze to my plan. She didn't much like it. "We can't spend much time on this. If you're so set on it, why don't you let our new stringer—what's his name, Daniel?—poke around."

"Daniel Smart."

She was right in one respect; I was burning energy on something frivolous. She and I were trying to cover about a third of the state, about thirty-five communities in an area the size of Hong Kong. Not to be funny, but Lee Ann couldn't even understand what people south of us were *saying*, let alone what they were thinking. A factor in her favor was that her responsibility was not to cover things so much as manage them. Our stringers covered the day-to-day news. She managed the process. As to big stories that broke, we had to be selective about the time we ourselves gave to them. Otherwise we'd go under. Sad to say, we hadn't had a big story yet, not as the new state desk team, anyway, so the issue was moot.

The more I thought about it, I just didn't feel right sending Daniel into those woods, on a mission like that, without me. If we were going to look, I had to lead the exercise.

"Let's say the boy really saw a person falling," Lee Ann said, indulging herself in my quixotic enthusiasm. "You have to wonder if he, or she, was alive, don't you think? Like maybe a parachute didn't open?" She frowned. "Or maybe the pilot was dumping somebody. It's happened, you know. They were dumping people out of airplanes in Argentina not so many years ago. Alive. Into the ocean." Her blue eyes stared at me. Her depression had just kicked in, like somebody threw a switch.

Her very sad personal history had involved seeing her husband shot dead in the street in New York City. Occasionally her mind and heart went to that. If anybody did see auras, hers would reflect that.

"Want to come along?" I asked. "It's actually very pretty down there. Tom Sawyer whitewashes the fences."

She looked up, shaking her head. "Are you forgetting about Injun Joe chasing Becky in the cave?" She thought for a moment, shaking her head. "I'm not going squishing around in some swamp looking for whatever's been in there for seven or eight days."

Her vivid imagination was, in this instance, part of her problem.

"Sooner or later you have to get down there, I said. "It's beautiful. Oak and hickory forests. Rolling hills. Beautiful lakes. Some swampland, sure; but that's not the main feature. It's a forest. You'd enjoy it."

"Tom Sawyer, huh?"

I had a hamburger. She had one too. Doing so, we got the top of the menu. Before she got into her burger she scooted away from the coat that had slipped off her shoulders.

"As I recall from high school physics," she said, "things fall at about thirty-two feet per second per second squared. That's in a vacuum, I mean. Let's say an airplane was at five thousand feet—"

I think I have a fetish for pretty shoulders.

"As I understand from jump school—"

"What's that?"

"Parachute training," I said.

She looked me in the eye, the burger suspended. "Parachute training?"

"Well, you go in the army, sometimes they offer you that. I took it, but I didn't stay in that line of work."

"I didn't know you were a paratrooper. As you understand it, what?"

"I wasn't a paratrooper. I took the training. Your body creates a lot of drag. The fastest you're going to fall is about a hundred and twenty miles an hour."

"They just told you that."

That was the Lee Ann I liked. Sly. Sort of sassy. And she wasn't worrying anymore about how I'd chosen to waste my Sunday. Or thinking about her husband getting shot.

FOUR

I was a few minutes late getting to Green Lake, and I wondered if the boys were already in there. To be honest I was anxious about them being in the forest alone. I had a bad taste in my mouth about southern lakes. I'd once driven by a beautiful lake in a forested area in Tennessee and stopped at a carry-out across the road and inquired about building lots. The young woman at the counter looked at me and said, "In *there?*"

I've often wondered what she knew, or feared. Whatever it was, her question sealed forever my interest in acquiring a secluded building lot in a thickly wooded area near a southern lake.

I hurried along the wooded path, the air heavy with the cloying smell of undergrowth. Thin shafts of sunlight pierced the thick canopy above me, spotlighting bits of ground cover.

Like the Boy Scout I'd once been, I'd come prepared. I was wearing laced-up boots, khaki pants tucked into my socks, and a long-sleeved shirt. In my backpack I had bug spray to ward off mosquitoes and ticks, a first-aid kit, work gloves, and tape to mark our trail so we could get back out. Hanging from my old army gun belt I had a canteen of water and a hunting knife. In my pocket I had a little compass. No Tenderfoot I.

My thoughts were interrupted by human sound—people on bicycles behind me on the path. Stepping aside, I watched a young couple peddle past. They wore backpacks. She smiled and waved. She was pretty—a wood sprite on a bike. He was square and dark. Didn't wave. Their passage diminished my discomfort in the setting.

Soon I got a look at the lake. Blue. Green Lake was blue! Just a few acres, surrounded by forest. Three boys were wading in the shallows with small nets, clowning around, apparently hoping to catch a small fish. I didn't see any boats on the lake.

Four teenage girls in shorts and halter tops had spread out a blanket near the water. They were laughing and talking and making a pretty good show of not being interested in the boys. After looking me over they went back to business.

The young couple I'd seen on the path had set down their bikes and discarded their backpacks near the edge of the trees. Beyond them stood my young stringer, Daniel Smart, and another young man, presumably his buddy Randy Perkins. They were gazing off into the trees. No surprise, I saw no sign of a younger boy. I went up to them, introduced myself to Randy Perkins, and asked after his brother.

"My dad's mad at him. He's always going off somewhere."

"I thought your dad was mad at *me*."

"Well, yeah; that too." He gave me a funny look and glanced at Daniel.

I asked what he thought his brother saw.

He turned back to me and shrugged. "Who knows? He's always got a story."

Daniel had walked away, heading down toward the lake. As I followed him down, one of the boys in the water shouted triumphantly. A tiny fish flopped around in his net. He moved toward the bank, pretending he was going to throw it in among the girls. They all shrieked. He dumped it back into the lake.

The boys' clowning around in the water brought to my mind that it could *in fact* be dangerous here, and that parents always ought to be interested in what their kids were up to.

As we watched, a pickup truck came down a gravel road to the lake, pulling a boat on a trailer. Seeing this, I assumed I could have driven my car in. The driver backed down to the lake edge and his small boat floated free. He had a 10-hp motor, a gas can, two rods, tackle, a cooler, a Styrofoam cup—worms, I guessed. Tying off the boat, he drove up and parked, then walked back down and pushed off into the lake. I envied him.

We walked back up to the edge of the trees. The young man and the girl were just standing there looking around. He appeared to be about eighteen and she maybe a year or two younger. She said hello. We said hello.

"Going on a hike in there?" she said.

In answer to her question I simply nodded.

"Wanna come?" Randy said.

Oops! He wasn't helping.

"Sure." She looked at her boyfriend.

The young man frowned. "We gotta get some firewood."

"Come on," she said. "It'll be fun."

Fun? More like a snipe hunt, I thought, with the possibility of something unpleasant ending up in the bag.

"Come on," she repeated, smiling at him. "We can get wood later."

He gave a little shrug. "Okay."

She was Caitlin. He was Arturo.

I couldn't come up with an excuse to say no. "I'm a reporter for the Post-Times in Stanton," I said. "I heard there was some illegal trapping going on in here." I gestured toward Daniel and Randy. "I asked these two boys to help me look, see if we could find any traps."

Randy looked cross-eyed again. I knew what *that* look meant: now I was spreading BS about animal traps.

Caitlin vamped Arturo a bit more, cranking up his enthusiasm.

"Okay," I said. "We'll spread out and keep our eyes peeled for traps. And do be careful. The ground cover could obscure them. You don't want to step on one."

The boy and girl nodded.

We went in, me mindful of snakes and whatever else was in there. A few minutes in, Randy yelled, "What does poison ivy look like?"

Daniel yelled back before I could. "Shiny green leaves. Pointy. Red edges. Waxy-looking."

"I think I'm in it," Randy yelled.

"That's why Mr. Morrison has his pants tucked in," Daniel yelled. "Ha, ha, ha."

"Rats."

Five minutes later I heard Randy say, "Wait up. I gotta take a leak."

"Look down," Daniel hollered. "Do *not* pee on a yellow jacket nest."

"What?"

"They'll follow you home. Just like in the funnies."

From time to time I caught glimpses of Arturo and Caitlin walking along together. Daniel and Randy, on the other hand, remained separated but couldn't tune it down. Yak yak yak. Or at least Randy, anyway.

"Hey, I found a fishing reel," Randy hollered.

"In here?"

"Yeah. No good anyway. All rusty."

A few minutes later I walked face-on into a big spider web. It wrapped around my head like silk. Forests have big, hairy spiders. I ran my hands over my face and neck and swatted my body all over. Then I stood still. Nothing moving. That I could feel, anyway.

We went on for a few minutes. I again heard Daniel's voice. "Watcha doin' up there?"

"Nothing. Just looking."

I guessed Randy had climbed a tree. I hoped he hadn't spotted a body up there. "Don't get hurt," I called.

About ten minutes later Caitlin cried out.

"What's up?" I called.

I got no answer. Then Arturo called back. "It's okay. She just turn her ankle."

"You want some help? I've got tape."

"No. We are okay," Arturo called. "You guys go on."

The boys and I walked on for about fifteen minutes and then moved over a few yards and started walking back. I figured there'd be a terrible smell if a body was lying around anywhere near us. All I saw and smelled was the new growth I occasionally waded through. The plants made it hard for me to breathe.

We got back to where we'd left Caitlin and Arturo. She called out that she was okay.

About five o'clock we got out of the woods.

If there were any secrets in there, the dense foliage had hidden them from me.

I suggested to Randy that he get some Calamine lotion for his legs. He nodded without rolling his eyes. He and Daniel split. Absently running my fingers over my body and through my hair, I sat chatting for a while with the young couple. They appeared to be in love, and excited about it.

***

On Monday I wrote a column about hiking in the Shawnee. I did relate my experience in the spider web. What I didn't mention was searching for a corpse.

The reason I gave in the column for the hike was the same one I gave Arturo and Caitlin: illegal traps. We hadn't found any, I wrote, but it had been an interesting day. I didn't name my fellow hikers; personal privacy and personal safety were becoming bigger issues, and we in the newsroom were sensitive to that.

Late Tuesday afternoon, after the paper came out and landed on doorsteps, I got three surprising phone calls. The first caller said I was an idiot. "How so?" I said pleasantly. He hung up. I wondered if it had been Dougie's father, one of the few people who knew what our hike was really about. Then I got a more interesting call. "Mind your own business." That was it. It was the voice of a grown man.

My third caller was Jake Tully, the new sheriff of Eagle County, which included a fair chunk of the Shawnee Forest, including Connerville and Everest.

"Mr. Morrison?" he said, "I think your column did a disservice to people in Eagle County law enforcement."

I hadn't yet met Sheriff Tully, but here he was, angry with me already.

"In what way, Sheriff?"

"What's this about illegal traps?"

"As I pointed out in the column, Sheriff, we didn't find any."

"Well, you left the impression that somebody's trapping illegally in my county and we're not on top of it."

"I'm sorry. But you know, Sheriff, there just may be something to it, because I heard from a couple of people before I heard from you—one of them telling me to mind my own business."

Long pause. "I'll leave it at that, Mr. Morrison. But if you know about a crime, your first job is to report it."

"I'll do that."

I was thinking, *in a pig's eye, Sheriff.* In my experience, sheriffs didn't make personal calls complaining about minor irritations. So why did he call me?

***

On Wednesday, darned if Eagle County deputies didn't go into the forest by Green Lake and run a boat along the edge of the lake. I knew this because Daniel called to tell me.

"They had bloodhounds!" Daniel said.

Bloodhounds? Huh. Why didn't I think of that? Of course, where do you go to rent bloodhounds?

"Were they looking for illegal traps?" I asked.

Daniel had no idea what they were looking for, or if they found anything. Yet, I was impressed that he'd called the sheriff's office to try to find out what was going on.

Lee Ann was pleased that I was giving Daniel his head. "We have to let the stringers do the work."

Thursday we printed what we had: *Bloodhounds employed in Sheriff's Department's search in Shawnee National Forest near Green Lake. No details being provided.*

Once again I chose not to mention Dougie Perkins' story of a falling man. The sheriff just might have been looking for illegal traps. I wanted readers to think so, anyway. It made it less likely that people would go in there looking for whatever Dougie might have seen.

***

It crossed my mind to go see if my friend Eric Sutter knew anything about the deputies and the dogs. Eric held down two jobs, one as a Lutheran pastor and the other as a crisis consultant with the Stanton police. A lot of law enforcement agencies, not just the Stanton cops, turned to him for help in resolving domestic disturbances, so he had a good sense of police matters across our circulation area. He also had FBI sources. All this made him a great source for me; I just had to be discrete about what he told me.

I would have tried to find him first thing Friday morning, but I got distracted by a confrontation with one of my associates at the paper.

FIVE

As I sat down at my desk on Friday morning, Franklin Harris, our city editor, sat himself down in the wooden chair that served my visitors. The chair wobbled a bit. He wet his lips. I had a hunch he was going to get after me about something. I'd worked for him for a while before coming to the state desk. I knew him to be smart but smarmy, fawning over people, his thick eyeglasses glistening, while he squeezed his subject cynically for information.

Our publisher, Gradison Ritchie, had moved me from the city desk to the state desk, cutting Harris' empire down to two—himself and one reporter. He was angry about his diminishing status. But as Mr. Ritchie explained, he wanted to put more focus outside of town, where circulation might more easily grow.

Harris had told Mr. Ritchie that moving me off the city desk was bad deployment of limited resources. "We need strong circulation where it counts. We can't be cutting city desk staff."

I didn't want to make Franklin Harris upset, and had said so to Mr. Ritchie. "Don't worry about it," he'd said. "He's just jealous. He's a useful guy, but he doesn't have your background." What he meant was, I'd developed skills in my army job that he hoped would enhance the work of the state desk. My army job, in a classified organization, had been to interview European applicants for technical positions with the U.S. government. Trained in interrogation, and with my background in communication research, I was occasionally able to get the truth out of people, it was true. That skill, he hoped, would put more zip in our state coverage.

"You and Lee Ann are a good team," Mr. Ritchie said. "That's the way I want it. Harris will settle down."

Well, he hadn't. Whether our publisher knew it or not, Harris and I were locked in quiet combat—he the experienced old editor who had come with the furniture, me the new and troublesome creature of management, with new and dubious ideas. That's the way he saw it, anyway.

"So how is our state correspondent this morning?" he said, giving me an inflated and imaginary title. His eyeglasses glistened.

"What's up?" I said.

"May I give you some advice?"

"Please do."

"Blundering into the woods with those kids, stirring up Sheriff Tully down there, is the worst kind of mistake, the kind that could ruin our reputation."

"I'm after a story, Franklin. What do you suggest I do?"

"I suggest you seek counsel from people such as myself who have some experience around here before you rush out and cause trouble."

"I was looking for firsthand information, Franklin. It seems to me if we suspect illegal trapping is going on, we should try to get the story firsthand." I wasn't about to tell him about the falling man; then he *would* think I was nuts. And, for all I knew, he'd find a way to tip Sheriff Tully to my real reason for traipsing into the woods.

"Well, it doesn't sound like much of a story to me. But if you feel you have to pursue such trivia, you can't go off half-cocked like that. Look, when you act like a bull in a china shop it works against us all."

"As far as I know, Sheriff Tully was interested in my column," I replied. "He called me about it. He even sent dogs in there." My nose was getting longer; I could feel it.

"My sources are not at *all* sure that Sheriff Tully favored the column," he said. "Nor was your little foray into the woods in the company of children wise in and of itself." He then oozed a little malarkey. "Don't get me wrong; I'm trying to help you here."

"Well, thanks, Franklin," I said. "By the way, who's telling you how Tully feels about my work?"

He stood up. "I'm glad we had this little talk, Brian." With that, he hiked it, leaving my question about his sources unanswered. He was from Cairo, down where the Ohio River joins the Mississippi, and the sound of the south was in his voice. But he had no trace of southern charm about him.

Having watched him depart, Lee Ann was eager to have her own chat with me. "We can use the conference room," she said.

The conference room, the back wall of the newsroom, had for many years been the private office of our editors-in-chief. Recently, however, our publisher, Mr. Ritchie, had had a new office built for the editor, glass-enclosed and positioned near the stairs. The new office not only provided a good view of the newsroom, it also offered easy access to the street.

Lee Ann and I squeezed into the dusty conference room. On the back wall was a darkening oil painting of Mr. Ritchie's father, who had bought the Times about fifty years back and combined it with his own paper, The Stanton Post, to create The Stanton Post-Times.

"Did Franklin help clarify things?" Lee Ann said.

"He suggested I seek his counsel, stop blundering about."

She smiled. "What do you hear from Tully?"

"Nothing since Daniel called in the lead about the dogs."

"So what are you up to?"

"I'm going to go see Eric. Find out what he's heard."

"Okay. You talk to Eric. Then what?" Her eyes flared just a bit. Her feelings were not hard to read: She wanted me to stop chasing a child's unlikely story and get back to work.

I called Eric at the church. He was there, and, yes, he had a few minutes for me.

SIX

Eric was pastor of a church called Christ the King, and had been for about five years. The handsome building was ten years old. The congregation was still paying off the mortgage.

I entered to the quiet of a big, empty place. Brightly quilted liturgical banners festooned the walls around the sanctuary. Eric stepped out through the door from the sacristy and greeted me silently with a hand raised. Coming toward me, smiling, he cut quite a figure. He was six feet two and handsome, a clotheshorse. Today's getup featured a soft tan linen suit over a light-blue clerical shirt with a blinding-white dog collar.

"You're looking natty," I said.

We walked into his cluttered office.

"I don't think they've found anything yet," he said. "A body would have to be dealt with. A forensic team would go in. Alerts would go out. None of that is going on."

I told him about the call I got from the boy's father.

"The guy's got a point," he said. "Would you have let one of the girls go in there with a stranger when she was ten?"

We parted company, he to a couple of visitors, I to a walk back to the office. What did I think? I thought my friend believed my intense focus sometimes obscured the bigger picture from me. He was right. Lee Ann, too. Me and my dumb ideas.

Lee Ann spotted me as I came into the newsroom from the stairs. Her beautiful almond eyes registered concern. "Oh, there you are. I was about to call the church. Daniel called. Somebody tried to snatch Dougie Perkins."

"Oh, boy."

"He's safe. They're looking for two men."

"What do you know?"

"He was at that lake in the forest with some pals."

"How come? School's not out yet."

"It's what they call an 'in-service' day for teachers. So, no school. Anyway, two guys apparently chased him into the lake."

"What guys?"

"They don't know. Dougie ran into the lake. I guess that saved him.

"The other kids saw this?" I asked.

"So Daniel said."

"I swear, that Daniel."

"Well, actually he got it from his friend Randy," she said. "Randy was there babysitting his brother because their parents were at work."

As I stood pondering, two men in dark suits showed up at the top of the stairs. You see FBI guys and you know. Our new editor in chief, Leonard Dudley, led them into his office. I'd been studying Lenny, hoping he wouldn't turn out to be like his predecessor, Frank Fosden, known to me as Fearless Fosdick, now happily late of the Post-Times.

Very quickly I was invited in. They were showing Lenny a couple of sketches. The sketches depicted the two guys as Lee Ann had described them. "We hope you'll put these in your next edition and invite comment," one of the FBI guys said. He handed Lenny a card. "Let's be clear. We don't identify people who call with tips. Anybody who helps us will be safe."

I smiled. That sort of promise always seems thin to me.

With apologies to Lenny for commandeering his office—thus politely suggesting he leave—the two turned to me. "We understand," said the slighter of the two, "that you've been pursuing a story line that maybe somebody fell from an airplane in the Shawnee Forest. Can you tell us about that?"

***

Thus, cordially, we began a conversation that eventually led to me going mid-morning Friday to the FBI office in Springfield. The reason I went was for a lie detector test. True story. One of the two, the smaller fellow, whose name was Marx—"Agent Marx"—specialized in conducting lie-detector tests. He was a slightly overweight and earnest-sounding man, around my age, I guessed, and he kept raising the stakes as we chatted, turning our conversation into a sort of adversarial debate, like he was slowly turning up a burner on a gas stove. In the end he suggested, in a friendly way, that I take a test, "so we can clear your name." This seemingly off-hand baloney confirmed for me that my pursuit of the falling-man story had got me on the FBI's short list of people who might possibly be connected in some way to whatever they were fishing for. I'm sure FBI agents are nice enough with their families and neighbors. And they do important work. Somebody's got to do it. But I've always felt that their friendly conversation is fake.

When I took the test, it involved not so much my answering questions while the equipment was running, but in Agent Marx gradually trying to convince me to confess whatever he had in mind "and get it over with."

I was aware from my army job that this was how lie-detector tests actually worked—the detection equipment being, in large part, a stage prop. I remained blandly comfortable in my story, reasonably friendly, not letting on that I knew Marx was trying to trick me into admitting I was complicit in whatever he had in mind. Thus the interview ended. My alibi, my position at the paper, and perhaps FBI awareness of my military background appeared to help satisfy the fibbies that I was clean. *Maybe* that was how they felt, anyway.

***

Although there appeared to be no new leads in Everest, two FBI agents had been down there poking around. I heard from Daniel that they were still there. Their presence kept me from going down there. Who knew what they felt "complicit" might mean?

The good news in all this, at least for Lee Ann, was that it reined me in to concentrate on other tasks. We were moving into the summer period of county fairs, with their endless judging of livestock, pastries, jellies, baton twirling—seemingly every product, animal, or skill that the judges could measure. To report all this news, we inserted extra state pages into the paper, and even used agate type, a smaller face, to publish details. I agreed to start concentrating on all this stuff beginning Monday.

We were doing the bread-and-butter part of the state desk job, and I recognized its importance. But I wanted a break in the falling-man case, and I wanted to be in on it.

7

SEVEN

About nine o'clock on Friday evening, as I dozed in a chair in my rental unit, occasionally aware of a noisy thunderstorm, I was brought straight up by a thunderous bang. I began hearing wailing sirens. Grabbing my raincoat, I got in the car and followed the wails.

The University Art Center was on fire. Most of the east end of the building was down. To the left of the mess, a banner hung on the facade of the building: "Salvador Dali: May 4-28."

The burning wing housed not the Dali collection but art from South and Central America and Mexico—a lot of it historic and rare. I'd especially liked a particular painting, "Los Sueños de mi Madre"—"dreams of my mother"— a montage of four moments in the life of a woman, always with the same young, smiling face. This painting had been destroyed, or at least damaged, I supposed, along with a lot of other beautiful Hispanic art.

As I'd arrived I'd seen an ambulance pull away. So at least one person had been hurt or killed. The thunderous explosion had awakened me at just about nine o'clock, so, unless the casualty was a firefighter, it was the watchman.

Shrouded in darkness, rain and smoke, people in raincoats were coming out with art works wrapped in plastic drop cloths. Other people were standing inside the tailgate of a semi, collecting the rescued art. The efficiency of all this impressed me.

WSTV was at the scene; two young guys had cameras rolling. As I watched they homed in on a man carrying a painting.

I saw city editor Franklin Harris arrive, looking disheveled. His young associate also appeared. A fireman pointed toward the street, apparently directing them to retreat. Smoke rose and soot fell, and black snowflakes covered firemen, trucks, and hoses. This wasn't my beat, so I stayed back.

A woman carrying art put it down in front of me, balancing it on her foot as she got a better grip.

"How bad?" I asked.

"Like a bomb went off in there," she said, and picked up the piece and went on.

A table had been set up under an awning. It held a coffee urn and bottles of water. I got myself a bottle. As I turned away from the table, near me stood campus reporter Melissa Meyer: work boots, bare legs, skirt to her knees, buttoned coat, watch cap, rain-drenched face. She was talking with a cop. She screwed up her face. When she turned away from him she seemed to be negating what he was saying, her arms waving awkwardly in the sleeves of the big coat.

I moved closer. "Melissa?"

"Oh, Brian."

Nobody calls me Brian, least of all Melissa.

"Oh, Brian."

I held her. "It's okay."

She gulped down tears. "Lee Ann—" She wept uncontrollably.

I had a stirring in my gut. "Lee Ann? Lee Ann what? What about Lee Ann?"

"She was here." She clutched me to herself, weeping.

"What?" I stood holding her. "What, Melissa?"

"She was here, Brian. She was— They found her. Up there." She turned and lifted a hand, little in the sleeve, toward the entrance to the museum. She buried her head in my chest.

I couldn't get it. A thunderstorm? Lightning? Lee Ann? "Lee Ann what?"

Melissa's muffled, snotty voice. "Up by the door." She pointed. "Right after the watchman—the watchman. They took him first."

I knew this much: It was about ten o'clock on a rainy night. We were at the scene of a fire at the art center. Melissa was crying. Rain was falling. I could feel it on my face. I was not dreaming. For some reason, Lee Ann had been here.

I shook her. "What?"

She shook her head.

I turned to a man carrying a piece of art. "Where do they take people?" I said.

"People? You mean like injured people? Well, to the hospital, I suppose." He had an NPR sort of voice. A woman joined him. "How may we help you?" She looked fresh and certain in the rain. In charge. She was about to tell me to retreat to the protective tape line. Looking at me, she thought better of it.

I got to my car. I thought about Melissa but turned on the ignition and left.

The woman in the hospital emergency room favored me with the hope of cutting through bureaucracy. "Well, let's see if we can find out."

In the end, Lee Ann Thomas, my boss, a person I loved, my hope for the future, however unlikely, was dead. She was dead. I sat in a chair in the emergency room too dumbfounded to weep.

EIGHT

I drove back to the art center and looked around, honoring the yellow tape. The rain had stopped. They were cleaning up. Melissa was still there. She bellied up to the tape and gave me a long hug.

"Do you have any idea why she was here?"

Melissa, always the reporter, said she had found out why, maybe. Lee Ann had misplaced her credit card, and thought she might have left it when she went to the Dali show. And, yes, she had. Anxious about it, she'd arranged to pick it up. Somehow, the job fell to the watchman. To get it from him, she arranged to be at the art center at 9 p.m., when he was locking up.

"Her credit card?"

Melissa nodded. "The bomb squad is here," she said. She looked at my coat, not my eyes, while she talked to me. "They've set up a command post in the Engineering building. I'm so sorry."

"It was a bomb?"

"Yeah, I think so. They're in there shooting film and picking up bits and pieces."

"You were in there?"

"Nobody's getting in. The television people are apoplectic."

"Who's talking to Lenny?" I meant Leonard Dudley, our editor, and the entire cast—the desk people, and so forth.

"Louis called in." She meant City Editor Franklin Harris's young associate, Louis Roper.

Lee Ann was dead.

Melissa put her arms around me, squeezed, turned away and plodded off in muddy boots.

In time, as I stood watching, two fire trucks pulled away, leaving just one. Art retrieval trickled down. I saw a white van coming and going. I figured it held bomb squad people, taking what interested them to the Engineering building. I remembered being here with Lee Ann, walking through the Mapplethorpe exhibit, having a glass of wine. She'd mentioned the Dali exhibit, coming back to see it. I could have gone with her. I could have paid. I could have. Hopeless tears flowed down my cheeks. I embraced Lee Ann's dark spirit.

When I came back to my senses I thought the storm had quit, but it came back, dumping more water on the half-destroyed building. A truck arrived with screeching brakes. Its logo, Flag County Emergency Supplies Unit, suggested that it provided, among whatever other things, emergency tarps that could be used to protect buildings and furnishings from rain damage after tornadoes and thunderstorms and such. Two men got out in rain gear and pulled down the tailgate. I retreated to the office.

***

On Saturday, we put out a bulldog edition. Everyone was focused, efficient, silent.

"Bomb Rips Art Center."

The heart of the story was this: About a third of the University Art Center, maybe seventy thousand square feet of it, was in ruins. One or perhaps several bombs were believed used in bringing down an entire section of the building. One person, Lee Ann Thomas, a Post-Times editor, had been killed in the blast, apparently a chance victim. She had been at the center to retrieve her credit card. The night watchman, found inside, had lost both legs in the blast. A fireman had been injured when a wall collapsed. Precious Hispanic art had been destroyed. Art center staff and docents had hauled a number of damaged art objects from the building and had moved other endangered pieces elsewhere inside the building. No suspects yet.

Harris and Melissa did a creditable job on the report, aided by notes taken by those of us who had also been on the scene. Even me. I did the segment on Lee Ann.

Who had done this? Why?

We assumed it was payback. Somebody was angry about the Mapplethorpe exhibit.

We reported the timeline: In the last days of March the county board votes 3-2 to let the Mapplethorpe exhibit go on. It opens in April. Sometime in the ensuing four weeks, while thousands of people from within and outside Flag County visit the exhibit, somebody stows explosives and incendiary materials around one end of the building. At 9 p.m. on May 15, when the center has just been locked up for the night, someone triggers a blast so powerful that people hear it more than a mile away. A third of the art center falls down. Yet, at press time, no one has called the Post-Times or the local TV station or the police to claim responsibility.

***

I went to the police station to talk with Eric. His eyes reflected his pain and sorrow—for Lee Ann, for me, for the madness of a bomber. He grieved with me, and I left the station and went to my rental unit to lie awake until dawn.

***

Melissa found a whiz on campus and invited him in to enlighten us as to how they investigate bomb and fire scenes. We had an extended staff meeting with him, a man about fifty or so named Arlen Lange. He'd been with the Justice Department before coming to teach at SU.

"Miss Meyer—Melissa— told me you would put up with a brief tutorial on this," Dr. Lange said to a newsroom gathering, "so I'll be watching for signs of fatigue. Then I'll invite questions.

"I know one of your editors was a victim. I am so sorry. The losses are heartbreaking, oftentimes collateral. Sometimes deliberate. Most times you don't know why some people lived and others died.

"A little personal history first: I was involved in a couple of bomb investigations in New York. I was part of the team at Sol Hurok's office when a man was killed and nine people were injured in 1972. Mr. Hurok was booking Soviet artists, and we thought that was a factor. If you don't recall the name, he was a world-famous impresario, managing and booking famous talent. We never did find out who did it. I was also involved after a bomb killed four people in 1975 at Fraunces Tavern. They picked it, I'm sure, because it's famous. You know Fraunces Tavern? George Washington made his farewell speech to his officers there in 1783."

He was right. No one in the newsroom appeared to know anything about Fraunces Tavern.

"About that tavern bombing. It was one of a string of forty-nine of them by the Puerto Rican national group, FALN. We didn't acquit ourselves very well on that one, either, but we got a few of those guys on something else a few years later. That happens too. Serial bombing. It's a calling for some people.

"What I'm telling you is that proving there was a bomb, and then finding and prosecuting the culprits, those are two different things. You can assure yourselves that the Department of Justice is involved with your people right now here in Stanton." He shrugged. "They hope to accomplish both those things: prove what can be proved about the bomb, and find the people who did it and put them away. Whether they get somewhere we'll just have to see."

Cynics in the room read between the lines: the guy's expectations, based on his experience, were low.

"Having admitted my former involvement in D.O.J. work," he said, "I want to be sure you understand I'm not involved now. So I'm more or less off the record here, and certainly so as regards actual events at the art center."

There were a few knowing smiles, his message being that he was not to be quoted. Journalists hate that.

"Now let me talk for a minute or two about process. First, the way you begin an investigation like this is vitally important if you hope to process the evidence. It's basic Who-Done-It work. There's no chance of a conviction if you don't do it right. To do it, you have to put together a team of specialists, you have to organize things, control contamination, and then go through a fairly exquisite process of identifying, collecting, and preserving things. It's like taking inventory, cubed.

"Second, the number of people who get involved may surprise you: evidence tech, forensic specialist, logistics person, medical examiner, photographer, procurement agent, safety specialist—plus, almost certainly, a structural engineer, looking at what the bomb really did."

I already knew what the bomb did. It knocked down the whole east wing of the art center and killed the woman I loved, Lee Ann Thomas.

"This takes time," Dr. Lange said. "You know how long it takes to investigate an airliner crash. It's like that."

He went on to talk about specific things all these experts did, including matters a layman might not think of, such as conducting a secondary search for explosive devices before doing anything else whatsoever at the site. "Some of this work has to be done even before they get wounded people out."

Then there was the matter of consulting with witnesses, he said, including not only victims but first responders and others who showed up at the scene, including media people and passers-by. Thus I assumed they'd get around to asking who from the Post-Times might have been there.

"You also have to talk to hospital emergency personnel, who may encounter things you hadn't realized. It's remarkable what people tell medical people.

"Finally, we make sure the package we've put together is complete and clear for anybody who gets into the case downstream. Reports go to the U.S. Bomb Data Center and other outfits that, based on the circumstances, need to know, like local police."

He talked about the second aspect of investigations, tracking down possible suspects. Again, there were complex and seemingly interminable steps.

My heart wasn't in the discussion. I was thinking about finding the guy myself.

Dr. Lange was summing up, in that professorial way, when he regained my attention.

"I'm not on this," he said, "so I can give you my opinion. People who deliberately bring harm to others are sociopaths. Sociopaths think they're better than you are, smarter than you are. They're dedicated to proving it. They're sick. The more successful they become at hurting people, or the more afraid they become of being confronted, the more dangerous they become. You, as media people, will be encouraged to stay out of it. Coming here to talk to you is my way of saying don't comply. Looking into things and keeping people informed can do a lot of good. But be careful. These are really awful people."

Strangely, as he said these things I thought of my old boss, Franklin Harris, whose enmity for me seemed odd. Why? I had done him no harm. Certainly not intentionally. I hadn't thought of him as a sociopath before.

"So. Questions?"

"What kind of bomb?" someone said.

"Well, like I say, I'm not on the team, but I'd guess a heck of a lot of dynamite would do it—against a supporting wall, enough to drop that wall and pull down everything linked to it. Maybe an incendiary device as well. I say that because there was a substantial fire. But, remember, I'm not on the job. One thing is obvious, though. The firemen had to put a lot of water in there, which of course is destructive in and of itself. That may have been part of the plan: destroy the art."

***

Lee Ann's body was shipped to New York on Monday to be buried beside the body of her husband. We had a memorial service for her at our publisher's house Monday night. Hardly anybody else in Stanton knew her. A couple of stringers showed up—"correspondents," as she called them. A few sent cards.

I began probing for news of the investigation. Eric kept me informed as best he could. It seemed to me they were getting nowhere. As the man said, investigations, like those of airliner crashes, take seemingly endless time. I would wait. But not forever.

NINE

In the days following the bombing we focused on telling every aspect of the story we could dig up or get someone to talk about. We ran an obituary on Lee Ann that dealt in part with the death of her husband at the hands of bank robbers in New York a year or so back, and how she'd chosen Stanton as a place to restart her life after her husband died. We ran several articles on the art that had been destroyed and the art that was being salvaged. We covered the University Board of Trustees as they considered their rebuilding options. We ran updates on progress in the investigation by the Department of Justice—admittedly not much. Lenny wrote an editorial suggesting better campus security. Tragic belated news was that the watchman, who'd lost his legs in the blast, had died. We reported that the injured fireman had been released from the hospital.

At a newsroom meeting I volunteered to find out who had been particularly strident at meetings of the County Board of Supervisors about the Mapplethorpe exhibit. I offered to write a column inviting help from readers in identifying vociferous Mapplethorpe opponents and also to see what I could learn off the record from a couple of supervisors I knew. Franklin Harris said "outing people" who expressed opinions at a county board meeting was inappropriate and might cause trouble. Lenny ducked the debate like Solomon, suggesting I just make the private enquiries.

Melissa came back from a meeting of university trustees with a quote by one of them, a former football hero, that she thought was pretty funny. When the guy heard the estimate of the cost of rebuilding, he said, "Are we nuts? For that kind of money we could add ten thousand seats to the stadium." The truth was, of course, that the university didn't have a terrorism rider on its insurance, so the cost issue wasn't funny to them. We didn't use the funny quote.

**

As we cast about for a person to replace Lee Ann on the state desk, it occurred to me that a woman on the sports desk might be a good candidate. Her name was Abi North. She gathered high school sports scores from across our circulation area. If she were to join the state desk, I had need for her right away; we had a regional quilt show coming up in a town called Center Ford in the next few days, and we had to show up for it.

I asked our sports editor if I could ask her. I was still being treated kindly because Lee Ann had died, so he listened.

"You want Abi because?"

"She knows the territory."

He waited.

"I'm serious. That would make her a great asset. And we need a *woman* on the state desk. And I need her right now because of some stuff that's coming up."

"I'd hate to see her go."

"All I've got to trade is a Carlton Fisk bubblegum card," I said.

"Pretty good card."

"But he signed it for my daughter and I'd hate to steal it from her."

"How's that?"

"We were at a game in Boston and she stuck the bubblegum in her mouth, saw his card, and waited him out at the locker room door. She was ten." That was Mallory, my athlete.

"Cute. Abi's around here somewhere. If you want to talk to her, go ahead."

When you interview somebody, you do some face studying. Abi North, a willowy, dark-haired woman, had light tan skin, quite striking, as if she covered tennis all the time. She was not exactly oriental-looking, but maybe one side of her family was from India, or maybe Thailand. Her big brown eyes betrayed a sense of humor, which I certainly was looking for in a colleague.

"I'm sorry about Mrs. Thomas," she said.

I nodded.

"Why me?"

"You show up all the time, seem to work hard. I hear you're pretty good."

"From whom?"

I pointed at the sports editor's desk.

"He okay with us talking?"

"You've been here what, two years or so? So he's willing to let you take a next step in your career."

Perfect teeth in a sweet smile. "Why would I want to work on the state desk?"

"Well, there's the travel, the association with a star reporter. Seriously, you'd get into a great variety of reporting opportunities. You've covered sports. Now you could do this. Add to your portfolio, as they say."

"How much?"

"I don't know. I'll see if I can get you a ten percent raise."

"Is there much travel? We only have one car."

"Some. We have a quilt show coming up in Center Ford this Saturday."

She smiled. "Is that typical, covering things on Saturdays?"

"Anything could come up. But we try to stay home and get the stringers to cover their events."

"When would I start?"

I laughed. "This afternoon."

"Who'll help out in sports while they look for my replacement?"

"There are one or two new people around who can sit in for a while."

"I'll tell you tomorrow."

"If you're signing on, I'll need you by Friday. The quilt show is Saturday. Now tell me, just for the record, who you are, where you went to school, what you studied, what you did before you came to the Post-Times. You married? Got any kids?"

She studied me with a hint of humor. "You're not supposed to ask about my personal life."

"Yeah. You've been working about thirty feet from my desk. I'm a good reporter. I can go over there and ask. I don't want a young mom sticking her neck out."

"Really? You need to read an up-to-date book on interview rules."

"Are you any good?"

"Am I any good? Yes, I am. You want background? I grew up in Virginia—and elsewhere. We moved around a lot because my father was career Navy. I got my degree in English from Virginia Wesleyan. Magna Cum Laude. I worked for the local paper for a few years, got married, came here with my husband, Fred, had a baby, a boy, Charlie, now six and tearing up the pea patch"— again that smile—"and I came to work. I'm a working mom.

Fred's a high school teacher. Does anybody around here know I'm good? I don't know. I take sports scores. My college honors suggest I'm smarter than most people. Is that good enough for you?"

She looked at me like she was considering ending the interview by punching me.

"Chutzpah," I said. "You'll fit right in. Tell me yes or no tomorrow."

I let her go. I figured she needed time to talk to a few people in the newsroom—about me, and about the state desk.

I dropped by the glass office and told Lenny I'd like to offer Abi North the job. He had no objection, and in fact seemed to think her moving to the state desk would solve his placement problem. Somebody to take sports scores would be easier to find. I had a sudden realization that maybe I was getting a pearl: Someone in each of our towns would know her name. And she could talk local sports with every stringer in the territory. They'd love her.

***

After talking with my candidate, and feeling reasonably good about my chances, I considered what to do next. Let's say you want to catch a bomber, and you're not the FBI, and you don't have their resources. What might you do? I called my friend Susan Mittleman, a retired psychiatrist who lived in Stanton.

"A bomber? Oh, you mean whomever it was that blew up the art center. Well, I'd look for a paranoiac, a grudge-holder, not so young, maybe 40 or so. Antisocial, I'd think. Someone consumed by hatred, a person who disparages others' beliefs. Maybe haughty, arrogant—I'm not sure. Maybe particular, fastidious, neat. That kind of personality."

I thanked her for the insights. "I'm going to the library to see what I can find on bombers," I said.

"I assume the authorities are working on this, that you're just snooping."

"You know me."

"Yes, I do."

That was the second time in a couple of days somebody called me a snoop. Sue Mittleman meant it kindly.

Actually, the art center wasn't even on my beat; coverage was in the courts of Franklin Harris, city editor, and Melissa Meyer, campus reporter. On the other hand, Lee Ann Thomas had been on the state desk, my turf.

TEN

The best library in Stanton was not the Flag County library but the Stanton University library. I had that on the authority of Melissa, who covered the campus for us with competence and flair.

When I'd arrived at the Post-Times in 1982, fresh out of my stint in the army, Melissa had taken me under her ample wing. Under her tutelage I broke the news that Garland Stevens, associate professor of agriculture, who at the time was about to reap a fortune out of peddling ground-up trash fish as a food source for the poor in developing nations, had neglected to report to the FDA that his process failed to remove excreta from the finished product. My stories went statewide and then nationwide and I suppose worldwide on AP. Exit, at my hand, "*Pescado Bueno Meal. Just Add Water.*"

I of course made an enemy of Garland Stevens—although, as Melissa pointed out, "If you don't keep people a little on edge you can't get their attention when you want it." She acted on her own advice. One way she got attention was to write a story she wanted to publish, and then call somebody in some college or department at the university whom she was homing in on and say, "Is this true?" At the first breath of affirmation, however hesitant, she'd hang up, send the story to the desk, and exit the office, making herself unavailable for frantic caveats.

Even if Melissa hadn't favored the university library, I probably would have gone there anyway. I'd just about lived in a university library during the three years I'd been a college professor—before I took the army intelligence job and then landed in Stanton as a newspaper reporter. A career going backwards, as my wife Cindy liked to point out.

The young woman at the reference desk smiled at me brightly. Her black hair was in a perky ponytail, and she was wearing a blue blazer over a white blouse above a khaki skirt. She was the perfect picture of a prep school princess.

"I've been asked to do a series of news articles on mental health issues," I said to her. Actually, this wasn't true, but I didn't wish to say I was fishing for ideas about why someone would blow up the art center. I laid my Post-Times business card on her desk. "I decided to begin here and see if you had anything to get me started."

She glanced at the card, squinted, cocked her head, pursed her lips. "Mental health."

I nodded. "Among the books and periodicals you've been receiving in, say, the past year, does anything in the way of anti-social behavior stand out particularly in your mind?"

She directed me to an area of shelved research volumes featuring behavioral studies and the like, and also told me where the library had its racks of recent scholarly periodicals.

I found myself looking at several shelves of books considering such subjects as the inner workings of depression and anxiety, psychological effects of trauma, development of criminal behavior over the life course, gender differences in antisocial behavior, paranoid schizophrenia, and so forth. Paranoid schizophrenics, I discovered, tended to display tendencies I'd learned about from Susan Mittleman. So that sounded interesting.

As I perused the possibilities a woman came by pushing a two-decker cart filled with books. She was shelving returned volumes. She waited politely so as not to get in my way.

"Sorry," I said, beginning to move to accommodate her.

"No problem." She smiled. "Can I help you with something?" It was a nice smile. She was tall and slim and attractive, maybe around thirty-five, with hair of a startling pale yellow color, like corn silk. I had the impression she was a patron, not a librarian. When she caught me examining her she grinned. "I'm on the library board. On Fridays I shelve books. They pile up back there because the librarians have better things to do."

"Ah. What do you do in real life?"

"I'm a dilettante."

I smiled. "And I find you here on Fridays?"

She nodded.

I was attracted to her. It wasn't just her beauty. It was poise, spirit—what people might call presence. I had gotten a kind of glow from Lee Ann, but this was different; I felt like I'd been tagged by a laser. I recalled an expression, "She turned on the charm." This was sort of like that, deliberate. What to say?

Lucky for me, the research librarian showed up beside us. "Here's a paper I found in the stacks on antisocial behavior," she said. "Hello?" She regained my attention.

"Oh. Good. Let me see," I said.

The young woman shelving books glanced at the paper the librarian was handing me, smiled, and pushed her cart on down the row. I watched her go.

"When you're done looking you can return the paper to me at the desk," the librarian said. She turned and departed, a study in innocence.

The paper she had handed me, by a professor at UCLA, said about five million American children had been identified with antisocial behavior problems. The issue was largely with boys, the paper stated. Boys exhibit more physical and verbal aggression than girls, whereas antisocial behavior in girls is more indirect, relational, involving harmful social manipulation of others rather than actual antisocial behavior itself.

I was about to leave the library when I decided to go to the card catalogue, where I looked up Edgar Cayce. There were three books on Cayce. As I got the story from glancing at one of these, Cayce, starting as a folk healer with a knack for applying grape poultices and such, had somehow been persuaded that his gift was far greater than folk medicine, and came directly from God. That is, he could give spiritual as well as medical advice.

I also read a little bit about auras. An aura is the distinctive atmosphere that seems to surround a person, the unique essence of that individual, as experienced by someone who can feel or see it. Well, if I couldn't *see* auras maybe I could *feel* them. I thought perhaps I just had, with the woman pushing the cart.

***

After leaving the library, next on my agenda was to learn what I could about people who had railed against the Mapplethorpe exhibit. I called two county supervisors I knew. I learned that about a dozen people had urged the county board to keep the show from opening, some of them, particularly a couple of women, becoming so agitated as to be warned to calm down or leave the meeting. My informants chose not to give me names.

ELEVEN

Friday afternoon, bored with facing stringers' envelopes, I decided to drive down to Everest. I wanted the fresh air. Haunting me as I drove was my image of the woman in the library. I couldn't get her out of my mind. I decided to tell Sue Mittleman about it. She was trying to find peace in retirement, no doubt. Maybe she'd ask me to find another shrink to consult with. I hoped not.

The little town of Everest was as simple as a Norman Rockwell painting. I parked and went into the tiny post office, which turned out to include the community library, a shelf of a dozen books or so. A woman watching me examine the books told me fresh ones came every week from the Eagle County library in Eldorado. Having just come from the University library in Stanton, I was reminded that people's expectations are relative.

I stood in line to buy stamps. In front of me stood a man with packages. Behind me was a woman talking to another woman about the bakery she ran from her home. I said good afternoon to them and told the baker I was with the Post-Times. She got right to the subject of the FBI being in town. She said it was common knowledge that a flying saucer landed or crashed in the national forest. "Everybody's afraid to go in there now."

I asked about her bakery. In describing the setup, she mentioned her sweet delivery person, Caitlin Butler. I recognized the name—the girl who was in the woods with us. That got the woman talking about Caitlin's dad, who she said was after Caitlin to break it off with her boyfriend, a Mexican boy.

"That would be Arturo, right?"

"He may be illegal," she confided, interested that I would know his name.

"May I ask you what the feeling is around here about illegals?"

She shrugged. "My own feeling? He's got a job. Works for a man with a portable sawmill. They get a contract from somebody who wants a tree down, Arturo cuts it down, the man brings his rig around and mills it on the spot. Then they haul it to his barn to cure. The boy's doing hard work, not causing any trouble."

"How do they get milling jobs? Why not the lumberyard?"

"Well, they cut down trees on private property. There's a chance there'll be nails in the trees. From No Hunting signs, things like that."

"So the lumber yard won't take private trees? Afraid they'll break a saw blade? Makes sense to me."

"Caitlin's mom likes Arturo," the woman said.

"Oh?"

"He got her a deal on a new stove. A top-of-the-line Kenmore."

"Really."

"Four hundred dollars. Delivered by Arturo and one of his buddies. That's a really good price."

I got my stamps and left the post office and drove north. The drive and the gossip had got me out of myself. I felt better. People in the newsroom glanced at me as I walked in, gauging my mental health, I supposed, maybe wondering if I'd do some actual work. I happened to see a book on Lenny's desk called *In Search of Excellence*, so I guessed he was "managing by walking around," as the book advised. I got to work. Sure enough, he ambled by. After smiling encouragingly at me, saying nothing, he moved along.

I could actually do some work. Why not?

Recollecting my impressions, I wrote a column about the little town of Everest, a lovely place from another time, where people visiting the post office ask you how you are today, share a little gossip, and nod pleasantly when you part. Some folks pick up or return a library book to a shelf that holds maybe a dozen books. Honor system.

I included in the column the gossip on a continuing mystery: What did a little boy see falling in the sky at Green Lake, just a few miles south of Everest and Connerville, on May 2? Some people were afraid to go into the Shawnee Forest, I wrote, because, as one woman told me, it was pretty certain a flying saucer had landed in there. What had the boy seen? Maybe time would tell.

***

Eric and Carol Sutter and I agreed to go to dinner. Eric and I knew the punch lines to each other's jokes. I liked Carol, too, so the three of us tried to get together for dinner every week or two. Not included in our dinners was my wife Cindy, who lived in our house with our two girls while I resided in a little rental unit. Cindy and I had not played well together for some time. She was disdainful of my apparently diminishing ambition. Cindy was a country singer who filled a niche. She had the voice, the looks, the ability to connect. Charisma. She'd recently been on a southern tour that had been fairly successful, and had cut a disc, *September Songs*, that had made the charts. I, on the other hand, was a reporter for a small-town newspaper. I didn't want to be a backstage husband, part of her entourage.

Our separation left our daughters dangling. On the weekends we three got together, and the two of them slept in sleeping bags on the floor of the living room of my little rental unit. If they had no all-consuming homework, we went to dinner and movies and such. I also attended school functions, and took them places on special occasions. The girls were sweet and smart. Cindy and I were blessed. The girls were getting older, though. Pretty soon they wouldn't be with me on Friday and Saturday nights. In fact, it was happening more and more. The hard floor didn't help, either.

***

For dinner Eric and Carol and I went to Tony Spuds, a very good local eatery that featured, of all things, potatoes.

"They need ten minutes," Carol said. Like Eric, Carol was good-looking and enjoyed fashion. Her choker and earrings, all of silver, glittered in the soft light. Eric was sans dog collar. I was sans tie. We looked okay. With lighted candles at all the tables, and something nice going on at the piano, the occasion felt grand to me. I also felt lonely. As often as not, Lee Ann had rounded out the group.

Waiting for a table, we ordered drinks at the bar. Some ministerial couples shy away from alcohol in public—not my Lutheran friends the Sutters.

People coming in for dinner greeted us at the bar, particularly focusing on the Sutters. Being both a clergyman and a police counselor had earned Eric visibility and respect. Carol, who had almost qualified for the Olympics as a college ice skater, occasionally led fitness classes. So, like Eric, she was something of a local celebrity. A few people commiserated over my loss of a colleague at the Post-Times. Carol kept an eye on me and changed the subject when the condolences got too heavy.

Eric carried his beer around to my barstool. "Don't look now," he said, "but when you walk into the dining room you will see and be seen by Jake Tully, Eagle County sheriff, over there in a party of six."

"How do you know Tully?" I asked.

"Illinois Sheriffs Association. Annual dinner last week."

"Ah." That also suggested to me how Franklin Harris might have access to the man. Harris probably belonged to every social and fraternal organization for fifty miles around. He was probably an auxiliary sheriff.

"Will you want to be seen with me?" I said to Eric. I didn't want people such as the sheriff to pay heed to the friendship between a clergyman associated with law enforcement and a reporter for a daily newspaper.

Eric shrugged off my concern.

Our party was called to dinner, and as it happened we didn't pass close to the sheriff's table, and so did not endure the bonhomie you sometimes witness when well-known people meet by chance in a public place.

Dinner was a bit stilted at first, with the loss of Lee Ann uppermost in our minds. We raised a silent toast. I then told them Abi North had agreed to take Lee Ann's job. We had a warm and pleasant dinner. I didn't mention the woman I'd met at the library.

Two martinis, plus a glass of wine, and I needed to visit the men's room. As I entered I saw the two guys from the sheriff's table at the urinals. I ducked into a stall. They were in the midst of one of those cross-urinal men's room conversations. I heard a bit of their brief exchange.

"Dogs had a nice outing, anyway. Now we got all these suits."

"Chasing who? Locals?"

"Why else would they stick around?"

Back at our table, I related what I'd heard to Eric.

"What's this all about?" Carol said.

"Who knows?" I said. "The 'suits' they mentioned would be the FBI, I think. Maybe the FBI thinks there might be something to the falling-man story. I think I'll call Daniel. See if he's heard anything."

"Your new stringer down there? Don't get him in over his head," she said.

TWELVE

The quilt show in Center Ford was going to take us a good part of our Saturday.

Before I picked up Abi for the drive down there I called Daniel. Got him out of bed, in fact. "Can you find out who the kid was who was playing with Dougie when he claimed to see the falling man?"

"Sure."

"That'd be good. No big deal."

***

I picked Abi up at 8:00 a.m., her husband coming out with their little boy, Charlie, to see us off. Charlie seemed like a nice kid. His father was thin, straight as a yardstick, and had hair like Einstein. I could imagine him teaching.

"I'm glad you could come," I said to Abi as we drove off. "Quilts are outside my ken. The other agenda is to talk to our stringer and see if we can meet some local people."

"Where is Center Ford exactly?" she said. "I've collected a lot of basketball scores but I haven't paid much attention to the geography."

"You and I talked about Everest, right? Center Ford is about fifteen miles northwest of Everest. Bigger. Population around 2,000. About forty-five minutes from here."

I learned as we drove that Abi's mom had been a quilter. If she had the time, Abi said, she herself would be a quilter. After we paid and went in, she led me through a couple of rows of quilts hanging on tall frames. It was obvious she appreciated what she was seeing.

A woman in a blue dress caught up with us. "Ms. Thomas?"

Abi turned to greet her. "Hi. I'm Abi North."

"I'm Lonnie Kimball." The woman looked confused.

I explained to her that Lee Ann Thomas had lost her life when the art center in Stanton was bombed, and that Abi was my new associate on the state desk.

"I'm so sorry. I didn't realize it was Ms. Thomas who was killed. I'm so sorry."

"Abi used to cover sports for us," I said.

Abi took Mrs. Kimball's hand. "It looks like a lovely show," she said. "I'm really excited to see the quilts."

I drifted away. At the end of the gym I found a little canteen. Presently a man of about forty, wearing a suit and tie, came up and asked me if my wife was a quilter. His approach suggested he played some role in the proceedings.

"I'm on the state desk at the Post-Times," I said, reaching for his hand. "My colleague, Abi North, is out there talking with our Center Ford correspondent, Lonnie Kimball." The word "correspondent" rolled right off my tongue.

"I'm Mr. Kimball, the high school principal," the man said. "Lonnie's my wife. My job is to look around for people who need help."

He got an iced tea and sat down. I cued in on a high school principal's need for respect, and addressed him as "Mr. Kimball."

A woman I judged to be about fifty, a positive spirit, came into the enclosure and got herself a cup of coffee. She looked inquiringly at Mr. Kimball. "May I join you?"

"Mr. Morrison has been interviewing me," Mr. Kimball said. "Of course everything is off the record."

She grinned as she introduced herself as Hattie Bush.

"So, you're a teacher?" I said.

"Geometry, algebra, Spanish."

"Spanish," I said. "Do you have a lot of Hispanic kids?"

"Yes, I do. I have Mexican students in all my classes. Which is a wonderful thing, for them *and* for the other students and for me. They learn spoken English and give us all a sense of their own language as it's spoken every day."

At this point we were interrupted by a man with a cup of coffee and no place to go, another lost male at a quilt show. I waved him to a chair. Mr. Kimball didn't look too happy about that, but done was done. I learned that the man was Melvin Crowley, father of a varsity basketball player, Melvin Jr., known as Sonny, best free-throw shooter in the district. From the quiet at our table I didn't think Mr. Crowley was being well received.

"What's up?" Mr. Crowley said, looking around at us.

Mr. Kimball picked up where we'd left off, answering my question. "We have two seniors, one junior, and five freshmen."

"The numbers are going up a little?" I said.

"We've seen the immigrant population increasing all across the state," Mr. Kimball said. "Illinois has maybe double the number of Hispanics that we had ten years ago."

"Increasing why?"

"We talking about Mexican kids?" Mr. Crowley said. "There's none of 'em comin' out for basketball, I'll tell you that." He laughed. "Get it?" He held out a hand palm down to suggest Mexicans weren't tall. Finding us unreceptive he became truculent. "We gotta find a way to get rid of these illegals. They are eating our lunch. Pretty soon, a white man won't have the vote in his own country."

Mr. Kimball tried to talk around Mr. Crowley. "People from Mexico and down into Central and South America are coming up here because they can earn more money, of course, but also because the U.S. is just a safer place to be."

"A lot safer before *they* came, I know that," Mr. Crowley said.

"I don't think you do know, Mr. Crowley," Hattie Bush said. "Studies going back a hundred years have shown that immigrants—regardless of nationality or legal status—are less likely than the indigenous population to commit violent crimes or be incarcerated."

He smiled. "I bet you got that out of a book, Ms. Bush."

"Yes, Mr. Crowley, I did." She paused. "The data show that for every ethnic group, without exception, incarceration rates among young men are lowest for immigrants. This holds true especially for the Mexicans, Salvadorans and Guatemalans who make up the bulk of the undocumented population."

"No wonder you're the teacher," Mr. Crowley said.

"Yes, it's a good thing, isn't it?" Hattie Bush responded politely.

"Beggin' your pardon, ma'am, I don't think so," Mr. Crowley said. "Look around. You see any American Indians? Before the white man came they owned this country. Millions and millions of 'em. Gone. Or drunk on the reservation. How're your grandkids gonna like it on the reservation? Come to think of it, we have 'em already. Whites hunkered down in the suburbs. All over the country."

He had silenced the table.

"How do the Mexicans get here, to Center Ford, I mean?" I asked Mr. Kimball.

"Most of them get to Chicago," he said, "and then some find it hard to get a job and come down here. Work here is seasonal, of course, but local families employ a lot of them in the off-season, too. They're hard-working, family-oriented, loyal, like the people who pioneered here."

"What kind of work?" I asked.

"You name it. Everything from farming to snow removal to helping on construction work. If you have a job, they'll do it."

"So, the atmosphere is friendly?"

Glancing uneasily at Ed Crowley, Hattie Bush spoke up again. "Hispanics are not well received by everybody. But most people accept them. And hire them because they work hard, and for low wages. That means they displace local people who are willing to do menial work. As to educating them, we had to enroll them. Congress forced it. And while drugs were an issue before, they're worse than ever now."

I found Hattie Bush interesting. After squaring off with Ed Crowley she was offering a balanced assessment of the situation as she saw it.

Mr. Kimball said, "We're trying to cope, just like every place else. Wouldn't you say so, Ms. Bush?"

She nodded.

Ed Crowley rolled his eyes.

After our little chat ended I caught up with Hattie Bush as she strolled around looking at quilts. "Is Ed Crowley typical?" I said.

"What can I say?"

"Whatever you say, it won't go further."

"He's a problem for my Mexican students. He, and his son, too, pour on verbal abuse as a matter of course. They're not alone."

***

It was just one o'clock as Abi and I drove out of town. We talked about our morning.

"You say Mr. Kimball doesn't want to deal with the Hispanic issue?" Abi said.

"I'm sure he's dealing with any number of people who think like Crowley. I doubt he wants to confront them openly; he'd only get people rallying on both sides. Then he'd have to deal with that. But I suppose that makes him a typical high school principal. Keeping lids on things is what they do. So tell me, how are we going to report the show?"

I learned that Abi and Mrs. Kimball had decided to divide the coverage; Abi would do the color and Mrs. Kimball would report who won what. Reading about the show in the Post-Times, quilters could bask in the warmth of a Stanton editor's delight in the event while getting the hard news from their local stringer.

I relaxed. We drove along in the afternoon sun. Farmland was greening up. Soon there would be corn, soybeans, tobacco, probably some hidden-away marijuana. I watched a rabbit hopping along a hedgerow, bait for a hawk. I recalled once seeing a hawk come down like a dart after a squirrel. The food chain in action.

Abi broke into my thoughts. "What are you planning to write about?"

"Well, you and Mrs. Kimball have the show covered. I think I'll do a column on Mexicans in southern Illinois, how they get here, how the numbers are growing, the work they do. The debate over immigration. I'll do a little research at the library."

She nodded.

I was learning how important local events were to our readers. I gave Abi my observations about this as we drove: If your name was in the paper, you clipped and saved the story. If your event got a warm review, you clipped the review, too. So, in our small

way, the Post-Times was like The New York Times—the newspaper of record—at least for our tiny slice of America. Who won
what at the quilt show, who won the tractor pull at the farm
festival, whose jelly won first place at the county fair, and how
the big-city newspaper—the Stanton Post-Times, that is—felt
about it, all of this was important to our readers.

Abi nodded.

***

After the trip to Center Ford, Abi and I chased other community stories, usually just one of us going while the other handled
the desk. Events ranged from the birth of quadruplets in one
community to a woman winning the Pillsbury Bake-Off contest
in another. Like Robert Preston in "The Music Man," we were
getting to know the territory.

The good news was, Abi was a natural with the stringers, more
comfortable with rural Illinois people than Lee Ann had been,
and even got a few of them to report matters that transcended
coverage of the Order of the Eastern Star. Stringers liked her,
and asked for her when they called the desk.

For her part, Abi was enthused about the job. "I didn't expect
to go running around southern Illinois like this, Mr. Morrison,
I'll tell you that. But I'm having a lot of fun. And Fred's okay
with it." She smiled. "So far, anyway. I worry a little about how
Charlie's dealing with it, though. He's not complaining. But it's
hard to know."

"I'm glad you signed on," I said. "I hope you stick around."

For my part, my heartache was perhaps less painful, but the
art center and the falling man were in the back of my mind.
I wanted something to happen on those two fronts. Whether
they'd intended to or not, they killed Lee Ann. And now the
night watchman. "Collateral damage," Dr. Lange had said. I
made a promise to myself. They would pay.

13

THIRTEEN

I spent Memorial Day with the girls. We went to the field-hockey team dinner on Tuesday, where Mallory picked up the Team Player award, meaning they all liked her. This had been her final season. She hadn't broken a leg or anything, so who could complain about that?

Her younger sister, Allison, came along with us. Allison had no interest in being an athlete. But she had advanced in the past year from worrying about her fingernails to reading world history. She also was sneaking a peek at herself in mirrors now and then. She was a good-looking child, maybe prom queen material, but she didn't flutter around to get people's attention about it.

The girls and I talked about Abi.

"I lured her away from the sports desk," I said. "Sharp. She went to school in Virginia, and worked for a newspaper there before her husband got a job teaching here. They have a little boy, six years old. Abi's father was career Navy, an admiral, I guess. I think her mother's from Asia—maybe Thailand or Burma, somewhere in there."

"Mr. North? I had him for homeroom," Mallory said. "He's nice."

***

A sensational murder trial in Arbor County, which was southeast of us along the Ohio River, suddenly captured Abi's and my attention. A boy was charged with killing his girlfriend. I took the lead. Not only was Abi new to court coverage, but she and Fred had only one car. Also, I knew a few of the players. The attorney for the defense was a man I myself sought legal advice from upon occasion. He had the colorful moniker of *Madrid Paris*.

As with other trials I'd covered, the early stages of this one had their lighter moments. Abi and I were on hand for a notable one. It was the Wednesday after Memorial Day, May 27. With the preliminaries taken care of, and the action finally getting underway, Mr. Paris asked to approach the bench.

"Your Honor," he said, "sunlight is coming through the blinds, bouncing off the shiny bald head of the esteemed counsel for the prosecution, and getting in my eyes."

It was true that the prosecuting attorney was bald as a billiard ball.

Gaveling down the laughter, the judge proclaimed that the blinds were to be adjusted as each day progressed.

"Mr. Paris," he said, "in the course of this trial you will be allowed just one more little witticism. Any more than that and you will be directed to a very dark jail cell for contempt, providing you with an opportunity to rest your eyes for a while."

More gaveling.

Mr. Paris's levity did its job. The jurors found him relaxed and likeable, which of course was just what he'd hoped.

"This is sort of like sports," Abi wrote on her pad.

I smiled. "Losing is tougher," I wrote.

I'd have liked to cover more of the trial but, as things turned out, I wasn't that lucky. After the opening day, I never went back.

So Abi was baptized by fire. I'll get back to my troubles in a minute here. But let me tell you how it went for Abi.

For three days, she covered the dramatic proceedings as they unfolded in the courtroom. Then, abruptly, the whole affair ended in chambers, where Madrid Paris was able to show that the shotgun-blasted girlfriend fell over not in Arbor County but in the county just south of it, Stone County. That is, the altercation between the two began in the one county and the girlfriend ended up dead in the other. As if that wasn't enough, the boy had had the presence of mind, or witlessness, perhaps, to turn over the wrong shotgun to the sheriff. Thus the prosecution had entered the wrong gun into evidence. They hadn't known, but Madrid Paris had. And he'd done further homework and found the interesting juxtaposition of the county lines.

Abi's report of the astonishing turn of events in the trial got her the lead on our front page. We almost never put state news on the front page. Quite an honor.

"He's a remarkable man, your Mr. Paris," Abi remarked to me later.

"He's a great guy to have on your side," I said, "especially if you're guilty as sin."

The two of us agreed the boy got away with murder.

As to why I missed the end of the trial, it happened because I got beat up. I got beaten so bad, in fact, I was a day or so getting my bearings.

It happened like this: I was returning in the dark to my little rental house, having gone to the office to write the story of the day's doings, and then getting a bite to eat. Parking in the dark in my gravel driveway, crunching along on my way to the house, I heard a couple of crunches behind me. I whirled around and faced a man.

"Morrison?" he said.

I was much too slow in responding, only half prepared to take his wrecking-ball punch in the stomach. A second guy reached around my chest from behind and yanked me up, pinning me, my feet dangling in the air. The guy in front put another fist ball in my stomach. Still pinned, but with my feet loose, I planted a shoe hard in the front guy's crotch. He doubled up and fell. I tried to flip the back guy, but he was as big as Michelangelo's David. I couldn't get my feet on the ground for leverage.

While the big moose held me, the other guy came back. "You son of a—" He didn't finish the thought as he swung for my head. I turned but still caught half of it.

"Listen up, Ace," the front man said. "Butt out." Up close like that, he smelled of pizza sausage.

The moose let go of me and I dropped onto the gravel driveway.

"If we have to come back it's gonna get worse," the front man spat. I got his spit on my face. For whatever good it did me, his voice sounded strained.

I watched them get in their car and drive off, not a care in the world. I got myself to my feet. Then I bent over and puked. I stood there, hunched over, hands on knees, alone in the dark.

After I got back into the house I looked in the mirror in the bathroom. I found what they call "contusions and abrasions," happily below the temple, to the side of my head and along my jaw line. My jaw worked. My teeth, one or two loose, were in place. My head hurt. My stomach ached. I stumbled into my shower, about the size of a voting booth, complete with security curtain.

I couldn't imagine why I'd been beat up. Whatever the reason, it wasn't for how we'd covered the Center Ford quilt show. I reviewed matters. The anonymous phone caller had told me to mind my own business. Then a guy said I should butt out. Of what? I could only assume it was the falling-man story. Chasing it, I'd scared somebody. The two FBI sketches came to mind. Were they the guys who beat me up? Maybe; I'd have to look at the sketches again.

I washed my face twice, and stumbled out for a towel.

FOURTEEN

Alone in my rental unit with my thoughts, some aspirin, some eggs, some peanut butter, and a modicum of gin, I took Thursday off, both to start healing and to do some thinking. How might I respond?

I didn't get much chance to think. By some miracle of social wiring, people I had deep personal connections with began to show up. Some satisfied themselves that I was okay and departed. Some hung around to console and care for me.

Who came? Eric, who just happened to drop by. My old pal Spike Rountree, to talk fishing. Daniel, to talk about his upcoming responsibility as editor of the high school paper. The Connerville and Everest school systems were being consolidated. In the fall, he'd be editing the paper at a combined high school and dealing with a lot of cultural circumstances new to him. Also ministering to me were Mallory and Allison, after learning from Eric that I'd gotten hurt.

Touched by all the concern, I told as much of my story as my painful jaw allowed. The occasion evolved into a pizza party, with me getting a cup of chicken broth and a glass straw. One interesting part of this for me was that the girls got to meet Daniel, my star stringer, a kid I liked.

As I considered all these well-wishers, I thought about the possible danger of pursuing the story of the falling man. Somebody had been angry enough about my digging to hire a couple of thugs to beat me up. So, in continuing to chase the story, was I putting people I loved at risk? Grandiose notions of investigative reporting can lose their luster in a certain light.

***

I hiked the stairs up to the newsroom on Friday and found people looking at me with worry and alarm. Abi looked up from her desk. She said not a word, but her eyes went wide and the palm of her hand went to her mouth.

Given the condition of my face, my smile didn't work very well. "I'm fine," I said to the general audience. "I took a little fall." Where is it men get that macho stuff? Somebody beat me up, and I hurt like hell.

When I got to my desk I discovered Franklin Harris sitting in my chair, piecing together some torn-up notes from my wastebasket. I thumbed him out of the chair and sat down. Carefully. He eased himself into my visitor's chair and continued his little search.

"What are you doing, Franklin?" I said.

"What happened to you?" he said, looking up.

"What is this?" I said, pointing to his jigsaw puzzle of note shards on my desk.

"It seems to me," he said, looking down at his handiwork, "that what we have here are some notes on your Everest campaign, steps contemplated, some already taken, that you've chosen not to share with the rest of us. It's obvious from all this that you persist in your foolishness. What are you thinking of, Brian?"

"You're going through my wastebasket, Franklin. That's what I'm thinking."

"Who beat you up?" he said, looking at me.

"Who said I was beat up?"

"You must be hurting," he said. But then he got back to his main thread. "You have to stop this stuff—whatever you're doing. You're ruining our reputation."

"Franklin," I said, "do you really think you should be going through my wastebasket?"

"Brian, I really do invite you to seek my counsel."

I shooed him away. Ye gods!

After he retreated, Abi came over. "What happened?"

"Remember the falling-man story?" I said. "The two men who tried to grab Dougie Perkins? I think somebody wants me to drop the matter, and beat me up to help make their point. At least I think it was them." My head was spinning. I didn't know a head could really do that. My jaw hurt, too. "This is about me, Abi. It's not about the state desk. Not about you. And I do feel better than I look."

As I was trying to soothe her I was thinking I'd go see Sheriff Tully. For one thing, it seemed to me he was more interested in the falling-man story than he was letting on. For another, my column on Everest, mentioning the mystery, must have stirred somebody up. I mean, somebody sent the thugs. Who? Maybe Tully knew.

"I'm gonna go see Tully," I said.

Abi watched me. "I could drive," she said.

"I can do it."

She reached out to touch my face, but apparently thought better of it. I extricated myself from the chair, a challenging task.

Standing by my desk, I dialed our Bartow stringer. Bartow was the Eagle County seat. I got her on the phone, and asked her if she'd had a chance to talk to the sheriff lately.

"It's like talking to a cigar-store Indian," she said.

I called the sheriff's office and asked the woman who answered the phone if Tully might have a few minutes for me. As it happened, he did. He'd see me in about an hour, she said. The woman's voice was familiar, but I couldn't place it. Easing my way down the staircase, I went out and got myself into my car and headed for Bartow. The car was sounding clanky. I needed to look into that. Black clouds boiled up southwest of us, a huge thunderstorm hanging like a theater curtain across the sky.

I made it down to Bartow in less than an hour, driving toward the storm as it made its way toward me. I was speeding, but prepared to tell anyone who stopped me that I didn't want to be late for a meeting with the sheriff. The square around the courthouse was dotted with lawyers' offices. A small movie theater sat among them. *Fast Times at Ridgemont High* was on the marquee. A clothing store window near the theater featured dresses on clothing dummies without heads.

Sheriff Tully—I focused my rattled brain on keeping his name straight—made me wait for fifteen or twenty minutes. Or maybe who made me go to a hard bench and sit was the woman I encountered in the front office. She was Mrs. Penny, formerly our stringer in Everest. I smiled, working on placating her.

The sheriff's greeting was cordial and his handshake firm. He was a rather small man, tough as old leather, with tired pale blue eyes, a straight thin nose, prominent cheekbones, good teeth that looked to be his own, and a square jaw. His speech, I thought, had a touch of the southwest, along with a slow cadence that anticipated respect. With nothing else to go on, I would have voted for him myself.

I survived his handshake.

"How'd you hurt yourself?" he said.

"I didn't hurt myself. Somebody did it for me."

"What happened?"

I told him.

"You report it?"

I shrugged. "You were at Tony Spuds in Stanton the other night," I said. "Two guys I saw at your table, deputies, I guess, were in the men's room later. They mentioned 'bad guys, maybe local' being sought by the FBI. Can you comment on that?"

"Can't say that I can."

"Sheriff, we're getting nothing out of you. My stringer here in Bartow. Me. Zip. Zero. That's why we're digging so hard. What happened when the deputies went in with the dogs? Did they find anything?"

"If you've read the Illinois police code," he said, "you know we have to maintain confidentiality. That means, even if somebody's dead, the deceased has rights. So does the family."

"Are you telling me you found a body? Why did you send in the deputies?"

"We were responding to concerns expressed by one of our Eagle County residents."

"Who? What concerns?" I said. "You have the code to deal with, and I understand that, but you also have a responsibility to the public."

"Look," he said. "This is not the big city. I'm not looking for advice or help from the media."

We didn't get any further.

Driving back to the office with the black sky tailing me I thought about Tully. Like some other law-enforcement people I'd met, and some politicians, he grouped all news organizations together, and judged them all to be bad. "The media." For people like Tully, the word conjured up a bunch of whores, I was sure.

So he kept his distance. From a distance, you can't tell a whore from a nun. By that I mean, seen from up close, some journalists are on the side of the angels.

I wondered if the feds would tell me anything. Nah. They wouldn't.

I had what was maybe an insight into Franklin Harris's constant awareness of what I was up to. Maybe Mrs. Penny was feeding him stuff. And, of course, he belonged to the Sheriff's Association. Yikes!

The black clouds boiled above me like cats in a burlap bag. Hailstones rattled the roof of my car. I was still hurting. I figured a martini would fix me up. Tully? I didn't like the guy. Like Lincoln said, maybe I had to get to know him better.

CHAPTER 15

About five o'clock Saturday morning, after troubled sleep in a night of noisy thunderstorms, I awoke to endless wailing. Stanton fire trucks were on the move—several of them. Afraid there'd been another bombing, I pulled on some clothes and followed the noise. It led me not to a Stanton disaster but south about nine miles to Tintown, a community of maybe a couple dozen mobile homes.

The first notable thing I saw clearly was the torn-up body of a panel truck. One piece of it displayed what was left of it's logo: "onder Bre."

All the trailers seemed damaged or wrecked. One appeared to be missing; there stood an empty lot featuring a rectangular grouping of stone blocks, a bicycle, a grill, and some other stuff. But no trailer. Looking for what might have departed that lot in the terrible storm, I spotted it—a trailer leaning vertically against a big oak tree. I imagined people inside when the funnel swooped down.

A Stanton fireman I knew told me the twister had nicked Hopeful, the Goddard County seat, about ten miles southwest, and then plowed up everything from there to where we were standing. As far as he knew, he said, the twister had killed a man and injured three other people, all of them here in Tintown.

I pointed inquiringly at the trailer up against the tree. He nodded. One person in there was killed, he said, and two others were injured. What a terrible way to die. Just like an airliner crash. You're alive but scared shitless, and then you're tossed into eternity.

The three people who were hurt, one of them a nine-year-old boy, had been taken away, the boy by helicopter and the two others, a woman and a man, by ambulance. I got names. I wouldn't use them until they were released; I just needed to know. I walked around, avoiding branches and debris. Water from the storm filled the ruts in the gravel road. By one of the trailers a Confederate flag hung limp on its slender pole. As I walked along I saw two people handing out bottled water. Following the water distributors, I sought out talkers.

"There appears to have been quite a lot of inflow." This from an old guy in skivvies who apparently had been listening to early reports of the twister on TV. "It was an F-2, I guess, not the biggest, but bad enough."

I'd have to start watching TV more, I thought, because I had no idea what an "F-2" was, or "inflow" either.

"The Four Horsemen of the Apocalypse, I kid you not." This from a young man who, I learned, was an English major at the university in Stanton. He asked me if what he'd said would be in the paper. I said the editor would decide.

"The police and firemen did a great job, these good people too," a young man said as he accepted a quart bottle of water that had a county label on it. "The thing was hardly gone and they were here." He carefully spelled out his name. He was about thirty, and appeared to be fit enough to apply for a position with the fire department.

Reporting hard news is not always about covering sensational murders, or about trying to sell more newspapers, either. Sometimes it's so sad it breaks your heart. I'd been beaten up the other night, and was feeling some pain, but these people's lives had been trashed.

It turned out Abi had also driven down, in the Norths' only car. I noted her tenacity, purpose, commitment, whatever. Along one of the rain-soaked lanes she had picked up a few sheets of typing paper. What she read on the pages, she told me, standing there in the muddy road, was screed, written by a hate monger. In covering the tornado, we apparently had tripped over some nutso, or at least his work. She was furious. In fact, she was so angry she wasn't being clear about what it was that was making her so mad.

I tried to calm her down.

"Morrison, we can't ignore this," she said. She spotted some other pages on the ground, went after them, and held them tightly in one hand. She tried tracking down where they'd come from, but no one claimed them.

"What? Ignore what?"

She was too busy searching for pages.

Back in the office, after we turned in our copy to the news desk, she took a more protracted look at what she had. While she was reading the soggy writing to herself she occasionally paused to read a passage aloud to me.

I was finally getting it. Race hatred.

Interspersed with her readings were her comments: "These people want a war on Hispanic immigrants," she said. "This is hate mail."

"It sounds to me like they're just inviting people to a meeting," I said after listening to excerpts. To help soothe her I said I'd go to the university library to see what I could find on resistance to immigration in general and about an outfit called Our Liberty League, which appeared to her to be behind the screed. In twenty minutes at the library, I found a fair number of relevant books. Resistance to immigration seemed to be linked to isolationism—especially whenever a significant number of Americans became weary of the wider world. I had read a little history, so I wasn't too surprised. President Roosevelt took on American isolationists as he campaigned to get the U.S. into World War II. Charles Lindbergh and other influential opponents said Hitler would win.

I went back to the office, and to her desk, and reported what I'd found. "Our Liberty League is someplace in Idaho. Nothing around here."

Abi waved the papers. "They are too here—ten miles down the road. Decent people believe they live in a safe and sane world, with no chance for some astonishing evil breaking out. But that's an illusion, Mr. Morrison."

"Aw, come on."

She looked at me. "You and I grew up in this country, safe, oblivious. My mother comes from Burma. I've heard stories from her that give me nightmares."

"You're pretty passionate about this," I said, defending my virginity, I suppose. I had no experience of despotism or dictatorship.

She put her finger on a page. "Listen. '*The establishment is planning to assure citizenship for millions of illegal immigrants, and their babies, illegally planted here. We must confront and defeat this treachery.*'"

"'Planted here'? Treachery? Pretty oily stuff, I admit." I said.

She read another passage:

"*'Spanish influence in America is spreading like a stain. We must blot it out. Otherwise, those of us who own this land are lost. God knows what will become of our children, and their children, under Spanish rule.'*"

The writer appeared to think we were heading into the Spanish Inquisition. "Pretty graphic," I said. "But this might be just one nut with a typewriter. I mean, what national outfit would operate out of a trailer in Tintown?"

She stared me down. "We don't know who the next madman will be, Morrison, or how he'll get something going. He could come from Tintown as easy as any other place. But he'll show up *somewhere*. Hitler came from Bavaria, you know. The big shots sneered at him. 'The little corporal.'" She waved the papers at me. "It could start in Tintown. Now. Today. Or has started already."

She was conjuring Yeats for me: *What rough beast, its hour come round at last, slouches toward Bethlehem to be born?* I wondered what her mother had experienced in Burma.

"You have to stamp this stuff out," she said. "The moment it starts. Before you get a U Ne Win, or a Pol Pot, or a Hitler."

"U Ne Win?" I said.

"The man who runs Burma."

The underbelly of the conversation was that I didn't know what she knew. Abi. From the sports desk. I was surprised.

"We have outfits that keep a lid on that kind of stuff," I said. "Really."

"The NSA, the FBI, the CIA—"

Her eyes flickered.

"This is America, Abi. Democracy wins."

"So far," she said.

"I'm gonna have to introduce you to my daughter Allison," I said.

"She feels like I do?"

"Yes indeed. She says people are lying to her, school books are lying to her. And nobody listens to her complaints."

Abi stood up. "I'm going down to Tintown. I am going to find whoever it was that wrote this, get an interview."

"What makes you think you'll find him?"

"I'll visit the trailers one by one."

She turned to go.

"Hey," I said to her back. "You'll need a car."

"Oh."

"Here. Take my keys."

"Really?"

"You're chasing a news story, right? I mean, you're not planning to attack somebody."

"That's right. This is breaking news, right here in Tintown."

As she left the office our noisy newsroom clock was announcing the hour. The point was to remind us of fleeting time. High noon. Put the paper to bed. The bongs evoked Frank Miller, arriving on the noonday train.

I admired Abi's spirit, in fact was amazed by it. But my own view was different. I was a third-generation American. In America we had freedom of speech. People could assemble to pursue their case against immigration. This nut in Tintown? In America we do love debate. We're like England in that way. I wondered if Sunday afternoons in Hyde Park in London were still as much fun as they'd been when I was there one day with a Bobby on hand to keep the debaters peacefully separated. Maybe not. As Abi was asserting, things change.

Frankly, I worried about Abi, on her own looking for some nutso. Southern Illinois is a peaceful place. We were long past the terrible crimes spawned by Prohibition, the coal-mining wars, the Ku Klux Klan, gangsters like the Birgers and the Shel-tons. Those days were long gone.

I had a flicker of memory: Lee Ann's body lying dead on the sidewalk at the art center.

Abi was driving my old clunker.

I looked out the window. It was still there. I could go with her. I tripped down our rickety stairs as fast as I could, but when I got to the sidewalk she was gone.

SIXTEEN

I shuffled papers for a while. I called my friend Eric Sutter. Saturday was a good day to try to catch him.

"Had lunch?"

We chose Bilbo's. Even the buns on the hamburgers were greasy, but at least they cooked them where you could see what was going on.

"I've been thinking about your falling man," he said.

"Yeah?"

"How much do you know about the Shawnee?"

"Now that I'm on the state desk, more and more. A huge forested area with a lot of private land mixed up in it. Three thousand square miles. Draw a line across the state, river to river, just south of Carbondale, and south of that's mostly the Shawnee."

"Close enough. What if your little boy didn't see a body falling? What if it was a shirt or a jacket, something like that?"

I stared at him, grinning. "You have a story to tell me. Something you got from your FBI pals."

"I do. Here's how it begins: On May 1, the night before the boy thought he saw the man falling, somebody knocked off Senator Hamilton Beets."

"Old news," I said, shrugging.

"What have you heard since?" he said.

"Not much. A couple of follow stories that said they're investigating. Of course, I've heard rumors about Beets and his highway construction contracts. But I've been hearing those ever since I got here."

"Right. And stories about shoeboxes full of money," Eric said.

"And roads paved right up to the doorsteps of his relatives and friends." I bit into my burger. "Those aren't just rumors," I said, after swallowing. "You can actually drive on 'em."

He nodded.

"As I understand it," I said, "one of those illegal paving jobs leads to his sister's fishing shack on Ferry Lake."

He put the burger down. "Ah, yes," he said, smiling. "Sugar Beets."

For a moment we considered Sugar Beets.

"Cindy's been practicing with Sugar Beets records ever since she first heard her," I said.

"Grand Ole Opry," Eric said. "1975?"

"About then, yeah."

He shifted gears, looked serious. "Okay. When the police got up to Beets' office in the senate office building they found him dead on the floor behind his desk with a bullet in his head, his safe wide open and empty. Plus they found the janitor dead in the hall. Shot in the face, like Beets.

"Yeah. All that's been in the news. How much did they get, I wonder."

"What I'm going to tell you is in confidence."

"Yeah."

"They're thinking as much as three million bucks."

My eyes went wide. "How'd they come up with that?"

Eric smiled. "I think it's about five percent of what the state paid for highway and bridge construction in Beets' district in the last year or so."

"That's what these construction companies were paying to get highway jobs? Five percent?"

"In Beets' district, anyway. That's what they're saying."

"Who's saying?"

"Contractors. They paid to get the jobs and now their money's down the drain, a lot of it, anyway. They thought they had some jobs nailed down and now they don't."

I loved it. Larceny so wide-open that people who bribed a state official could go public to complain about outcomes that didn't seem fair. "He had their payoff money but the contracts weren't awarded yet?"

"Some of them, yeah. Beets dead. Nothing to show for it."

"And I can't print it." I started laughing.

He looked at me over his hamburger. "It's time for my recorded message to you: I hear things. I provide some of what I hear as background to you, off the record. Because I do that, you are better informed. Hopefully, good government is served. But you can't use what I tell you unless you go out and prove it on your own. And under no circumstances can you attribute anything to me. Ever."

"I love when you talk dirty," I said. "So what's all this got to do with the falling man?"

"Let me finish," Eric said. "One of the Senate office building cameras picked up a plate that was seen later on a car apparently abandoned at an airstrip in Sharpsburg."

"So?"

"So when they followed up in Sharpsburg, one of the locals recalled hearing a plane taking off that Saturday morning, from the sound of it, heading south. So, if it was headed that way, it could have been over the Shawnee around ten o'clock.

"So?"

"So, maybe the killer, or killers, arrived in Sharpsburg in the car and left in the plane."

"Where'd you hear this?

"I read an FBI bulletin."

"Which said?"

"It said a ranger in the Shawnee heard a plane and glanced up and saw something falling. She thought the plane was falling apart. But it kept going."

"You think she saw the falling man."

"Well, yeah, I do."

"What kind of plane?"

"She didn't know. Just a plane."

He had my attention.

We paid up and I thanked him for the tip.

But where was Abi?

SEVENTEEN

When I got back to the office, there she was. She looked pooped. She said she couldn't find the seditionist, or whatever he was, but she'd tracked down a woman who admitted knowing him. "Biblically, I mean."

Biblically. Abi was just full of surprises.

"I got to talk to her. Big woman. Raw-boned, I guess you'd say. Good-looking. She pointed out his trailer. It's across the road. I went over there, but nobody answered my knock."

I'd been thinking of Abi as a naïve young woman, fresh from the sports desk. How could she drive all alone down to Tintown in my bummed-out Ford, hoping to interview an extremist, find his trailer, end up talking with a neighbor, and conclude she was involved with him?

"So where is the guy?" I said. "Is the trailer habitable? Is he staying there?"

"He's there sometimes, at least. She says it's a mess. A couple of tree branches fell on it."

"She's been in there?"

"Well, yeah." Abi gave me a look, like maybe I hadn't gotten her point.

"So, what's in there? Did she say?"

"She said there's a couple of folding tables in there, like four or six feet long, in the main room, covered with bed sheets."

"Dust covers? Hiding something?"

"She doesn't know what's under there; he told her to mind her own business. She thinks he's sort of a Nazi."

"What do you mean?"

"She says he talks about 'the coming time in America, after we get all these wetbacks out'— his words, not hers. I think she's a little scared of him, to tell the truth."

"The coming time?"

"I guess when all the illegals are gone. She said he calls immigration 'the invasion.'"

"So, what happens now?"

"She believes she'll see him again."

"Is she looking forward to that?"

Abi giggled. "I suspect she has a streak of—what? You know. Marquis de Sade."

I looked at her.

"BDSM." She looked at me. "What? I have to spell it out?"

"No. I get it." I was embarrassed. This was Abi?

"She knows I'm spying on the guy. She enjoys the intrigue. I think she'll let me know when he calls."

After listening to Abi's story I shared Eric's theory of the heist, and what the forest ranger saw. "All this is just between you and me," I said. "Just so you know. What Eric tells me is just for background—always."

Abi gave me a look, something like the one I got from Randy at Green Lake. I had the feeling she thought I was naïve.

I went back to my desk. Abi's news from Tintown, Eric's news of the investigation, Daniel's report from Connerville. Too much stuff flooding my head.

If I were the FBI, I'd know by now that it wasn't a body; it would smell to high heaven, and vultures would be circling, signaling where to look. So I'd send a bunch of agents in to beat the bushes where the ranger thought something might have fallen. I'd also be researching general-aviation aircraft, and how something might fall off of one, or out of one. I'd also be looking into who owned such planes.

I got up and went back to Abi's desk and told her what I'd been thinking.

"If they don't think it's a body," she said, "maybe they're thinking about the loot. Loot would trigger the coonhound effect."

"Coonhound effect?"

"You ever seen coon dogs hunt?" She cocked her head a little, listening for what I'd say.

"In Virginia? You know about that?"

"Sure."

"Okay, I have a question," I said. "They tree the coon. Do they shoot it and eat it?"

She shrugged. "It's an acquired taste."

I went back to my desk. Coonhound effect. It was about the money. Why else would Tully be so interested? Why were the feds hanging out down there?

I imagined the murderers hauling three million dollars to a plane. It could be in anything—flight bag, rucksack, suitcase, cardboard boxes, whatever.

I called a friend, Doris Noble, a teller at my bank. "Doris," I said, "how many bills in a one-inch stack?"

"Why do you want to know?"

"I don't know; say somebody's hiding money in a drawer."

"You shouldn't be hiding money in your drawers, Morrison. Bring it in here. It'll be safer in our drawers." She giggled.

"How many?" I was getting tired of people putting me on.

"Actually, I know the answer," she said. "About two hundred and thirty new bills to the inch."

"And you know this because?"

"Bank drawers are built to hold money, honey."

We parted. She was a wiseass, but I did like her.

I figured illegal transactions were in cash, hundred-dollar bills, a denomination that took up less space and was easy to count. A few calculations told me that for three million dollars you'd need something like a standard-size suitcase, canvas, Samsonite, whatever. The suitcase full of the bills would be heavy, maybe sixty-eighty pounds. I imagined it crashing down into the Shawnee. Dougie didn't talk about *hearing* anything, so it must have fallen some distance away. Not in the water. He'd have heard a splash.

The phone rang.

"Hi, Mr. Morrison. It's Daniel."

"What's up?"

"A kid found a pair of glasses in the lake."

"Eyeglasses? Near the campground?"

"Yes, sir."

"Found them how, Daniel?"

"He was netting—you know. The glasses got into the net."

"What'd he do with them?"

"He was going to put an ad in the paper."

"The weekly there in Connerville?"

"Yes, sir. Lost-and-found. The ads are free."

"So how did you find out?"

"He told Randy."

"How did Randy get into it?"

"He was there, looking for Dougie."

"Dougie's missing?"

"No, no. He was at a friend's house."

"Who has the glasses now?"

"Randy. He told the kid he'd take them to the lost-and-found at the Ranger station."

"And then Randy told you what he had."

"Yes, sir."

The kid played hide-and-seek with his father. Not so cute. "Can you get them from Randy?"

"Yes, sir. I already did that. I'll give them to my dad. He'll put them in the lost-and-found."

A body in the lake wouldn't smell so bad. Nah. I was sticking with money. It was money.

"Oh, there's another thing," Daniel said. "The guy who went into the woods with us? I guess he went back in again, Saturday."

"Arturo? Where'd you hear that?"

"Randy. He saw him go in.

"So, did Randy happen to talk to him?"

"He just saw him go in was all. He was looking for Dougie."

"Huh." Had Caitlin's twisted ankle been a ruse? They were deeper into the woods than the boys and I. And finding treasure like that? They'd have been excited, confused. A suitcase full of money.

EIGHTEEN

I drove to my rental unit. As I got to my door, my neighbor, a guy maybe ninety years old, called over to me. "A lady named Cindy has been looking for you."

"Cindy?"

"Yeah, I guess. A couple in a yellow car?"

A couple? That didn't ring any bells. But "Cindy" did.

"She said it was about Allison?"

Cindy never came looking for me. She just didn't. I went in and called the house and got no answer. I ran back to the car. When I got to the driveway I saw Allison's bike by the curb. A dozen broken spokes protruded like porcupine quills from the bent rear wheel. I ran inside. No one was home.

A neighbor lady knocked and came in without waiting.

"They've gone to the hospital."

I looked at her.

"They took her in an ambulance."

I ran back to the car.

When I got to the hospital I was in a state. I couldn't lose Allison. She resided in a trauma bay, comatose from a sedative. Her right leg was elevated by a couple of pillows. It seemed twisted. Wisps of her blonde hair hid one of her closed eyes.

My heart pounded. I kissed her. Cindy held her hand and delivered soft talk.

"What happened?" I said.

Cindy shook her head. "Broken leg. Up high. Maybe more."

"Is she all right?"

Cindy shrugged, pain in her eyes.

Gradually, Allison became alert, in pain. As I was deciding to try to get help, the surgeon showed up, a pleasant-looking bearded guy. He walked in, his focus completely on Allison, his dark eyes registering concern. "That's got to hurt," he said.

She nodded.

"We'll get you something for it." He scribbled a note and handed it to the nurse, who went out.

"What is it?" I asked him softly.

He held up a finger. He asked Allison to wiggle her toes.

I got it. Circulation.

"I'm Dr. Sherwood," he said to us.

He took us aside and showed us the X-rays. "It's a clean break, but the bone is twisted up against the hip, as you can see here, so I've ordered pre-op traction. We're concerned about blood loss in femur breaks," he said, "so we're setting up an IV for the morphine and will be prepared for transfusion if that's required. Shortly here we'll get her admitted and taken to a room."

"Does she have other injuries?" I asked.

He shook his head. "I'd say no. Nothing notable."

My heart was slowing down.

"When will you operate, doctor?" Cindy asked.

"We'll do the surgery on Monday morning."

"Why wait?" Cindy asked.

"We want Allison stabilized. Just a precaution. How did this happen?"

"She says a car hit her bicycle," Cindy said. "Right out in front of our house."

The doctor turned to Allison, who was breathing easier in the glow of a morphine drip. "How did it happen, Allison?" he asked.

"I don't know. It just hit me."

He looked surprised. "By your house? In your neighborhood?"

While we live in a suburb, our street fronts it. Lots of traffic.

"How fast was it going?" the doctor asked. "Any idea?"

"We have no idea," Cindy said. "It was a hit-and-run."

"What else do you know?" I asked.

"Did you see her bike?" Cindy asked me.

"Yes. But I didn't take the time to examine it."

Talking around us, the doctor asked Allison how much she was hurting now, offering her a numeric scale.

"A little," she mumbled. "Four? Five?"

"Do you have any health issues we should know about—high blood pressure, asthma, that kind of thing?"

"She's in perfect health," Cindy said.

At this point, people came in with a contraption to provide skeletal traction. I retreated with Cindy and the doctor to the hallway.

"What's the recovery time?" I asked.

The doctor's eyes took in both of us. "Most femoral shaft fractures take four to six months to heal completely. Some take longer. We'll know more after the procedure."

"Oh, dear." Cindy looked stricken.

There went Allison's summer.

"She'll be mobile pretty quickly," the doctor said. "She'll be limited in what she can do, that's all. Lots of people go through this. It'll be okay."

He told us the surgery would take place at six o'clock in the morning, and might take an hour or so. Given the issues of anesthesia, we might see her by ten o'clock, he said. "Don't worry; she's going to be fine."

After the doctor left us, Cindy and I watched them elevating Allison's leg. In about twenty minutes they had it in place. She took all this with morphine-induced equanimity.

Cindy settled in by Allison's bedside.

I went out. I'll find the guy. I'll kill him.

NINETEEN

To find a hit-and-run driver you begin with the police. Well, no. I took several pictures of Allison's bike, focusing on a smear of pale blue paint I found on the crumpled silver fender.

Our next-door neighbor, Bella Hurst, answered some questions.

"I was in the laundry room," she said. "The drier was going, but something got my attention, like a baby crying, you know? When I got to the front window I saw her down on the ground with her bike. Maybe I heard a car, I don't know. Poor thing. I stayed with her while Cindy called for help. She was all tangled up with the bike, you know? The medics were careful but she did cry a little."

I couldn't find any other neighbors who'd seen or heard anything. One child, however, a girl of five, Carla Billingsly, who lived across the street, had been playing in her driveway and saw the collision. She'd run to her mother.

"Carla is so shy," her mother said. "She's not going to come out here and tell you. I went to the front window. I would have gone over there, but Bella was there."

"And Carla?" I asked, "what did she say?"

"Oh!" Mrs. Billingsly laughed, shyly. "She said a car 'bumped' a girl across the street. I got out her crayons and we drew cars. From the colors she chose, I believe she saw a blue car, a very light blue."

I'd seen that streak of light-blue paint on Allison's bike, but thought it might be old news. "May I see the pictures?"

Carla's cars all looked like Volkswagen beetles, but light blue they were.

"You might want to put queries in business places up at the strip mall," Mrs. Billingsley said.

I went in the early evening to the police station and filed a report. Then I called my insurance agent. Then I went back to the house. I found a Coke in Cindy's fridge. In there with the Cokes I saw a six-pack of Corona. Cindy and I didn't drink beer. Corona was expensive, like around a dollar a bottle. The creep was driving the yellow car. Me? I wasn't there for my daughter.

Coke in hand, I wandered around the empty house. A couple of game boxes and a practice-guitar on the coffee table. My den neat. Mallory's room neat and tidy, an SU pennant and some other stuff on the walls. Spare clothes on Allison's floor. In Cindy's room, my room, a framed photo on the night table. I picked it up. It was a studio head shot of a guy whose hair was too long. "Love, Mark." Somebody in the business.

I sat in the living room. I'd match the light blue paint, smear it on a bunch of business cards, and hand them out at every auto repair place I could find. I would pay five hundred dollars cash to anyone who reported being asked to repair a damaged vehicle

of that color. At the same time, I also would look for a car dealer whose vehicle colors included the one in question.

Mark? Lover Boy? Unh.

Anyway, I had a way to begin.

TWENTY

Sunday night around ten the phone rang.

"Morrison," I said.

"I understand you're looking for the car that hit your little girl."

"Yes, I am."

"I told you to butt out."

The phone went dead.

Was it the voice of the guy who called me at the office? How about the guy who beat me up? When they go after people you love, what then?

I would never get off them. Not ever. Some people blew up the art museum. Lee Ann got killed. They didn't care. But *these* bastards actually *went after* Allison. After I settle with them I will go after the people who killed Lee Ann.

***

On Monday morning the surgical procedure and recovery went as the doctor had predicted. Allison went to the ICU to get her senses back. Mallory, who had been planning for several months to fly with two girlfriends and one of their mothers to New York City for three days of shopping and theater hopping, felt safe to go, and did. Cindy and I hung out in shifts at the hospital.

Safely past the operation, I reported the phone call to the police. The FBI got into it.

A couple hours after the FBI entered the case I got a visit at the hospital from the two agents who'd grilled me after Dougie was accosted at the lake. The three of us went to an empty visitors' waiting room. They wanted to know my story, *exactly*. A couple of pit bulls. I told them my family and I were the victims, not the criminals. To the fibbies this kind of thing becomes a blur. They start mixing up the chess pieces. Bottom line: try never to come to the attention of the FBI. Or, for that matter, any other law enforcement agency.

The Post-Times allowed the public perception to stand, that the injury to Allison might have been a mob hit. For all we knew it was true. Watching the noon news on TV in Allison's hospital room, Cindy saw a little blurb on the TV. A nurse was with us. Allison was asleep.

"Is that what you want her to see?" Cindy said to me. "That she was the victim of a hit by the mob?"

The nurse rolled her eyes.

"Are you trying to find out who did this?" Cindy asked.

I told her the hit-skip car was light blue, and that I'd painted business cards and taken them around.

"Do you think all this publicity is a good idea?" Cindy asked.

I went out and got myself a Styrofoam cup of very bad coffee one floor down. When the machine delivered just half a cup

I pounded on it. This did not make things better. Why? Why was somebody so anxious, so furious, so determined to get me to back off? Why would they do such a reprehensible thing? For three million bucks, was that it? A lot of money. Also the odor of politics.

***

Monday afternoon Allison was still resting well, sedated. I hit the road. In Huston, just north of us, Pop. 409, according to the sign, I pulled in to talk to a shade-tree mechanic. I liked the look of the place. I explained my mission: find a hit-and-run driver. He looked at my paint-stained business card and said, "What's the deal?"

"Five hundred bucks if you lead me to the right car."

He squinted at my card, then at me. "I just repainted an '82 Merc. Medium blue. Could be your car."

"Where do I find this guy?"

"You gotta go to my paint shed."

I had wondered where he did his spraying, because it couldn't be done under a canopy of trees next to a shack. "Why?"

"That's where the paperwork's at."

I suggested we go together.

He shook his head. "I gotta get some stuff done." He riffled through papers on the messy and greasy counter. The counter appeared to be the back of a junked church pew, or something like. "I got an address here somewhere. My painter's shed."

"He got a phone?"

"Nah. It's just a shed." He found the address and scribbled it on a piece of paper.

"Will he want some money?"

"Nope. This was my job. Tell him I sent you."

"Okay." I gave the guy a hundred bucks on account.

The sliding garage door on the painter's shed was locked down, and there was no sign of the painter. When I drove back to the shade-tree shop the mechanic said he had no idea how to get hold of him. What a way to run a business.

***

The car he'd painted was an '82 Merc. I went to a Ford dealership and found such a car, a Cougar wagon with a 112-horsepower V6. It was cream-colored, not blue.

"Yeah, you can find these cars," a salesman told me, "but not as sweet as this baby. Look at that luggage rack. This automobile will take you and your family on some great trips." He opened the driver's door and checked the odometer. "Only fifty thousand and change."

"Got one in blue?"

"Lemme call around."

We went to his cluttered cubicle and he made a few phone calls.

"Nope," he said. "These babies move!" Sharp pencil in hand, he addressed a blank notepad. "Lemme tell you what I can do for you on this one right here, including the paint job."

I stood up. "Thank you, no," I said.

His manager was striding toward me across the showroom with a big smile.

It took me five more minutes to get out of there.

I started cruising the streets of Stanton, looking for light blue Cougars. I knew I wasn't making sense.

21
TWENTY-ONE

On Wednesday morning Allison, a plaster cast encasing her right leg, got from her bedroom to the kitchen on her new crutches. She was still on acetaminophen, and stronger pills if she needed them, but she was managing the situation and the pain. I told her I understood bed rest is the only way to heal a broken femur. She said the doctor had told her that too. People had already started signing the cast. It was going to look like a railroad overpass. I liked it that people loved her as I did.

I finally heard from the shade-tree mechanic. I was again to go to his paint shed, where the car in question got its coat of blue. I drove back up to Huston and then to the shed, where I got the name and address I needed. This led me to a development a few miles west—a planned suburban outpost. The signs and bunting proclaimed "Holiday Park, Your Holiday by the Park." The house I sought was a new ranch-style white frame laminate structure with a carport. I thought if it caught fire it would melt rather than burn. Nobody was home. I spotted a model home a few houses down and drove over and parked in front of it. The breeze helped spray water from a sprinkler onto new grass.

At first I was uncertain about sitting in my car waiting for trouble, but the longer I waited the less I worried. What tough mob figure lived in a laminated house in "Your Holiday by the Park"? Just after 11 a.m. I got my answer. Along came a newly painted blue Cougar, and when it pulled into the carport out climbed a small woman, maybe 70. She reached back in and hauled out a sack of groceries. Collecting herself and the bag, she entered the house from the carport.

I pulled in behind her car, got out, went to the front door and rang the doorbell.

She peeked through the panel next to the door. Immediately she shrank back. I again rang the bell. I heard the side door of the house opening. The woman was about to discover that my car blocked her car in the driveway. No escape.

Moments later she opened the front door a smidge. "Down, Blackie," she said to an imaginary dog. "We don't donate to curbstone callers," she said toward me. She closed the door.

I rang the bell. "Ma'am," I said to the door, "if you talk to me I may not have to get the police in on this."

After some seconds, she opened the door. "Police?" Her aging gray face had come around the door and her eyes were big. "Why in heaven's name would you involve the police in whatever you're doing here?"

"Ma'am, you know, and I know, that you hit my girl's bike with your car. What you may not know is that she's just now out of the hospital. She'd have gotten there a lot sooner if you hadn't left without helping her. The question is, did you hit her deliberately?"

Her eyes went even wider. Then she blinked, and began to cry. "I have no idea what you're talking about. Someone hit your little girl? Deliberately? Oh, my! How bad is she hurt?"

"She had surgery for a femoral fracture. So far, she's doing okay. But she's facing several months of bed rest and post-operative care." I wanted the woman to feel terrible, and she apparently did.

"Oh, that's awful! My husband is in a nursing home. He has Alzheimer's. I have no money." She glanced at the table where her purse resided with her bag of groceries.

"You have a brand new house," I said.

"Friends are developing the park," she said. "They're letting me stay here."

"And you work?"

"I'm a nurse. When I'm working. Now I'm not. I'm seeing to Jacob."

I gave her a look. "And you left my daughter in the street?"

She started crying again.

"Look," I said, "This has to come out. But let me ask you a question. "Who was it called me up and tried to scare me off?"

"Whatever you're about, young man, you seem sincere. Why don't you come in?"

I did so. I sat on her brightly printed sofa, feeling the stiff fabric, probably sprayed to protect it from spilled food, and thought some more. "Did you tell anybody about this?"

She shook her head. "Are you okay?" she asked, giving me a funny look.

This question, *Are you okay?* is the most common question in the English language—and has been translated into seventy-eight other languages as well. I made this up, but just keep your ears open, wherever you go.

"Look. The police are going to question you," I said. "There's no getting around it. You know nothing about someone calling me?"

"I'll get you some water."

And she did.

"Now," she said, "why would you think I hit your child's bicycle?"

"You repainted your car."

"Ah." She actually laughed—a little titter. "I work for *Health at Home*, a nursing service. They told me I had to get a new car. For the image, you know. I told them the one I had would look like new if I had it painted. Even *that's* expensive. Didn't you see the *Health at Home* logo on the door? I'll bet when I opened it you missed it."

My face was red.

"I apologize," I said, getting to my feet. "I've apparently mistaken you for someone else."

"Well, you must have had good reason to believe I did it, or you wouldn't have stalked me."

Now there was a word. *Stalk.* I had done that. That was exactly what I'd done. I stood there mortified. Pulling myself together, I gave the empty glass to the poor woman and convinced her to take one of my hundred-dollar bills to help tide her over while she took care of her husband.

She followed me to the door, embarrassed but thankful for the money. "I'm so sorry," she said. "Tell your daughter I'm praying for her."

I drove to the shade-tree shop and got my hundred dollars back. The mechanic was nice about it. We even talked about the little banging noise I was hearing around the right front wheel and the slight instability I felt in the steering.

"Sounds like ball joints."

I was torn. More important to me than ball joints was the guy who called me in the night, implying the hit-and-run was deliberate.

"Can you do them now? Today?" I said.

He looked at me, then at his watch, then at the Ford. "Sure. Let me get the jack."

I liked it that you could still take your car to a guy like this and get it fixed.

A half hour later he said, "Look at this."

Mechanics always show you what they claim are the leftovers. Sort of like cats showing you what they just killed. They looked like old ball joints to me. I guess.

TWENTY-TWO

While I was chasing my tail on the hit-and-run, I was losing my focus on Everest. I was nervous about Daniel, my new stringer. Maybe I was asking too much of him. Maybe he was taking risks. On Thursday I called him to see how he was doing. He said the FBI agents appeared to have left, as I'd guessed they would. Current FBI focus was on the art center bombing. He told me he was trying to track down the thugs who'd attempted to waylay Dougie Perkins.

"We've got our eyes peeled, Mr. Morrison," he said.

"Who's we?"

"Kids who saw them down at the lake, other guys I know."

"Wait! Wait! You asked a bunch of kids to look for a couple of thugs?" Shades of old *Our Gang* movies.

"Mr. Morrison, there are posters up all over the place, sketches of those guys on every telephone pole in Everest, and here in Connerville, too. They're not going to go after some kid that looks at them funny."

"I guess you're right, Daniel. I just don't want anybody getting hurt."

I brought him up to speed on everything I could think of, including Allison's injury. "I'm trying to track down the hit-and-run car," I said.

"Somebody hit her on purpose?"

"I think so, yeah."

He was silent for a time.

"If it was deliberate, Mr. Morrison, maybe somebody stole the car to do it, and then got rid of it."

"Good thought, Daniel. We should see if anybody reported a car stolen the first few days of June. You cover the sheriff's annex down there. I'll check the police up here in Stanton."

"The paper carries police reports every week. Stolen cars get listed."

"Your weekly down there?"

"Yes, sir. I'll check it out."

I also asked him to check, unobtrusively, to see if Arturo Soto and Caitlin Barber were around. Arturo might be cutting down trees and Caitlin might be delivering pastries, I said. If Daniel happened to spot Arturo I'd ask the young man why he went back into the woods.

"I'm laying a lot on you, Daniel. But I don't want you sticking your neck out. I'm also changing how we pay you. We're going to triple your rate."

"Thanks. Tell Allison I'm sorry she got hurt. Would it be okay if I come see her?"

"She'd like that. Again, please be careful. It's not too far-fetched to think somebody could come after you."

"Me?"

"These people, whoever they are, are nasty. Just keep an eye out, okay? You can't be too careful."

After disconnecting, I went out and searched through Stanton Police logs and then looked at logs at the Flag County and Goddard County sheriffs' offices. I learned that several cars had been reported stolen lately, not unusual, I was told, and that several had been found abandoned and been towed.

The two counties and their towns had a common impoundment lot. At the moment it held about two dozen vehicles. When I got in there to look I didn't see any blue ones.

"Nobody picks 'em up in ninety days, we auction 'em off or sell 'em for scrap," the aged attendant said. "Pays my salary, anyway."

"Do you recall seeing a blue car?" I asked.

"We had a nice-looking Chrysler Imperial in here—light blue." He looked at his ledger. "Yeah, it must have been traced, because it was hauled out yesterday. Just like that. In and out." He got an inward look. "Seems like I seen it before. Well. They come and go. Always busy."

"Who paid the towing charge?"

He scanned his ledger. "Says 'J. Wright.'"

He gave me the VIN number. I gave him five bucks.

When I looked up the details on the VIN I found that the Chrysler retrieved in the name of J. Wright was a 1981 FS model, the "FS" standing for Frank Sinatra. Wanting to know more about what I was looking for, I dropped by the library and found books on car models. The car was sexy looking, and when you bought the FS model you got a little bit more. For an extra thousand dollars or so you got three cassette trays, sixteen Frank Sinatra cassettes, gold FS medallions on each of the front fenders and also on the trunk lid, plus a Mark Cross leather-bound cassette carry case with capacity for fifty-six tapes. The exterior was limited to Glacier Blue. One of the seat-cover options was Corinthian leather. I recalled Ricardo Montalban, a Mexican actor, stroking the ad copy in his exquisite English: "...seats available even in soft, Corinthian leather." This leather did not come from Corinth. They made up the name. The things I learn.

I went off in search of Mr. J. Wright and his car, and discovered that his house was located in a subdivision I was familiar with, Oake Runne Estates, where my publisher, Gradison Ritchie, also happened to live. Oake Runne was the most exclusive residential location in the territory.

I called the newsroom and then Mr. Ritchie's house. He was home and we talked. He had a "waving" relationship with Mr. Wright, he said, and after I explained my mission he called the man to pave the way for a call from me.

Mr. Wright agreed to see me.

"Would seven o'clock this evening be convenient?"

"Yes. That's fine," he said. "What's this about?"

"Your stolen car."

"It appears we got it back."

"I can explain when I get there."

"That's fine."

***

The Wrights' house, set back in the trees of a huge lot near a small lake, was big and handsome and brightly lighted. The housekeeper ushered me in. The interior looked like an art museum, with oil paintings decorating a lot of walls. I'd chased a story some months back that happened to immerse me in such art. What I saw represented a lot of money.

"They're out by the pool," the housekeeper told me, leading the way.

The day had cooled but the fading sun embraced the garden and patio. Mr. Wright rose to greet me, introducing himself as Jeff and his beautiful wife as Olivia. They looked to be about sixty or so. Olivia appeared to be operating on two or more cocktails.

Mr. Wright introduced two young men present: Nathan, whom I guessed to be about twenty-five, and Justin, maybe thirty. Both seemed like their father, handsome and in control. And then there was Julie, quite beautiful. Thirty-five? Forty? She was tall and slender, with straight hair the color of corn silk. A longish face, narrow nose, wide mouth. She wore no rings, so I wondered if she was unmarried. Then she made eye contact, a quarter-whammy. The library. The girl pushing the cart.

Mr. Wright caught the exchange.

"Mr. Morrison and I met at the library," she said. "I was shelving books. Small world."

Mr. Wright smiled at me. "I guess you have a couple of questions about our wayward car," he said. "Maybe you can tell us what it's been up to."

"How did it get lost?" I replied, equally fatuous.

"Why are you even pursuing this?" Julie said. "It was stolen. We got it back. That doesn't sound like big news to me."

I gathered my wits. "I think it may have been involved in a hit-and-run," I said.

"Oh? Was somebody hurt?" Jeff Wright said.

"My daughter," I said.

They were silent for a moment.

"What happened?" Julie said.

"I don't know for sure," I said. "She got hit on her bicycle. She ended up in the hospital with a broken leg."

"She okay?" Jeff Wright asked.

"Mending well, I guess," I said.

"Glad to hear it." He paused. "Is this personal, not about news?"

"I'm chasing a news story," I said. "But, yeah, I'd like to get the person who hit-skipped my daughter. Allison is her name. She's sixteen."

Julie Wright was the same magnet to me she'd been at the library. I had wobbly knees. But my focus was clear. It was on Allison.

23

TWENTY-THREE

"Why our car?" Jeff said.

"I'm not even sure it's your car I'm looking for," I said. "Tell me, did one of you run out of gas? Maybe the police found it before you could retrieve it?"

"Well, no," the younger son said. "Somebody stole the damn thing."

"Nathan!" his mother said.

She seemed wired. I wondered if she wasn't drunk but nervous.

"As far as we know," Jeff said, gazing at the others, then at me, "somebody broke into the garage, helped himself to the car, used it for whatever purpose, and then abandoned it out by the quarry."

The quarry, as I happened to know, was a gravel pit on State Route 48, near the state penitentiary, about five miles north of town.

"Kids go there to swim—as you probably know," Jeff said. "I think some pretty wild things go on." He smiled, shaking his head. "I should be around more; maybe I'd find out what my family's up to."

"It would be nice if you were home more," Olivia said.

The conversation was like a dance, with Olivia just a little out of step.

"Nobody took it to go swimming?" I said, as if I was amused.

The young men shook their heads. "Maybe the car thief," one of them said. "Kids, I bet."

I tried to imagine someone getting into Oake Runne Estates, coming onto this property, getting into the garage, and stealing a car. It seemed unlikely. Had to be kids.

"Do you leave your keys in the cars?" I said.

"They keep them in a box in there," the same son said. He smiled. "It keeps us from losing them."

I had the feeling he thought keeping track of keys was amusing.

I imagined a big garage, and a lot of key rings. Another problem with being rich.

I stood and thanked them. I nodded to Julie. "Nice seeing you," I said.

She smiled. I felt it.

Jeff and the older son stood to shake hands. The younger son sat and watched. He looked confused. I couldn't blame him. Yet, I marked his expression. Surprise? Why?

The housekeeper led me to the front door. Exiting the house, I turned and walked on the cobbled drive to the detached garage. It was huge, with four vehicular doors. I entered. In a lighted section of the vast space a man was polishing a shiny black Lincoln Town Car, one of perhaps a dozen vehicles in the place.

"I'm sorry to bother you," I said. "If I may, I'd like to look at one of your cars."

"You are?"

I stuck out my hand. "My name is Morrison. I'm a reporter for the Post-Times. I'm trying to find a hit-and-run car, and I understand you have a car here that was stolen and may have a damaged fender."

"Bert Long." He glanced at his hands, perhaps felt they were dirty, and didn't extend one. He was a small man—maybe 150 pounds or so—dignified, with dark hair and eyes and a small goatee. "We do have a car that got dinged up a little," he said.

"May I take a look?"

He pointed toward a car.

Lights went on in that quadrant. I saw that the garage was indeed immense, with vehicles parked three- and four-deep. The car I made my way toward was a nice-looking two-door, trim and clean, pale blue. I wanted some time to look it over, but the hour was late, and even under the lights the area where the car sat was dim. "Maybe I should come back tomorrow," I called to the chauffeur.

"Take your time. I have things to do here, anyway."

He went back to the Lincoln he'd been polishing, leaving me to look at the damage to the Chrysler. The right front fender was slightly bent, its paint chipped and scratched. I was able to break off a thumbnail-sized fleck. I compared it under the light to the paint on the business card. Hard to see. I wrapped the chip in a handkerchief and walked over to where Mr. Long was working under a pool of light of his own.

"You have a lot of cars to take care of," I said.

"Mr. Wright is a collector. Somewhat random. Vehicles he admires."

"A couple of questions?" I asked.

"Certainly, sir."

"As I understand it, someone came in here and took the Chrysler sometime before May 30, and you got it back on June 2 or 3. Do I have that right?"

"They towed it in here yesterday." He walked a few steps, opened a door, went into a room, and came out looking at a page in a binder. "Yeah. Here it is." He showed me the entry.

"When was it was taken?"

"I don't know. It wasn't signed out." He waved his hand around. "We have thirteen vehicles, including two motorcycles. They come and go."

"Wow. How do you keep track of them all?"

"If they don't sign them out, it's hard."

"Ah. So people sign the log, take the keys, return them to the drawer when they come home, and sign back in?"

"Yes. That's what's supposed to happen."

"But you have no record of the Chrysler being signed out."

"As I said. And if somebody stole it, well…" He laughed.

"It was up front, by a door, easy to take out." I waved at the garage doors.

"Yes."

I unwrapped my handkerchief to show him the paint chip. "I took a chip."

He nodded.

I tucked it away. "Can you tell me anything about the car?"

"They want to sell it."

I don't know what I expected, perhaps something along the lines of how long they'd had it. But not a sale announcement. Given the state of my Ford, the appeal of this car, and the fact that it had caught the eye of a collector, all of that combined to interest me. "How much?"

He smiled. "I don't know. Ten thousand?"

"Why are they selling it?"

He smiled again. "Mr. Wright didn't confer with me."

I looked at my watch. "I better let you go," I said. "Maybe I'll be back."

"That's fine."

I went out. Apart from probably being the hit-and-run vehicle, the car looked sharp. Strange night. I'd gone to the Wrights' focused on the hit-skip, run into Julie, and come out thinking about buying a car. It was the one that hit Allison, I was pretty sure. Was somebody messing with me?

TWENTY-FOUR

When I got to the office Friday morning I stopped by the desk of Melissa Meyer, campus reporter, the best reporter I knew, and told her what I'd experienced at the Wrights'. I caught her with her mouth full. With her fat fingers she had just pushed the last bite of a chocolate-frosted doughnut into her mouth. The doughnut box had migrated from the copy desk.

"That's pretty rich turf, Oake Runne," she said when she was able to speak. "People like that don't like being pushed around."

"What do you suggest?"

"Hey. You're a fisherman. Give the guy a little time; let him take the bait. If he's your man he'll tug on the line soon enough."

"How?"

"Well, for one thing, he could question your competence."

"Like?"

"Well, how about, *'Is it true, Mr. Ritchie, that your reporters are free to just barge in and ask impertinent questions? That man Morrison who came to my house? It was about some inconsequen-*

tial thing—a car that was stolen from our garage, I believe—but his questioning of me and my family was, well...'"

"Yeah. I could imagine something like that," I said.

She nodded. "Then, if he gets really anxious, he'll trot out his lawyers. You can't afford a lawsuit. He can."

"Sue me for what?"

"Slander. Or, if we print something, libel."

"Slander? Where would he pick up on slander?"

"Listen to yourself around here. All you'd need is for someone to take a few notes." Her eyebrows went up as she looked me in the eyes.

We both knew she was talking about Franklin Harris. Would he really do that? I don't know. Maybe.

"So, what would you do, Melissa?"

"Like I say, keep things quiet, let him stew. If he's guilty he'll get curious about what you're up to, maybe approach Mr. Ritchie. *'Say, whatever happened to that stolen-car story your man was working on?'*"

"Meanwhile?"

"I don't know. They've got help, right? A butler? A housekeeper? Find a way to get chummy. But keep it quiet."

Maybe the housekeeper, or Mr. Long, the chauffeur. "Thanks."

She nodded. "No charge. Meanwhile, remember. Keep your mouth shut."

I headed for my desk.

Abi had shown up, and I told her the whole story.

"Maybe you should work on this full-time," she said.

I smiled. "You've been on this desk two weeks and you think you can handle it all by yourself?"

"For a while? Yes."

"What'll you tell Lenny?"

"We'll just not tell him," she said.

"Don't stick your neck out," I said.

"I'll be okay."

***

Poking around for something quiet to do, I called Eric.

"What do you hear?"

"About Beets? The FBI is talking about doors on planes."

"Doors on planes?"

"Auxiliary doors. Stowage doors. Access to luggage, tools. Apparently, people have been known to take off with these doors not properly latched, meaning they might blow open. If that happens, you might get a wind tunnel in the cabin."

"Pretty scary."

"That's what they say. They tell pilots not to get distracted— Just try to keep the aircraft under control. And here's the thing. If a door bangs around it probably gets damaged. Assuming you land safely, you may still have to go to a dealer for the fix." FAA rules on fixes are pretty strict."

"And thus you fall into the arms of the FBI."

"That's what they're hoping."

***

I called Daniel to tell him I thought I'd found the car. His mother answered.

"Mr. Morrison," she said, "I don't know what you've gotten Daniel into, but he and his friend Randy Perkins have taken horses into the forest to find somebody. What in the world is going on?"

"I have no idea, Mrs. Smart. I'm learning what a go-getter he is. I'll try to slow him down."

"Nobody can slow Daniel down," she said. "The question is, is he old enough to be doing what you're asking him to do?"

"I asked him to look for that Mexican boy, Arturo, that's it. I have no idea what's going on."

"I'll talk to his father."

"Tell me," I said. "Is this about Daniel and his pal riding horses for fun or about looking for Arturo?"

She relaxed a little. "Daniel's father handles timber management. That involves looking around. There are always things to look for. He's always on the lookout for possible risks of fire, for example. There are places you can't go in a motor vehicle. Daniel likes to ride. But he looks for trouble spots, too. He reports them to his father."

"Any way to contact him?"

"Sometimes he gets to a phone and calls things in."

"If he calls, would you ask him to call me?"

"I'll try."

I got up and got a cup of coffee. I stopped by to tell Abi what was up.

"I got a call from the woman in the trailer park," she said. "She has a date with the Nazi."

"When?" The poor man had become *the Nazi*.

"Tomorrow night."

"Good."

"Good?" she said.

"While they're out to dinner or whatever, I'll visit his trailer, see what's under those sheets."

She laughed. "Oh, my, Morrison." She sobered up. "I'm covering the Tintown story, remember? Not you."

"You want to find out what he's up to? We've just had an opportunity served up to us."

She looked me over. "What if it's locked? How do we get in?"

I didn't miss the fire in her eye. "I have my ways."

"What did you do before you came here to the Post-Times? Really."

"I was a professor of linguistics."

She shook her head. "Ha, ha. I repeat, the Tintown story is mine. You get back to work on the falling man."

"Um hmm."

She was talking like a boss. I didn't miss that, either.

TWENTY-FIVE

Just before noon I got to talk to Daniel's father. He said Daniel had called. He and Randy had been riding along Green Lake.

"Can they ride anywhere they want in there?"

"When they're working for me they can. In fact, I want them to. They're looking for tree problems. Apparently, this time, they're also trying to find this Mexican boy you're looking for."

I wondered why they were looking for him in the forest. I imagined the two of them camping, gazing up at the stars at night through the hickory and walnut and oak. "I guess I ought to come down," I said.

"I'll either be home or at the station."

I headed south. The sky was clear. Windy. Maybe a front coming in. I passed a cemetery. Little flags fluttered near a few headstones. It was an anniversary of D Day. Almost fifty years ago.

When I arrived at the house, I saw Ed Smart out in his yard. We didn't get to start a conversation, because Daniel and Randy came riding up the street right then, cloppety clop.

Daniel called out, "Hey Dad, Hey Dad!" He pulled up, looking down at his father. "We found a dead guy in there, Dad."

"What?"

Daniel looked at me. "Mr. Morrison. It's the guy we went hiking with."

Ed put a hand on the reins of Daniel's horse. "Come on in the house. You, too, Randy."

The boys swung themselves out of their saddles and led the horses to a fence rail and hitched them up.

***

It was cool inside, a house of southwestern furnishings. The living area faced a big stone fireplace. Heads of half a dozen deer posed above it.

"Now tell me," Ed said.

"Shouldn't we be calling the sheriff?" Daniel asked.

With a touch of impatience his father waved off the question. "You two found this man dead and came straight here?"

"Yes, sir."

"He was under a tree," Randy added. "It fell on him."

Ed raised a hand. "One at a time, please."

"We were riding where that big boulder sticks out of the water," Daniel said. "About half a mile south of there we saw a tree down." Daniel dropped his head. "He was under it, Dad. His back was caved in. There were vultures on him, bugs."

Daniel rubbed tears from his eyes, and his father got up and went over and wrapped his arms around him.

"His face was all blue," Randy said.

Betsy Smart came in, and I stood up.

"The boys found a body in the forest," Ed said. "I'm going to call the sheriff."

She hugged her son, then went over and hugged Randy. "Come on. I'll get you some cocoa."

"We should take care of the horses, Mom."

"I've done that. Let's see about cocoa."

I followed Ed into his den and listened as he called the sheriff.

"We've had an accident," he said. "As I understand it, a man is dead. Near Green Lake, maybe half a mile south of the big rock. I'll see you there." He hung up. Then he picked up the phone again and alerted the ranger station and said he was going to meet the sheriff.

We walked into the kitchen.

"Horses good to go?" Ed said.

Mrs. Smart nodded.

"Daniel, why don't you and Randy stay here with your mom?" Ed said. "We're going to ride out and meet the sheriff."

I stroked my horse's neck—sort of like petting the fabric on a sofa—and swung myself into the saddle. I tried to remember how long it had been since I'd gone horseback riding. A while. Leaving the driveway, we arrived at a two-rut dirt road, then walked the horses along it into the forest and onto a trail to the lake. My horse wanted to wander off. Then she got edgy as we passed the big rock. Before we got to the tree and the body she began to shy. I got down and tied her off. The decay was fouling the air. Furry animals scurried for cover and vultures flapped to a safe distance.

We walked close enough to make things out.

"I believe that's Arturo Soto," I said.

"You knew him."

I nodded, my eyes not leaving the body.

"Well," Ed said, "it looks like he was doing some illegal logging in here." He gestured at tree-cutting equipment scattered about. "It's interesting that the tree fell on him. He shouldn't have been standing there. And he should have heard it falling."

"Maybe he ran the wrong way?"

"Don't know," Ed said. "Got to wonder why it played out like that, that's all."

"Why was he cutting trees in here?"

Ed laughed. "You're talking to the timber management chief for the district and he doesn't know."

I wanted to get to a phone, dictate a lead, and talk with Abi. Also, somebody had to get to Arturo's girlfriend, Caitlin, and perhaps find Arturo's parents, before this got out.

A rough-terrain vehicle came down the narrow gravel road that I'd seen the man bring his boat trailer down on my first visit to the lake. The RTV had an Eagle County Sheriff's Department logo on it and held Sheriff Tully and a couple of other people.

Studying the ground, the sheriff walked toward the body and gave it a long look, then gazed all around, his eyes going momentarily to the horses and finally resting on Ed and me. He pulled Ed away. They talked.

The sheriff paused in his conversation with Ed and spoke to one of his deputies, and the man approached me. "Let's talk for a minute," the deputy said, leading me off a way. "Please tell me who you are," he said to me in that polite but distant cop voice, "how you happen to be here, and everything you know, start to finish."

Another RTV arrived, and crime scene people began taping the area and searching the ground.

I told the deputy that I recognized the victim to be Arturo Soto, a young man I'd been hiking with when we looked for illegal traps.

A man who appeared to be the coroner stooped down by the body.

Arturo's life had been short and hard. I said a prayer for him.

TWENTY-SIX

It was coming on two o'clock as I talked to the deputy. My mind went to how to break the news to Caitlin, and also how to get away to dictate a lead to the desk. As I pondered, here came Daniel from the house. He was riding a bicycle, wobbling along, coming down the trail we'd ridden. I was past being surprised at the initiatives he took. He put down the bike and raised a camera and stood behind the yellow crime-scene tape taking pictures, as coolly as if he were shooting a sports event for the school paper. His lens caught the coroner bending over the body.

"Hey!" the deputy said, turning away from me. "No pictures."

"Sir, I'm a reporter for the Stanton Post-Times," Daniel said.

"Just stay here until I clear it." The deputy went to talk to the sheriff and returned. "No more pictures. And stick around. Don't go further than the house," he said. "He wants to talk to you." He glanced at me. "You too."

I took this as my dismissal from the crime scene. I got on my horse and followed Daniel out of the forest. It was slow going for me. When I finally climbed off my horse at the house, feeling a little bit like I was in a movie, Daniel told me his mother had left to deliver the film to the Post-Times.

"Your mother?"

"Yes, sir. I told her I had to stay here."

"You talked to the desk about Arturo?"

"Yes. To the lady you work with. Mrs. North?

"Abi. Good."

"We just hung up."

"Well, I appreciate your work. And your mother's, too." The Smarts were always interesting. I got on the phone and talked to Abi. She said Daniel had covered it all, and that if his mother arrived in time with the film, maybe the photo would make the paper along with the story.

Sheriff Tully came into the house and signaled to Ed that he wanted to talk with him. They went to the den. Ed came out and the sheriff then talked in the den with Daniel. It appeared to me that the two conversations didn't go well.

When it was my turn, the sheriff asked me about my dealings with Ed Smart, with Daniel, and with Arturo. He asked me if I was in any kind of business relationship with the Smarts.

When the sheriff was done questioning me, Ed Smart said to me, "The sheriff suspects that Daniel and I were engaged with the boy in lumber theft." He rolled his eyes. "I'm going to call my lawyer."

I thought the sheriff was off his rocker.

Yet to be dealt with, as Ed and I knew, was how Arturo had come to be under the tree. I had a hunch Ed wasn't going to raise his own suspicions about that until he talked to his lawyer.

"Ed," I said, "I'm going to go find Caitlin Barber."

The sheriff said nothing, so I left.

I drove the three or four miles from Ed's house to Everest and rolled down the main street, glancing left and right. I came upon several cars and small trucks parked along the edge of the road, and a couple of bicycles dumped in a yard. News travels fast in a little town. Caitlin's mother invited me in.

"You're from the paper," she said.

"Yes, ma'am. I'm sorry about Caitlin's friend."

She told me I'd find Caitlin down the hall.

I went down there and tapped.

"Go away."

"Caitlin?"

After a minute the door opened. Inside with Caitlin were two other girls. She lay on the bed, curled up, sobbing. One girl sat beside her.

"I'm sorry about Arturo, Caitlin," I said. "Call me if you want to talk." I dropped a business card on her nightstand, nodded to her friends, and went out.

As I drove north to Stanton, rain began to fall. When I got to the office I went to Abi's desk and sat in the visitor's chair. "The sheriff thinks Arturo and the Smarts were stealing lumber," I said.

"You want to get that into the story?"

"No."

We sat, reflecting. I barely knew Caitlin. The young aren't expecting death.

Franklin Harris came at us. "What's this about moving Roper?" he said.

"Huh?"

"You heard me." He looked at me. "Don't smirk at me, young man. I guess this dead boy was with you in the woods. Is that right?"

I ignored him. When he was gone I turned to Abi. "What's going on?"

"Lenny asked me how I was doing and I said we were swamped. Then he came back and said Louis Roper would be coming over to help us."

I grinned. "You do good work."

"Somebody has to tell Arturo's parents," she said. "Does the sheriff's office do that?"

"I don't know. I'll call down and ask around."

"You said Arturo had friends," she said. "Maybe they'll know how to get hold of them."

Louis Roper, the young man on loan to us from the city desk, was standing there, listening, taking all this in.

"What do you want me to do?" he said.

We smiled at him.

"Sit down at my desk, Louis," Abi said. She lifted some mail from stringers out of her in-box. "Let me show you."

27

TWENTY-SEVEN

The night of the break-in at the trailer was at hand. I had plenty of time before dark to reflect. Diluting the anxiety, I took Allison and Mallory to *Saucy Pizza*, Allison doing pretty well with her crutch. As we waited I told them Daniel and his buddy Randy went horseback riding in the forest and found Arturo's body under a felled tree. I tried to report his death gently, but that never works.

We switched gears and Allison and I listened as Mallory painted scenes for us from her visit to New York City: Times Square, Fifth Avenue, the theater district, Central Park. "Just the noise," she said. "You go outside your hotel. The people, the traffic, the banging, the building going on. It's so alive. And the Mets. Did you know the Mets are hot?"

"That's a New York baseball team, right? Like the Yankees?" Allison said.

Mallory bubbled on. "When I get out of college I'm going to move to New York."

"Not here?" Allison said, alarmed.

"No problem," I said. "All you need is money." College was getting expensive. But Cindy was emerging as a successful country singer. She was endorsing western apparel. She was so well known now that she'd been advised by friends to take precautions about the girls' safety. Considering the possibility of a celebrity kidnapping was a whole new game for us. Cindy and I needed to talk about it. The hit-skip had made me paranoid.

"Tell me about Daniel," Allison said.

Well, well. "He's going into his senior year. He's a good reporter. He has curiosity and he takes initiative. Imagine one of our other stringers riding into the woods like that to look for a missing person, then coming back in with a camera."

"I looked him up in his high school yearbook," Allison said.

"Where'd you get that?"

"I borrowed it through library exchange."

Talk about taking the initiative. More to worry about.

Between bites of pizza we touched on my search for the hit-and-run driver, and for a moment I got back on the subject of their safety. I said I thought my colleague, Abi North, had stuck her neck out by going alone down to Tintown to look for the nutcase. "Things are not always as safe as we assume," I said.

"Dad," Mallory said. "Enough."

But Allison took off on a tangent. "We were talking in class about Norman Rockwell," she said. "His paintings were all about American innocence, right? Fairy tales. I'd rather get the truth."

I laughed. "You didn't say that about Santa Claus."

"Seriously, Dad. High school history books may be telling the truth, but not *all* of the truth, I know that." She giggled. "Somebody ought to write a romance novel about George Washington. We know where he slept, but we don't know the rest of the story."

I gave her a look. But it *was* funny. "You think he slept around?"

"People think he was dull. What if he wasn't?"

The kids had a point. It wasn't just the sexual exploits of presidents that got hushed up. It was anything that didn't fit the biases of people who approved textbooks.

My conversations with the girls, as they got older, had fewer holds barred. We learned things from each other and laughed a lot. We ate a lot of pizza. Sometimes, the best way for one of us to get a point across was to catch the others with their mouths full.

One particular comment by Allison gave me a jolt. She said she'd read a book by a Wall Street Journal editor. "Nine out of ten letters they get at the Journal aren't even rational. According to him, anyway."

"Not rational how?" I said.

"A lot of letters are about conspiracies. People just don't believe what they're being told. They think the government lies about things."

"Give me an example."

"Well. There's the Kennedy assassination."

"Other than that."

"Just about everything, Dad. If nine out of ten letters to the Wall Street Journal are irrational, maybe they're rational, you know what I mean? Like it's the other ten percent, and the editor, who don't get what's going on."

"She's got a point, Dad," Mallory said.

I glanced at my watch. "Oops. Gotta go," I said. "Got to get ready for a meeting."

TWENTY-EIGHT

I took the girls home, gathered up some of my dark clothes—out of my former closet—and went to my rental unit, where I dressed myself to look like a jewel thief in a Hollywood movie. When I walked toward my car, there stood a figure in black. Oh, no! Not again! But it wasn't the thugs. It was Abi. She had decided to join me. Like me, she was wearing black. Jeans and a dark turtleneck, fashionable but functional. Her family's car was parked by the curb.

"What the hell are you doing here?" I said.

"The Tintown story is mine."

"This is a break-in, Abi."

"You have to fight fire with fire," she said.

"What about your family? What if something bad happens?"

"I told Fred we had to go to Tintown, that I'd only be gone a couple of hours."

After sidestepping my point like a bullfighter, she suggested we take her car; it was a lot quieter than mine, even fixed as it was. I agreed, and took a paperclip and my little lock picks from the glove compartment of my car.

"This is crazy, you coming," I said.

She grinned, "Yes, but stupid." She was amused but anxious, clowning around for cover. I hadn't seen this side of her.

Lights were on in the woman's trailer, but all was dark at the man's. After we cased the neighborhood for sound and movement, I took the paper clip and picks from my pocket, and, putting on my gloves, cautiously took a few minutes to open the door to the trailer. You'd think lock picks would be hard to get, but I'd discovered you could order them, claiming you'd use them in your work restoring old motorcycles. That made them available to burglars, too.

Abi looked at me and my little tools.

"Touch nothing," I said.

She smirked and displayed gloves.

The place smelled of mice—that is, unclean, stale, moldy, and probably infested with the little rascals. Overlaying that odor was the smell of bleach. I turned on my penlight, shielding the beam with my hand, cautiously letting light peek out. From the state of things, I guessed the man was housing himself elsewhere. I hoped so, anyway. I didn't want to encounter him.

Abi lifted the covering sheet from a table, extracted one piece of paper, and re-draped the stack.

I lifted the sheet from the other table. More papers. I took one, and replaced the sheet. I tucked the paper under my shirt. Abi put hers in her pocket.

Car lights caught the window. We held our breath. The car went on by.

"Wait." I went to the end of the trailer, and was about to enter the bedroom.

"Lights!" Abi hissed.

Beams lit the house and then the driveway, wheels crunched gravel. I considered our options. I could scare the poop out of him as he entered. Might work. Nothing else came to mind. I moved toward the front door. Next to it was the light switch.

Abi picked up a wine bottle off the sink. Holy Moses! She was going to hit him over the head. I put up a discouraging hand. We stood like characters in a wax museum.

The beams bent away from the driveway. Somebody turning around.

"Come on!" she said. She put the bottle back.

"Wait." I went into the bedroom, penlight shaded. There were sheets and blankets on the bed. He was living here. I opened the top drawer of the dresser and found two shirts, then the second drawer, which held two sweaters, then the third. In this drawer, under some underpants, socks and tee shirts, I touched and extracted a Rolodex. With my penlight I was able to read names, addresses, phone numbers.

"Morrison!"

Starting from the back of the Rolodex, I flipped through the cards a second time. The name "Wright, J" showed up, No. 14 Forest Road, Oake Runne Estates, Stanton, Illinois. I returned the Rolodex to the drawer.

We tiptoed toward the door. Here came a guy walking, his feet crunching gravel. Like a couple of shore birds trying to steal bait from a bucket, we froze. He opened the door and walked right in, and saw Abi.

"What!"

Abi's scream did him one better.

"Wait! Wait!" I said. "This is your trailer? We are *so* sorry. Oh, wow! We thought all these trailers were empty. Because of the tornado, I mean. We'll get out of here. I am so sorry. Wow."

Glancing into the bedroom, registering the neatly made bed, no doubt, he returned his gaze to us.

"We just got here," I said, trying to look embarrassed. With my hands behind my back I removed my gloves and stuffed them into a pocket.

Abi giggled. "Oh, Johnny," she said. "You and your ideas."

I tried to look horny. You had to be there.

"Get out of here."

We got out of there and hurried to the car. As we left, I turned on the headlights.

"I think I wet my pants," she said. She giggled.

We drove in silence. My adrenaline spike was subsiding.

"Why did he let us go?" she said.

"He didn't know what to do."

"What do you mean?"

"Consider. He walks in. A guy's standing there. In the dark! At first he's terrified. But there's a girl with the guy. Ahhh! A little hanky-panky."

"Yes. But after we leave he starts to wonder," Abi said. "He gets it: we were snooping around."

"He's not going to do anything, Abi. He's scared."

"You think?"

Wouldn't you be, if you were him?"

"He."

***

At my rental unit, we sat still and silent for a few minutes at the kitchen table.

Abi giggled.

It dawned on me that she giggled when she was nervous. She got up and got a diet soda out of my fridge. I got up and put ice in a glass and added a glug of bourbon. We sat some more. Soda can in hand, she got up and turned off the light and went to my front window and scanned the street. After a while, she turned the light back on and sat down. We considered what we'd taken from the trailer.

The flier that Abi picked up, one page, big print, called for a meeting of a "U.S. Patriots Forum." It gave a date and a place, Wicker Lake, Idaho, where "the Forum," which would consist of "a thousand leaders, maybe more," would consider how to respond to the "invasion of the illegals." The flier was signed "Finis." On the back were directions to Wicker Lake and details of arrangements to be made by persons making "the pilgrimage." It appeared they'd be roughing it like doughboys in tents to be erected on leased farmland there.

"It feels like a revival meeting," Abi said. "You know. Get some converts and get them roiled up. Remember the guy at the quilt show? Mr. Crowley? People like that."

She had me thinking about Nazis.

We next considered what I had, a handbill to be mailed with the flier, supporting the case for the Idaho gathering. Millions of Mexicans and other Hispanics were flooding the country, to America's peril, the handbill said, and the government was failing to do anything about it.

"These immigrants are undermining the American way," it said. "We have congestion, environmental chaos, increasing crime rates, health risks, rising health care costs, significant pressure on our educational system, job losses." Interspersed with text were graphs and charts supporting various points being made. The closing words were a call to action: "Americans know the truth. Our government is helpless. It is time to act."

I'd heard the government maligned in many ways. "Helpless" was a new way of putting it.

Like the flier, the handbill closed with a signature line: "Finis."

I had another drink. Abi just sat there looking anxious.

"The guy in the trailer didn't write this," I said. "It's well written, and it's persuasive. From the feel of it, I'd say there's a think tank behind it—some political research group."

"So what do we do?" she said. "We can't write a lead that says we broke into somebody's trailer, stole some papers, and here's what they said. Maybe we should go to the FBI."

"About what? Sedition? I don't think so. Maybe in wartime."

"So where does that leave us?" she said.

"I found a name," I said. "J. Wright, on Mr. Buford's Rolodex. You remember J. Wright? The guy in Oake Runne Estates?"

"You didn't tell me about any Rolodex."

"It was in his dresser."

"Wright? The vice president of the railroad? The guy that owns the car you think hit Allison?"

"Yeah. That J. Wright."

"I don't believe it," she said. "He's a successful businessman. Why would he be mixed up in something like this?"

"I don't know, but he is."

"I keep imagining my mug shot on the Post Office wall," she said.

"I want to look up 'Finis'," I said.

I came back to the kitchen with my Merriam-Webster's dictionary. "Jefferson Davis, president of the Confederacy, often signed his papers 'Finis'," I said. I considered the irony of this guy using the name. "That was the most deplorable time in American history. As I recall my high school history book, it was glorifying people like Robert E. Lee." I thought of course of Allison.

But she was on a new page.

She shuddered. "This is about darkness in the world's greatest democracy. Right now."

"That's pretty heavy," I said. "Maybe it's about some people trying to make themselves heard."

She shook her head. "Hate-mongers," she said. "Hate campaigners. Brownshirts. Sturmtruppen."

I was surprised again by what she knew. We'd talked about the Sturmabteilung, and Hitler's rise to power, in a class at Monterey.

"Hitler got things going in Bavaria," she said. "The establishment sniffed at him. 'The little corporal.'"

"To get that sort of response, you have to touch a national nerve," I said.

"As you yourself pointed out," she said, "this is a well-conceived mailing, perhaps going to more people than you and I imagine."

"If everyone they had listed on that Rolodex is some sort of nut, and they all get this mailing, and they have nutty friends, they might be right in imagining thousands of people at their gathering in Idaho," I said. "Maybe the anti-Woodstock. Without the music, I mean. Without Janis Joplin, The Who, The Grateful Dead, Joan Baez, on and on."

"Those were the days," Abi said.

"You were there?"

"No. But I wanted to be. It was the summer of 1969. I was fourteen. Mom and dad had me on a short leash."

"I'll bet they did."

TWENTY-NINE

On Monday morning Caitlin Barber, looking awful, met me at a place called Mom and Dad's. It was ten o'clock in the morning. The two of us had the place to ourselves. Blinds kept the sun from Caitlin's eyes but left her in striped shadow.

She let her coffee and the sweet roll sit.

"I have kids your age, Caitlin," I said. "I think I know what you're going through."

She studied her coffee.

"So, who's going to arrange the funeral?" I said, trying again. She was too young to be planning a funeral. "Do you know how to contact the family?"

She spoke, in a tiny voice. "I know his friends— Raúl, José Luís, and another boy, Juan, I think. Raúl's the one helped him move the stove."

"How do I find these guys?"

"They all work."

"Where?"

"Here and there. They cut grass, do construction, dig foundations, shingle roofs, that kind of stuff."

"So where do they live?"

"They rent a house off Snake Road."

"Snake Road?"

She poked with her finger at the apricot filling. "I think it's Eagle Street," she said. She smiled a tiny smile. "Everything around here is named Eagle Street, like we're in Eagle County, you know?"

"Who named it Snake Road?"

"They close it in the spring so the snakes can migrate, get across the road. They just call it that."

"Oh? What kind of snakes?"

She got more animated. "All kinds. The ones to watch out for are copperheads—or the cottonmouths, timber rattlers. Those guys get *huge*. Six feet. That thick." She made a circle about the size of a saucer with her hands. "There's all kinds. Worm snakes, blue racers, ring necks, king snakes, milk snakes." She was lecturing me, enjoying it. "Milk snakes look like coral snakes, but people say they're not poisonous."

"You know a lot about snakes," I said. I took a sip of my coffee. It wasn't so bad. "Why do they migrate?"

She put sugar in her coffee. "There's a big swamp, west of the road? They cross it to mate on high ground. It's blocked this time of year. Five or six months. Not that anybody'd want to drive in there. We get a lot of snakes. You don't want to build a house on a snake nest, I'll tell you that."

"On a snake nest?"

"The woman I work for knows a family that built their house on a nest. You open a cabinet and a snake slithers out. Or worse, you reach in and get a surprise. Or, you wake up and feel a heavy weight across your ankles."

My discomfort got her further into it. She actually grinned.

"They got hundreds of snakes, I don't know, thousands, living in their place—their den, whatever—and these people built a house right on top of it. Why, I don't know. Anyway, they got snakes in the basement, snakes in the walls, snakes in the pantry, forever, man. Snakes in their life."

I thought about the boys living on Snake Road. Cheap, but not too good a place to live.

"Let me change the subject here, Caitlin," I said. I cleared my head. "I'd like to know what was going on with Arturo. For example, why'd he go back into the forest?"

For a while she just sat there. Then she answered.

"Remember I hurt my foot? He took my ankle bracelet off to rub my ankle." She was looking inward, leaning, remembering him. "We forgot it. So we went back to get it."

"When was that?"

"The day after."

I thought about that. It would have been before the deputies went in with the dogs and the thugs chased Dougie.

"So when did he get the idea to take down a tree?"

"When we went in there with you. It was a walnut. He looked up at it and went over and touched it. He wanted the wood."

"What for?"

"To make things, like folk harps and things."

"Why wasn't he using a power saw?"

"I don't know. Power saws make a lot of noise. Big crosscuts need two people." She took a big gulp of nothing, air. "I guess nobody wanted to help. It's illegal, you know. Cutting a tree in there. If they catch you you're going back to Mexico."

Her eyes got wet. She started to cry.

I gave her a paper napkin. I was being too pushy, but she'd clarified something for me. Arturo and his friends were illegal and she knew it.

After a while I asked her a question: "How was he going to get it out?"

She ignored me.

I gave it a minute, and she composed herself.

"Help me here, Caitlin. Maybe I can understand."

She stirred her coffee, sniffing. "Look, I have to deliver some buns. Can we talk about this later?"

"Sure. Just one more question. He bought your mother a stove. That was a nice thing to do. How did he happen to do that?"

She blew her nose on the napkin. "Because he was a sweet man, Mr. Morrison. Mom's stove went out. She needed a stove and he got her one."

"Just like that? Did he do that a lot? Help people?"

"Yes. When he could."

"May I ask where he got the money?"

"You think he was a thief? That what you think? He didn't steal things." Her face was blotched with red.

"I'm sorry. I just wondered where the money came from, Caitlin."

"His parents sent him money. They're rich."

"Ah. That would explain it."

"I gotta go." And she was up and gone.

I paid for the coffee and rolls. Then I drove out to Snake Road. A barricade with a sign with fine print about snakes and the environment told me to drive no farther, and to walk at my own risk. I decided I didn't need to see the boys. They probably weren't home anyway.

I drove over to see Ed Smart. Betsy said he'd be home for lunch shortly. Would I like a cup of coffee?

I gathered Betsy was no longer so angry with me. "Just had some, thanks. With Caitlin. Where's Daniel?"

She laughed. "At the lumber yard. They called him in."

"The sheriff is off your case?"

"Yes, he is. No apology, though." She paused. "But who would kill a boy like Arturo?"

"Good question," I said. "What about a funeral?"

"Somebody's arranging the service."

"Somebody?"

"We have several Roman Catholic families around here."

Ed and Daniel walked in together.

"I forgot my lunch," Daniel said. "I have to get back."

Betsy waved me along toward the kitchen with the others.

I protested, but southern hospitality has its way.

"Ed, what's a walnut tree worth?" I said from a stool in the kitchen.

"It's complicated. As that log lies there, black walnut, it's probably worth several hundred dollars."

"I think he was selling wood for stringed instruments, furniture, gun stocks, that kind of thing," I said.

"Could be," he said. "Just for starters, it's a nice, clean tree. But then you have to get it out of there. He felled it near the lake. It's possible to cut it up, drive along the shore and get it, I suppose. Or float it out of there, I don't know. But then the wood has to be milled, reduced to lumber, air dried. And there's the question of market. Did he have buyers lined up? If he did, he might have done okay."

Daniel got up to go. "I got the glasses, Mr. Morrison." He went to his room and came back with them. Metal frame. Tinted lenses.

"Let me see them," Ed said. He washed the glasses, took off his own, put them on. He picked up a cereal box and read some text. "These are for a nearsighted person. Like me."

"I was wondering why somebody lost them in the lake," I said.

"We had a guy swatted his off when a hornet got after him," Ed said. "I could check lost-and-found to see if anyone reported his missing."

"I'd appreciate it."

Ed took the glasses.

Driving home I noticed a new sound in my car. It didn't sound like a rattlesnake so I dismissed the thought that I might have picked up a passenger at the end of Snake Road. I called the shade tree mechanic.

"Could be tie rods," he said.

"Tie rods. Hmmmm. So what could happen?"

"Oh, a wheel might fall off."

THIRTY

Wednesday was Mallory's birthday. I showed up a half hour early for the party but she was at the hairdresser, so I lazed away the time with Allison, whose cast had signatures and symbols all over it. I asked about a scribble that looked like a mountain and a stream.

"That's Stone Mountain Rivers, Dad. He and mom are going to open the county fair. It's a last-minute thing. Sugar Beets was going to do it with him but she's in mourning, you know? Since Senator Beets died? Actually, Mom and Mr. Rivers sound pretty good together."

That suggested they'd been rehearsing within earshot of my housebound daughter. "Mr. Rivers has been here, in the house, rehearsing with your mom?"

She smiled. "Mr. Rivers is gay, Dad. All his friends know it. He's just not out there with it, you know?"

I didn't mention the photo signed "Mark" I'd seen on the nightstand. I was sure Allison didn't want to talk about it, either.

"A lot of these country singers live around here, don't they? Stone Mountain Rivers too?"

"Sort of," Allison said. "He lives down around Everest, I think. He flies his helicopter up here to rehearse with mom. He uses it mostly to commute to Nashville."

"Parks it where?"

"Up here? At the fairgrounds."

The way some people live. I tried to envision where Mr. Rivers might keep the thing. In his barn? And then roll it out to go to meetings in Nashville? Or to come up here? Maybe Cindy was right about me; she and her friends were out of my league.

Mallory showed up, hair cut nicely, and she and Allison and I considered the supplies we'd need. Then we ordered pizza for the evening from a new franchise, *Papa John's*.

Mallory's current boyfriend showed up. No hat on backwards at least, and he seemed polite enough. Shortly after he arrived the Smarts pulled into the driveway. They were the only people I myself had invited; I was facilitating Allison's secret romance with Daniel.

Allison, gimping around, greeted everyone with a glorious smile, looking a lot to me like the actress Meg Ryan. She introduced me to Mr. Rivers. If her leg was hurting, I couldn't tell. The Smarts signed her cast, Daniel last as "(heart) Smart."

Cindy gave Mallory a gold toe ring. Okay, whatever. Mark of the Signed Photo did not make an appearance. The party was over not long after dark. When everybody was gone I told Mallory I had a present for her.

"Michael Jackson is supposed to be in St. Louis in March, and if I'm still in the good graces of our publisher, I believe I can get you two press passes. If I get them, he will no doubt expect me to write a review. Not having seen the show, I'd probably interview you."

That evening during the party I got free passes to a concert myself. Stone, with whom I had a good time recalling off-color ballads from our college days—he from SIU, me from Emory—gave me a handful of wristbands for up-front seating at the opening-night musical extravaganza at the county fair.

More important to me, he told me something that gave me a possible angle on the falling-man story. When he'd been rehearsing with Sugar Beets, Stone said, she'd been bemoaning the murder of her older brother. "She said they killed him because he changed his mind on a bill. He was going to vote no so it wouldn't come out of committee. Then he told them he'd changed his mind. He was going to vote yes."

"And somebody killed him for that?" It seemed far-fetched, but I'm no politician so how would I know. It occurred to me that Senator Beets had been considerably older than Sugar. She was maybe thirty-five, and he, I guessed, had been closer to fifty.

"That's what she believes. With his negative vote, the bill wouldn't have come to the floor. But with his positive vote, it would have. But now, with him dead, it's bottled up, and probably won't come to the floor this year."

"What bill?"

"Driver's licenses for illegal immigrants."

"Tie vote in committee?"

"That's what the situation is now, Sugar said."

Beyond my astonishment at ruthless politics, I was puzzled. It seemed dumb to me to kill the bill. There were millions of illegals in the U.S.; no way we were shipping them all home. If they could get transportation to a job, everyone would win, it seemed to me. They'd get wages, pay taxes. Plus, they'd have to get auto insurance, I assumed—another winner all around. "So who wanted the bill killed?" I asked.

Stone frowned. "People who want the illegals stuffed."

"And who might they be?"

'Where I come from, just about everybody, man."

"So why was Senator Beets going to change his vote?"

He laughed. "You ever been to Springfield? Votes get traded like baseball cards."

As he said this I thought back to the abortive attempt by the Post-Times, just a year or so back, to establish a Springfield bureau. For a month or so—no more than six weeks—I'd been the "State Capitol Correspondent." Then our publisher, Gradison Ritchie, had abruptly changed his mind and closed the office. It cost too much, he said. I didn't much like Springfield anyway. But, yes, I'd had a little glimpse of Springfield politics. Enough to be wary of the intrigue. I'd also gotten a little insight into the newspaper business: television news was coming on; it was a tough time for newspapers, including ours. Our publisher, trying to spread our wings, had gotten them clipped.

Eric and Carol were at the birthday party with their kids. I had a question for him.

"How can we get the news to the dead boy's parents?" I said.

"There's an agency that tries to find relatives. I'll see what I can find out," Eric said.

That was my only private moment with him that night. We had a house full of people and it was Mallory's birthday and, along with my wife Cindy, I was a host.

***

As I walked into the county fairgrounds for the grand opening of the fair on Sunday night, the air was warm and the sky was clear. I was accompanied by family and friends, and our mood was festive. The fairgrounds were crowded, and the atmosphere was redolent of that film fantasy, *State Fair*: straw on the dirt, the odor of livestock, the noise of the midway—garish organ music, shouts, laughter—and the orbiting lights of a Ferris wheel, its benches gently swinging, carrying mostly couples into the sky and down, into the sky and down.

A vast amphitheater had been fashioned for the opening extravaganza. People, most in family groups like ours, were bringing in their own folding chairs and blankets and getting as close to the front as they could. Down front, close to the stage, chairs had been set up for VIPs, among whom we counted ourselves.

Stone and Cindy had the country sound and the heartbreaking duets, and they had the crowd. I figured eight hundred or so.

The two of them were singing away, everybody having a sweet time, when an astonishing thing happened. Down the center isle strolled Sugar Beets, who had pulled out of the show because she was grieving over the death of her brother. Now, here she came. As she danced and twirled her way down the aisle, smiling widely and waving grandly, heads turned, and people gawked and applauded. Stone, up on the stage, signaled the band to switch to welcoming music. Soon enough the three of them were together on stage. Sugar told the crowd her troubles, in the intimate way she had, and said, "But I couldn't stay away." People loved her, and here she was, uninvited, unannounced, but welcomed even by the two singers she'd overwhelmed.

Our family broke for a couple of hours of carnival—rides, games, cotton candy, the works—taking turns pushing Allison around in her wheelchair. Sugar came with us, which slowed us down for autograph parties. Cindy and Stone also drew attention. Republican vice presidential candidate Dan Quayle was rumored to be at the fair. If he was, I bet he was jealous of the fuss made over us.

I got Sugar aside, conveyed my condolences, and asked her, off the record, if she thought her brother's death had been politically motivated.

Open person that she was, she didn't hesitate. "He was gonna get a bill out onto the floor for these poor immigrants. She sighed. "For once in his life, he was gonna do the right thing. And they killed him for it."

"Who they?"

"I don't know, but I know the rats in the senate who were workin' to kill that bill. They been guests of mine at Ferry Lake. Most all of 'em."

"Have you dug into this?"

"No. I don't know yet who to go after."

"So how are you going to narrow it down?"

"I thought I'd invite 'em to dinner, nice an' all, kind of a memorial dinner, and see who shows up. I'll listen for the false notes, you know?"

I smiled acknowledgement. "Interesting. I wish I could be there."

She tilted her chin a little at me. "Ya know, I think I'll invite you. What's your name?"

"Morrison."

"What do you do, Mr. Morrison?"

"Just Morrison. I work on the state desk for the Stanton Post-Times."

She looked surprised. "Gosh, I hope I didn't spill the beans."

"Don't worry. I have good reason to be on your side." I told her how I thought Allison had been injured.

"How terrible."

"Yes," I said.

She smiled, a remarkable vision. "I'll call you."

THIRTY-ONE

On Monday, Daniel, sounding a lot younger, called and said Tully had ordered an autopsy. "He's talking about murder," Daniel said.

"Want me to call him myself?" I said.

"No, no. But I'm learning this isn't exactly like covering high school sports."

I wanted our stringers to cover their territory. But I realized there were things they weren't equipped to do. I had to be careful here, or Daniel might get in over his head, as Eric's wife Carol had warned me at dinner.

"The Sheriff wants my dad to hold up on removing the tree," Daniel said. "I guess that fits with the rest of his thinking. By the way, there's a funeral mass for Arturo at the Catholic chapel. Two o'clock Wednesday."

"In Everest? I'll come down," I said.

Before we quit, Daniel said he was coming up to Stanton to look into enrolling at the university and hoped he could stop by Cindy's to see how Allison was doing.

I said I thought he'd be welcome.

Within an hour Daniel called me back with his story. "I got talking to Mrs. Penny—you know, the lady who had this job before me? She's nice. She really likes working for the sheriff. She told me 'forensics' seemed to point to murder, and they were getting fingerprints off Arturo's tools and looking at getting DNA samples. That's what she said, 'DNA samples.'"

I told Daniel I was pleased that he was talking to Mrs. Penny, but that we had to be careful what we reported based on anything she said because it might be inaccurate and, further, the sheriff might detect a leak. "And don't tell her any of *our* secrets."

We went to press with the autopsy story, saying the sheriff suspected murder. I wondered about the sheriff's pronouncements. He'd certainly been wrong about criminal complicity among Arturo, Daniel, and his dad. But, like Daniel's dad, I had to admit how Arturo died was uncertain. There was an aura of violence around us: the murder of Senator Beets, the attacks on Allison and me. And now perhaps Arturo's death.

To avoid exposing Mrs. Penny's indiscretions to the sheriff, we didn't drape the story in speculation about tire tracks and DNA.

Meanwhile, there was news right in our own newsroom. I say this tongue-in-cheek, yet it was serious in its way. I found out that Lenny, our editor in chief, was removing "Calvin and Hobbes" from our comic pages. I liked Calvin and Hobbes. So when Lenny was managing by walking around I asked him why the strip was getting the gate. Some parents were complaining, he said, that there was code in the strip that would lead kids to consider "alternative behaviors." Yikes! Secret code in our funnies! I told him I was sorry he was killing Calvin and Hobbes, because to my mind, at least, the strip was actually worthy of thought, whereas most strips were not.

Joining the conversation by my desk, our new society editor, Helen Beaulieu, expressed support for Lenny, saying editors had responsibility for community leadership, including what went into their funnies. I was surprised by her point of view and passion about it. I'd had her pegged as not too swift. Maybe not.

Although I was in favor of laissez-faire policy, and hence on the other side of the fence, I didn't have time to get into Calvin and Hobbes with them. It was all I could do to focus on the falling-man story. But it occurred to me that, in failing to defend Calvin and Hobbes, I was abdicating a responsibility to defend freedom of thought and expression. Because of specious complaints to editors all over America about various comics' so-called hurtful insensitivity to this or that sacred cow, sharply drawn and funny comic characters were one by one being replaced by bland blobs dealing in drivel.

I harked back to my conversation with Allison and Mallory about high school history books, and how they omitted more and more actual history, perhaps because people who controlled the educational process thought it wiser or safer or better not to include this historic fact or figure, or this incident or that.

It seemed to me that, more and more, famous people in history were being measured not by the standards of their own time, but by those of the present time. So, by that logic, today's history books could be out of date by tomorrow morning. A phrase becoming popular about this new style was "political correctness." The two words captured the sensitivity pretty well. I would say, "God help us," but God seemed to be under fire, too, so maybe I couldn't say that. Freedom of speech? It appeared to be going down the drain. Freedom of religion? Seemingly headed that way too. Pretty soon, it seemed to me, I could maybe count the four freedoms on two fingers.

THIRTY-TWO

That afternoon, Lenny sat himself down in my visitor's chair and said he'd had a phone call from Mr. Jeff Wright.

"He's wondering why I would send a reporter to check out something as unimportant as a stolen car. I said I'd talk to you about it."

"Yeah?"

"The question is, was it a good idea for you to involve Mr. Wright?"

Oh, boy. I reminded Lenny that the Wrights' car was almost certainly involved in the hit-skip in which my daughter was injured.

"And why did you involve our publisher?"

"I needed to get through the gate at Oake Runne," I said.

"Why not come to me?"

"Well, I didn't think you had anything to do with the gate at Oake Runne."

"Is this personal business," Lenny said, bridling a bit, "chasing this hit-and-run?"

"Yeah, I suppose it is," I said. "But I think it links directly with the falling man story."

"Why is that?"

I reminded him of the anonymous call I'd gotten after Allison got hurt, indicating that she'd been hit deliberately. "As you may recall, Lenny, the FBI is looking into that." I paused. "Although nothing's come of it. Far as I know, anyway."

"Speaking of that story, Morrison, Franklin Harris tells me you're getting nowhere on it and making enemies for the paper."

"Harris is jealous, Lenny. He's lost his staff—first me, now the new kid."

"Helen Beaulieu has been raising her eyebrows, too."

"Who?"

Lenny frowned. "Our new society editor."

"Her? Did you know she reads auras?"

"What?"

"Never mind," I said. "How the heck did she get into this?"

"Helen is making some contacts at the university, and not all of the people she meets are fans of our paper, some citing you as a case in point."

"Really. Who constitutes 'not all of them'?"

"A Professor Garland Stevens comes to mind."

I almost spit out my coffee. "There are some things you don't know, Lenny. But rather than bore you with a recital of these facts, let me get a file for you from the morgue."

"Okay. I'll take a look."

I went straight to the morgue, borrowed the folder on *Pescado Bueno Meal*, and dropped it on Lenny's desk. My reporting had not only exposed a reprehensible idea, but had pretty much tanked Professor Stevens' hopes of getting tenure.

As I gave Lenny the folder I suggested he beware of Franklin Harris and also keep an eye on the society editor, who appeared to me to have an agenda we didn't know about.

He nodded. "Um hum."

With that, I visited the desk of my mentor, campus reporter Melissa Meyer, and told her where things were headed between me and Lenny. I said her observation that Jeff Wright might find ways to put pressure on me seemed prescient. "It's like you wrote the script."

"So what does Mr. Wright's call suggest?" she said.

"That Mr. Wright is scared."

"And what does *that* tell you?"

That Wright was hip deep in this thing, I thought, and had started using power tactics to extricate himself from the slime.

"You mentioned Helen Beaulieu," she said. "That woman's name keeps popping up on campus. I'll have to find out more about her."

So I thought Melissa would start demolishing Helen Beaulieu posthaste. But no. That was not what happened at all. Over the next few days Melissa seemed to soften toward Helen.

"I guess what she needs is a friend," Melissa was saying to people.

I hoped that Melissa, in focusing on Helen Beaulieu, hadn't decided she liked her, maybe fallen in love. Helen Beaulieu *was* cute. You never knew with Melissa.

I dropped by Abi's desk, and she said "the Nazi" told the woman he was seeing that someone broke into his trailer.

"I told her it wasn't me," Abi said. "She said she knew that. She was lying, but then both of us were. I asked her to keep me posted, and she said, 'This Mata Hari stuff is scary, honey; the guy's a Nazi!' I told her maybe she should break it off with him and she said she didn't think that would be so easy."

"You think she's in danger?" I asked.

"She wonders about it. I do too. Who's Mata Hari?"

"A spy the Nazis shot in World War II."

THIRTY-THREE

Late Tuesday afternoon, as I was about to leave the office, Sugar Beets called. "Dinner on Friday, darlin'. Glad rags. Seven o'clock."

"Who all's coming?"

"Some of my political friends, and their spouses. Bring your dear wife."

"How about a reporter?"

"Who?"

"A woman named Abi North. She replaced Lee Ann Thomas on the state desk with me."

"Of course. Seven o'clock."

No sooner had I put down the phone than Ed Smart called. "Somebody asked about the eyeglasses," he said. "I'd like to give you the name, but I'd feel uncomfortable doing that."

"How about Daniel delivers the glasses to the owner?"

"Morrison, you find more ways to get my son in the soup."

"Yeah, you're probably right. How about I visit lost-and-found when the guy shows up."

"That might cause trouble."

"Maybe the guy had nothing to do with it," I said.

"Maybe not," Ed said.

"Can you arrange for a pickup at a certain time?"

"I can try."

He called me back. "Wednesday. Two o'clock."

Unfortunately, that was the time of the memorial service in Everest for Arturo. Maybe Abi could show up at lost-and-found while I went to the service. "You have a forest-service magazine, don't you, Ed?" I said. "Could Daniel do a little photo feature on forest services, like lost-and-found?"

He laughed. "Yeah, I suppose that can be arranged."

So, just before two o'clock on Wednesday, I dropped Abi at the ranger station at Connerville to observe the pickup of the glasses, and I drove to Everest for the service.

In a chapel that looked like they'd laid two Nissen huts end-to-end, a woman played a tiny organ. The place was stifling, two fans working to not much effect. Mass was not in Latin but in Spanish. Yet, the little place was packed with as many Anglos as Hispanics.

As the service ended, I positioned myself at the door to talk to the boys. My Spanish and their English didn't cut it, and they were suspicious of me, so I got nowhere. As Daniel's mother came out, and then the priest, we three conspired to ask the boys if they might like to come to dinner at the Smarts' residence one night. They understood that: a home-cooked meal. They nodded and tried out their smiles and their English. "Okay."

I bet Hattie Bush would come if I asked. We'd have an interpreter.

THIRTY-FOUR

As Daniel's father expected, a man came and picked up the eyeglasses. But when Daniel tried to get a photo of the guy, he declined. I got there too late to see all this.

"He was a big guy," Daniel said. "Maybe six-four or -five."

I wondered if he might be the big thug who picked me up and dropped me.

Ed Smart joined us on the steps.

"I guess we didn't get anything," I said.

"I have a plate number off his truck," Ed said, surprising me. I guess he figured that, while the name of a caller was private, a number on a license plate in the parking area was fair game.

***

Thursday I wrote a column on the memorial service, and Abi worked on tracking the license number. After I finished the column I started calling old army buddies. I was looking for a headhunter, somebody in the executive-search business. I figured headhunting would be a natural occupation for people who did what we did in the army. I was over my head here, and needed a little help from my friends.

The first guy who called fit the bill. He was Harrison R. Holman III—Hal Holman—a guy I remembered as smart, good-looking, rich, sly, and funny, and who drove a Mercedes 300 SL around our post in Stuttgart while the rest of us were driving VW beetles and Morris Minors. Turned out Hal's family owned a radio station, plus a famous ski resort, plus who knew what all. These days he was finding high-level executives for Fortune 500 companies.

I returned his call right away.

After we got down to business I said I wanted to find out what I could about Jeff Wright, vice president of the Illinois & Southern Railroad. He said he'd look into it.

I left the office and headed for a place with tuxedos for rent. Looking in the mirror, I felt like a stand-in for James Bond. At a wine shop I bought a bottle of red wine that had been around for a few years. About broke, I headed back to the office, where I found that Abi had already scored on the license plate of the man who lost his glasses.

She saw the bag with the tux and peeked at the wine bottle. "It's for?"

"When you and I go to dinner Friday at Sugar Beets' place."

"I'll have to ask Fred."

Late in the day, she opened a bag that held a gown.

"Where did you come up with that?" I asked.

"Consignment shop," she said. "Fourteen dollars."

"Put it on the tab."

***

The car Abi had identified from the license plate number was owned by one Antony Biro, thirty-four years old, who surprisingly had an address only a mile or so from my little rental house—that is, near the railroad tracks, among the lower-class rentals. Why, I wondered, had his glasses been tumbling along the bottom of Green Lake?

At dark I cruised by Antony Biro's house, which didn't look a lot different from my own—a cheap box with clapboard siding. I found a place on the street to park and watched the house. I fell asleep in the car and woke up about three o'clock in the morning with a crick in my neck and went home and took two aspirin and went to bed for a few hours.

The sun was well up when I got to the office. Abi had called the Spanish teacher. She was going to come, and hoped to bring a couple of Mexican kids with her.

35

THIRTY-FIVE

Abi and I were as elegant as William Powell and Myrna Loy as we arrived at Sugar Beets' place Friday evening. Abi's dress was white and her earrings were the deep red of garnet.

The place was a palace that had appeared, as I recalled, in some magazine. I'd occasionally heard it described as Sugar's "fishing shack." If so, the Taj Mahal was a bowling alley. Isolated it was, on a lake shimmering in the moonlight, the dock sparkling with tiny lights.

We had driven down in Abi's car, mine having a wobbly front left wheel, and had found the mile-long private road to Sugar's house to be smoothly paved with asphalt.

Leaving the car to an attendant, we walked through a garden oozing flowers. The path divided to wrap around a massive Roman fountain in which bronze nymphs splashed in erotic play. That's what I thought was going on, anyway.

The butler was dressed at least as well as I. As we emerged from the hallway we were among people crowding an inlaid hardwood bar as smooth as a lacquered shuffleboard table. A trio was playing soft-as-cotton jazz. Sugar, dressed in white like Abi and wearing lipstick that accented her generous mouth, gave us kisses on the cheek, assaying Abi like an auctioneer preparing to parcel her off. The two appeared to click: southern chanteuse meets attractive and somewhat dark and mysterious guest of her newfound friend the reporter.

On offer from wandering servers were some local delicacies, including crayfish. Apparently, these mini lobsters invaded southern Illinois fields where farmers grew rice. Yuck. Like eating stewed grasshoppers.

Led by Sugar, we mingled. We met three state senators, two members of the House, the lieutenant governor, several people who did lobbying for this cause or that. The women were well dressed, as I'd expected, in gowns that probably cost more than fourteen dollars.

We, as Sugar introduced us, were Brian Morrison, doing academic work in media, and Abi North, a publicist. Sugar figured if we were seen as newspaper folks we'd hear precious little from cagey pols.

***

As we walked toward the final introduction, Sugar whispered that the couple we were about to meet were "very interesting" to her. I took this to mean they were the most likely people in the room to know something about what happened to her brother. My job, as I saw it, was to try to ferret out what that might be.

The guy's name was Lincoln Chen. He introduced his wife, Chuntao Chen, a knifelike sylph in an emerald green sheath who spoke English, but not too well.

Mr. Chen's attention remained fixed on Abi for a long moment. Attractive she was, but that's not what I read in his gaze. It was more like curiosity. I wondered if he thought she might be Chinese, like him, or have some Chinese blood. He turned to me. "You've known Sugar long?"

"Not long," I said. "We met after her brother was killed."

"Oh?"

"We were at a county fair," I said. "My wife was singing. Sugar joined her on stage."

Mr. Chen turned to Abi. "Ah. You are a singer."

Abi grinned. "I am not his wife."

"Ah."

"Morrison is from academe," Abi said. "I am his minder."

"Ah."

"And what is it you do?" I said to Mr. Chen. "May I call you Lincoln?"

He smiled. "Link. I'm a political consultant."

Mrs. Chen touched Abi's arm. "And I am Joy."

Maybe she liked "Joy" better than "Chuntao." I did. Joy Chen.

"Did you work with Senator Beets?" I asked Link.

He hesitated. "I work with quite a few legislators."

"Oh? That's interesting—how legislators and lobbyists interact. How does that work, basically? May I ask you that?"

He chose his words. "Sure. If I have a client whose interests correspond with those of a legislator, I try to get them together."

Abi was tuned into this conversation, but Joy was not. It appeared the drinks were catching up with her.

"So, let's say you had a client interested in how a road would be laid out," I said to Link, "or widened or whatever, you'd try to arrange a meeting between legislators involved and your client? See if they could accommodate each other in some way?"

Chen laughed. "That's a little bald, but it's sort of how it works. I might go to a legislator's office manager and ask if there might be room for discussion. Then, if the process was at a stage where my client's views could be heard, perhaps there'd be further discussion." He laughed again. "All open to public scrutiny, of course. The rules are the rules. Lobbying is an art, but the rules are strict and precise."

"I'm sorry. I'm naive about the political process. I hope I haven't offended you."

"No, no. Not at all."

"So. Let me ask you this then. Were you working on anything with Senator Beets recently? Like, would any of your clients be interested for whatever reason in the proposed driver licensing bill, the one that would allow illegals to drive?"

Chen's eyes flashed for an instant. Then he smiled. "There's apparently a lot of interest in that bill. My guess would be that even if it got to the floor it wouldn't have passed. At least, that's the sentiment I was hearing. But me? No. I don't have any clients interested in the bill, one way or the other. So I don't know much about it."

***

Abi and I were seated with Link and Joy at dinner. Abi expressed sadness at the loss of Sugar's brother.

"He was the quintessential politician," Link said.

"'Quintessential.' That's interesting," I said. "Do you think politics has an essential essence? What might that be?"

"Um," he said, clearly wondering, but not asking, what I meant.

"That's why he has me for a minder," Abi said, laughing.

"In that context," I said, "I've been considering what I've been hearing about the murder. Do you suppose it was about how Beets practiced his politics?"

"How he practiced his politics? I guess I'm lost," Link said.

Now it was Joy Chen who burst into laughter. "You right. They kill him for vote. Money extra."

"Sweetie, you've had a little bit too much to drink," Link said. He waved a hand and made a face suggesting she was off base, uninformed.

"I did hear they stole a lot of money," I said. "Maybe three million dollars." I turned to Joy. "You think getting the money was just a lucky break for the killer?"

"Oh, yes. Lot a money," she said.

Link said, "I'm sorry. It's been a long day. Chuntao is tired."

He tried coaxing an exit, but she wasn't leaving us so easily.

"Pretty lucky," she said. She winked.

Excusing himself and his wife, Link pulled back her chair, took her by the arm, and led her from the dining room. We watched as the two of them ascended the staircase to the second floor, Joy bouncing up the steps on his arm like a pogo stick.

Dinner was breaking up, so most guests were otherwise engaged and missed the show.

Guests were invited to have an after-dinner drink from the bar, dance, perhaps walk along the dock under the stars. Abi and I walked. Tied up to the dock with a couple of bumpers protecting the hull was a mahogany Chris-Craft. I took a long look. Down the way, at water level, was a shed for it. Further on I saw a rack holding three canvas canoes. I could imagine going out in one as mist rose from the water in the early morning, casting for bass among the weeds.

Abi asked after the powder room, and was directed toward the staircase. She went inside and up the stairs.

I drifted along the dock and encountered a couple who had impressed me earlier when we were introduced. We chatted. She worked for a defense contractor. Her husband was a retired Air Force colonel.

"What do you think is going on in the state legislature?" I said.

"About what?" she said. She seemed interested, not just cordial.

"I heard somewhere that Senator Beets was on a committee working on a bill," I said, "something about driver's licenses for illegal immigrants."

"Oh, the Licensing bill," she said. "Ham's committee was considering whether or not to bring it to the floor. At first he was going to vote against it. Then I heard he was going to vote *for* it." She smiled. "His was the deciding vote, either way, because three of them were dead set on killing it and three wanted to position it for a floor vote. But now that Ham's dead, the issue is moot. The bill died with him. Unless, of course, one of the anti's changes his vote. Nobody thinks that's going to happen."

The woman's knowledge and insight intrigued me. "Do you think Lincoln Chen, this lobbyist here tonight, has any interest—"

"Nice meeting you," her husband said, "but we'd better mingle." He smiled apologetically as he took his wife's arm.

So, for the second time in the evening, a woman was led away from me—more gently than Link had led Joy, or Chuntao, as he'd referred to her, but away, nonetheless.

Abi came back. "Joy is in a bedroom up there, lying down," she said. "I wonder if she's okay. I saw some bruising on her arm. I didn't notice it earlier. Her cheek was red."

We alerted Sugar to Joy's possible indisposition. She said she'd have someone look in on her. She told us she hadn't gotten any leads. "But I did hear people wondering who *you* are." She smiled that wondrous smile. "How did you get on with Link?"

"What is it that you think connects him to—" I hesitated.

"Well, darlin', lately, every time Link and I saw each other, he'd ask me where I thought Ham was on the licensing bill."

"That's interesting," I said.

"What makes you say that?"

"He told me he didn't have any interest in the bill, one way or the other."

***

The party began winding down, and we approached Sugar to say farewell.

"Before I go," I said to her, "one more question?"

"Yes?"

"Has the FBI questioned you about your brother's murder?"

"Yes, they have. I told them what I told you. They've also approached some of these people. A couple of them have told me so."

I asked her for a copy of the guest list.

"I'll send it," she said. She kissed me on the mouth, quite vigorously. "Call me."

The attendant went for our car.

As we waited Abi said, "You appear to have made a friend."

"Felt like it," I said.

THIRTY-SIX

We drove through the late evening mist. "There's something about you I don't get," Abi said, her eyes on the road.

"What don't you get?"

"Well, you say you focus on one thing at a time, but that's not true. There's the falling man. You're interested in that. And the Tintown guy, the Nazi. You're interested in him. And Sugar's brother, the senator, him getting killed. You're interested in that. That's just off the top of my head—three things."

"No kidding."

"And the Mexican boy. Arturo something. You're interested in him. That's four."

"Arturo Soto," I said.

"And his girlfriend. Caitlin. Five."

"Caitlin Barber," I said.

"Yeah. And the answer to my questions is?"

"I do try to focus on one thing at a time. That's true. That's why I'm so confused right now."

We arrived in Stanton and headed for Abi's house, where my Ford was parked in the street. We pulled into the driveway. The porch light came on.

"Here's a better answer to your question," I said. "My mind sort of takes snapshots, and then arranges them in some kind of order, I guess. Tonight I was focused on those people we met, Lincoln Chen in particular. He was a snapshot for me. As for Tintown, you're in charge of that, right?"

"Not any more, I'm not. We broke into somebody's house. Isn't that sort of like Mr. Harris going through your wastebasket?"

"Hmmm. Well, thanks for coming with me tonight," I said. "It just wouldn't have worked—me by myself, a loner at the dinner."

"What did we learn?"

"Don't you think Mr. Chen got agitated with our little exchange? And didn't he slap his wife?"

"Maybe it's time to go to the FBI," she said.

"They're already on it; you heard Sugar; they're questioning 'people of interest.' And they're hanging out in Everest. To them we're just a sideshow—those dumb media people. And maybe they're right; I sure don't have a fix on any of this."

"Just be careful."

Fred came out on the porch under the light. I got out of the car, waved and said goodnight, and went to my car.

As I drove to my rental unit I considered Abi's view of the Tintown break-in. Maybe she was right: justice in a democracy requires adherence to the law. Breaking into the guy's trailer was wrong. Perhaps going to a dinner and fishing for information under false pretenses was wrong, too. It's easy to slip into the ways of the wicked.

THIRTY-SEVEN

I drove to my rental unit, telephoned the house, and found Cindy still awake. I told her there was a possibility somebody might be targeting me. She was not too pleased. "If there's any trouble," I said, "it will almost certainly come directly to me. I just wanted you to know."

***

As I got into bed I put my handgun on my night table. Listening to Abi had alerted me. There were more than a few snapshots, lining up like Tarot cards, in my mind. As I say, I'm not a particularly spiritual person, but I do know that things can line up sometimes such that you're in trouble.

Nobody showed up in the night, but I wanted the gun with me. Illinois concealed-carry laws were strict, so I put it in the trunk, not loaded, and put two loaded mags in the glove compartment. This was not immediate protection, but I could get it and put in the bullets if I had time. And, of course, I was, if not paranoid, neurotic.

***

When I got to the office on Saturday I found a note from Abi. My buddy Hal had called Friday, and told her what he had on Jeff Wright. I scanned the note: Mr. Wright grew up in Utah.

After college he got himself connected with a financial firm. He leveraged that into "various ascending positions," and now was a vice president of the Illinois & Southern Railroad, a vast transportation and land-development empire, with his offices in Stanton. Apparently, he was essentially a lobbyist for the railroad. The three target cities in his work were equally accessible to him from Stanton—Springfield, Illinois, by car; Washington, D.C., by plane, and Chicago, by rail.

As to his personal life, Mr. Wright was married to Olivia Fredericks, who'd been a Philadelphia debutante. Their children had gone to private schools. He was a member of a few soup clubs, like Rotary. His favorite pastime appeared to be "wealth management." This was another phrase, like "political correctness," that was oiling its way into the public consciousness.

***

No sooner had I digested the news about Jeff Wright than Daniel called, excited, pleased to find me at the office. The sheriff had released the body, the autopsy having uncovered a *huge* surprise: Arturo had died not by murder, not by accident, but of a heart attack. The world is full of surprises; to me, this was a *big* one.

I called the coroner's office in Hopeful. His wife answered, and he came to the phone. He told me his phone rang at his home when he wasn't at his office. That's what being coroner gets you. No question in his mind, it was a heart attack. Such deaths among the young are rare, he said, but when they happen it's often during strenuous physical activity, such as sports events. For a variety of reasons, he said, the heart can beat out of control. Such beating of the heart risks instant death.

Why Arturo? He said the boy's coronary arteries were connected abnormally, which compressed them during heavy work, reducing blood flow to his heart. So, in his opinion, Arturo's effort in felling the walnut tree had killed him. Which of course was why he hadn't gotten out of the way when it dropped.

I told Daniel what I heard from the coroner and he wrote the lead. Sunday paper. Byline and all. Heady stuff for a 16-year-old.

***

Eric called. "I talked to a man at the Mexican Consulate in Chicago," he said. "A Catholic search agency traced Arturo's family. They're shipping his body home for burial."

"Who's paying?"

"The agency. The family has no money."

I gave Eric the most interesting news I had—that the autopsy had uncovered Arturo's heart attack.

"Your heart may get *you* killed, too," he said.

"They messed with my daughter."

I heard him take a breath. "I think you've got yourself screwed up," he said. "If you're going after these guys, go after them because you're a journalist exposing crime, not because you're a father seeking revenge. I think I'm making the same point your editor made when he asked you if this was about Allison. You are bigger than a vengeful father, my friend."

I thanked him for his advice and signed off. To Daniel's lead I added the news about the Catholic agency shipping Arturo's body home.

***

I was able to get out of the office by midafternoon, but I had another obligation that night; I was to meet Hattie Bush and Arturo's three friends at Daniel's house at six o'clock. I worked around the house and forgot the time. Late and scrambling, I hurried down to Connerville, hoping my tie rods, or whatever, would hold up. When I got there, already assembled in the living room were Daniel, Hattie Bush, two of her students from Center Ford High School, and Arturo's friends Raúl, José Luís, and Juan. Betsy Smart had put out beef barbecue, potato salad and slaw for us. We were to have at it after our meeting. She'd also made chocolate-chip cookies.

"Go ahead and eat those cookies," Betsy told the young men.

Living alone in a rental unit, I'd forgotten the incredible taste of homemade chocolate-chip cookies.

In her fluent Spanish, Hattie Bush handled the introductions. As things got underway she served as my translator. I began with the news about Arturo, making clear the coroner's finding of heart failure, and that Arturo never knew what hit him. I also reported he would get a proper burial in Mexico. I spoke slowly, so Hattie could translate. Even with the calming news I had for everyone, things were awkward. Then, cautiously, the boys sought clarification. Among their concerns was their own personal security. No snitches here? No trouble? This is just about Arturo?

As they sat silent, pondering the responses they got, Hattie took a Rosary from her purse. "Let's pray for Arturo and his family," she said, translating the Spanish for me. "Ten Hail Marys." The boys gave the responses. All in Spanish, the prayers at first seemed quaint, but the refrain soothed me. At the conclusion of the prayers, everyone waited in silence for someone else to begin.

Gradually, curiosity got the best of the boys. They began asking each other questions about life, jobs, school, sports. Not about girls, of course. Not in front of us adults.

When things got rolling Hattie turned to one of the boys who had come with her. "Tell us how you came to be here in the States. In English now, just like you told us in class." I figured the question was a rehearsed prompt.

The boy's somewhat shy comments, occasionally translated to make things more clear to all, helped break the ice, and the other boys started to play a sort of "Can You Top This?" Out came stories about tough times in Mexico, leaving home, dealing with human coyotes who led dangerous treks across the border and into the U.S., surviving in a confusing new environment, in some ways as desperate and difficult as things had been for them back home. The two boys who had come with Hattie made much of the fact that she had helped them.

The constant crossovers between Spanish and English improved my Spanish, I'll say that. Between Hattie's warmth and charm and Betsy Smart's homemade cookies things got more relaxed, the chatter punctuated by laughs and guffaws.

"Tell us about Arturo," Hattie said to the Everest boys. "What was he like?"

Arturo, they confided, was strong, the leader, honest, a person who shared what he had. Also a wisecracker. Sometimes a little moody, but pretty soon laughing. They hooted about him picking up snakes, tossing snakes. "At us!" Cruel or not, it was a game he played. Their revelations made things clear about Arturo. Not only was he a kidder, a joker with a bit of a mean streak, but he was never selfish, and he led and helped them in this strange land.

The words "duffle bag" popped up in a translation by Hattie.

"Tell me about that," I said.

The boys hemmed and hawed for a moment.

"He put it under the house," one said.

"We were not to go near it," another said.

"What's in it?" I asked.

Laughter. "Lots of snakes down there," one boy said. It appeared they didn't know.

I had the feeling they felt uncomfortable discussing Arturo's duffle bag. That suited me. I didn't want them to focus on it, either.

"Arturo wanted to carve walnut wood?" I asked, steering the conversation away from the bag.

The boys said Arturo thought walnut wood in the U.S. was better to work with than walnut in Mexico. Taller trees. Fewer knots. Better. He made carvings of the Virgin Mary, the saints, even devils.

"Did he sell the carvings?"

Some, and he also made musical instruments, they said.

"Gifted," I said. The boys didn't understand. "Clever. Smart," I said.

Hattie translated.

"Fearless," I said.

"Yes."

"Smart ass," one of the boys said in perfect English.

"Yes, yes."

Much laughter.

Our hosts broke out the food.

THIRTY-EIGHT

Monday morning I found Louis Roper, who looked and acted like Opie from Mayberry, focusing on tedious but obligatory state desk matters. I was thus freed up to focus completely on the falling man.

Before I faced into the issue, I wanted to get my Ford squared away. With Eric following in his car, I drove to the shade-tree mechanic's place in Huston. The mechanic and I agreed he would work on the tie rods. He also planned to change the oil, and said he'd need six quarts. Did he not have oil? I asked. Yes. But when he changed mine out he'd need more. An interesting arrangement. Go get your own oil. Somehow I liked the whole deal.

Eric took me back to Stanton and I borrowed his car, a dark blue Buick Century, so I could get the oil. I drove the Buick to Auto Shack, a parts store relatively new to Stanton, and went inside to get the oil. A small man with a black goatee—Bert Long, the Wrights' chauffeur—stood at the counter ordering spark plugs for the Wrights' Lincoln.

As he turned to go we greeted each other. I asked him how they were doing trying to sell the Chrysler. I had a hunch it was going to be a classic. I mean, how's Frank Sinatra's initials on a car, the big FS, for an automotive pedigree? If I could only figure out how to get Mr. Sinatra to sit behind the wheel once!

"Mr. Wright is advertising it and we're getting some response."

"A car like that, not quite an antique, not so easy to get rid of," I said.

He shrugged.

"How much does he want for it?"

"He's asking nine thousand."

I'd heard *ten* thousand before.

"He'd like to get rid of it."

"Okay," I said. "I'll go to the bank tomorrow and see about a loan. Eight thousand."

He smiled. "Eighty-five hundred."

"Deal."

"What are you driving now?" he said.

"That Buick out there."

"Where is the Ford?"

"My mechanic's got it up in Huston. Tie rods." Picking up my bag containing the six quarts of motor oil, I told Mr. Long about my shade-tree mechanic, and about the tie rod problem.

"You sure that's what it is?"

My turn to smile. Another guy who knew more about cars than I did.

We parted company with a handshake on the Chrysler. As he walked away from the store in daylight, I wondered if, like Abi, he was a person of Asian heritage.

I drove up to Huston to deliver the oil. I mentioned to my mechanic that I was buying the Chrysler, and he said something about the carburetor. Preoccupied, I paid no attention.

***

That afternoon I decided to talk again with Caitlin. Although she was still grieving, I wanted to get clear on some things before her memory faded. I drove the Buick down to Everest. Caitlin was at home, moping, I supposed. I talked her into going for a Coke.

"How are you doing?" I said.

"I miss him."

"I wish I could help you, Caitlin. I think I told you I have two daughters about your age. One of them got hit by a car a couple weeks ago. Broke her leg. She's got a cast up to here." I indicated ankle-to-hip. "I can't help *her*, either."

"Does it hurt?"

"She doesn't complain. She scratches where she can. I got her a back scratcher from the wood shop up at the state prison."

That got her interest. "They got a store?"

I told her about the store, open to the public, where prisoners made a few bucks.

She took a sip of the Coke. Tears had welled up again in her eyes. How do you try to console a person who's lost someone forever? Anything kind I'd say would be trite, presumptuous. Arturo had begun to be part of her life. Her mother had liked him. Now his body was going back to Mexico. The flowers she and her friends had laid in the woods would wither and disappear. I wondered if she'd ever find another boy she'd love as much as she loved Arturo.

I felt guilty. Engaging her in my falling-man case so early in her time of grief was self-serving. But I rationalized: my interests might be a distraction for her.

"I have to get clear on something," I said.

"What?" She lifted her head. How beaten down she was. When I'd first seen her at the lake, how pretty and smart and alert she'd been. A gamer. Randy had certainly been charmed. He'd invited her to come on the hike with us. Now she was pale, listless, sad, her spirit diminished, like a tree in winter. I couldn't help myself. Lee Ann came to me. *O lost, and by the wind grieved, ghost, come back again.*

I got a grip on myself. "I think Arturo found some money," I said.

"No!"

"I can't see it any other way, Caitlin. I think you two stumbled on a duffle bag full of money when you hurt your ankle."

"No!"

Tears welled up but I pushed it.

"He went back in for it. The very next day, right? You were with him. You wanted him to leave it. But he didn't want to do that. All that money. It was just too exciting. Somebody else might find it. But after he took it he didn't know what to do with it."

She sat watching me.

"I think I know how he felt, Caitlin," I said. "All that money. But what could he do with it? Spend some? On what? Give some away? Word would get around. Whoever it belonged to might be bad people. But if he took it to the police they'd look into his status. So what could he do? He'd hide it. He'd have time to think."

I sipped my coffee.

After a moment of silence, she nodded, not so much at me as agreeing with herself: That was the way she remembered it too.

"I'm working on a big story, Caitlin. Murder's involved. It has nothing to do with you and Arturo. But the fact that you were with him when he found the money implicates you, whether you did anything wrong or not. You can't use the money. Giving it up won't hurt you in any way. Keeping it will. Arturo knew that. You do too."

"A murder?"

"Whoever stole it killed somebody, yes."

"You a cop?"-

"No, I'm not. Somebody ran down my daughter. Deliberately. They didn't care whether they killed her or not. I'm going to find them."

Big eyes. "Why'd they do that?"

"I was chasing a story. That's why Daniel and Randy and I went into the woods. Looking for whatever was in there."

"So you gave us some cock-and-bull story about illegal animal traps."

"I'm sorry."

She was quiet.

"How did he get it out of there?" I said.

"It was in a suitcase. He forced the lock."

"He walked out with the suitcase? It wasn't broken?"

"It was smashed up, leaking money. That's how we found it. Locked but leaking money. But he had to break the lock. Then there was all this money. He had to put it in a duffle bag." Her eyes were round. "So much money."

"He left the suitcase there, in the woods, where you found it?"

"No. He went back for it. He threw it in a dumpster."

We sat there thinking about the money.

"Can you not talk about this—while I try to sort it out?"

She smiled. "Can I trust you?"

"You don't want to put your girlfriends at risk," I said. "You will if you tell them about this." I was telling her the truth. I hoped she'd listen.

As we left she glanced at the Buick. "You driving that road apple?" She laughed. "I've been in one of those." She swayed her hips, rocking as she did so.

My father had a Buick Roadmaster, the 1956 model. Caitlin obviously had one in her background too. Only a young lady, such as Caitlin, familiar with an early Buick Roadmaster, with its extra-long wheelbase, could move her torso like that. I hoped I could get the moves somewhere near right to show Eric.

My eyes were wet. I headed for Stanton.

THIRTY-NINE

Tuesday morning I called Eric. He had time to drop me off in Huston to pick up the Ford, now with new tie rods. When we got there I gave it a little test run. It did seem better. Less wobble, less noise. I told Eric he could go on. But after he drove off I thought maybe the steering still wasn't right.

The guy started talking about steering racks and steering arms, and how there are a couple of kinds of steering systems. I said "Okay! Okay! Just fix it." Ye gods! I was buying a whole new Ford, piece by piece.

I told him again about the Chrysler.

"That's the FS model, right? I'm thinking it has CFI."

Now that I was buying it, I was attentive.

"Continuous-flow electronic fuel-injection," he said. "It was a great idea but it wasn't reliable. It might stall around twenty-five miles an hour. It might get affected by magnetic fields around power lines. Things like that."

"Really?" Allegations about the strange effects of power lines always interested me.

"Yep. The fuel system might go rich and shut the car down." He smiled. "I remember now. Frank Sinatra had one. He got a free one. He wasn't happy."

"You know a lot about cars," I said. Forget about trying to get Frank Sinatra behind the wheel.

"I love cars." He gave me a wry look. "Maybe that was my problem with my wife. Anyway, with one trick or another, you could keep it running. Or," and here he shrugged, "you could change out the EFI system for a carburetor. We could do that."

Good grief. He was already thinking of repair jobs on it.

"You want to sell the Ford?" he said.

My smile became a grin. "Maybe."

He had a rental for me, a '76 Nova. Twenty bucks a day. A deal, he said, because he was working on my car. I gave him forty dollars and left the Ford with him. I hoped the Nova didn't belong to one of his customers.

It handled okay, and, not being recognizable as my car, it was good for a stake-out. I drove to the thug's house and parked for a while. Getting bored, I drove back to the office. I told Abi about my conversation with Caitlin. But she didn't have time to talk, she said. She was off to see the woman who lived in the trailer in Tintown.

"She was with the Nazi last night," she said.

"I wouldn't be confronting Mr. Buford, if I were you," I said. "He may remember you from our little tryst in his trailer."

"It was dark in there," Abi said. She giggled.

Franklin Harris gave us a sharp look.

Abi headed toward the stairs.

"Be careful," I called after her.

I asked Louis Roper how he was doing, and he made a face. "The state desk is really boring, Mr. Morrison."

"It's just Morrison, Louis. Hang in there. Something interesting will come along."

I encountered Franklin Harris.

"What's going on between you and that married woman from sports?" he said.

"Get lost," I said, and went to my desk.

My buddy Melissa Meyer waved me over.

"Ever hear of Krebiozen?" she said.

"Yeah. A big scandal at the University of Illinois, right? Back in the fifties? A so-called cancer drug. Reason I remember, they were thinking it was actually horse urine. That got around, so the boys in my room started calling anything we were suspicious of horse piss."

Melissa laughed. "You were about eight, right? Sounds right for eight. I think we have another case like that brewing."

"Here? At Stanton?"

"Yeah."

"Good as fish meal?"

"Maybe better. There's a visiting professor from Ukraine claiming a little concoction of his can clean out your arteries."

"A visiting professor from Ukraine?" I smiled.

"I hear there's a lab report that breaks down what's in it. I'm trying to get hold of the report and put it on the wire. That would knock off 'ArtiClear' before some fool at the university says its worthy of further study. The report, as I understand it, is under lock and key somewhere. The people who did the analysis are supposedly afraid to go public. Fear of defamation suits, libel suits, that kind of thing."

"Go get 'em," I said.

"By the way, it involves your old friend Garland Stevens. I don't know how yet. I'll keep you posted."

I went back to my desk. Louis paused in his string calculations, making himself a note. "Mrs. North just called," he said. "They found a stiff in Tintown."

"AbI called? Somebody's dead?" I gave the desk people a heads-up and raced downstairs. The darn Nova wouldn't start. I ran back up. "You got a car, Louis?"

"Sure."

We hurried to the parking lot and climbed into his VW beetle.

"Let's roll," he said.

I laughed. "Like I've been telling you, Louis. Something's always coming up."

"Yes, sir!"

When we got to Tintown I counted two deputy-sheriff cars and three emergency vehicles. Further down sat Abi's car. I hurried over, Louis right behind me.

She held up two fingers. "The two of them are dead," she said. "Her trailer. At least I assume it's them." She seemed distraught—stress, guilt, whatever.

"Not your fault," I said. "I'm sorry, too." I recalled Daniel's anxiety when he covered Arturo's death. Covering the news can be hard, especially on new reporters.

We spotted the sheriff. Like Tully down in Eagle County, this sheriff was new, but we were on pretty good terms.

"What can you tell me, Sheriff?" I said.

"Two dead. Man and a woman. A shooting."

Abi elbowed me aside. "Domestic?"

"Can't say."

"Where were the bodies?"

"Both in bed."

"Where are the wounds?"

"Both in the head."

"Did you find a weapon?"

A microphone and a television camera were suddenly in the sheriff's face.

I hate it, but officials who have to run for re-election react to a camera like a dog to a biscuit. The woman with the cameraman turned to face the camera. "Two people are dead in a Tintown shooting," she said breathlessly. "Sheriff Clements told us what's known so far—"

Louis Roper appeared to be enjoying himself. Action News!

"You up for a little B&E?" I asked him.

"That's breaking and entering, right?" His eyes glistened.

"Yeah."

Louis and I crossed the road and headed for Buford's trailer. We were alone. All the other people on the street were engaged in the death watch. I pulled out my handkerchief, fiddled with a bent paper clip and picks, and got the door open.

"Wait here," I said. "Let me know if anyone's coming."

I went into the trailer. The fliers and handbills were gone. So was the Rolodex. Wiping down the places I'd touched, I backed out, backed Louis out of there, and locked the door.

As we began the drive back to Stanton, he eyed me. "What's going on?" he said.

"I don't know, Louis." I told him about Abi finding the papers in the road and thinking maybe there was a story in it.

"There must be something to it," Louis said. "Two people dead like that."

"Maybe so," I said. I didn't mention the missing Rolodex, fliers, and handbills.

***

Abi came back shortly after we did, and did a fair job on the story. But we didn't have background, either on the woman or the man.

"She had a sister in Cerro Gordo," Abi said. "They were able to reach her. But when I tried to call her nobody answered. Maybe I can get the information through the funeral home."

When I decided to try to go home, the darn Nova actually started. Ran fine. Cars.

That night the big news on local TV was "the mobile home murders." I turned it off; they didn't have anything earth-shaking. I sat thinking. My handgun was still in the trunk of my car at the shade-tree mechanic's. Not too smart. The Nazi, as Abi perceived him, and maybe he was, was dead. A "neo-Nazi," they'd say. But who was he? How did he get involved? Did he get the fliers mailed? To hell with it. Bedtime.

FORTY

When I got to the office on Wednesday I was groggy after a night of troubled sleep but able to type. As Melissa Meyer had pointed out to me in earlier days—and had demonstrated—if they dump you at your desk you're good to go, no matter your physical or mental state. I dashed off a column for the afternoon edition, providing my own insights into the Tintown tragedy.

Outtakes
By Brian Morrison

Yesterday we reported that two people died in a shooting in a mobile home in Tintown—a woman who lived in the trailer and a man who was visiting—both shot in the head.

It looks like a classic murder-suicide, but no gun has been found, or at least the sheriff hasn't reported finding one. Finding no gun would suggest somebody killed them both.

The man who was shot lived in a trailer across the road from the woman. He was said to be a social activist— planning to mail fliers inviting people to a rally in Idaho to discuss "the immigration prob-lem."

The fliers may or may not have made it to the Post Office. We don't yet know.

So, my question is this: Was social activism—or someone's determination to abort it—a factor in the shooting? Maybe. There is a lot of heat around the immigration issue—in fact, it appears to me, a lot more heat than light—on both sides.

From what I've been able to determine, allegations of fraud surrounding the Immigration Reform and Control Act (IRCA) are probably what's driving activists—again, on both sides. IRCA was signed into law by President Reagan last year to control massive illegal immigration. Detractors say the law isn't working.

I also have to wonder who, or what organization, is behind the rally proposed in the flier? (You'll notice I'm not naming the place or the date here; I'm not on the invitation committee.)

So here's a thought: Law enforcement agencies have been looking into the robbery of several million dollars of state highway construction money from the safe of State Senator Hamilton Beets when he was murdered May 1. Is there a connection?

Senator Beets was on a committee considering legislation that would allow driving privileges for illegal aliens. Now that he's dead, that bill probably is dead, too, not likely to come to the floor of the Senate in this session, anyway. What motivated his murder? Was it the pending legislation, or the money?

As we know, immigration is a complex issue, and illegal immigration is a significant problem. There is no avoiding the reality that the flowing into the country of large numbers of immigrants, legal and illegal, creates costs for taxpayers. Among other things, immigrants heavily utilize social services and welfare funds. Most immigrants also take low-paying jobs that American citizens might otherwise do. And frankly, institutions such as churches and other charitable organizations that support assimilation are not as big, active, and rich as they once were.

Of course, in the long run immigrants are good for the country, as a reading of American history attests. But that's in the long run, and citizens want political focus on immediate problems. "What have you done for me lately?" is a question politicians routinely hear from their constituents.

So. Who dunnit? Why? What's happening?

I showed the column to Abi .

She handed back the copy. "Before we print this you better buy body armor."

Knowing the desk would want the column vetted, I took the copy to Lenny. Using a brand new toy he called a "facsimile machine," he forwarded it to our cowardly attorney, Thomas Pickens, whose office was three blocks away. He turned out to be another facsimile machine owner. Alexander Graham Bell makes his first telephone call.

Upon reading Lenny's missive, Pickens got on the phone to us. "This is a dangerous story," he said.

I got on an extension line.

"Can we print it or not?" I asked.

"It's got a libelous feel to it."

"Whom does it libel?" I asked. "The man and woman are dead."

We had a long pause before he said, "Nobody directly."

"That would be nobody, right?"

"It has a sleazy feel to it."

"We are not creating the sleaze," I said, "we're reporting it."

"When you spray poison into the hole the rats come out," he said.

"Good point. That's what we want."

"That's a danger to the newspaper, to you, to Leonard Dudley—"

"So if Lenny is game and I'm game, we go to press, right?"

"I can only warn you, as the attorney for the Post-Times, that it's a risky business, and it may also sour Post-Times readers as a piece of junkyard-dog journalism."

"That's your legal opinion?"

We got off the phone.

"I think Gradison Ritchie should read this," Lenny said to me.

We called, and he was at home. I read the column to him. Over the past year or so he had come to enjoy his position as publisher of a newly courageous and combative daily newspaper. If he okayed it, we'd go to press.

"No," he said. "You're putting yourself in the middle of the sheriff's murder investigation. The gun is at the heart of your argument, and, until the sheriff talks about it, the column's too speculative. It's not worth putting you and Lenny in any kind of danger."

That was the first time our publisher had vetoed one of my columns. I'd hoped to cause a little trouble, and he'd picked up on that. I had to like him.

***

By the blessing of my banker, the Chrysler now sat in the street outside the Post-Times building. I looked down at it from a newsroom window. A couple of passers-by were standing there admiring it.

I went down, got in, and drove it by the house, where I picked up a few of my things. I asked Allison if she'd like to have the Ford.

"*Would* I?" But then, glancing down at her cast, she said, "Drive it how?"

To get past the moment, I took her to my favorite ice cream parlor, *The Ice House*. Daniel had just shown up at our front door, so I invited him, too.

After slurping the bottom of his shake three times with his straw, Daniel watched Allison polish off her soda. I slurped my malt one time, the adult maximum.

We talked about the falling man.

"I've been wondering," Daniel said. "Do you think all this might be connected? It seems to me that all of a sudden there's a lot going on."

Out of the mouths of babes. I gave him a nod.

***

Thursday morning Abi managed to get hold of the slain woman's sister in Cerro Gordo, a town set in rolling hills about twenty miles northeast of Stanton. They talked for a while.

"She has a letter from her sister she's willing to let us read," Abi said. "Could you go?"

Abi was abdicating control of the Tintown story. Maybe she and Fred were having second thoughts about the state desk.

I headed up to Cerro Gordo. The first people I encountered as I entered the little community were a man and, I guessed, his two young sons, riding their bicycles, single file, across the main intersection. I waited for the wobbly little parade to pass. Then I waited some more as two other little boys, bats on shoulders, gloves attached, walked across the street toward a school playground. I went through the intersection, crossed a set of railroad tracks, and shortly arrived at the woman's small, narrow house.

"I thought it would be Mrs. North," she said after I helloed through her dented front-door screen.

"She wanted to come," I said through the screen, "but her little boy had a dental appointment so she asked me. I work with her."

The portly woman sighed in indecision, then pushed the screen door open to invite me in. She indicated the couch as a place for me to sit and plopped down in a rocker. "She seemed very nice," she said. The wistful message was that she guessed I'd have to do.

From her apron pocket she produced a crumpled letter. "I got this Monday," she said. She stretched out her hand to me, and I took the page. She wiped away tears as I unfolded the letter. Seeking relevant passages, I scanned the tightly spiraled writing:

"I have found out some things about my neighbor, the so-called Mr. Francis Buford. It turns out Mr. Buford may not be who he says he is. A card in his wallet, issued by "Our Liberty League," whatever that is, is in the name of George Robert Styles.

I considered this. She had gone through the man's pants pockets.

"She was beginning not to trust him," her sister said, pausing in her rocking.

I read another passage:

"He seems to know something about that Stanton museum. I heard him talking about it on the phone. Something about this Edgar Cayce, too. Do you know about him? Strange. What could Edgar Cayce have to do with the Stanton museum? Anyway, I wondered if you could put up with me for a few days. I'd like to see you."

"This is very interesting," I said, holding up the letter. "May I keep it?"

"Should I be worrying about this?" she asked.

"About someone harming you, you mean? I don't think so. Whatever was going on, you weren't involved. And who would know about this letter? But it might give us a lead on who killed your sister. Did she ever say anything else about him?"

"Well, at first she was all optimistic about him, but he disappointed her soon enough. Then she got anxious, as you can tell. It appears she wanted to get shet of him." Again she wiped her eyes. "I don't know that I want to pursue it."

"Maybe we can help find whoever killed her."

She thought for a moment. Then she nodded, almost to herself. "I think we know. It was that awful man."

"They don't know yet," I said.

"Keep the letter. Keep me out of it."

"I'll do my best, but the police may want to talk to you, you know, regardless of this letter. So may I take it?"

She nodded. She and her sister had been close. She worked her way up and out of the rocker and saw me to the door.

I tucked the letter into my wallet and thanked her.

FORTY-ONE

That night, under a waning moon, the air warm, the sky hinting rain, I planned to change clothes and go stake out the guy who picked up the eyeglasses. I mentioned my plans to Eric, and he invited himself along.

"I thought you could use a little back-up," he said.

"I appreciate it," I said "but I don't really think you need to take the trouble."

He laughed. "Carol and Cindy were talking, and Cindy told her you warned her to protect herself."

"Cindy overreacts. What I said was, if there's trouble, it will come to me. I specifically said that."

"Well, that's why I'm here. Cindy is staying at our house."

I frowned.

"Let's go eat," Eric said. "Then, while you head for your stake-out, I'll take a chair in your bedroom."

"Why?"

"Maybe I'll meet whoever's dogging you."

"That makes you the target."

"But I'm a police officer and a better shot than you are, and we're positioning me at a point where violence is more likely to occur."

"Don't you have better things to do?"

"I'm on call. I'll call in and leave your number.

"Well, I do appreciate your concern. By the way, are you packing?"

"Yes."

"Two?"

He pulled up a leg of his pants and displayed his ankle gun.

I confessed I'd left my gun in my car at the shade tree mechanic's.

He shook his head. "We'll get it first thing tomorrow."

He gave me his ankle gun, and I pocketed it.

"What's that you're driving?" he said.

I bragged on my new Chrysler. We drove it to a Chinese take-out and got sweet and sour chicken. After we ate at my place I left him and drove over to the thug's neighborhood. I was betting he was the thug, anyway. All I had was the eyeglasses and my intuition. It wasn't yet dark. I had brought a book to read. I figured the thug wouldn't recognize my car even if he saw it.

The dark came and went, and as dawn arrived I was getting myself together to leave. A car rolled into the driveway. Apparently, the driver was alone. Gun in hand, I got behind him as he got out of the car. He was a very big man. "Don't turn around or I'll shoot you," I said. I nudged his back with the barrel of the little weapon.

"What?"

"We're going to walk over to your front door and you're going to open it, drop the keys, and step away."

"Why?"

"Pretend your life depends upon it."

We entered the house and went to his bedroom. I told him to lie on his back crossways on the bed with his head over the edge toward me. He gave me some bad language as he maneuvered around but soon he was looking at me upside down. He was one big, mean galoot.

"Stretch your arms out wide. That's it. Stay put. Remember, I will shoot you."

His eyeglasses glittered in the light of the ceiling fixture. I reached for his phone, tucked it in my ear, dialed the rental unit, and told Eric I was entertaining the guy.

The guy started to roll over and I fired a shot into the mattress, away from him. Not too noisy but convincing, without doubt.

"Hey!" He quickly resumed the position.

"Hey what?" I said.

"I'm gonna split you like a chicken."

"You're the one on the spit here, not me," I said.

Eric came in and checked him out. "That's new," he said, indicating the man's supine position on the bed. He sniffed. "Who shot what?"

I pointed with the gun barrel to the hole in the mattress.

"You're gonna regret this," the guy said. "The both of ya."

"Was he carrying?"

On my advice, the man on the bed remained still as Eric checked him out, finding a lump. He extracted a gun from the guy's pocket, "Hmmmm. Beretta." He sniffed the barrel. "Trade you," he said. I got the Beretta. Eric got his ankle gun back.

The man's upside down eyes were shifting as he tried to keep us in focus. His glasses were more of a hindrance to him than a help.

"What's your name?" I said.

"Roger Touhy."

"Chicago gang boss. Died around 1960," Eric recalled. He had a mind for dates.

I tapped the Beretta with a fingernail.

"Antony Biro."

"Who do you work for?"

He tried to look tough. Upside down, it loses something.

"Here's what I'm going to do," I said. "I'm going to call Sheriff Tully down in Eagle County. I'm going to tell him we have one of the two guys who chased the kid into the lake." I waited for denial. None came. "I think he'd be happy to meet you. Or, we can let you go and forget the whole thing. The price to you is just one name."

Eric looked on with a slight smile.

"Who do you work for?" I said.

"You're gonna find out soon enough."

I displayed the Beretta.

"A guy in Springfield."

"Who?"

"Hey, this sucks." He rolled his head around.

"Tell me about the guy."

"Come on. A guy in a restaurant."

"Give me a name."

"I don't know."

"How did you lose your glasses?" I said.

"What's that got to do with it?"

"I think you lost them when you went into the lake after Dougie."

"What?" Again, no denial.

"Who's the guy in Springfield?"

He looked at me upside down.

"One name. And you get out of here."

"Henry."

"Henry who?"

"Henry. That's it."

"Henry. How do you connect with him?"

He was tired of this, but he also wanted out.

"I see him at noon on Fridays at Felix's."

I considered this.

"Lemme up!"

"If I find out you had anything to do with running down a girl on a bike, I'll find you. I am not kidding, Antony. I will find you."

It took him a minute to sit up. "Gimme my gun back," he said.

"Take off your clothes," I said.

"What?"

I put a second hole in the mattress. Noisier with the Beretta.

I got him down to his boxer shorts, threw his clothes in the kitchen sink, and turned on the water.

He stared. Upside down it took some neck stretching. Eric was staring, too.

"We're leaving," I said. "If you come running out of here I'll shoot you."

He looked at me like I was a madman.

I went to the wall and pulled out the telephone cord.

As we left the house the sun was coming up. "I'm going to go see Henry," I said. I looked at my watch. "Matter of fact, I better go. I want to be sure I catch him."

"Go see him and do what?"

"I want him to name *his* boss for me. If he does, I'll let him up."

"You *do* chase sticks," Eric said.

FORTY-TWO

Felix's Restaurant had a small parking lot but I found a space easily. Inside, the walls were art deco. It was 1940 all around. A man in a double-breasted pinstripe suit with wide lapels sat by himself at a table in a back corner. It had to be Henry, but if he'd been at Sugar's party I sure didn't see him.

"Henry?"

He gave me a questioning look.

I continued to stare.

He shrugged me into the seat opposite.

"You are?" he said.

"My name is Morrison. I'm a reporter for the Stanton Post-Times. I'm chasing a story about Senator Hamilton Beets."

"How would I know anything about that?"

"I met one of your employees this morning. That didn't work out for him. He sent me to you."

"Why are you bothering me?"

"His name is Antony Biro," I said.

"What do you want?"

"First, don't send any more thugs to see me. Second, why do you want to shut me up?"

He shrugged.

"If you listen up you can get a free pass," I said.

He laughed. "A free pass? What kind of talk is that?"

I looked him over. "Listen, Henry," I said. "My newspaper is on to this. You can *be* the news, or you can *read* the news. Your choice."

He smiled. "You talk a lot."

"Why beat me up?"

He shrugged.

"Who hired you, Henry?" I said. "The name gets you the free pass."

"We appear to be done," he said.

"See you in the news," I said.

I went out and found a hamburger joint. Wouldn't you know it? After I left, the Chrysler stalled. I got out and looked around. Sure enough, power lines crossed the road. I walked a couple of blocks to a gas station and borrowed the phone and dialed the shade-tree mechanic. Whatever number I'd dialed, I got a voice I didn't recognize, urging me to say who was calling. I hung up.

I called a Chrysler dealer, right there on the outskirts of Springfield. It took a while but they towed the car to their place. Once we got there they said they'd fix it. Did they know how? They hadn't even looked at it. But, a dealer's a dealer. I decided to leave it.

Eric picked me up. He said he had bad news, then gently told me my shade-tree mechanic was dead. A bomb had gone off in the trunk of the Ford and killed him.

A few deep breaths got me some air. A bomb? In the Ford? The poor guy was dead? Good Lord. It should have been me.

But there it was. A nice guy who had nothing to do with anything was dead. I imagined him examining the car, opening the
trunk for a look-see, before making me an offer. My mind went
to my catechism, a line right out of terror novels: *Watch therefore:
for ye know not what hour your Lord doth come.*

Now I had another score to settle. There was a verse for that,
too. *Vengeance is mine, sayeth the Lord.* I thought for a moment
about my S&W .459, tucked away in the trunk of the Ford.
I also thought about the ammo in the glove compartment. It
would have popped its rounds if the car caught fire.

FORTY-THREE

When I got to the office, two FBI types were waiting for me. I felt bad enough. Now this. For the second time in six weeks, they took me to their Springfield office.

A car explodes, killing a guy? What was that about, they wanted to know. Had the bomb been planted to kill him? Kill me? Or had he been *installing* a bomb? They'd sent fragments of the bomb to a lab. They were still trying to tie me, and whatever I was up to, to organized crime, and I guess, on a level, I couldn't blame them. Who knew what was going on?

It seemed to them I'd been too quick to get into the forest to chase a story they now connected—as I myself did—to the murder and robbery of Senator Beets. So I was hip deep in this. That they knew. They just didn't know why, or how.

Interesting to me, as they questioned me they made no mention of finding a handgun when they picked up the pieces of the Ford. Magazines, either. If the mags had been in there, and the bullets got heated sufficiently, they'd have sprayed lead like tommy guns. The site team would have noticed the residue. So, I concluded, the bomber found my handgun, then looked around for the mags and took those, too.

The questioning went like this: Why was my car in the mechanic's lot? When did I leave it there? What did I know about the mechanic? Why would somebody want to kill me?

For several hours I resisted their insinuations, their blustering assertions, their personal attacks. A handful of agents, including the two who'd questioned me after the thugs confronted Dougie at the lake, came and went from the room. Who killed a state senator and stole big money? Why did someone run down my daughter? Who blew up the car? I wanted answers to those questions myself.

The interrogation made one thing clear: The FBI wasn't any closer to figuring out what was going on than I was. And they were arrogant and sly. They never asked me open-handed questions, questions that might suggest respect for me, my knowledge, or my opinion. They didn't talk about an airplane, or ask me where I thought the missing money might be.

And they apparently hadn't yet considered that all this might be linked somehow to the Tintown murders. My stringer, Daniel Smart, just a high school kid, had given it more thought than they had.

For my part, I felt abused. Here I was, feeling terrible guilt, and they were after me. I felt stupid. But I was not a criminal. I took all the abuse they dished out, and they got tired of me and drove me back to my rental unit in Stanton. It was lonely. Hot and lonely. I pushed up the lever for the air conditioning and got myself a drink. A stand-in for a friend.

***

When I walked into the newsroom on Saturday morning I got treated like a lost dog found. Dogs know how that goes: they give you the big, warm reception, but at arm's length, and then you get the bath.

I learned that the mechanic and his wife had split five years back. I located her, shared my own grief, learned she had two kids, told her I was going to bring back the Chevy Nova and settle up. I would help her and her kids somehow. What help I might provide, I had no idea. I turned to helping Louis Roper with the mail.

***

Saturday night I went by Cindy's and found Allison and Daniel and Mallory and Jock—her latest boyfriend—in the third or fourth hour of a Monopoly game. Daniel broke away to tell me he had found Dougie Perkins' buddy, the kid who'd been with him at the lake. "His name is Stanley Hirsch. I guess Stanley is like Dougie. Anyway, both of them wander off. Stanley's uncle was babysitting him, so Dougie took me over there."

"You went to the uncle's house? A guy named Hirsch?"

"Yes, sir. He's not a very nice man."

"Tell me."

"Well, when we got there Stanley was playing in the front yard, and I guess his uncle thought he was going to go off with us. He came tearing out of the house and grabbed me by the shirt. I got a close enough look at him, I promise you. I think he could be one of the guys in the posters."

"What? He grabbed you?"

"No kidding. I thought he was going to hit me."

My eyes were wide.

"I got him off my shirt and told him Randy and I were just looking for Stanley, because the Post-Times was chasing a story and Stanley might be able to help us. Then he really got mad. He really was going to hit me." Daniel grinned. "Randy said his old man was going to come over and beat the tar out of him. He didn't say tar, either. He backed off then."

Well he might. I myself had experienced a breath of the wrath of Randy's father, Mr. Perkins, after I invited his son Dougie for a hike in the woods. Now I'd almost gotten *Daniel* beat up by Otto Hirsch, a guy I believed to be a thug and maybe a hit man.

"I'm glad you weren't hurt," I said.

"My fault."

"No, no. Not your fault, Daniel. Mine. I wonder why Dougie didn't tell the FBI his friend Stanley's uncle was one of the guys at the lake."

Daniel shrugged. "I don't know. Maybe he thought they wouldn't believe that either."

I had to laugh. Except now Otto Hirsch knew Daniel. Not so good.

FORTY-FOUR

On Monday I drove down to Everest and asked the postmistress where I could find a man named Otto Hirsch.

She smiled like I'd let her in on a secret. "You're with the FBI, right? After Hirsch?"

I gave her a half-smile in return, the kind I'd seen FBI agents use.

"He's got a box on the wall over there." She looked at the clock. "If you hang around I think you'll see him. But nothing in here, okay?"

I thanked her and poked around.

By and by a scruffy guy came in. The few people in the small room appeared to shy away from him, like they knew him and didn't want to get into conversation with him. The postmistress gave me a little nod. I remembered him. The look on his face. How he sauntered over to the car after he beat me up. Cocky. And Daniel had nailed it: he looked like the poster image. He got his mail and I followed him home. He walked up to his door, oblivious to me, speaking as he did so to a small dog that came up onto the porch. He was the guy. I was sure of it. I came up behind him. The dog growled. He whipped around, but his hands were full of mail.

I put a fist with all my strength into his stomach. Mail went flying. As he faced me, his face red with rage and pain, I hit him again, with everything I had, in the mouth. My hand hurt. He doubled up, trying to protect his belly. I brought my hands together and drove them down on the back of his neck.

He staggered, done for. I pushed him inside. I shoved him down onto his stained and sprung couch. The couch, him riding it, hit the wall, crushing plaster. I guess he hit his head. If he tried to get up I'd punch him again. He knew it. He didn't have it in him. At least not yet. I'd have been pleased to hit him again.

The place smelled like his sink drain could use a little Arm & Hammer. Except for hurting my hand, I felt great. I had exorcised some of my demons. That is to say, this guy had paid for some of his sins and some of mine, too.

"What the hell?" he grunted, rubbing his neck and sucking air.

"Who sent you after Dougie Perkins?"

"What're you talkin' about?"

"You know."

He sat up straighter, still soothing his head.

"They're treating it as attempted kidnapping," I said. "You know what that means?"

"What the hell you talkin' about?" He was mumbling out of the right side of his mouth. I understood most of it. His lips on the left side were all bloody and puffy.

"The little boy at the lake," I said.

He breathed some. "We wasn't tryin' to snatch no kid."

I reached for the phone. "Maybe we can sort this out."

"We was gonna pay 'im."

"For what? To find something in the woods?"

He was sizing me up, but decided I'd be quicker, so he leaned back, looking weary.

"Somebody hired you to snatch the kid. Who? Why?"

"Hey. It was no snatch. We was to *ask* the kid to show us what he seen in the woods."

"So you *were* going to snatch him."

"No." He started to shake his head, but quit. "We was gonna give him ten bucks to show us. Ask 'im. He'll tell ya."

"Why did you think he knew where to look?"

"I was tole that by my brother's boy, Stanley."

"By who?" I would have said 'By whom?' but how would that have helped? Anyway, I believed him. I put the phone down.

"My nephew, Stanley Hirsch. Him and Dougie Perkins is pals."

"What exactly did Stanley say?"

"He said Dougie tole him he saw somethin' fallin' an' claimed he knowed where it landed. He said Dougie said it was a person. Stanley tole me he didn't believe it."

"They went in there, the boys?"

"Nah. Stanley said no way he was goin' in there lookin' for some *body*. Which is why we was gonna ask Dougie to show us. Go with 'im. Protect him, like."

"Why did you care about a body in the woods?"

"I dunno. We didn't know *what* it might turn out to be. We was curious."

"Come onnnnnn."

"Okay. We was tole to get 'im to go in there with us and find what he seen."

"Ah. Tell me how *that* came up."

"I tole Dougie's story to a guy in Springfield."

"You bragged to a man named Henry at Felix's Restaurant that you might know where a body or something fell into the woods, and he told you to go in there and look."

He looked up at me, surprised that I knew all that.

I can't certify that I heard everything the man said. He talked like he had his mouth full of mashed potatoes. Part of it was my fault. "You better put some ice on that," I said, pointing at his face. I paused. "And don't be messing with kids, you understand?" He understood, all right. If he went after Daniel or Randy I'd be back.

He was still rubbing his neck when I left, and rubbing his stomach, too. Me, I felt better, although I wanted to go soak my hand. I was putting part of the puzzle together: not one but two groups—the sheriff's people and the thugs—were looking for the money. What neither group knew was that Arturo had already found the money. And taken it. The FBI was into it, too, starting with what they thought was a kidnapping case, then sniffing around for the money. Me, I happened to know exactly where the money was. My plan was to get it, and use it for bait.

FORTY-FIVE

Monday night I slipped into the "visitation" for my mechanic at a small funeral home in Huston. I signed the book but didn't greet the family; I just wasn't ready for that, and perhaps the ex-wife would not wish to greet me either, the person whose automobile had figured in the man's death. The ashes were in an urn on a pedestal. I wondered how much of the poor guy they'd scraped up. For about a half hour I sat thinking about him, a man I'd liked. *Requiescat in pace.* Comforting Latin, a remnant from my past. I gazed around from time to time, but saw nobody that aroused my curiosity. When the clergyman walked toward the lectern I slipped out.

***

Tuesday morning I got a call from Sheriff Tully. He wanted to know why I beat up a guy in Everest.

"Are you charging me with some crime?"

"No. But I'm warning you again, Morrison. If you know about a crime you report it."

Tully was looking for more than a confession that I'd beat up
a thug. I had a feeling he was dancing around me like a prize-
fighter, not wanting to get stung himself.

"He hit me," I said. "So I hit him back." Never mind the
number of days between his hit and my hit.

"You're a wise guy," he said, "and you're trouble. And I think
you're getting that boy in trouble."

"What boy?"

"You know who. The forestry guy's kid, Daniel Smart."

"What do you mean, trouble?"

"You've got him sticking his neck out."

This suggested Tully knew Otto Hirsch had threatened Daniel. I was ever more curious about Tully. Was he a bad guy or
not? I wondered if Hal, my headhunter pal, would look into his
background for me. I called and asked. He agreed to do so.

He was quick in getting back, and his report was simple.
"Tully was a Viet Nam war hero, a tunnel rat. Battlefield pro-
motion. Bronze Star. After he got out of the service he went into
law enforcement. Was a deputy in Dallas County. Good record.
Married. Two children."

I thanked him

"No problem," Hal said.

I knew he meant it. Hal and I and a few other guys covered
each other's backs. Off the record and off the books. Without
rhyme, reason, or rules. That was something we learned in the
army. We were just keeping it going. Bless the 3807. Our call
sign.

We signed off.

I knew about tunnel rats. They went alone into underground
passages in Viet Nam. They encountered spiders, rats, snakes,
knife traps. Tunnel rats were unusual people. Tully's war record

helped him get to be sheriff of Eagle County, but I didn't know how he might help or hinder my quest.

***

I called Susan Mittleman. I knew she liked to hear about what I was into, and to give me motherly observations and advice.

"Do you know anything about tunnel rats," I said, "the guys who went after the Viet Cong in the tunnels in Viet Nam?"

"In fact, I do," she said. "A couple of them have been patients of mine. Do you know someone with that sort of background?"

"Yeah. One of the sheriffs I run into. I find him difficult, secretive, uncooperative—"

"Well," she said, "I can only talk about the two I dealt with. Their job was killing people, you know. Not with a bomb or a cannon. Personally. That's versus the common military experience. Most soldiers who go into combat don't even fire their rifles. They don't want to kill anybody. But tunnel rats, as I understand it, are special. They're selected for their personalities, their willingness to kill. They carry a knife and a handgun, and when they encounter a person in a tunnel—Viet Cong, I guess—they kill him. Tunnel rat training builds that in, killing. You see someone, a threat to you, you kill him—or her. Stimulus-response, stimulus-response. This taps into the part of the brain that is central in dogs. 'Throw the ball. Throw the ball.' What we humans call the midbrain."

"I think airline pilots get training like that," I said. "Emergency-respond, emergency-respond." I thought back to my own training. I was a trained killer too.

"Well, that's what they do," she said. "In certain jobs, you have to react properly when you're scared out of your wits. If you're trained, your animal brain takes over in a crisis. You're right. Pilots react with their midbrain. They either make it safely or they're still responding when the plane hits the ground or the water."

"So how about these tunnel rats returning to civilian life?"

"I would think that when these guys are frightened or angry their conditioning kicks in."

I thanked her. Sheriff Tully, from what I'd heard from her, was carrying a lot of freight. But he wasn't like the people I was looking for. At least I didn't think so. The people I was looking for were terrorists. Sociopaths, actually. He was a courageous loner, almost certainly with a midbrain set to kill. So. I might not like Tully, and he well might be dangerous, but he was sort of like Sergeant York, who got the Medal of Honor for knocking off Germans in World War I. Such people were rare. I would honor Tully for his service as a tunnel rat in Vietnam until he gave me reason to think he might kill me.

***

In the afternoon I drove down south to make sure Daniel was okay. It turned out that while I was down there he was up at my house in Stanton making sure Allison was okay. Things happen quickly, as parents learn.

While I was down there I went to Wal-Mart to get some sunscreen. Snake boots were on sale for $9.98. Snake boots?! They protected your lower legs with a hard shell of some sort. As I learned from a saleswoman, realtors wear snake boots. I learned there were several kinds. The ones I was looking at tied on like shin guards. Say you walk through a vacant lot. A rattlesnake sees you coming. If it strikes, it hits a plastic shield. I thought about Abi saying I needed body armor. Well, here it was. I bought the things. I tried them on. Not too uncomfortable.

When I got to the office, Lenny called me in.

"Is it true you bought a car from a subject?"

"Huh?"

"A person the Post-Times is investigating."

"I don't know. I bought a car from the Wrights."

"Franklin Harris told me that. Do you understand the problem here?"

"Huh?" Franklin Harris. He was like a horsefly.

"Morrison, you're chasing a story and, using your influence, getting an automobile from people under the market value."

I looked Lenny in the eyes. "You're serious, aren't you?"

"I think you need time to think about this. I'm putting you on paid leave and asking you to get a medical evaluation."

"What?"

"Effective immediately. Please give me your press card."

It's hard to stand in your editor's office being told he thinks you're in poor mental health, or even dishonorable. Nevertheless, there I was, on paid leave and advised to get medical help. As my friend Melissa had advised, they come at you in mysterious and creative ways. How do you protect yourself against psychological warfare? It's more insidious and evil than being physically assaulted.

I called Susan Mittleman again. "Am I crazy?" I asked. I explained my new circumstances.

The essential question in sanity, she said, is does a person use common sense.

I waited for her verdict.

She laughed. " I will say you're creative. And you display some itsy-bitsy problems. You know, a neurosis, but not a psychosis. All in all, I think you have most of your marbles."

"You're a pal," I said.

So, as far as I was concerned, I had been to the doctor and gotten a clean bill of health. I mean, nobody's perfect.

Yet, I was on leave. I had no press card, no right to approach people in the name of the Post-Times.

***

I gave Abi the news.

"What am I supposed to do without you?" she said.

"Seems to me I can help you as long as I don't have to show a press card."

"Maybe."

I worried about her. I didn't want anybody to think she was now the one to go after to shut up the Post-Times.

"Maybe I should try to get an interview with Mr. Chen," she said.

"You?"

That was probably the wrong thing to say. Or the wrong emphasis. Something.

"Yes, me." She scrutinized me sort of like Lee Ann sometimes did. "You're not the boss. You're on leave."

"Interview him about what?"

Upon reflection, that was not the way to put it either.

She spoke carefully.

"Maybe the Wrights and Chens are friends," she said. "Both those guys are lobbyists, perhaps working the same streets. Chen and I could talk about that."

I was right to worry. She was an independent thinker.

FORTY-SIX

Nothing better to do, I went by the Y Tuesday night. A handball court was open, small miracle, and I went in and started slamming the ball around. Pretty soon an older guy stuck his head in and we played three games. He was great, and beat me 21-7 in game one. I came back in game two and beat him 21-19. He won the tiebreaker 11-2.

In the locker room I learned he was on the faculty at the university. When we exchanged names he asked me if I was the reporter who upended Garland Stevens' plan to cook ungutted trash fish to feed the hungry.

"He's still talking about that, is he?" I asked.

He laughed. "He's got a little stickpin doll in his office with your name on it."

I thought about that as I buttoned my shirt.

We agreed to play again, checked the desk and set a date.

***

When I got up Wednesday morning, except for a few aches and pains I felt pretty good. I called Hal, and joshed with his associate, Jade, for a couple minutes before he came on the line.

I asked if he'd please vet a woman, Olivia Wright née Fredericks, Philadelphia debutante.

"Might be a day or two before I get to it. What's up?"

"Olivia's married to Jeff Wright, a guy you checked out for me.

"I'm checking out a lot of people for you. That's okay. But I'm wondering what you're up to."

"We had a murder that involved a robbery, or a robbery that involved a murder, I don't know which, and I'm covering the story. Somebody dynamited the art center here at the university. Brought down half the building. Killed a reporter friend of mine. More than a friend, in fact. My daughter's bike was hit by a car and she got hurt. She could have been killed. It may have been deliberate. Not long after that, two people died in what may have been a murder-suicide, but maybe not. The other day my car was in for repairs and somebody blew it up. My mechanic was killed in the explosion. All of this seems connected somehow."

"That's awful. Awful. And your daughter? Sounds like the Mafia."

"This area's had its gangs and gang wars," I said. "But all that was back in the '20's and '30's. This is different, or at least I think it is. Anyway, I want whoever's behind it put away—in a hurry. I appreciate your help. I don't want you to think I'm wasting your time."

"I'll put Olivia Wright on top of the pile. You want me to come down there?"

He meant it, I was sure. "Send Jade," I said.

He laughed. "You're *already* in trouble."

"Call me at home," I said. I gave him the number.

"Why's that?"

"I'm on medical leave. They think I may be nuts."

"True story? You sure you got things under control?"

"You're the second friend who's asked me that."

***

After I got off the phone with Hal I called the Chrysler place. They said I needed to change out the EFI system, and that they could do it. They'd had it since Friday, and probably wanted to get it off their lot.

"How much?"

"I don't know. We'd have to price the parts."

"Why don't I come in?"

"Any time."

Eric found time to drive me over there. In contrast to the informality of the shade-tree shop, there was no way I could talk to the mechanic. Ah, well. The guy I talked to was about forty and had dirty fingernails, which was a good sign. He introduced himself as Ted, the shift manager.

"What you got," he said, "is a continuous-flow electronic fuel-injection system. It was a great idea but they aren't reliable. They stall around twenty-five miles an hour. They get affected by magnetic fields generated by power lines along roadways. Other things."

"No kidding." Everybody knew about my car's quirks but me.

"Somebody just sell you this car?"

"Yeah."

"Shoulda told you it don't take regular. Because of the EFI, I mean. When we change it out it won't be stalling on you."

"What you're telling me is that this car was designed to use regular gasoline but the EFI system really needs higher octane?"

"You got it. You got a car that takes regular but with the EFI actually needs premium. I think you'll want us to fix the fender, too."

"Yeah. I suppose. I should have gotten the people to fix it before I bought it."

He took me to his manager's office. Clean fingernails. He figured the price. Total: $560.17 for the fender, $412.00 for the carburetor. Altogether, $972.17. Plus tax.

"Why so much for the carburetor?"

"Labor. We got a rebuilt carburetor and what else we need. That comes to $212. Then there's the labor."

"Will it work?"

"Ninety-day warranty."

Sounded like a thousand bucks to me.

"Why don't you hold off on the fender?" I said. "Can you install the carburetor while I wait?"

"Okay. There's coffee out there." He pointed to a waiting room. Free coffee. I felt like my car was in an operating room. I guess it was.

It always amused me that car repairs at dealerships were predicted to be precisely this much or that much. Down to the penny. Anyway, they got the conversion done. But the Chrysler was going to end up costing me about ten grand, not the eighty-five hundred I'd laid out for it.

***

As I drove home from the dealership I got stopped for speeding. Isn't that the way? You're feeling great, on top of the world, living in the moment, and you lose track. The cop said I was ten miles over the limit. That was a kind assessment, I thought.

"Let me see your headlights." He'd seen the ding near the passenger-side headlight.

They worked. He retreated to his squad car. I knew what was going to happen next. When he came back he asked if it was my car.

"Yes it is, officer."

"It's registered to a Jeffrey Wright."

"I forgot to register it." This meant I wasn't insured, either.

Demonstrating that he was a nice guy, he let me drive the car about a hundred yards to a grocery store lot to park it, rather than pay to have it towed. While I was parking it he checked further. Again, this took time. Now the grocer had a squad car with flashing lights in his lot.

"Your car has quite a history," he said, coming back to me, chatty now that he had found me peaceable in the process of getting a ticket. Also, I thought, maybe it had occurred to him that I was connected—a friend of Eric's.

"Oh?"

"A Julie Wright, who I assume is Mr. Wright's wife or daughter? I've stopped her twice for speeding in the past five or six months."

"In this car? Really."

"Anyway, forget I said it, okay? This place will have it towed in a couple of days, so you better get it registered and insured pronto and get it out of here." He paused, like he was going to tell me something else.

"Anything else?" I asked.

"You sure they weren't unloading it on you?"

"What do you mean?"

"Well, I guess it's been impounded a couple of times."

"Huh?"

"It got towed in Sharpsburg, and then it got towed again, on Route 48, up near the quarry. You always wonder why a vehicle is abandoned. Out of gas? Motor problem? Stolen?" He dug some more. "Here it is. Stolen. Not once but twice. I gotta say, it's a nice-looking automobile. Joy riders, maybe."

I nodded.

"You need a lift?"

"Can you take me to the Post-Times building?"

I rode in back. He dropped me off. When I got to the top of the stairs I saw Lenny in his office. I stuck my head in and told him a psychiatrist was willing to certify my sanity. "Does that get me off?" I said.

"I'll tell you when," he said. "And let me be clear. It's not your sanity I'm questioning, it's your common sense."

Oh, oh.

I went downstairs to the parking lot, and once again the Nova started. Hallelujah! I drove around town, taking care of the registration and insurance. Following that, with a lift from young Louis Roper, the guy filling in with Abi on the state desk, I retrieved the Chrysler from the grocery store lot. I drove to my little rental house. What a day!

While I stuffed a load of laundry into my washing machine I considered the checkered past of my FS model Chrysler Imperial. I also thought about guns. I was still carrying Otto Hirsch's Beretta, but I needed to get rid of it. I'd have to ask Eric how to do that.

47

FORTY-SEVEN

While I was doing the laundry I got a call from Hal. He had turned up some stuff on Jeff Wright's wife, Olivia, ex-Philadelphia debutante. "That woman is pretty strange," he said. "As a teenager, she fell in love—literally—with a character in one of Ayn Rand's novels, the guy named John Galt. She'd actualized him, if that's the word for it. But it's stranger than that. She felt that he wasn't *returning* her love. That's when the first psychiatrist entered the picture. Then, when Ayn Rand died, she figured her affair with Galt was hopeless. So she tried to off herself."

"In love?" I said. "I recall the character. He's in *Atlas Shrugged*, right? I started to read it. I put it down, never finished it. It felt like a sales tool for her political views. Boring. At least to me."

"Well, I read it," Hal said. "Finished it. "As you probably know, Ayn Rand was big stuff for teenagers. Anyway, Olivia's family decided to get her some help. And get her married off. That's where Jeff Wright comes in—an ambitious and up-and-coming young man who wanted a social connection. They hooked Olivia up with Jeff within three months of her release from the home."

"The home?" I was astonished at what Hal could find out. Scary.

"Whatever. A residence for rest and relaxation."

"How'd you like to be married to someone with a problem like that?" I said.

"Well, he could have done a lot worse. Marrying Olivia, he connected with a Main Line family. Old Money. Marrying into it is quite a trick."

"The upwardly mobile banker," I said.

"Fact is," Hal said, "I finished that book, *Atlas Shrugged*. As I remember it, Galt shows up toward the end. He's overwhelmingly superior, so much so, in fact, that he has no need, or even awareness, I guess, of other people. So, there he is, noble and unobtainable, kind of like Lancelot in *Camelot*. Imagine that image as bait for a dreamy teenager. You can adore him and he won't get in your pants. The romantic ideal for a kid."

***

It wasn't too late, so I called Abi, just to check in, and we talked for a minute. I asked her about Chen. She said she finally got past the receptionist, but Chen claimed he was just too busy to meet.

"What do you make of that?" I asked.

"He's afraid of something," she said. "Lobbyists enjoy meeting people. I know from being around my father. It's in their blood."

I told her what I'd learned about Tully—that he was a loner, perhaps dangerous, but maybe a better guy than I'd thought. Then I reported Olivia Wright's love affair with a guy in a book.

"John Galt? By the time I was out of my teens I'd rejected what Ayn Rand believed." She reflected for a moment. "But there *is* something attractive to me about John Galt."

We disconnected. I'd have to take a closer look at Abi's husband.

***

On Thursday morning I drove by the Wrights' house, and there was Bert Long collecting mail from the box by the road.

I stopped to chat because he'd seen me. "I thought you were the chauffeur," I said, smiling in my best neighborly way.

"Also the mailman," he said. "On occasion, the butler."

I told him what it had cost me to fix the car. "You can get a good steak dinner for just the tax I'm paying on that," I said.

"You have a question?" he asked, noncommittal about the car. In the morning sunlight, his complexion seemed sallow, akin to Abi's.

Well, why not have a question, I thought. "Does Mr. Wright commute to Chicago and Washington?"

"Yes. Why do you ask?"

"Just curious. His job must take him to Chicago and Washington quite often. Flying out of Stanton doesn't seem convenient."

"Mr. Wright flies his own plane."

"Expensive," I said. "To have your own plane, I mean."

Mr. Long smiled. "He can afford it."

"No kidding." I gazed around, admiring the grandeur of the house and its setting. "Nice talking to you."

***

It rained all day Thursday but cleared up overnight. Friday morning I awoke to bright sunlight. It was the 3rd of July. Such a day, I thought, might find a lot of people cleaning their barbecue grills, cutting the grass, and making other preparations for the holiday. After washing and waxing the Chrysler, I drove to Sharpsburg. I wondered as I drove if the FBI had yet figured out what make of private aircraft might have carried the stolen money over the Shawnee.

The Sharpsburg airstrip looked charming as I approached it—neat, trim and clean. One white airplane was taxiing, rolling into position for takeoff. I watched as it took off, wings dipping left and right as it lifted up and up. A Quonset hut housed the office, and a young man behind the counter, apparently the only person present, greeted me with a nod. A standing fan blew noisily, the air aimed at him. I told him I was trying to learn what I could about a takeoff that occurred on May 2.

"Actually, I don't pay all that much attention," he said. "But it's interesting. The feds were in here asking the same question."

"Oh?"

He nodded.

"Did they ask about a car that was abandoned near here, or about strangers coming in here?" I asked. "Yep. Same questions. Couldn't help 'em there, either."

"Are there regulars that hang out in here?"

"Sometimes. But I don't think they were able to help much, either."

I looked around. "What's the draw here?"

He mused, not taking offense. "You're wondering with all this quiet how we manage to stay in business. Well, I'll tell you. My brother and I are crop dusters. Do some deliveries. Take people hunting. That sort of thing. We rent out hanger space and tie-downs." He smiled. "We get to fly."

"Can you help me find one of the regulars?" I took out my card, wrote Abi's name on it, and laid it on the counter.

"What's going on?"

"I'm looking for a lead on a hit-and-run."

He smiled. "A hit-and-run? Seems like a lot of interest in it. The FBI, you."

I smiled back. "Well, I don't know what else these people might have done."

"You leveling with me?"

"Yes, I am. I'm a newspaper reporter." I pointed to the card. "We're tracing a stolen car and a plane that might have flown down to the Shawnee."

"That's the story?"

"Pretty much."

He pointed toward the front window. "Follow the road along the strip to the blue frame with the big porch. That's Hank Durbin's house. Tell him I sent you." He thought for a moment. "And call me when your story breaks, will you? What station?" He picked up my card and squinted at it.

"You get the Springfield paper? It'll be in there," I said.

***

Hank Durbin was mowing his lawn. He shut down his tractor and came over to my car. He said he and his pals had been interested in "the kerfuffle," so they'd gone out to look at what the FBI was up to. They were wearing gloves, going over a car. Then they were getting it towed. "Come to think of it, the car looked just like yours."

I smiled. "It's a long story, but, yeah, this is the car. It happens to be mine. Did you see the plane?"

"Nah. Can't recall even hearing it, whatever I was doing."

"If anything else occurs to you, let me know, will you?"

"You're from a newspaper, eh?"

I found another business card, and wrote Abi's name on it. "If you hear anything, talk to her, will you? I'd appreciate it."

I went back to the airstrip office and told the man at the counter I might want to catch a ride over the Shawnee.

"Two passengers?"

I nodded. "Probably."

Driving back to Stanton, I felt sad. The guy at the airstrip had said, "What station?" TV news—quick, simple, exciting—was capturing people's attention. Woe is us.

FORTY-EIGHT

As I drove home I heard on the car radio that a Nazi named Klaus Barbie had been sentenced to life in prison for war crimes so despicable the news reader wouldn't go into them. I knew about Barbie; his name had come up in class in Monterey as we discussed the use of informants in counter-intelligence. The U.S. used Barbie for a while after World War II. Then he ran off to Bolivia. The Israelis tracked him down. They could track a rat in a sewer.

I made a mental connection: Whoever blew up my car, killing an innocent auto mechanic, was a sewer rat. Whoever struck down Allison, an innocent kid, was such a creature. I would find him.

Eric said I was a journalist, and I should be chasing a story, not seeking revenge. Actually, I was a hunter, tracking a sociopath. I agreed with the Israelis. You hunt the killers down: Mess with me and your ass is grass. Where does that expression come from? The person you kill and bury decomposes, and fertilizes your lawn. How about that?

***

Eric and Carol had invited the girls and me to a 4th of July weekend house party. During the barbecue Saturday afternoon I asked Daniel if he could get his father to pinpoint airstrips in and near the Shawnee for me.

About four o'clock, while we were playing softball in Eric's back yard with a 16-inch "Chicago softball," Eric got a call from the station. A woman named Melissa Meyer, a Post-Times reporter, was trying to reach him.

"My friend from the paper," I said. "She's trying to call me and thought you might be a contact."

I went inside and called her at home.

"I attended a reading this afternoon," she said.

I asked Eric to tell the others to go on with the game. "Yeah?"

"I got invited to, guess where, the Wrights'."

"Really." Now I understood why she'd been sucking up to Helen Beaulieu.

"Seven of us. Helen, me, Julie, plus a couple I didn't know, and—guess who?—Franklin Harris. And his wife."

"No kidding."

"Helen told me Gar Stevens called Julie to say he couldn't make it."

Gar Stevens? "So what happened?"

"Interesting. First we did some ums—"

"Huh?"

"You close your eyes, um for a while, and relax. Which, by the way, I never got the hang of. That went on for a while. Then Julie did a reading about dreams. Maybe ten minutes of that. Then people talked about their dreams. The guy I didn't know recalled a dream where somebody brought him a dead horse. Somebody said a dead horse is bad news. So that went on. Then Harris said he dreamt he shot two duck decoys. Julie said this was a *very* bad dream. I don't remember why. Then we um'ed some more. So. That's it. Next session will be on reincarnation."

I did an um myself. "All this took how long?"

"An hour or so. Maybe an hour and a half.

"No sign of Jeff Wright or his wife?"

"Nope."

"Look, Melissa. I've got to get back with these people here. I'd like to talk more about this. I'll catch up with you at the office, okay?"

We disconnected.

When I went outside, the softball game had deteriorated into Piggy Move Up. It was not long before we walked off the field and sat at the picnic table. Eric told our little group that he played Chicago softball when he was growing up. "You pitch high and inside," he said, "and the batter hits high fly balls to left field. You need a good pitcher and a good left fielder."

Daniel, alert to the call I'd gotten from Melissa, asked me what was up.

I told him a colleague had been to an Edgar Cayce meeting. "It's for spiritualists."

"Some kind of séance? That kind of thing?"

"Well, not exactly." I gave it some thought. "Cayce's dead. About 1940, I think. He was a folk healer. If you had a bellyache, maybe he'd recommend a grape poultice. Somebody suggested to him that he was more than just a healer, more like an instrument of God. So, he would put himself in a trance, his wife would ask him questions, and he'd talk about dreams, psychic phenomena, health, reincarnation. She kept track of what he said, and when he died she had it all on tape. What he'd said led to readings, where people would listen to something he'd said, or what she'd written down, meditate on it, then talk about their dreams and listen for people's thoughts.

"Cayce believed dreams are meant to guide us," I said. "His thinking apparently appeals to certain spiritual seekers—people who want inside information. Like you can be a Methodist *and* a Cayce devotee. Cayce offers spiritual insights that are more personal than you get in church, or tries to. So he connects with—among others—university people. People who want the inside scoop."

"You hear about people handling rattlesnakes," Daniel said.

I grinned.

"So why are you involved in all this?"

"These meetings connect in some way or other to what I'm looking into."

"What do you mean?"

"I wish I knew."

The others had gone inside. I suggested we follow suit. We joined a card game. I don't know how you play cards and hold hands, but Daniel and Allison managed it. As we played the game I admitted to myself that I had a twinge of interest in Cayce. What if I told Eric? Yikes!

***

After the fireworks Saturday night, Daniel gave Allison a kiss that I thought went on a second too long, then headed home to Everest.

***

On Monday morning Daniel called me at the rental unit to tell me his dad had pinpointed five airstrips. He and his buddy Randy were going to "ride out and take a look, see which ones are being kept up."

Another campout. I envied and worried about them. "Do *not* do anything risky, okay?"

***

I stopped by the house to pick up some of my books. When Allison heard Daniel and Randy were going to camp out in the forest she wanted to go. She was getting frustrated about her leg. I was not too displeased that she couldn't go with them. And I reminded her—once again—that her leg had to heal, that surviving a femoral fracture was a delicate process, that if she wasn't careful she'd end up with a limp. Blah, blah, blah. Do kids listen?

When I dropped my books off at the rental unit I called the guy at the airstrip in Sharpsburg. "How about Friday?"

Shortly after that I got a call from Hal, whom I'd asked to glance at the history of our society editor, Helen Beaulieu. He had discovered that she came from a wannabe-prominent Ontario family. The guy who ran the soft drink plant here in Stanton was her third husband. No surprise, given my take on her. She was pretty cute in her pastel suits.

Thinking Lenny might be inclined to put me back on active duty, I went up to the newsroom to tell Abi what was going on. As I expected, Lenny called me into his office.

"I think by now you ought to have the message," he said.

"Absolutely. I'm back on the job?"

"Yes."

The Cowardly Lawyer walked in as I was leaving Lenny's office. "Am I missing something?" he said.

I opened my mouth to speak. I caught a warning flash in Lenny's eye and walked silently out.

Abi was happy to have me back. Melissa and I chatted about her experience of Edgar Cayce readings. "I don't get it," she said, "but I can ummmm with the best of them."

***

By Wednesday Daniel and his buddy Randy had visited three of the airstrips his father had pinpointed on the map, and Daniel got to a phone and told me what they'd seen.

"One of them's apparently being turned over to farming," he said. There's one fairly close to Green Lake, too, but it's all grown over. I don't think anybody could put down in there. But there's another one about eight miles south of Green Lake, close to the river, that looks good. There's a house on the property, pretty nice, and a big red barn. An interesting color, kind of a purplish-red."

"Tell me some more," I said.

"The strip is mowed and sharp-looking. The house has a big screened porch, overlooking the strip. I could make out a couple of people in there."

"Be careful, Daniel."

"I used binocs."

"No, no," I said. "Reflections will give you away."

"Well, we probably have the same problem with stirrups and bridles," he said.

"Keep your distance," I said.

"We want to see a few more."

"Having fun are you?"

"Yeah. We found a leather jacket. Pretty nice."

"What?"

"Hanging on a bush. Just like somebody put it there."

"Can you pinpoint the location?"

"Yeah. A couple miles south of Green Lake."

"Did you touch it?"

"Randy's wearing it."

"Oh, boy. Have Randy take it off, please. Put it in your duffle. How soon can you get back to your house?"

"We're not too far. Tomorrow, about mid-morning? What's the big deal?"

"It may be a clue in the falling-man case."

Daniel laughed. "There was nobody in it."

"Daniel?"

"Yes, sir?"

"Be careful, you and Randy. See you tomorrow."

FORTY-NINE

I pondered the jacket. Who should I call? Sheriff Tully? The FBI?

I called the FBI.

"My name is Morrison. I'm a reporter for the Stanton Post-Times. I need to talk to Dennis Walker."

I got Walker's gruff hello.

"A couple of boys found a leather jacket—maybe a pilot's—hanging on a tree in the Shawnee."

"Tell them not to touch it."

That's what I mean by FBI style.

"They're on a pack trip, but they're coming in. They'll be at the Smarts' place, down in Connerville, on the north edge of the forest. Ten o'clock tomorrow."

I got there about nine.

Betsy was not happy with me. "Ever since Daniel got mixed up with your newspaper—"

"Betsy," I said, "Daniel is an adventurous person. He had that trait before I met him."

She shook her head and walked away.

At nine-thirty a helicopter landed in the road, making a lot of noise and kicking up all kinds of dust.

There was a loud knock on the door. Ed waited a few moments for the dust to settle and opened it.

The man in the doorway glared. "FBI. I am Agent Marx and this is Agent Walker. May we come in? Is Daniel Smart at home?"

Apparently Agent Marx didn't like being left waiting while dust settled.

"Come on in," Ed said. "They'll be along shortly."

"They?" said Agent Marx. He still had that hard look they get.

"Daniel and his friend Randy Perkins," Ed said.

"Who's Randy Perkins?" Marx said.

"Quit harassing people," I said. "When I heard the boys found a jacket I told them to pack it away and come to the house with it. Then I called Agent Walker. He's standing right beside you and knows all about this."

I got Marx's hard look but no verbal abuse.

We waited. The dining room clock ticked.

"Anybody want coffee?" Ed Smart said.

"I'd like a cup if it's already made," Agent Walker said.

Somehow his request helped bring balance to the situation.

I looked at the Smarts' beautiful paintings, and all the deer heads. I thought about the jacket.

The second hand went around.

Twenty minutes passed. Agent Marx ground his teeth.

Clop clop clop

Ed went to the door. "Here come the boys."

We went outside. A couple of people were in the road, looking at the helicopter. A surprise. Ed's neighbors, their houses hidden in the trees.

"Hi! We're home!" Daniel hollered. He and Randy looked exulted. The horses were spooked but they calmed down. The boys swung themselves down, looking a little sore in the legs. They turned the horses out in the fenced backyard. Betsy got some water into the trough, and for each horse she peeled a banana. She had grain for them, too.

Horses like apples, as I knew from watching movies. I knew nothing about bananas.

"Have they been grazing?" she asked.

The boys nodded.

"Drinking?"

"Yes, ma'am," Randy said. "We made sure they had plenty of water."

"Where's the jacket?" Agent Marx said.

The boys moved to get it and he told them to stop. Agent Marx went to get it from the duffle. We all watched as he put on medical gloves to do so. The leather jacket looked like a pilot might wear for warmth and comfort. Fleece lining.

"Why are we just now learning about this little excursion?" Agent Marx said.

"We post our plans each evening for the next day," I said. "You have to read the bulletin board."

Agent Marx squinted at me. "We can bring you in for impeding an investigation."

Walker looked amused.

Daniel rolled his eyes.

Walker got a briefcase from the helicopter. "Boys, we need your fingerprints," he said. "Okay?"

Daniel's mother made a face.

"Can we go back inside to do this?" Walker said.

"Yes, sir," Daniel said.

The fingerprinting was a solemn and careful process, but the boys looked at each other and smiled.

"Was the jacket zipped up when you found it?" Agent Marx asked the boys.

"No, sir," Randy said. "We didn't see a body, either."

"Can you pinpoint the spot?"

"Yes, we can," Daniel said. "I'll go get a Geological Survey map."

Armed with the marked map, the men stowed the jacket and and lifted off in the helicopter in a cloud of dust. The boys calmed the horses. We all shielded ourselves and watched. I felt like we were in a movie.

***

When I got back to the office I found Abi at her desk and filled her in.

"It was a leather flight jacket," I said. "I'm assuming it fell out of a plane. What do you think?" I paused, got no response, and continued. "When Dougie saw the falling man? He might have seen the sleeves flapping. Arturo found the money close to Green Lake. The boys found the jacket about a couple miles south."

She cocked her head. "New lead?"

I shook my head. "Nah." I didn't want to spotlight the boys.

"It's your story." She shrugged.

I called Sugar Beets, and, remarkably, found her at home.

"What's up, Darlin'?"

I reminded her she'd promised me a copy of the guest list. I also asked if she knew if Lincoln Chen had a private plane.

"Yes, he does. I've flown with him a few times. We go hunting."

"You do? Where?" I imagined her in camos and boots. That image made her more approachable somehow.

"On the southeast side."

"He's got an airstrip in there?"

"Private land, by the river," she said.

"Nice place?" I asked. "With a screened porch overlooking the strip? A couple miles south of Green Lake?"

"No, that sounds like Eddie Beecher's place," she said. "Chen's is south of there, maybe five miles. Rustic. I swear, there's about eight miles of gravel road going in. You'd think he'd have it paved. Gray frame with a lot of glass. Birds hit the windows. Breaks their necks, poor things."

"What kind of plane is it?" I asked.

"A Cessna."

"Do you know what kind?"

"A Cessna."

She was doing her best.

"Does it have stowage doors?" I asked. "Can you stow things from outside—without going through the passenger doors?"

"I have no idea."

"Well, how do you carry hunting guns?"

"He keeps 'em at the lodge."

"Sugar, we need to get a look at that Cessna. We need to see if it has stowage doors, luggage doors, whatever, on the fuselage, and, if so, if one of them is damaged."

She mumbled to herself, like she was committing my request to memory.

I loved her voice. Jade was sexy but Sugar was softly southern, sweet.

Lee Ann? Lee Ann was assured. Willing to put up with you.

***

Jade called, speak of the devil. She said her boss had asked her to tell me that Mrs. Harris—Harriett, wife of Franklin Harris—

had been arrested three times in the past year, for shoplifting. "Apparently, nothing's ever come of it."

"Shoplifting? Shoplifting what?"

"Lingerie." She giggled.

Interesting. But my mind didn't go to Victoria's Secret. And why would a string of charges be dropped?

I told Abi about the shoplifting. We agreed we didn't want to print a belated story about three shoplifting arrests that had come to nothing. But I was going to talk to Franklin Harris about it. Getting past that, I told Abi I was going to fly over the Shawnee on Friday morning, and she was welcome to come. It turned out that, with all that traveling as her father moved around in the Navy, she'd never flown in a small private plane.

**

Friday morning Abi and I drove to the airstrip at Sharpsburg. Our pilot was ready to go. His brother was manning the desk. The plane wasn't cheap to rent, with pilot, for half a day, but I was satisfied the trip would be worth the money.

After we got in, me in front and Abi in back, our pilot checked to see that we were strapped in, and then climbed into his seat. By this time the cabin felt like a sauna. He released the brakes and we lurched forward.

Over the grass and up we went. Abi and I cringed as we climbed over what looked like a telephone line at the end of the field. We continued ascending and reached a cruising altitude of three thousand feet, the pilot told us. To me it seemed too high for looking down and enjoying the scenery, but the air was cooler and the engine noise had quieted. He passed me a set of headphones. I asked him if he could fly at a lower altitude, and he took us down to two thousand. Much better.

Our ride was fairly smooth. The weather was calm and clear with a few clouds. "Ideal," he said. When we got to the Shawnee we dropped down to about a thousand feet and flew south along the Ohio River. It was a big river. You could sense from up where we were that it was wild and dangerous. You hear about the Mississippi, but the Ohio is big and serious, too. When it pours into the Mississippi south of Cairo it adds muscle to the mix.

"This should be the first strip," our pilot said, pointing. "I'll drop down so you can get a better look."

We got low enough to see fine detail. The place looked abandoned, as Daniel had promised. We went on. The next strip was obviously Beecher's, trim and beautiful. No sign of life.

"Pretty," Abi said.

"Those people paid two million for that place, what I heard," our pilot said. I passed this on to Abi, more or less in a shout. Soon we got to another spread along the river. A flight of ducks passed below us.

"They can fly much higher, and can be a danger," our pilot said. "In a plane this slow you can usually see and avoid them. It's not the propeller that's the problem. They come through the windshield. So right now we're in their space and we're over a flyway. But its Spring, and they're down on the ground making love. Except those guys. Autumn months are when it's bad. Anyway, if they're heading right at you, you're supposed to slow down and pull up. They tend to dive.

"Chen's," I said. "Has to be."

The pilot nodded.

"Can you get closer?" I asked.

He eased us downward.

"That's a horse," Abi said in my ear.

"Where?"

"Edge of the woods. Just north of the barn."

"Run by it again?" the pilot asked.

He circled. Going a bit lower and slower, we cruised over the tree line and over Chen's bright red barn. Magenta. Very pretty.

"Those two people coming out of the barn," I said, "are Betsy Smart's adventurous son Daniel and his buddy Randy."

"One of 'em's leading a horse," Abi said. "The other one's got a camera."

"That would be Daniel," I said.

"I thought the trail ride was over when they turned over the jacket," Abi said.

I just shook my head.

FIFTY

Driving home from Sharpsburg, we stopped at a restaurant and I called Ed Smart and urged him to get the boys home. I doubted I'd win Betsy Smart's affection by suggesting I was worried about them, but I couldn't help that.

"They were over by the river, you say? I don't know," Ed said. "Might be a while."

"If you do talk with them, ask Daniel to call me, will you?" I said.

Seeing the two boys poking around Chen's barn had unnerved me. What in heck had they been up to?

Arriving in the newsroom, I plopped down in the chair by Abi's desk.

"I've got to straighten Daniel out," I said. "We can't have him sticking his neck out like that."

Abi smiled. "Maybe some of your style has rubbed off on him."

"That's what his mother thinks." I switched subjects. "I've been looking into that Ayn Rand business," I said. "Here's something weird. Did you know this John Galt, the character Julie's mother got wrapped around, is at the center of a cult? I mean right now, today. Apparently you see billboards in Kansas—*John Galt lives!* The story is, people in that part of the country keep just two books by the bed. One of them's *Atlas Shrugged* by Ayn Rand, published about fifty years ago."

"I give," she said. "What's the other one?"

"The Bible." I paused to watch her consider that combination of books. "Interesting, don't you think? I mean, the two messages seem antithetical to me."

"Where'd you hear all this?"

"My headhunter friend."

She shook her head. "What's going on?"

"Beats me. After I talked to him, I called the Kansas City Star. A guy said Galt is a thing out there. He said the Galt movement favors laissez-faire capitalism—not exactly a subversive idea, you know. They have a motto, or pledge, or whatever it is: *'I support a society based strictly upon voluntary association.'*"

She laughed. "Not exactly electrifying. What does it *mean?*"

"Between the lines it means look out for yourself, and *only* yourself. And the only job your government should have is to protect your rights—not superimpose others' rights on yours.

"That sounds like Libertarian dogma," she said.

"Ah, I asked that very question. But Ayn Rand considered Libertarians anarchists, which she definitely was not."

Abi considered. "The Bible on the nightstand with that book? If you think about it, the bottom-line message of the Bible is to get yourself to Heaven. Period." She grinned.

"I know you like setting me straight," I said, "but aren't you forgetting the parable of the Good Samaritan?"

"Rural Kansas?" she said. "Places like that? People don't *have* any neighbors."

She sounded at that moment like my lost love, Lee Ann.

Louis Roper broke in. "Do you people have nothing to do?"

"Strategy meeting," I said.

"Want to give me a hand with these clippings?"

"Why not?" I took a pile of envelopes.

Abi joined us.

As I opened envelopes my thoughts wandered. Bert Long apparently routinely picked up the mail from the box at the end of the drive; that meant he could sift through it before he took it to the house.

***

Daniel called me Saturday.

"What were you doing in Chen's barn?" I said.

"Oh, that. Dolly threw a shoe. I was trying to find something to get the nails out."

Here I was, ready to lecture the kid. "Was she hurt?"

"No, but I needed to get that shoe off. She could have hurt that foot real quick."

"So what did you do?"

"Lucky for me, Mr. Chen must have horses around sometimes. There were a couple of empty stalls in there. I found a rasp and clippers. I found some duct tape, too. I pulled the shoe and wrapped her real good and walked her home."

"Duct tape." I laughed. "You couldn't ride her?"

"Oh, I could have. The ground in the forest is pretty soft. But I didn't want to risk her getting bruised or turning her foot."

"Did anybody see you?"

"No. At least I don't think so. I got some pictures. I'm going to develop them as soon as I can."

"You? You have a darkroom?"

"Yes, sir."

Daniel. What didn't he get into? No wonder his mother was anxious. But he was an intelligent kid, more grown up than his mother knew. He was like his father, I thought.

***

Monday I found Abi at her desk and told her about the horseshoe problem.

***

That afternoon I got a call from Sheriff Tully. "What's this about finding a coat in the woods?"

"Somebody found a jacket in there. The FBI didn't tell you?"

"Why am I just now hearing about this?"

"Sheriff, why is that jacket interesting to you?"

"Don't push me, Morrison."

"We're trying to do the right thing, Sheriff. We could use a little cooperation from your office."

"I ought to lock you up."

He hung up.

He knew about the money. He definitely knew.

***

On Wednesday we had our now-and-then newsroom meeting. Lenny was grumpy about Helen Beaulieu's work. He asked her point-blank about a couple of big mistakes on the society page, one of them the wrong name under a wedding photo.

"Sorry, Leonard. There's a lot going on," Helen said. She was a sweet young thing, doing her number. Or so she let on.

"A little less socializing on campus and more attention to editing would help. The mother of the bride was in tears."

"Yes, sir."

Later in the day I was talking with Melissa.

"She's a social climber," Melissa said. "And she can't write worth a damn."

"I thought you were chummy, talking about auras, going to readings."

"Hey, you were the author of that. She's up to something. I don't know what. I want her off my campus."

Well, well. This was the old Melissa. I wondered what Helen had done to get her so mad. Spurned her in romance? I guessed not. In all fairness, Melissa was right; she'd gotten close to Helen at my behest to try to find out what she was up to. I decided to have a cup of coffee with our publisher, Mr. Ritchie. I got myself invited to his house and told him how Melissa felt.

"I'll talk to Lenny," he said.

I couldn't read Mr. Ritchie. But it seemed to me he was becoming more aware of who was who in the newsroom. Or, maybe he was just more aware of Helen Beaulieu. He had a reputation among us, or at least with me: a good guy but a lech.

***

That night I got a call from Sugar Beets.

"I went by the hangar," she said. "I said I left a bracelet in the plane."

"Great. What did you see?"

"I walked all around the plane, darlin'. There's no luggage door or any such thing as that."

"Huh."

"You think that lets Chen off the hook?"

"So it would seem."

"Is there anything else I can do?"

"Maybe. I just don't know what that might be. Not yet, anyway."

"I love what you're doin' for me," she said.

Life was interesting. I'd just asked a woman who made the cover of *People* magazine to talk her way into an airport hangar, sneak a peek at an airplane, look for any luggage doors and damage, and call me and tell me what she saw. And she'd done just what I asked. Even though she had a high interest in finding out who killed her brother, and knew I was trying to help, I still couldn't imagine a superstar being so accommodating. To my mind she wasn't just pretending to be down home. She really was. I had a little frisson—a little surge—of excitement about her.

FIFTY-ONE

I told Abi I had an idea. Melissa could go to a Cayce meeting and drop a hint that might bring somebody out into the open.

"Like what?"

"Maybe recall a dream featuring me finding three million dollars."

"Come on. That's not a good idea," she said.

I approached Melissa.

"What a caper," she exclaimed. She loved getting stories by bamboozling news sources.

Given her enthusiasm, I figured the gambit might work. I started breaking in my snake boots. I mean, that's why I bought them, right? To go after the money. If something broke I'd need to be prepared. I also bought a paperback at Barnes & Noble, *Snakes of North America.*

A Cayce reading was held that very Friday, and Melissa attended and dropped the hint. At least, that's what I hoped. Afterward, she and I went for coffee at The Press Club.

"Franklin Harris and his wife were there," she said, "and Julie Wright, of course—and me, and Helen Beaulieu, but not her husband."

What made Melissa's day, however, was that the guy she didn't know had showed up again, and turned out to be the man behind ArtiClear, the research venture at the university she thought was bogus and was trying to dig into.

"He doesn't know I'm onto him. Oh, and Garland Stevens, your pal from the ag school, he was there."

She was referring to the creator of *Pescado Bueno Meal*, the trash fish diet supplement I'd derailed a year or so back.

"So there were eight of us," she said.

I was interested in who got drawn to Edgar Cayce. Spiritualism, around for a hundred years and more, had gotten past the crystal-ball stage, past the Ouija boards, and was presently pretty much the province of spiritual advisors. Cayce was such a person, a spiritual advisor, whether he'd seen himself that way or not. Drawn to Cayce readings were people of the middle and upper classes, notably university people, journalists, and the like. Spiritualism was in. Thus the mix of people at the readings at the Wrights' house was no surprise to me.

"So?"

"It was just like last time," Melissa said. "We got into ums, meditation, interpretation of dreams."

"How did your dream go over?"

"Pretty good, I think. I told them I dreamed about work. You and I were talking—"

"Me? Morrison? You were talking with me? In your dream?"

"Yes. You and me. You were wearing a mask, kind of like the guy in *Phantom*, and you had this huge sack over your shoulder. Let me think."

"Phantom?"

"Phantom of the Opera. A musical. In London. University people are into it big time. So they knew what I was talking about. Anyway, money started spilling out." She laughed.

"That was in your dream? Money spilling out of a bag I was carrying?"

She nodded. "And they asked me why I thought I had this dream, and I said you were working on a big story about a murder and robbery, and in my dream you knew where the money was."

My eyes were wide. This was no little hint. "Pretty bald, Melissa," I said. I rubbed my neck.

"Well, there were other dreams, too. So mine was just part of the mix, you know? Just another dream. Helen Beaulieu dreamt about butterflies. Julie said dreaming about butterflies signifies something elusive, like butterflies in real life."

"Really."

"Oh, and another thing happened," Melissa said. "The Arti-Clear guy, Hryhory Andrusiv? Is that how you pronounce it? Anyway, he handed out his cards. I have mine here." She produced it.

Hryhory Andrusiv
Chemistry of Body and Soul
Institute of Human Awareness
Kiev, Ukraine

I did laugh. "In the middle of a Cayce meeting he hands out his card?" I looked it over. It was a con artist's calling card if I ever saw one. "In English, that's Gregory Andrews." I got into it. "Ukrainians take *Scamming I* and *Scamming II* in their first two semesters in high school. If they get exceptional grades they go into the Foreign Service, anything that will get them overseas. Their job abroad is to steal everything in sight."

It was her turn to laugh. "Sounds like him. He said he dreamt up ingredients that could be brought together to help heal the human spirit."

"A kind of mental-illness potion," I said.

She laughed again. "After the meeting he told me he could get me a journalism fellowship in Kiev. Really. He said that. Then he asked me if we had any old computers here at the paper, or that I could get at the university, that we could give to Ukrainian universities. All we'd have to do is ship them over; he'd handle the Ukrainian end. What do you think?"

My turn to laugh. "So he gets free computers and sells them in Ukraine, conning people in his own country while he's conning us."

"Sounds like it," she said. "I just want to break the ArtiClear story before he does any real damage."

***

On Saturday, Daniel invited my darling daughter Allison down to his house to learn about developing film, so I took time to question her about it.

"Oh, Dad," she said.

Her mother and I, skeptical but trusting, you know, talked to the Smarts and then said okay. Off she went, hitching along lopsided on her crutches to his car. Do they have etchings in darkrooms? I wondered. Nah, he's a nice boy, I thought.

***

My own journey into the dark with a lovely female began Saturday evening. Returning a favor for Melissa, Abi and I had covered a Suzanne Vega concert at the University. Abi reported on the music; I did the interview and the color. The young woman talked like she sang—all on the same note. Or so it seemed to me.

Afterward I stopped at a homeopathic-remedies store to pick up a bottle of wintergreen liniment for aches and pains that lingered from the beating. I had left the store and reached my car when I felt a nudge in my back. I looked in the car window and saw Abi's frightened face.

"Run," she cried.

What was sticking into my back was a gun, I had no doubt.

"Get in. Try any funny stuff and she gets it first."

A masked person sat beyond Abi in the back seat.

"Don't turn around," the gunman warned. In the dim light, a hand, palm open, presented itself. "Keys." While he was at it, he ran his other hand over me to satisfy himself I had no gun.

Not willing to "try any funny stuff," as he put it, with Abi there, I gave him the keys and got into the back seat next to her. She was gulping and sitting straight up. I was sweaty-palmed.

The guy who had been at my back went around to the driver's seat. The backseat guy had a gun too.

I was sorry I'd fixed the carburetor.

"Put those on, backwards." We were handed a couple of balaclavas. I could feel Abi trembling beside me.

In one of the Travis McGee novels I'd read, McGee could tell blindfolded where he was, and guess where the bad guys were taking him. Not me.

"Where we going?" I asked. They had tossed the wintergreen liniment onto the front passenger seat, which meant it wasn't accessible. So I could not bang somebody over the head with the bottle, or maybe spill some of the fiery fluid in somebody's eyes.

"We're goin' to get the money. One funny move and the lady gets it."

Abi and I remained silent.

"So where is it?" the guy sitting on the other side of Abi said.

"Tell them," Abi said. Her voice told me she was terrified. Up until that moment in my life, I hadn't known I could actually sense my heart sinking.

"We can do this, and you can go home," said the driver.

"Let her go," I said. The little deception we'd concocted for Melissa had turned from a lark into something ugly.

How frightened Abi must be—and thinking about her little boy. She'd been right. The dream caper was a dumb idea. Our predicament was not funny at all. "We're going to get out of this," I said.

"Shut up," said the driver.

I knew the driver's voice.

FIFTY-TWO

"So where is it?"

"If I knew, which I don't, and told you, which I obviously can't, what would happen next?"

"When we get the money, we let you go. Where is it?"

"I haven't got a clue."

A laugh. "What you talking about? Where's the money?"

"Here's the deal," I said. "You let her go, right now, and I tell you where I *think* it might be." The man sounded like he hadn't heard about the money dream. If he wasn't lying, that seemed to eliminate the people Melissa tried to con at the Cayce reading.

Again, the laugh. "You ain't got no chips. Your young friend. Daniel, is it? He'll be okay if we get this done quick."

Daniel? They had Daniel?

Abi sucked in her breath.

That confirmed that the guy talking, the driver, was Otto Hirsch, Stanley Hirsch's uncle, the man who'd thought about beating Daniel up. So the guy in the back was Antony Biro. Of course. I doubted they had Daniel, but I didn't want them considering hurting Abi, who was close at hand. But I couldn't play my hand like they didn't have Daniel, because in fact I didn't know.

"I think the Mexican boys have the money," I said.

The car slowed.

"Mexican boys?" the guy in back with us said. It was Antony Biro. I was sure.

"Friends of the Mexican boy who died," I said.

"Greasers? Some wetbacks have it?"

"Oh, shut up," I said.

A surprised yelp came from Abi. "Stop it!" she cried.

"Yeah?" A snicker.

I leaned over Abi to the guy. "You'll be the first one I kill." I chose not to try out his name.

***

Silence. Abi breathing.

"Listen," I said. "I believe I can get the money. But you have to let this woman go. She knows absolutely nothing about anything. You have to do that now."

"Where is it?"

"Stop and let her out."

"No dice."

"I'll kill you both," I said.

They both laughed.

The army had drilled this into me: *Take your chances when the time is right.*

"Everest. East of town," I said.

"Where exactly?"

"Buried. Beneath a house."

"And you know this why?"

"Because the guy told me."

***

I tried to think. These two guys worked for Henry, the film noir detective at Felix's Restaurant. Henry worked for Lincoln Chen. But who had led them to believe I could get the money? Caitlin, perhaps? Excitement gets people whispering to friends. It happens. And Otto Hirsch lived in Everest.

Otto said, "Okay. Where now?"

"Eagle Street."

"Snake Road," he said.

Otto Hirsch would know that. The two of them had tried to drag Dougie into the woods. Now this. Was Henry behind this, or were they freelancing? I'd beaten both of them up. Getting even was probably part of this. I didn't like that part.

The roadway turned to gravel, then wound around for a couple miles. They stopped the car and Hirsch opened the front door.

"Get him out," he said.

They pulled me out my door. I could smell the snakes.

"Go get it, wise guy."

"I don't have a shovel," I said.

"Figure it out."

They were sure I wouldn't run away and leave Abi. Another reason, the road led nowhere but to a house next to a swamp. Otto Hirsch would know that.

I took off the balaclava. I didn't look at them.

"Go get it."

That sounded like "Fetch!" to me. I began walking down the road. Although we'd driven for a while over gravel, this was asphalt, old, cracked, and broken. My legs wobbled. I was walking into the unknown, and I was afraid. No matter. I went slowly and spoke softly to whatever was down among my feet. "Hi, snakes. I'm just walking here. I'm not going to hurt you." I whispered this over and over. The night was black, so black in fact, that I could not see a thing. We were in southern Illinois, where nothing lightens the dark night sky.

***

For warmth, snakes like to lie on blacktop roads at night. Also, they don't like rude awakenings. I learned all this in my book about snakes. Also, if you spook them, they go nuts. Left to their own devices, when the road cools off they slide away. Right now it was still too warm to trigger exits.

Because I could not see where I was walking, I had to feel with my feet that I remained on the asphalt. The downside was that I might just step on a snake, or trip in a rut. Some distance along on my timid journey, concentrating on nothing but my feet and the pavement beneath them, I began to sense movement. I sensed, more than saw, a few small shapes that made serpentine retreats, then a big one. Big. Maybe as long as me. Very slowly, slushing my feet softly to tell him I was coming, I approached him. He held his ground. I stopped, watched. I whispered my mantra. He moved. Slithered off.

The following is as true as I can write it: A snake jumped straight up, levitated. Landed. Splat! I didn't know snakes could jump.

Then I came upon a water snake. Wham! He banged my shin guard. I cried out as he struck. In fact, I almost fell. I was terrified. Whipped.

After he backed off, I stood silent.

"Hey," one of the thugs shouted.

I moaned.

"Hey!"

I didn't respond.

"We're sending the lady."

The lady? I considered. Maybe she wouldn't encounter a snake. I'd scared a lot of them off the road. Here was a chance to get her away from the goons. I groaned, but said nothing.

I heard them open the car door, and slam it shut, and heard her: "Morrison?"

"Abi," I replied, trying to be feeble about it. "Take it slow." I kept talking, helping her home in a little on my voice. Sooner rather than later I would get my hands around their necks: sending a woman on a mission they were afraid to undertake. If she got to me, I could pick her up. Carrying her, how far would I have to go to reach the house? Twenty yards? Fifty yards?

"Morrison?"

"You're okay. Keep coming. Take it slow."

"Oh!"

She'd apparently seen one.

"Give him time to go."

After a long pause, I heard her slow shuffle and then I made out her shape, a shadow in the dark. I walked slowly toward her. "Shhhh. It's okay. Keep coming."

I reached down and swept her up into my arms.

"Oh."

"It's okay. I've got you."

A shout: "Okay, lady? Get the money."

"Tell them you're helping me."

Which she did.

"You're okay?" she said.

"Yes."

I carried her, continuing to whisper. "We're okay, we're okay."

She was light, but not that light. And there be demons, as Eric sometimes said. But we had a better chance now. She clung to me.

FIFTY-THREE

"I think that's the house," she whispered into my ear.

I sensed it too. A dark shape looming in the night. No light from within. No electric. Squinting at the house, I took my attention away from the snakes. Not for long. I felt something alongside my shoe.

"You look for snakes," she whispered. "I'll see where we're going."

I got past it. I touched wood with the toe of my shoe. "Here." I felt a stair and took it. Another step. Three. Four. My foot felt a larger surface, a porch. The shadow of the house had brought back blackness. (Country nights can be black. Go out in a black night; take a few steps; try to get back. Better bring a flashlight.)

Abi was getting heavy. Would a snake hit the back of my legs?

"Door," she said.

I paused, she turned the knob, and I stumbled in. Pitch dark. Silence. Somebody's house, dark as pitch, in the middle of a snake-infested cypress swamp. Surely the boys didn't have a gun.

I tried to put Abi down. Her feet didn't want to touch the floor. I breathed out. Sounded like a wind tunnel. She touched down. Ooof.

Silence.

"Hello? It's just me, boys. Morrison. From the Post-Times." What if they weren't home and I couldn't find the money?

I heard someone come into the room. Cat's feet.

"Qué pasa?"

Ah! I understood. The voice was boyish.

"Yo soy amigo. Morrison. From the church. From the meeting with Señora Bush. La maestra." That's the right word. La maestra. "We need help. Pronto." I was mixing and matching languages. What could I say?

"Por qué?"

I tried some more. "Los hombres malos estan en el camino, tratando de matarnos." I threw in "Alerta! Cuidado!" *Bad guys are on the road, planning to kill us. Be alert! Be careful.*

Silence.

"Help us, please," Abi said.

Then a shout from outside. "Ten minutes. Ten minutes!"

The boy called out something, I guessed to his pals. For all I knew he said *"Get the gun."*

I thought I heard him go, probably back to the bedroom. He was crying out. Maybe it was *"We got a crazy gringo in the living room!"* We heard other voices. In the dark I could see shadows and hear talk.

Light! A gas lamp?

"What's going on?" said a voice. A boy in skivvies.

It had to be the boy who translated for me at the chapel, the boy who had spoken English at Daniel's house. I squinted past the lamp. He began to translate for me as I yammered. "They want the duffle bag. We can save ourselves."

Spanish words flew around like bats out of a cave.

I learned this: You need patience when other people are deciding your fate in a language you don't understand. I don't know how often in life you will need that information, but there it is.

"Andele! Por favor!" I said. I knew those words well enough: *Hurry! Please!* Then I said, in slow English, "They will shoot us if we don't give them the duffel bag."

After more chatter the spokesman said "What do you want?"

"Where is the door under the house?" I said. "We need to get the bag."

After some more yammering the boy, lamp in hand, showed me the trapdoor. I pulled it open. I understood one thing: he knew I meant business about the bag and the guys outside.

Dim. But I smelled them. It smelled like the snake house at the zoo.

"I need a hanger," I said. "A coat hanger."

The boys watched me, my interpreter talked to them. Then they got me a hanger. I straightened it.

"I need you to hold my legs," I said.

This concept, from English to Spanish, took some time to develop. As I knelt by the opening they got the point.

The boys were beginning to get the overall picture. I was going to fish among the snakes for the duffel bag. From their murmurs in Spanish and their glances at me I guessed they thought I was brave or stupid. It also seemed clear to me that they didn't know what was in the bag. It was just Arturo's bag. They felt my urgency. Get it.

We accomplished the leg-holding arrangement and I peered down. One of them held the lamp closer so I could see better. I faced what must have been fifty snakes, I don't know how many, on top of each other. I sensed heat. Hence the congregation, I supposed. Some of the snakes were big. They featured several combinations of colors and designs. I never liked them in zoos, either. They moved around. They smelled awful. Little forked tongues.

Nestled in among them was what I came for, a big duffle bag, the kind you could get at a surplus store. It looked heavy, impossible to get. I stuck my head in just a little for a closer look and I heard a loud rattle. I jerked my head back. Testing the situation, I extended the wire hanger again, moving it slowly toward the handle of the duffle. The big rattler coiled. A couple of other snakes moved away. I snagged the handle, and began to draw the bag closer. It didn't feel right.

I pulled back my arm and looked around the room, fixing my eyes on the woodstove.

"I need that pipe," I said, pointing to the woodstove chimney. This caused confusion.

"No. Wait," I said. I pulled up a leg of my pants and unstrapped a shin guard. "Please. Strap this to my arm. Give me a towel."

After chatter, the boys got the drift. Abi, calming down, joined the team. They wrapped a towel around my arm and affixed the shin guard atop it. It was like a straightjacket on my arm. The wrapped towel protected my hand. I hoped so, anyway. They lifted my rear end to allow my arm to go down through the opening, like they were moving a statue through the door. We slid me into place. One of the boys got a flashlight and shone it down into the pit. The colors of the snakes became more apparent to me. I recalled Caitlin's descriptions of local serpents. The gang's all here, I thought.

With my shoulder in the opening and the towel wrapped around my fist, I again moved the coat hanger toward the bag. The rattlesnake struck at my arm. The hit was hard, like a hammer blow. I cried out, and almost lost the hanger. Spit flew. The snake had lost a little venom. I had a woman and three boys watching me, so I had to look courageous. I thought they could see my arm shaking. The snake struck again, surprising me by reloading so fast. But I hooked the handle of the bag. It was heavy, but it folded over toward me. Pulling harder, I got it to budge a little. Keeping it up, I slid it slowly toward me. The dirt under the house was dry and loose and that helped. As I dragged the bag, other snakes struck at it and at my arm. Some scattered. Then the big rattler struck at me a third time. How to explain the shock? Like somebody slapped my hand hard.

I was scared. My armpits were dripping wet. It is possible that I peed my pants. But who could smell that at the mouth of a snake pit? Other snakes, agitated by the moving duffle in their midst, became even more aggressive. A new player, with a brightly banded body, tried to bite me. Caitlin had talked about snakes like him, ringed in several colors. Not good. Finally I got the handle of the bag directly below my face. Snakes were slithering all over the dirt floor and each other directly under me, around the bag. Getting the hanger in place on the handle of the bag, I asked the boys to pull me straight up, because, as I tried to tell them, I couldn't bend my arm. "Slowly," I said. "Slowly."

A heave, and out came my arm and the hanger. But no bag. The weight had bent the head of the hanger, and the bag had fallen back. No bag. I was flustered. Failure. From my vantage point, with my head in the entry to their hideaway, the angry snakes seemed like crocodiles. Watching. Waiting. New game. With a punch I was learning about.

I tried again. Having my hand wrapped made me slow and awkward, but I fenced around with the hanger, moving the snakes back with it. Then I dropped the hanger, and put my wrapped fist through the bag strap. The big rattler struck for the fourth time, hitting my toweled hand hard. I didn't let go.

The boys cheered as I hooked the handle. I was shaking as they pulled me and the heavy bag out of the pit. Snakes smell even worse when they're mad. I can tell you.

We heard a distant shout. "Five minutes!"

"What in five minutes?" Abi said.

I shook my head. "They're afraid. Otherwise they'd already be here."

I was sweating like the proverbial pig. I took a minute to collect myself. We pulled off my shin guard and I got to my feet and opened the duffle. While the boys stared, astonished, I dumped bundle after bundle of hundred-dollar bills onto the floor.

The boys yammered in Spanish so rapid and alien to me that it confounded my senses. I practiced studied aplomb, sweat dripping down off me.

"Hold on. Hold on! We're not done yet," I said. I held up my arms like a football referee.

The boys went silent—looking at the money, looking at me.

"We are not done," I said. "When we are done, each of you can take one bill. One. Uno." I held up a bundle and displayed a single. "But we are *not* done." I waggled the finger.

Translation brought impatient commotion. They were confused about the money, and about my command of it.

"That big one struck at me three or four times," I said. My translator was staying with me more confidently. "So I think he's out of venom. For a while, anyway. You all know about snakes? You know that now he can bite but probably not kill?"

After a few moments of rapid translation I got some nods.

"I am going to catch him." I pantomimed choking someone.

Translation followed, then wide-eyed wonder, much rapid Spanish. They were watching a bull fight.

"Por que?"

Abi echoed the sentiment. "Why would you do a crazy thing like that?"

"We are going to scare the poop out of those bad men."

My translator got stuck on "poop," so I tried another word, "caca." They laughed.

"First, has anyone got gloves? Please get me a thick glove, a winter glove."

I hadn't thought of gloves before, but maybe they'd have some.

"Quick. Those guys have guns. They will kill us."

"Esta bien! Claro! Andele! Andele!" Words I understood.

We affixed my snake boot to my extended arm and the boys put two padded work gloves on my right hand, one smaller glove, tight, one larger one over it. I could open and close my hand.

"I don't think this is a good idea," Abi said.

My mind flitted to our trailer break-in. "Yeah. But stupid."

She actually smiled a little. She looked like she was about to get a penicillin shot.

Down went my right arm. If the snake struck, and its fangs penetrated towel and gloves, I would perhaps get some venom. And it struck! Venom splashed around like spit. Now I'd had six or seven hits. I went straight for its neck, scooping with my right hand, drawing the thing toward me, then throttling with my left. What happened then was writhing frenzy, like when a worm goes on your hook, only gigantic.

Have you ever wrestled a twenty-pound catfish out of its hole in the bank of a river? I have seen it done. There is nothing docile about a wild thing when it thinks it's facing death. You're fighting energy several times the creature's weight. The snake I was choking wrapped itself around thin air and pulled fiercely for its life. I cried out for the boys to hold on tight to my legs as my torso folded into the pit under the snake's almost overwhelming strength. Another snake struck at my protected right arm. Others slithered away. As I'd read, snakes don't think much. What my huge rattlesnake did know, however, was that something was choking it to death.

"Pull me up!" I cried.

With the heaving of two boys, and then a third, the snake and I came tumbling together onto the floor of the room, me holding fiercely to its neck. We were a slithering mess. I was trying just to keep its head away from my body. The fight was scaring me about out of my wits. "Grab it! Grab it!" I grunted. It actually rolled me over with its force. But by then the boys were grabbing hard at its body, anything to make it stop writhing. Six hands. Plus mine. Suddenly, without preamble, it just went quiet. At least for the moment.

"Hold it! Hold it!" I screamed, not relaxing my hold on its neck.

With all our hands gripping its heavy body, my own around its throat, the snake, exhausted, remained still.

"Abi. Get the bag," I said.

The boys yammered away and held tight to the snake. They saw themselves in control. Here was good sport.

"You're nuts," Abi said, but she got the duffle bag open. Tail first, we started folding the huge, thick body in.

"Push! Push!"

The snake began to fight again, but less fiercely. Suddenly it just quit. It was exhausted. Waiting for its next opportunity. In it went. I hoped I hadn't killed it.

We heard a shout. "Time's up. Get out here."

At that moment I was sliding my gloved and toweled left hand over the big snake's head, pushing hard with my right. In it went. Abi buckled the bag. Snake in a bag! *BIG* snake in a bag. From what I'd seen, it was upwards of five feet long and as big around in the middle as a coffee can.

I pulled off my gloves and ripped the shin guard off my arm. Telling the boys to stay clear of the bag, I went outside to look. Headlights told me the car was rolling toward us down the asphalt road. The thugs had figured out the snakes were gone.

The snake in the bag remained still. It was snug inside there in the dark, presently feeling pooped but not immediately threatened. Perhaps it felt like it had been swallowed.

Just like the boys, Abi looked at the bundles of money all over the floor, her eyes wide. But I did not have to remind her she was next to a very big snake. It kept her attention.

"It really stinks," she said.

"I'll be back," I said. I lifted up the duffle. It weighed about what the money had weighed, and I went outside with it. It really did stink. But the snake stayed quiet and still.

"I'm coming. I'm coming."

I walked gingerly out onto the road, not wishing to arouse the snake. There was just a bit of a moon now. It appeared that the road-visiting snakes were gone. I limped toward the car.

"You want me in back?" I said.

"Where's your girlfriend?"

"You want this or not?"

"Gimme the bag," Antony Biro said. He was in the back, where I was also to be. I withheld the bag. I climbed into the back seat, holding the bag.

"The girl!" said Otto Hirsch from the front seat. He had a gun trained on me.

"You want this?" I asked again.

Otto Hirsch said, "Gimme. Wow. Something stinks." Antony Biro slammed the door behind me.

I hoisted the heavy bag over the seat.

Otto Hirsch unbuckled the bag and reached in.

"What? Oh!" His eyes lighted up.

The big snake, exposed and touched, erupted from the bag, a monstrous jack-in-the-box, jaws immensely wide. Striking.

"Aggggh!"

Otto embraced his wounded hand. The snake struck again.

"Aggggh."

Otto's terrified eyes shone."Agggh!"

Car doors flew open. Antony Biro fled westward down the road. Otto Hirsch stumbled out. He stood doubled over, his stomach embracing his punctured hand. Through the front door Otto had opened, the snake slithered down and out. Huge. It looked to me like an elephant's trunk.

"Lie down," I yelled at Otto. "Lie down."

I glanced in the direction Antony had been running, then back at Otto, who stood terrified. Lucky for him, the snake had slithered past him.

"Lie down. I'll get help."

Otto stared at me, then went to his knees. He looked around some more, then slowly laid himself down on his side on the broken pavement, walleyed in his search for snakes.

I climbed over the seat into the front of the car. My bottle of wintergreen oil had fallen out of the car with the snake and broken open. The lotion had pooled around Otto and on the ground. A new stink. I wondered if the poor snake was covered in wintergreen. If so, it had to be burning. Nothing I could do about that. I got the car started and edged away from Otto's prone body.

"Hey," he shouted. "Hey!"

I ignored his pleas. I left Snake Road and drove to Daniel's house, a run of twenty minutes. I wasn't thinking too straight. I rang the bell, pounded on the door.

Daniel came to the door.

"There's a guy bitten by a rattler on Snake Road," I told him. "In front of the Mexican boys' house. Get help." I paused, trying for the right question. "Ah, Allison. Back in Stanton, right?"

He nodded. "Yes, sir."

I got back in the car and drove back to Snake Road. I felt stupid. I should have explained to Daniel why I had been on Snake Road in the middle of the night, and why I'd come to his house. Ah, well. I pulled over onto the edge of the road just before I got to Otto, who was still on the ground, doubled up. All the snakes seemed to be gone. Our ruckus had caused a little kink in their sex lives, that's all. Plus Mr. Big was probably covered in wintergreen, sad to say.

Abi was still sitting at the kitchen table trying to communicate with the boys, packages of hundred-dollar bills on the floor all around them.

She looked up at me. "They're gone?"

"Yes."

"That was some snake."

I held my arms wide. "This big."

The one boy translated. The other boys laughed and carried on.

"One bill." I held up the finger. "Uno."

"No mas?"

I gave them the same perspective I'd given Caitlin: keeping the money would be wrong, and perhaps get them killed. They reluctantly agreed to take just one bill—$100 apiece.

When they each had extracted a bill I suggested they now give their bills to me. "For laundering," I said. I tried to explain laundering. "I'll give the money back to you in fives, tens and twenties. Soon."

They conferred. I was the big snake killer. They gave me their hundred-dollar bills.

"Got a pillowcase?" I asked.

They found two. We filled one and then the other with bundled bills.

Looking like Santa with my bags, I thanked them.

"Where you going?" asked the spokesperson.

"To find a safe place for the money."

"Ah." They looked confused. The bad guys were toast. Why did I have the money? They still weren't sure. "I'm taking it to the FBI," I said.

They understood "FBI."

"Maybe there will be a reward, and you'll get a little more," I said. "But not if you talk about it. Silencio. Silencio." I put my finger to my lips, then drew it slowly across my throat.

The boys hated to see the money go. They had sweat equity in it and loyalty to their late friend Arturo.

But, carrying the stuffed pillowcases, Abi and I departed.

Outside, men were loading Otto Hirsch into an ambulance. They paused to glance at us. Abi and I walked around them, got into the car, and drove off. I felt like we'd just made the Final Four.

FIFTY-FOUR

A Jug of Wine, a Loaf of Bread—and Thou
Beside me singing in the Wilderness—
O, Wilderness were Paradise enow!

I don't usually wax rhapsodic, but these lines from Omar Khayyam came to me as we arrived safely at my little rental unit. I was somewhere around drunk, which was a medical miracle because I'd had nary a drop to drink. Flooded with happiness— Abi unscathed, Daniel untouched, money recovered, *huge* timber rattler bagged, three Mexican boys confused and disappointed, but *thrilled* by the exciting extraction of the dough, two thugs foiled—I popped the cork on a bottle of wine of uncertain heritage and got out a couple of empty jelly jars, some cheddar cheese, and a sleeve of saltine crackers.

Abi was as giddy as I was. "You are quite a hero to those boys," she said, then had a cheese cracker and sipped from her jar. "And, I have to say, me, too. You cut a fine figure, Morrison. But you stink."

"You too." I glowed like a 100-watt bulb.

We stroked each other some more, and I drank more wine. I was way, way over the top. Abi controlled herself better.

"What are you going to do about Stan and Ollie?" she asked.

She was alluding to a couple of British standup comics, Laurel and Hardy, who always managed to screw things up. It was a fitting allusion, I thought.

"I think we can learn some things from them," I said.

"Like what?"

"I'm going to visit Otto Hirsch in the hospital and see."

"And the other guy?"

"Antony Biro? Beats me. Last I saw he was running like hell. I know where he lives. Or at least I did know. But I can get my hands on Otto Hirsch."

"I'd better go home," she said.

"What are you going to tell Fred?" Dawn was upon us, and Suzanne Vega, whose show we'd covered, was probably home in bed in New York.

"I've been thinking about that," Abi said. "I'll tell him the truth; nobody could make up a story like that."

I drove her home.

I slept with the two pillowcases full of money. They were a little lumpy.

***

Sobriety brings clarity. Or so one hopes. After sleeping the morning away I was sober, and debated with myself taking the money to the FBI. But then I thought, no. The money represented the leverage I'd been hoping for, and if I turned it over to the FBI I'd lose it.

So. Where to hide it? In the woods, right where Arturo found it? At Grad Ritchie's house? In some cabinet in the Post-Times morgue? Or, how about beneath the house on Snake Road, right where I found it? Who would think of that? Then I thought about facing a replay of my fight for the duffel bag. No way.

How about right here in my little rental unit? What the heck. I punched up the pillows to get the look just right, and spread my blanket. Cozy.

FIFTY-FIVE

Wind was whipping thin white clouds across a pale sky as I hiked a vast, vehicle-jammed parking lot to the main entrance of Stanton General Hospital. It was hot out. I got inside the building and cooled off for a minute as I waited at the desk. An elderly female volunteer directed me to the elevator. I got off on the fourth floor and got lost.

With help from a guy in hospital attire, I arrived at Room 432 and walked in on Otto Hirsch, the only patient in the two-bed room. He was snoring away, so I took a chair. By and by he became aware of me and rubbed an eye. He winced as his movement tugged on the needle in his arm. It was attached to a bottle on a hanger.

"Whada you want?"

"I want the story, Otto, everything you know, start to finish."

He laughed a guarded laugh. "How is this not like ratting me out to the feds?"

"Well, I could kill you. That was my original plan, you know. You are a snake, Otto. Snakes don't think about much, I know, but I want what you recall. If your memory is good I'll reconsider my plan for you."

With this gentle nudge, he began to review things for me. He'd been hired by a guy named Henry in Springfield to do some dirty work. And so on, and so on. A few things he mentioned to me were worthy of attention—for one, how he'd come to guess a lot of free money was loose. It went sort of like this: Rumors about Senator Beets' money-filled shoeboxes had been around for a while, so his murder had stirred up a lot of talk. Also, people began to believe Dougie Perkins' story about something falling in the sky; after all, the sheriff had right away sent in dogs. Then, after that, Henry told Otto and Antony Biro to get together with "this kid Dougie," who was pals with Otto's nephew, Stanley, and go look for whatever was in the woods.

"So we got nowhere with that, as you know, and then we was told to tell you to butt out. So we did that. Then, when you still didn't listen, Henry told us to add some muscle. Which we did."

"Nice job," I said. "I wondered at the time what I was supposed to butt out of."

"Well, we really didn't know that either. But we figured you knew."

"And then what?"

"Ah. Then, Antony and me, we put two and two together. It was about the dough, we decided. That's why we were supposed to get some cooperation out of the kid. Since we'd been asked to get your attention, we figured maybe you really did know where the dough was. And how would Henry find out if we went after you? Nor likely, right?" He smiled carefully. "So Antony and me picked you up. And the lady, because there she was."

"Involving her was a *very* big mistake, Otto."

He rubbed his forehead and glanced around. "Here we are, so I guess so."

I reminded him that he and Antony had threatened to harm Daniel. "You're lucky I haven't killed you."

"So, last I recall," he said, ignoring the implicit threat because now I apparently looked benign, "you and the lady were in the house lookin' for the dough. D'ja get it?"

"Yes we did, Otto, and it's safe in the hands of the FBI, so you can quit worrying about it."

"Well, I told you all I know," Otto said. "I still get the shakes about that snake."

"Shock therapy," I said, getting out of the chair. "Maybe it'll do you some good."

Having completed my mission, I left the hospital. And, no, I hadn't turned the money over to the FBI. Nor was I going to. Not yet, anyway. But Otto might tell Henry that I had done so, and Henry might go up to Chen's office and repeat the story. In theory, then, nobody would come after me to cough it up. For a while, anyway. Or so I hoped.

FIFTY-SIX

I dropped by to see Eric at the church and asked him how it went with the FBI and the jacket. He held up a finger as he said goodbye to someone on the phone. When he hung up he pointed to a coffee pot on his hot plate.

I poured a cup and took a sip. "Very bad," I said.

"Pour it back in the pot," he said. He leaned back in his swivel chair. "I do have news about the jacket. They got several prints off of it. The boys' prints were all over it, of course, and there were some they couldn't identify. But here's the weird thing. Got 'em stumped. They got prints that apparently belong to some international fugitive, somebody the Chinese are looking for. Looking for pretty hard, in fact."

I stared. "Prints on the jacket? I'm assuming this fugitive is Chinese. Right? And what do they mean, 'fugitive'?"

"Well, maybe that's my word. Someone 'absconded,' is what they said. I would think an escapee, a runaway, a deserter, someone like that. They're even running ads about him—or her. Or so the FBI thinks."

"The FBI thinks it might be a woman?"

"No, no. Somebody who absconded. A man or a woman. I'm just an equal-opportunity observer here."

"Ads?" I said. "Like newspaper ads?"

"Yeah. Sort of like 'personals,' In Chinese-language newspapers in New York. Here's what they say." He peered at his notebook. "'A corrupt official has absconded. We are investigating passports, money flows, and family movements. The corrupt are brought home to justice. Giving themselves up, the corrupt can expect leniency.'"

I laughed. "I wouldn't want them looking for *me*," I said.

"It's odd, isn't it?" he said. "Assuming the jacket fell from a plane involved in a heist, maybe somebody wanted by the Chinese government was on that flight—or at least touched the jacket that took the trip."

"International spin for my falling man," I said. "Maybe it was a Chinese guy that fell."

Eric gave me a look.

I thanked him for the information, went out into the heat, and walked back to the office. When I got up to the newsroom I told Abi about the fingerprints.

She was as amazed as I was. "Mystery upon mystery." She had some Chinese news herself. "We may have Joy Chen coming to talk."

"How'd you swing that?"

"Melissa got the dean of the Asian Studies department to agree to introduce her. That made Joy feel important. She said she couldn't refuse."

"Clever," I said. "A luncheon where?"

"Why not the faculty club?" Abi said. "Prestigious."

"I'll see what Melissa can do," I said.

But Melissa waved off the idea. "Closing the club for lunch would irritate a lot of faculty people. They'd blame me. How about *The Chinese Imperial Inn*. I know the owner. Nice lady, Mrs. Wong. She could close the place for a classy luncheon. Her regulars would be impressed. Word would get around."

I smiled. Melissa saw around corners.

She closed the deal with the restaurant owner.

"I need to get the right dress," Abi said.

"Like what?" I said.

"Long sleeves, high neck, flat shoes. Formal look."

"Maybe darken your hair a little," Melissa said.

"Hmmm," Abi said, squinting her eyes.

"Nice," I said. "Inscrutable." The truth was, Abi really could deliver the look.

While all this was going on, the Chinese fingerprints on the jacket were in the back of my mind. Someone who absconded. Someone who had stolen something, maybe? How about three million dollars? But why would the Chinese government be involved in that?

***

While Melissa and Abi were arranging a luncheon featuring Joy Chen, I was researching the guest list I'd finally gotten from Sugar. Fourteen guests plus spouses and their "significant others." That was a newly minted expression for whomever you showed up with. Lincoln Chen was listed as "political consultant and independent lobbyist."

I called Mr. Ritchie and asked him if we could spend Post-Times money on a headhunter to check out a few of these people.

"Executive searches? Why? You want to hire one of them?"

"No, no. Sugar Beets had them at her place for dinner after her brother was murdered. A sort of commemorative event. It wasn't clear to me—"

"You went to her place, to a memorial dinner for Beets?"

"Yes, sir. Abi and I went."

"Abi? Your new state desk staffer? You two went to a dinner at Sugar Beets' mansion?"

"Sugar calls it a shack."

"You're on a first-name basis with Sugar Beets? Really? She had these people over to pick their brains?"

"That's what she said. She's interesting, Mr. Ritchie. Powerful."

"You might want to call me Grad, Brian."

"Thanks. People call me by my last name, you know."

"They do? Really? Mr. Morrison?"

"Just Morrison."

"Well. Yes, I think we can do that. Have the bill come directly to me."

"Yes, sir."

***

I called Hal. Jade answered. I told her I needed to get some background on Lincoln Chen and Henry Lockmann. I told her my publisher would pay for all these searches they were doing for us.

"You're actually going to pay us?"

"Yep. Can I hear from you in a week or so?"

"Heck. Maybe tomorrow."

***

That night, Daniel and Allison came by my rental unit. Daniel showed me some prints from the pack trip. One shot, no doubt taken by Randy, showed Daniel bent over in Chen's barn extracting a nail from his horse's shoe, which was hanging loose.

What popped out at me, though, was not the horse or the hanging shoe but what was in the background of the photo: Beyond the horse, a stepladder stood next to a small plane. A stowage door in the fuselage hung open, clearly broken. The damaged door was out of focus, but there was no doubting what it was.

Allison was leaning over my shoulder, looking at the photo. "Isn't that interesting, Dad? I had him print it to show you."

I smiled at her over my shoulder. "It's a great picture."

I got a magnifying glass and studied the photo. I could see that one hinge of the stowage door had snapped off, and that the door was hanging by its other hinge. It was a wonder to me the door hadn't blown off. I imagined how people must have felt when the door came loose—like a shrieking banshee had got into the plane. The plane was being repaired at Lincoln Chen's retreat. No doubt about it.

Daniel was standing behind Allison as we looked at the photo. "Pretty good, huh?"

"Remarkable," I said. "May I have this one? You removing the shoe from your horse's foot?"

I decided not to tell Daniel what I saw in the photo. Knowing the truth could get him killed.

FIFTY-SEVEN

On Tuesday I got a call from Hal. He told me Lincoln Chen appeared to have a clean record. "The only interesting thing I found out about Mr. Chen is that his bank balance shows regular withdrawals—a thousand dollars a month—for the past three years."

"Huh. I wonder why," I said. "Mortgage? Car payments? Something like that?"

"Nope. Nothing like that. The checks are made out to cash. He could be, ah, renting an apartment for a friend."

Henry Lockmann, the other guy Hal had looked into, ran a "full service" security and detective agency, "offering expertise and assistance in matters ranging from armed security to surveillance." It was easy to imagine how Otto and Antony got on Henry's payroll. They probably saw a classified "personal" ad in a newspaper: *"Yes!* **You** *Can Have a Career in Security Systems!"*

***

I called the Wrights and asked to speak to Julie. An hour or so later she called me back. I turned on such charm as I had. "I don't need a book from the library," I said to her, "and I don't know yet who took your car, but I was hoping you could help me with something else."

"And that is?"

"I'm going to dinner with friends, and I wondered if you might like to come."

"Me? Why?"

"Well, you meet a pretty woman at the library—beauty and brains, you know?"

She laughed. "When is this dinner?"

"Tomorrow night. My friends Eric and Carol Sutter and I are going to Tony Spuds, and I wondered if you could join us. He's a minister and she teaches fitness classes. We go out fairly regularly." I didn't mention that Eric was also a cop.

"You need a fourth wheel?"

"Yeah. But one I'd enjoy going around with."

She laughed. "Okay. Dress?"

"One click up. I'll pick you up at seven."

***

During my post-proposition pondering, the name "Mark" entered my mind. I had a moment of sorrow, or maybe angst, or anger. Maybe all three. My world was in flux. Lee Ann was gone, my marriage was on the rocks. Now I'd gotten myself a date with a woman from a family I was investigating. First I got their Chrysler, now I was going to dinner with their daughter. I wondered what Lenny would say. But I told myself this was research, that I wanted to know more about Julie Wright to get more insight into the family. That had been Melissa's advice, after all: connect with someone in the house. So I was doing just that. But, to be honest, Julie had caught my eye at the library. I hadn't had a date in more than two months. Thinking about her, I was excited.

***

Wednesday evening, as color faded from the summer sky, I stopped by the Wrights' mansion—there was no other word for it—and picked up Julie in my shiny Chrysler and drove with her off to Tony Spuds. She looked beautiful, kind of skinny but sexy, pale blonde hair falling a little bit over her eye. She wore a silver-blue silk dress with spaghetti straps and a bare back; the bra must have been padded. Five-inch heels. I recalled an old movie where Veronica Lake dropped a hand grenade in among her minimalist boobs and strolled into a cave full of Japs. Julie looked like that: a slender, gorgeous blonde with perhaps a devious purpose. Abi's erotic insight into the woman in the trailer park came to mind.

I did wonder why Julie had agreed so readily to go out with me. She might be doing a little legwork for her father, who appeared to be wondering what I was up to. Or, maybe she just wanted to go out with me.

We walked into Tony Spuds at eight. Eric's wife Carol, in something of a darker blue with no straps at all, had her shoulders covered with a scalloped white lace top. She was a knockout; no other word for it. She was younger than Julie, I thought, maybe thirty-five, and retained that blush of youth. Julie seemed to handle it okay. Eric had chosen not to wear his dog collar. He and I wore jackets, no ties. We looked all right.

The waiter took drink orders. Julie, like me, had a martini. So, I thought, she either enjoyed booze or felt she needed a stiff drink—an approach that, as we know, sometimes gets people in trouble. The ordering over, we turned to small talk.

First, Carol disclosed that she was a stay-at-home mom with a clergyman for a husband, but that she did lead fitness classes, more or less as a hobby.

"What do you do, Julie?" Carol asked.

Julie laughed. "I told Brian I was a dilettante. I guess that's about it."

Inquisitive smiles.

"Julie and I met at the library," I said.

"The university library?" Eric asked.

"I'm on the board," Julie said. "That was my father's doing. Plus, I volunteer one day a week."

"I love that library," Carol said.

"Volunteering there has its rewards," Julie said. "As I shelve books I occasionally get lucky."

I laughed. Julie had a compelling intensity and charm. And she was witty. Sitting close, watching her, I felt drawn to her, as to a magnet. What is that rush you get with certain women?

Long pause. I leaned closer to her.

"Lucky, as in getting to consider books you're filing?" Carol said.

"Sometimes you pick a winner."

We got quiet.

Julie sipped, put down her glass, and set a new course. "This may sound weird," she said. "I've been reading books about madness and mass delusion."

I wondered, instantly, if she was interested in the subject because of her mother's adolescent loss of touch with reality. Hell, I thought, her mother is still out of touch.

"Tell us," Carol said.

"What I'm finding in my reading? Well, I don't want to bore you."

"No, no," Eric said. "Your take on that kind of stuff just might help me in my work."

"Your work?"

"I'm a family counselor. I help the police deal with domestic crises. I confront angry people now and then—some of them probably deranged."

She considered this. "So there you are, standing on somebody's front porch, and the guy suddenly points a gun at you."

Carol shuddered.

"To complicate things," Julie said, "there's no possible way you can figure out what the guy might do; there is no one thing that constitutes madness. Or so I read, anyway."

Eric bowed his head and looked up. "You're right. At least, I've had that feeling."

"So, what do you do?" Julie asked.

"I try to soothe people." He smiled. "I also carry a gun."

She laughed. "Pragmatic."

"So where does all your reading take you?" Eric said. "What's the larger understanding?"

"Sadly, I don't think there is a larger understanding. There are all kinds of sanity tests, and shrinks are forever using them. But insanity defies analysis." She paused. "Consider Ted Bundy. The serial killer? He killed thirty women. Thirty. Early on, a psychiatrist had an opportunity to pick his brain. He found nothing abnormal, nothing."

We sat silently.

"And mass delusion?" Eric said. "What have you learned about that?"

"Aha. There is something to be learned about that! It's clear from history that people with superior minds can manipulate others. Ceasar, Ghandi, Lincoln, Jesus Christ, Churchill. You know what they accomplished. Vast groups, entire nations, like individuals, can be manipulated into embracing an idea. Consider Hitler, one of the most charismatic leaders of all time. Whether he was maniacal or not, he was certainly manipulative.

"We could talk all night about your compilation of leaders," Eric said.

"What's an example of maniacal manipulation going on today, right now," I said.

"I'll give you one," Eric said. "This mania that's sweeping the country about abuse of children at day-care centers. It was started by just one person, a demented grandmother. Heaven knows how many people have bought into what she said. People have gone to jail over it. Day-care centers have closed—"

Carol interrupted. "You think children aren't being sexually abused—"

Now *he* interrupted. "Of course they are. There's no disputing it. Children are targeted, all over the world. It's been going on forever, probably in every country on earth. It's evil—beyond terrible, arguably the worst personal crime there is. But's that's not what I'm talking about. I'm saying that madmen can, and do, manipulate the masses by distorting facts around hot-button issues. They take something like child abuse—a perfect case in point—and find ways to confuse the issue to advance their cause. Suddenly child abuse is not an individual issue but a day care center issue, a horse for the accuser to ride. This is a classic case. It's still simmering. This woman"—

Now Julie interrupted. "What woman? Who are you talking about?"

Eric smiled. "You're testing my memory. This was five or six years ago." He reflected; we waited.

"Ah. I do remember," he said. "The initial charges were made in 1982 by a woman named Mary Ann Barbour, the step-grandmother of two kids in California. She said the children had been used for prostitution and child pornography, tortured, forced to watch snuff films. This woman had a history of mental illness. Nevertheless, God forgive us, she—her ideas—captivated a lot of people, because sexual abuse of children *is* a hot-button issue. Law enforcement people jumped in on her side. Now, a lot of innocent owners of day-care centers have been falsely accused. One maniupulator. Suddenly a cause célèbre—"

"No harm intended here," Julie said, "but who's being manipulated, the people who believe harm is done at day-care centers, or the people who believe, with no possible measure of the facts, that it can't be happening?"

Enough is enough. I interceded. "I wonder if delusional notions were connected somehow to the bombing of the art center."

"Oops," Julie said. She'd sloshed her martini onto the tablecloth.

We put a napkin over the wet spot, and I caught the waiter. "Would you please get the lady a fresh drink?"

"Good question. Why *did* they blow it up?" Eric was taking my cue.

The waiter took our dinner orders. Julie ordered another martini. I had one also, just to be social. That's what I told myself.

After the waiter left, Carol spoke up. "I'd think there are two possibilities. One, it was a statement against the growing Hispanic influence in our country. They destroyed the wing that held Hispanic art."

"And the other?" Julie asked.

"Mapplethorpe," Carol said. "Some people were furious that the exhibit had gone forward against their wishes."

Julie nodded, sipped her drink.

"What do you think?" I said to Julie. "Does your look into psychoses offer clues to the art center bombing?"

"I don't know about psychoses, but I'm with Carol," Julie said. "Only I would think *both* things. Who in his right mind would display Mapplethorpe's work? And, while I'm at it, the art center is quite small; there's nowhere near enough room for any significant display of American art, or of our own southern Illinois crafts and such. So why does this museum display Hispanic art? I don't get it."

"Did you have fun flying over the Shawnee the other day?" Eric said to me—hard over on the tiller, bringing our sailboat about.

"I loved it," I said. "Maybe I'll book a fishing trip to Canada, or Alaska."

"Just for the ride?"

"No, no," I said. "But that's part of it. A lot of fun." I turned to Julie. "Your father flies his own plane, doesn't he? Commutes now and then in his job?"

Julie picked up an iced shrimp, dipped it in hot sauce, took a small bite. "Oh, occasionally he does. Just a few times a year. Mostly he's goes to the office, nine-to-five, right here in Stanton."

"But, when he does commute, he flies his own plane, a Piper, I guess?" I said.

She popped the rest of the bite into her mouth and nodded as she sipped her martini. "But rarely."

"So the plane is hangared here in Stanton. Can you fly it? It would be fun, I would think."

She laughed. "Well, I got my license. But do I fly? Not routinely, no. I'd rather see the world from the ground, thank you very much."

Dinner came, and Eric and Carol took the opportunity to adjust their blood pressure. I, in the afterglow of my martinis, cozied up to my fearless, interesting, and beautiful guest.

FIFTY-EIGHT

I took Julie home. We sat in my car in her driveway with the front windows rolled up, a sudden, remarkable thunderstorm rattling the roof. Her slight body was against me, her thigh against mine. The rain was coming down so hard we couldn't see the driveway.

"I think I was talking too much," she said.

"What do you mean, talking too much? When were you talking too much?" I put an arm around her shoulders. Lightly.

"All night." She laughed. "I had two glasses of wine on top of a couple of martinis. Talk, talk, talk. People don't want to hear it." She laid her head on my shoulder.

She was, in truth, a little high. From more than just "a couple" of drinks.

"What you had to say was interesting," I said. "Fearless, I think. Are you a rebel?"

"Everybody's a rebel, don't you think?" she said. She looked up at me.

"About what?" I said. I'd had a few drinks myself.

"Nobody likes to hear other people's viewpoints. Especially after a few drinks."

"I think you're right."

There we sat, a bit muddled, but electrified. The night, the drinks, the storm. I got a radio station, even in the rain clear enough. Diana Ross and Lionel Richie, *Endless Love*. A little static, but music is everything. I put my hand on her bare shoulder and pulled her to me and kissed her. She was lovely. Smart and lovely. I had met a few charismatic people in my life. She had that about her. Her beauty, her intelligence, her scoffing attitude. I was as lost as that one sock in the dryer. Rain kept drumming on the roof. The music was soft. We were moving to a gentle waltz.

"Like teenagers?" she breathed. "Right here in the car?"

Like teenagers? I lifted my head and leaned toward the steering wheel. As gently as I could, I released her and gripped the wheel and pulled myself up.

"We could get in the back," she said.

But she knew, or felt, that I had tripped over some distraction or other. She sighed, straightened up. "That was sweet," she said. "But there's always the first-date question." She was trying to be funny, but she was miffed.

"You're right. You're right. The first-date question."

After a while she said, "Your friend Eric. Did I hear him say he was a minister but worked as a police officer?"

"Eric? Yeah. Umm. Ah. Yeah. He's a Lutheran pastor. Christ the King. Just west of my office."

"Fairly liberal," she said.

"Yes. Very."

"Split personality," she said.

"Oh. Ah. Well, it's complicated."

"Pretty smart, though."

"Yes. Yes. He is one smart guy."

"But they have a lot to learn, those two," she said. "He and Carol. Don't you think? You can be smart but naive, you know?"

"Meaning?"

She was quiet.

"You might want to read *Mein Kampf,*" she said.

I sat up straighter still. If you want to cool down from a little sexual adventure, try hearing the words *Mein Kampf.*

"What? Hitler's book?" I said. "I doubt I could find it in the library, Julie, even if I wanted to." The rain had slowed to random drips. I was recalling what one of the county board members said to me. He said one of the folks who tried to block the Mapplethrope exhibit invoked Hitler, quoting the Nazi leader on the subject of art. It would take knowledge and guts to go to a county board meeting and quote Hitler on any subject, I thought.

"Was it you who invoked Hitler at the county board meeting?" I asked.

She was quiet for a few moments.

"You pretend not to see racial inferiority in these Hispanics. Am I right?" she said. She was more together now. Her spaghetti straps were in place.

"Well, I don't know that I'm pretending," I said. I looked at her. In profile, she was thin as a cookie.

"Don't you see that we have to expel all these Mexican people? There are *millions* of them flooding in here. Do you not *see* that? Soon it will be too late. Zip me up."

I obliged, trying to be tender about it. I was overwhelmed by the passion in her voice. "You're ahead of me, Julie." I wondered how we'd gotten from our hands on each other to this. I was very confused.

"We Americans have created this false dichotomy that if you're not for open borders you're a racist," she said. She got a pack of Pall Malls from her purse and lighted one.

I tried to connect with reality. Where were we? Didn't you light up a weed after good sex?

"The madness of the mob," she said softly, blowing smoke. "Hitler saw that, you know, mob madness. 'Herd mentality.' Your friend Eric brought it up at dinner. Individuals latch onto ideas, and share them, and pretty soon entire communities have an indefensible viewpoint. Do you see that? I see it happening, right now, right here in America. Right here at the university."

"And Hitler," I said, "how do his actions fit into your thinking?" I studied her face.

"Struggle," she said. "If you read George Orwell, who read *Mein Kampf* early on, you'd see that he saw the brilliance in Hitler. Hitler was a genius, you know. We're just not allowed to talk about it." She smiled. "Or even think about it."

The rain had stopped, so I cracked the window.

"Hitler caused a world of trouble," I said. This was my last stop on this subject. But I was impressed, not just by her knowledge, but by her passionate beliefs. In a way, in her style, in her passionate and articulate presentation of her thinking, she reminded me of Allison. Poor Allison. Intelligent. Passionate. But, still, childlike. There was the risk that she would worship this woman. Smart, articulate, convincing. Youthful worship is a problem. You haven't been there yet. You seek guidance, allegiance. You just might bond, like a young bird, or animal, to the first bright person you meet. There's a certain joyful compulsion in bonding. And great peril.

"Hitler didn't envision a good time for everyone, certainly," Julie said, more forcefully. "A fight, that's what he anticipated. He said either Germany wins or Germany ends. But he was all in. No prize for second place." She drew on her cigarette, blew a thin stream of smoke.

"Germany ended," I said. "He caused it."

She lifted one eyebrow, moved a little bit away. Ground out her cigarette in the ashtray. We sat quietly.

She opened her door. "I'd better go," she said. She got out of the car.

Damn, damn, damn.

I said goodnight, looking to catch her glance. She had that charismatic absence in her eyes, like she was someplace else in her head. I watched her go to the door of the house. She had a way of walking. Like the rest of her, it got my attention.

I waited for her to get safely into the house. As I pulled away I thought how easily my daughter Allison might be swayed, not necessarily by Julie, but by some smart, attractive, passionate person. A rebel. I was afraid for her. She was a seeker. I wanted to keep her close, at least for a year or two. Maybe she'll go to Stanton, I thought. I smiled. I was coming back to earth.

Eric called late. "What do you think?"

"Pretty deep into abnormal psych," I said, skirting him a little.

"Uh huh. What else?"

"I don't know. "Attractive? Rebellious? Passionate? Interesting."

"You told me her mother read Ayn Rand, right? Fell for one of the characters?"

"Yeah. John Galt."

"You notice any similarities?" he asked.

"Between Julie and her mother? I've met her mother. There *are* no similarities. They're two different people. Different generations. Different styles." Different, I wanted to say. Different.

"No. I don't think so," he said. "I've read Ayn Rand. Ayn Rand was against social help. Live for yourself, she said. She demonized the poor, the 'moochers,' as she called them. She called altruism 'a basic evil.' What you have here are the Ayn Rand sisters. Mother and daughter. They're the same. They're missing a little thread that mentally healthy people have."

"I'm sorry?"

"Sorry? What does that mean? Don't be sorry. Just listen to me. Keep in mind the social imperative. A lot of the people that people like Julie are denigrating are decent and hardworking but impoverished and in need of help. They need the help of their neighbors and friends. People get sick, old, and in need of such help. That's what society is for. Helping people in need. They're to be taken care of. People like Julie don't get it."

"She's different from you and me, Eric. She's also a bright and beautiful woman. She happens to be a rebel—"

"I'm afraid you've had a brain transplant," he said. "Or maybe you need one."

"Oh, come on."

We didn't sign off like we usually did. But I wasn't totally missing his point. We are drawn to the fire. It had been a while for me. I recalled a poem by Robert Service, *The Cremation of Sam McGee*. "It's the first time I've been warm," says a corpse in Alaska, after it's been tossed into a fire. The poem is funny as hell. I guess you have to read it.

As besotted as I was, I did remember that Julie's father had his own airplane, and that she could fly it. She could be in love with Hitler, I thought. Hell, maybe she was.

59
FIFTY-NINE

The luncheon for Chinese women got scheduled for Friday, July 31—only a week or so away. A Friday was chosen because Joy Chen said Fridays were lucky. But our luck seemed bad. First, Link, her husband, decided not to let her speak. Then the issue of saving face came up. You can't just cancel; you're invited by the dean. So she would speak. Then Link planned to attend, to monitor her behavior, I was sure. But Sugar did something for me: she called some senator and asked him to arrange an appointment with Chen for the particular day and hour. So he wouldn't attend. So then he decided Joy must read a speech that would be written for her. And that's where we were when the merry-go-round stopped.

"He's going to write her a speech?" I said.

"He's getting a speechwriter," Abi said.

"There's not enough time for all that," I said.

"Yes there is," Abi said. "My father was always being asked to give speeches. The Navy had speechwriters in the woodwork. In two or three hours they could write a speech for him that sounded great but said absolutely nothing. So he agreed to give these speeches and never got in trouble with the big brass for saying something out of school. I'm sure Lincoln Chen has access to a speechwriter like that."

***

Before Abi headed off to the luncheon I checked her out. She wore a black pageboy wig and a sheath dress. She had that Oriental look.

***

Afterward, she told me how things went wrong.

"At first, Joy was animated and forceful, but after the first few lines, which she probably memorized, she wasn't able to deliver them without sticking her nose in the text. So we had about ten minutes of that. Stick your nose in, read a line. Stick your nose in, read a line. And of course the speech said nothing.

"Then she saw me waving my arms to get her to stand up straight. So she started ad-libbing.

"I had encouraged her to keep her lips and throat lubricated, so she paused from time to time to take a sip of her plum wine. Mrs. Wong, who runs the place, provided her with a fresh glass whenever she emptied the one she had. I counted. Three glasses. Four. Have you ever tasted plum wine? Very sweet. After her third glass she started eulogizing Beets. She said, 'That poor Senator Beets. They kill him, you know. Because he flip on bill.' That's what she said. 'Flip.' I guess it sounded funny to her, because she started to giggle. There were about forty women there, and from the back of the room, where I was sitting, I could see them all sitting up straight in their chairs.

"Things calmed down, and I thought maybe she could survive, but five minutes later she was talking about attending a reception at the Chinese embassy in Washington. She got tearful about how she was treated. She was ad-libbing again. I wrote it down, word for word: 'They greeting us, all these gentlemen and ladies, senators and wives, all kissy, but when they get to Link and me they pull me aside and say they wanna see my papers.' She used an adjective in there I won't repeat. Then she started giggling again. People were gasping, I'll tell you."

I could imagine.

"I couldn't see people's faces," Abi said, "but I was sure they were horrified. Mrs. Wong fired herself out of the kitchen. Boom! There she was, applauding, smiling, bowing, lifting her arms to get everybody standing and applauding. There was darn little of that. People were scooting for the exit."

"Wow!"

"Truly. Mrs. Wong and I worked on her with cold towels and told her how good she'd been. I took her to my house for a nap. It was quiet. Fred was picking Charlie up at school. After she woke up we had some tea, and after a while she got past the post-speech dumps. Then she opened up to me. 'Link is changed,' she told me. 'He like Senator Beets.'

"I asked her if Link was being blackmailed, or paying off an extortionist or something. She was taken aback that I said that. But it was true. I could tell. What I finally got from her was that somebody saw Chen at the embassy and accused him of spying. That started all her husband's strange behavior, she said. She said he was afraid for his relatives."

"Did he become an informant? Did she say?"

"I don't know if she knows. But I believe she loves him, either way."

"Okay," I said, "let's say he was there when Beets was shot. Let's say he didn't shoot him. *Somebody* did."

Abi threw up her hands.

"He's paying someone off," I said. "Let's print it."

"I have to think about it."

**

While hearing Abi's report of Joy's drunken speech and revelations to Abi, my mind went to Allison. Oh, oh! I looked at my watch, ran down the rickety stairs and headed for Dr. Sherwood's office. She was still there, but just barely. She was standing on her own without the cast in the waiting room, one hand on her mother's shoulder, the other on a crutch. She radiated relief. I could see that her abrasions had healed, disappeared. She looked great. I gave her a hospital hug. I watched as she took a couple of hesitant steps.

Cindy was smiling too, even at me. "He says she's good as new—just has to see him once a month. For a while, anyway."

With Cindy and me in cautious attendance, Allison rode in a wheelchair to the building exit, got into her mother's car, and went off to whatever awaited her as a temporary invalid. Watching all this, I got a little sunshine in my soul. It could have been a lot worse.

SIXTY

After yet another night of sleeping on lumpy pillows stuffed with hundred-dollar bills, I went into the office on Monday and got a shock. To my astonishment, Helen Beaulieu, our society editor, was gone. She had cleaned out her desk on Sunday and left us.

I felt guilty. I'd gone over Lenny's head and complained to Grad about her, and she'd packed up and left.

I asked Lenny what he knew.

"I don't have any idea," he said. Leaning back in his swivel chair, he eyed me with interest, as if I might know more than he did about this strange turn of events. Why he might have a feeling like that I had no idea whatsoever. He reached into his desk drawer for a folded piece of paper and tossed it at me. It said, "*Thank you for hiring me. I learned a great deal while I served as society editor. Now I must resign. —Helen Beaulieu*"

"Strange," I said.

"Indeed," Lenny said, still watching me.

I went out into the newsroom and stopped by Melissa's desk. "What do you think?" I said.

"Haven't got a clue. Or maybe I do. Two people at the university have cleaned out their desks." She thought for a moment and made a note to herself, then looked back at me. "One of them is Hryhory Andrusiv, however you pronounce it, and the other is Garland Stevens, your fish guts guy."

"What? Gone? Both of them? Stevens, too?"

"That's what I'm told. It appears they got canned. The Food and Drug Administration has built a case against Andrusiv and his *ArtiClear*, and the university has found sufficient cause to terminate not just him but the two of them." She picked up and read from a note she'd gotten hold of that had been privately circulated among the administration and board of trustees: "'... colluding to defraud, violating research principles, publishing deceptive papers.'"

She dropped the note. "They were ousted yesterday, escorted off campus. I'm not hearing any squawks from the AAUP, either."

I wondered, but didn't ask, how Melissa had gotten hold of the private note. She had better contacts than a car battery. "Did you have a hand in it?" I said.

"Heavens, no. I wanted to publish a story, not punish people. That's somebody else's job. And now, publish I will." She pulled out a manila folder. The tag said 'ArtiClear.' The folder was an inch thick. "I've got enough for a series, and this"—she tapped the Trustees' note—"tees it up."

"Nice job," I said.

She nodded her head sideways, sort of an acknowledgement. "So I was wondering," she said. "Do you think this might connect with Helen leaving? She spent a lot of time with those two guys. Then she joined the Cayce study group, in which both of them participated. Now I'm wondering if there was more to her than I understood. I'm going to dig into it."

I parted company with Melissa, went to my desk, called the bottling plant, and asked to speak with Mr. Beaulieu. They told me Mr. Beaulieu was not employed there.

After checking in with Abi, I called the Ritchie residence. Mrs. Ritchie said her husband was busy.

"I need to see him for five minutes," I said.

"Okay. Be quick about it."

I drove over there. Mrs. Ritchie came to the door and pointed me toward his study.

"I know you're busy," I said to him, "but I have a quick question. Did you fire Helen Beaulieu?"

"No."

"Do you know why she left?"

He looked me over. "We're off the record?"

I nodded. What can you say to your publisher when he asks a question like that?

"This is a rather convoluted story," he said. "Helen Beaulieu is not Helen Beaulieu, and she doesn't have a background in journalism."

"Say again?"

"She's connected somehow to the FDA. They approached me, said they needed cover for an FDA agent to get on campus. We couldn't make her the campus reporter so I told them she could be the society editor."

"Oh, wow, Grad." I thought for a few moments. "She's not from Canada?"

"No."

"She's not married to a guy who worked at the bottling plant?"

"I doubt there ever was a Mr. Beaulieu at the bottling plant."

I started to laugh but checked it. I thought about my head-hunting friend, Hal Holman. He'd reported to me that Helen Beaulieu came from an "upwardly mobile" Ontario family and was on her third husband. Obviously my friend had been duped by a well-placed cover story. I was impressed, both with the FDA and with Helen Beaulieu, whatever her real name was: chasing around campus looking like an idiot social climber, remarking on Lee Ann's aura, joining the Cayce group, apparently just to connect with the ArtiClear guy. Clearly, she was a master of deception. Mistress of deception? Whatever. Whatever her real job for the government was, she was a first-rate spy. In my old Army outfit we'd thought we were pretty good. She just might be better, I thought. She'd kept up the deception for weeks, with a lot of people.

"She nailed the ArtiClear people," Grad said.

"I heard that." I told him about my conversation with Melissa.

"We *cannot* talk about this," Grad said. "If it gets out it might jeopardize the FDA case against a couple of very bad people."

"Screw the FDA," I said. "Think about this from our perspective."

"Oh?"

"By letting her work under cover as a Post-Times reporter you've broken some pretty fundamental journalism rules. We're hanging way out. You need to tell your friends at the FDA that you're going to deny complicity. She applied for a job. You filled a job. Period."

"We just gave her a job, that's right. What's the matter with that?"

"Do you know what people call 'the newspaper test'?"

He shook his head.

"Whatever you do, well-intended or not, if it's going to look bad in the newspapers, don't do it."

"What newspaper?" he said.

"Ours."

"What do you mean, ours?"

"Melissa will chase this story forever. And demand we print it in the Post-Times. Failing that, she'll take it somewhere else."

"Really. Our own reporter?"

"If I were you, I'd tell Lenny to put out a memo that says Helen quit for personal reasons. And, if I may suggest, don't just call him, and don't send him a note. Go over to his office and tell him in person."

"Really?" he said.

I headed back to the office, practicing a look of honesty and innocence.

SIXTY-ONE

When I got back to the office Abi handed me her copy.

"Read this," she said.

I scanned it. It was a great story: a senator's murder is linked to politics by the wife of a lobbyist.

"I'm still wondering if I should turn it in," she said.

"What?"

"We enticed Mrs. Chen to speak," Abi said. "We got around her husband. I sat by while she had too much to drink. I pumped her while I was sobering her up. So I feel terrible about it. And if we print this it will come to the attention of the FBI."

While Abi was deciding what to do, Grad came into the newsroom, creating a little stir, as always happened when he showed up. He went in to talk with Lenny, and pretty soon a note from Lenny started circulating. It said Helen Beaulieu had resigned for personal reasons. People around the room initialed it and passed it on.

Rip

That was the first sound I heard as Abi began tearing up her story.

I called Chen's office and left a message.

Then Lenny called me into his office and said he'd just heard from Chen. "He said he was going to sue us if we print anything about what Joy said at the luncheon."

Grad, seated there like George Burns playing God, was listening attentively. Then Abi came in. Then we were joined by Thomas Pickens, Cowardly Lawyer. Lenny's office was pretty grand; it held the five of us.

"What do you think we should do?" Lenny said to the assembly.

"Maybe it'll go away," Pickens said. "We just have to lay low."

"Oh, come on," I said. "Chen's not planning a lawsuit. He's bluffing. He's scared, and he's trying to scare *us*."

"*I'm* scared," our lawyer said. "You know what it costs to defend a libel suit?"

I turned to Abi, who nodded, freeing me up to share her news. "In fact," I said, "Abi's decided not to turn in a story about the luncheon. That means Chen's going to think he won. I want to talk to him now, right away. It's the perfect time to catch him with his guard down."

"Not a good idea," said our lawyer.

I thought Grad was going to examine an unlit cigar and say something profound, but he just sat there.

"I'll call Chen and say we didn't hear anything newsworthy at the luncheon, so we don't have a story anyway," Lenny said. He picked up the phone. "That ought to set him up for you, Morrison."

I was beginning to see Lenny in a new light. Quick. Smart. Maybe he was going to be good.

Our lawyer threw up his hands and left. You have to see somebody throwing up his hands to know it actually happens.

Late in the afternoon, Chen's secretary returned my call. He had agreed to see me Tuesday afternoon at his office.

***

On my way home from work I stopped at the Piggly Wiggly to get some groceries, and as I trouped the aisles my cart bumped into a woman's cart.

"Why, it's Mr. Morrison," the woman said, smiling.

"Hi!" I enthused.

"You don't remember me, do you? I'm Maddie Foltz, the Wrights' housekeeper, or was." Two little girls with her stood politely.

I smiled at the little girls.

"I've got the girls for a few days."

"How about I take you all to *the Press Club*," I said. "You girls like that?"

The two girls, maybe seven and nine, were definitely up for pizza. They were Kati and Dani, the baby. Kati gave me another one of those smiles. Dani gave me the once-over.

***

The girls wanted pepperoni with extra cheese. Maddie and I were okay with that. Watching a couple of kids about the age of Eric's was entertaining. They were trying to be polite and almost made it.

As we waited for the pizza I asked Maddie how things were going at the Wrights'.

"I quit, you know."

"Really? What happened?"

She continued to talk softly. "There were some indecent goings-on."

The girls were busy with crayons, filling in characters on their paper placemats.

"It's bad enough her mother's crazy," Maddie said, "but Julie's a strange one, too. Quite independent. Doesn't listen to her parents. Why she still lives with them, I don't know. My heavens, she's a grown woman. And then, no sooner do they hire this guy, the two of them are thick as thieves."

The chauffeur? Julie and the chauffeur? Getting past my emotions, I tried to put him in the mix. Julie believed in the Nazi ideal of racial purity, and, in my thinking, had perhaps fallen for Hitler. So how did the chauffeur fit in? Was he submissive, someone she could master? If he was weak, and love-struck, well, she could easily draw him in. I knew that.

Mrs. Folz regained my attention.

"I go into the garage one day and they're in there smooching. That's not all. I go in another day and there's a pistol lying there on the work bench. A pistol. Like it was a wrench or something. And the two of them are nowhere to be found. Excuse me? I didn't know what was going on, but I wasn't going to stay and find out."

"How long has this—liaison—been going on?" I said.

"I don't know. Ever since he showed up." Her cheeks went red. "I finally gave notice. I just told Mr. Wright I needed to look after my nieces a little more. Actually my grandnieces, you know."

"Where'd he come from, the chauffeur? Do you know?" I said.

She gave a final swipe to her mouth with her napkin and dropped it on her plate. "As I understand it, he was living here when they hired him, but I think they met him a year or two ago in Washington. I think he was working in a garage there. And then he moved to Stanton. That's when Mr. Wright hired him."

"Julie and her father met this guy in Washington, working in a garage?"

"That's what I heard."

"So, what are you doing now?" I said.

She smiled. "There's a couple always asked me to come work for them. I'm over there now." She saw the girls getting restless. "Come on, you two. We better go."

The girls slid out of the booth.

"Say thank-you to Mr. Morrison," said Mrs. Foltz.

Julie and Mr. Long? Interesting. I wondered if he came to Stanton to be with her, and she persuaded her father to hire him. So now he lived over the garage. Convenient.

SIXTY-TWO

Tuesday afternoon I drove to Springfield for my meeting with Lincoln Chen. I didn't want to be late; it might give him an excuse to duck out. The two-story building, of yellow brick, was near a cluster of government offices. Four other occupants were listed, including a loan company, a portrait studio, a travel agency, and, lo and behold, Lockmann Systems, a business being operated, as I knew, by Mr. Henry Lockmann, provider of muscle for security work of all kinds.

Turning right on the second floor I passed through a frosted-glass door discretely labeled "Lincoln Chen Systems" into a small but elegantly furnished waiting room.

As promised, Chen showed up, smiling. "Nice to see you, Mr. Morrison."

As we walked to his office he said, "You've joined the Post-Times?"

"Yes," I said. "It provides opportunities for me. To verify communication theory, I mean."

"Oh."

He sat himself down behind a walnut desk, his back to a window overlooking sunlit Capitol buildings. I sat in one of the two white leather wingback chairs that faced the desk.

"I was pleased the paper won't be covering the luncheon," he said.

"I heard them making that decision in the news-hole meeting," I said. "I didn't catch much of it."

Big smile. "So then. Sounds like we don't need to meet after all."

"I'm not sure I understand, Link."

"You're not here about my discussion with your editor?"

"No, no. That's not why I called you."

"Really?"

"I'm working on a different issue," I said.

"Oh?"

"It involves research I'm doing. I thought you might be an excellent source. It's about Chinese citizens who've come to the U.S.—how they're adjusting, their relationships with relatives back home, how they're dealing with the Chinese government, that sort of thing."

"Oh."

"There's a lot of uncertainty among Chinese Americans, as I'm sure you'd agree. My research is into the complexity of that—and, of course, how those issues might affect state government here in Illinois."

"And how would that concern me? I was born here. I'm a U.S. citizen."

"I assumed so, yes," I said. "Do you have dealings with the Chinese government?"

"Why would I?"

"Lobbying, perhaps?"

"You think I'm a lobbyist for China? Why would you think that?"

"I'm sorry. I just heard you had a connection. You occasionally visit the Chinese embassy in Washington. Isn't that so?"

"What's this about?"

"It's about what I've tried to explain to you, Link—relationships between Americans of Chinese origin and the Chinese government."

"Why come to me? It seems presumptuous of you to come in here like this. You should have made clear to me in advance what you wanted to talk about."

"Link, there's a Piper Cherokee with a busted storage door in your barn," I said. "What happened to it?"

He sat straighter in his chair, like I'd slapped him.

"What the hell business is that of yours? And what's it got to do with your so-called research?"

"Maybe a lot. Let me explain. Two different people—a little boy and a forest ranger—saw something falling over the Shawnee back on May 2. The story is, what they saw may have been the loot from the Beets murder—which may have fallen through a broken storage door of a private plane."

"What are you talking about?" he said.

I could tell he knew very well what I was talking about. I saw fear in his eyes.

"Here's the connection to my research," I said. "There's reason to believe a Chinese fugitive may have been on that plane."

"What?" He looked like he really was astonished.

"You commute between your home here in Springfield and your retreat by the Ohio River?"

"Wait! What's going on here? Who's telling you this? Who are you, really?"

"I'm who I say I am, Link. A guy who works for the Statnton Post-Times, doing some research into Chinese Americans. Their influence in Springfield. I'm just trying to get clear on things."

He was so taken aback I was able to get some more words in.

"Sugar Beets tells me you've taken her on trips to your lodge. Is that true? Hunting deer, razorbacks, that kind of thing? I suppose you take other people, too."

He responded like a boxer who'd been hit hard, twice.

"Sugar told you that? I fly over the Shawnee. In my Cessna. Sometimes she's with me. Other times, others."

"You fly a Cessna? I wonder why that Piper is in your barn."

He got a sudden cagey look, like he had to think fast. "You've been snooping around my property? Trespassing on my land? Journalists! I think I'll talk to my attorney about you."

"You sure?" I said. I had a liar on the ropes.

"Well," I said, standing up, "I'm sorry to have troubled you, Link." I paused. "Henry Lockmann, the guy down one floor from you? He runs a detective agency, right? He has thugs for hire. Did you know that? They beat me up one night. That was an experience, I'll tell you."

I turned and took two steps.

"Wait."

I turned back.

"Sit down," He was sagging in his big chair. "You think I robbed and killed Senator Beets? You plan to write some sort of exposé, win a big prize?"

"I am a journalist, Link. I'm trying to find out what happened to Senator Beets. But I'm not lying to you. There is a Chinese angle. I'm trying to find out what it is."

He turned and looked out his window. He sighed. "You're right," he said. "I used to visit the Chinese embassy."

I waited.

He swiveled his chair back around to look at me with deep sincerity.

"Consulting. Helping the Chinese get American viewpoints. But they turned on me. I don't know why. They started claiming I was guilty of 'foreign infiltration' into Chinese government affairs. That's what they said. 'Foreign infiltration.' Whatever that means. Then a guy, one of their agents, came to me and said I could make amends by doing some lobbying for them. Like I needed to make amends. That was crazy. But, let me tell you, it scared me. I *am* scared. Right now. As we sit here. I'm scared. They could hurt my family, ruin my reputation."

"I figured they had something on you, Link," I said, "like maybe you've got some relatives in China, something like that, or you wouldn't have had any dealings with them." I wondered about the Chinese agent. "Was the agent a guy named Long? Bert Long?"

Chen nodded. "He started claiming I was a member of 'a major criminal gang that seriously disrupts public order.' That's what he said. They punish people for that kind of thing. They go after your family, your friends. So I started 'paying a fine,' as he called it. A thousand bucks a month." Chen put his hands to his face. "They're driving me nuts."

I thought again about Mr. Long.

Chen spoke again. "They got interested in my lobbying business. Why, I don't know. They always have their reasons."

I tried to soothe him. "Link? Link? Here's an idea. Let's go to the FBI with this."

He sat rubbing his eyes with the heels of his palms. "No! That's what they want—me to complain to U.S. authorities. That's when they put the arm on your family."

He'd been sucked into a whirlpool of fear.

I thought of Eric. I wondered if he could help.

"There's a place I know, Link. Christ the King Lutheran Church, over in Stanton. My friend Eric Sutter is the pastor there. He can get help for you. FBI help. And he won't rat you out. I know that's true. Or I could call another friend, a lawyer. A guy named Madrid Paris. He's a great guy. There are people who can help you, Link. What do you say?"

Chen took his hands away from his eyes. He stared at me. His eyes got wider. Then he boiled over. "Get out," he shrieked. He exploded out of his chair, slamming it back against the credenza. "Out."

He was frenzied—like his car had gone into a river's swift current and he was trapped inside. Terror was in his eyes. Apparently, in churning up his agony, I'd knocked him off his head.

I got up and left his office and walked quickly past his wide-eyed receptionist, down the steps to the first floor, and out to my car. I got it started and got out of there.

I hadn't had my tape recorder running for the interview. I got it out and started dictating. Chen hadn't connected the dots, but it wasn't hard for me to do it. He and Bert Long had gone to Beets' office. Beets got shot dead. His safe got cleaned out. The two of them flew to Chen's retreat, but lost the money when the storage door broke en route. There was no other way to see it.

SIXTY-THREE

When I got to my little rental unit I discovered that Allison had let herself in.

"How'd you get here?" I said. "You're not trying to drive with that leg yet, are you?"

"It's okay, Dad. It's Mallory's car. There's lots of floorboard room. If I manage the stoplights I don't even have to use the clutch." She laughed. "Third gear, all the way."

I tried to imagine a person with a leg fresh out of a cast driving a car.

She showed me her hand. On her ring finger was what appeared to be a gold band.

My eyes probably registered alarm. Then I realized it was her right hand. "Very nice," I said.

"Don't get excited, Dad. It's a friendship ring. It kind of means that if I decide to get married I'll give Daniel the right of first refusal." She provided that smile. "I thought it was sweet."

"Hmmmm. Of course it's sweet. Just stay out of the darkroom." I laughed like I was kidding.

"Oh, Daddy." She laughed too.

***

On Wednesday I got a surprise that took my breath away. Abi was deserting me! She was leaving the state desk, moving to the society desk. She whispered the news to me just before we walked into a morning staff meeting that explained things. Franklin Harris was to retire. A new guy named Mike Hutmier was to be city editor. My young friend Louis was to return to the City Desk and work for Hutmier. Abi was to be society editor, replacing Helen Beaulieu. Another newbie, a guy named Alex Fletcher, was being added to the sports desk. He was a runner, a two-miler who held some records. We would advertise for a new state desk reporter.

I was stunned. I had begun to feel good about Abi's work, and had thought she did too. Apparently she hadn't felt as good as I did. You never know what other people are thinking. I concluded that the Joy Chen speech had been a turning point for her as to what she would and would not do. After the staff meeting I didn't bother to tell her about my interview with Lincoln Chen. I ducked out of the office and walked down the alley to Tony Spuds. It was about noon, but it must have been five o'clock somewhere. London, England, seemed like a safe bet.

I got a stool at the bar. Along about the second martini, Abi took a stool next to me. "Hey."

I kept my own counsel.

"You're a great teacher, you know? And the state desk is fun. I've learned a lot."

I shrugged. "Six weeks isn't enough time to get it."

The bartender brought her a Coke.

"Fred says what I've been doing is too far out, that it's okay to work, but we've got a little boy to think about. He didn't ask to get born. We did that to him. Fred's my husband, you know? My best friend. He knows journalism is my love, but he says what

I'm doing is not wise for a mom with a six-year-old child. Out at all hours, sticking my neck out. He's right. Charlie is my life. I'm his life. The society desk I can handle."

I took a sip. "We are *that* close to getting a good story, maybe a prize winner." What I was thinking as I said this was that her husband probably thought I was nuts, a good person to steer clear of. He wouldn't be the first. I needed a little sign for my desk: Beware—Occasionally Goes Crazy.

She laughed. "Yeah. But what we're doing. Getting kidnapped. Wading through snakes. Going out of town together. Going on a sort of date to a dinner party with Sugar Beets. Hustling Joy Chen to get her drunk in front of the Chinese women. Fred says I've got my neck out. Charlie's too.

I smiled and nodded. "You're right. The state desk is no place for a young mother." What I was thinking was, she thinks I need a sign, too.

"Anyway, that's what Fred is feeling," she said.

I looked at her. "I think you'll make a fine society editor."

"I am a good reporter," she said.

"It'll be interesting for you, being society editor," I said. "If you can cover a wedding honestly, like we cover other news, it'll make the wire. Maybe the Trib will pick it up. Maybe the Times." I was on my third martini. Not good.

"We're friends" she said. "I don't want that to change."

I smiled. "Me neither." I imagined her reporting a speech by a best man, spouting whatever came into his head after three or four drinks about marital bliss. We'd go national.

She gave me one of those side hugs, her arm around me, pulling my shoulder to hers. Then she took off, leaving her Coke

***

Finding a competent journalist usually requires saying no to a good number of nice people. That's why headhunters work as middlemen in searches for executives. But an entry-level job at a newspaper isn't in the headhunter league. On a hunch, I called the Dean's office in the College of Communication Arts and talked to the secretary. Did they post jobs for their graduates? She said yes, that they ran classifieds in their alumni magazine: "Journalists seeking positions in media, and media seeking journalists. We publish bimonthly."

"What is that? Twice a month or every two months?"

She laughed. "Every two months is what we mean. In fact, we're about to publish."

"Can I send over a classified ad tomorrow?"

"Absolutely. Send it to me personally."

I dashed it off.

AVAILABLE: Reporting position on community daily. Start immediately. 30K range. Growth and excitement along with some tedium. Positive, aggressive, award-winning newspaper. Southern Illinois. Send brief letter and one-page résumé *to: Newsroom Position, Box 202, Stanton, IL 61800*

The woman had told me any letter for me would thus come to them, not to me, and be redirected to me.

So, off went my ad.

I said farewell to Louis, thanking him and encouraging him, then started opening stringers' mail and laying out state pages. The interesting work lay fallow.

***

We had a farewell party at Mr. Ritchie's palatial home for Franklin Harris. I showed up and raised a glass. Bon voyage, you jerk.

From my perspective, Grad was doing good things for the paper these days. Handing Harris his hat was one of them. Jealous and frustrated in his life, Harris had gone sour. I had become the embodiment of his demons, so he took his frustration out on me, going out of his way to slander me every chance he got. Hounding me like the cop in *Les Miserables*, as he had, he'd driven himself a little cuckoo, I thought.

After the toasting round I told Harris I knew he'd failed to report his wife's shoplifting. I told him I figured he'd probably had some sleepless nights over it, so that was torture enough. I told him I wasn't going to pursue the matter for the paper. He nodded without comment.

All was quiet at the party regarding the abrupt departure of Helen Beaulieu, so maybe Grad had dodged a bullet there. Melissa was writing an outstanding series of stories covering the saga of ArtiClear, and apparently had forgotten, at least for the moment, the little mystery of how Helen Beaulieu joined us and then abruptly departed.

SIXTY-FOUR

Résumés started showing up. A couple of them lay unopened on my desk. Looking at them reminded me that I'd lost Abi.

It was hot and muggy in Stanton, with no rain in sight. My only relief was in occasional encounters with Mallory and Allison. Mallory told me she was no longer going with Jock. Good; he hadn't looked like son-in-law material to me. I was glad I'd suggested she not tell him about the possibility of getting Michael Jackson tickets.

***

Caitlin Butler was on my mind, so I called her house. Her mom gave me the Everest baker's phone number. I called her there. She agreed to meet me. I drove down, and met her at the little Everest restaurant. She looked like a bunch of flowers, all fresh and bright.

"I went to Snake Road and got the money," I said. "Soon it will go to the feds. I wanted to tell you that. I didn't want you wondering what was going on."

"Okay."

"Snake Road was interesting," I said. I gave her a blow-by-blow.

"Holy—" She hesitated, seeking a word. "—cow!"

I smiled. "But we still can't talk about it, okay? I just wanted you to know what's happening."

She cocked her head. Her face was radiant. "You're a nice man. You know that?"

Caitlin? Joyful? Feeling blessed?

"Mr. Morrison, I want to tell you something. I told Arturo I loved him and he told me I could move on now."

"I'm happy for you, Caitlin," I said, and I was. But I was bewildered. I am not a spiritual person. Relationships with the dead are comforting to people, I guess, but they're beyond me. Thoughts of Lee Ann crossed my mind. I missed her. But we had no spiritual connection. She was just gone.

"You look good, Caitlin," I said. As I studied her in the light from the window I thought her faith had helped her. It was helping me, too. Reflected happiness.

"I'm learning to bake," she said.

"I'm glad to hear it. But isn't the bakery owner afraid you'll compete?"

"Oh, no! I'm going to work for her."

Driving home I thought about small towns. Nobody would try to upstage the baker.

***

I called Eric and reported on my interview with Chen. While I was now ready to distill possibilities, he was not.

"You haven't got much," he said. "Just some self-serving dramatics."

So, he was in no mood to help. Maybe he was still upset about my attraction to Julie.

"I do know one thing," he said.

"What's that?"

"It may be a coincidence, but the Department of Justice team says the materials in the art center bomb, and the way it was put together, tell them it's identical to the bomb that blew up your car."

"How in the world did they come up with that?"

"The FBI guy on the art center bomb worked the car bomb case."

"Can I print it?"

"Not so fast, Red Ryder."

I smiled. Like Calvin and Hobbs, Red Ryder was a comic strip character. He had a sidekick, Little Beaver, a kid with a headband and a feather who spoke pidgin English. The strip disappeared when I was in high school.

***

A couple of days later I interviewed a young woman named Sarah Albright, an applicant for the job being vacated by Abi. Sarah, a 1982 Stanton University alum, had been a newscaster on a TV station in Indiana. She'd been laid off, and was hoping to work for a newspaper. She was straightforward and pleasant and seemed smart, and willing to dig in and get things done.

We parted company with the mutual assumption that she'd probably come to work for the Post-Times. I did a little checking at the university, talking with a professor of journalism, a guy named Bob Sink.

"You're lucky to get her," he said.

"So why is she leaving the station?" I said.

"Television? They want a slim young maiden. Sarah's beautiful, but she's sturdy.

"Just looking at newsreaders," I said, "I get your point."

"She's smart, sensitive, caring, a go-getter. You'd be getting a winner."

"If your wife dies I'm going to look into the circumstances," I said. "Meantime, I'm going to offer her the job."

***

I penned a note to Lincoln Chen, who had chased me out of his office only a few days back.

Dear Mr. Chen,

The other day in your office I tried to give you some advice. You chose not to take it. I am offering you another chance.

Here's what I believe, what I advise, and how I can help:

I believe you and Bert Long went to Senator Beets' office on May 1, at Mr. Long's request, to get Beets to help abort the licensing bill. I think Beets refused, and Mr. Long shot him. I think Mr. Long knew killing Beets would lock up the bill. With Beets dead on the floor, Mr. Long stole about three million dollars from his safe— money subsequently lost when a luggage door failed on the Piper Cherokee that Julie Wright was piloting carrying the three of you to your retreat near the Ohio River. I believe Mr. Long and Julie Wright planned to use the stolen money to help fund anti-Hispanic activism. Because you were present when Beets was shot and his safe was robbed you are an accessary to murder. Do think about that.

The following is perhaps more speculative, but I believe it.

You've been duped, Mr. Chen. Mr. Long is no more an agent of the Chinese government than I am. He is just a guy who absconded from their embassy in Washington. In fact, they are looking for him. So the "fine" you are paying is a fraud. He just wants your money. I believe he went AWOL from the embassy to be with Julie Wright.

To try to worm his way back into the good graces of the Chinese government, he's decided (with or without their blessing) to stir up some trouble for the U.S. by helping Julie with her anti–Hispanic campaign.

If I'm right, Mr. Long has killed several people to help her with her wrongdoing.

You may wonder what happened to the three million dollars from the Beets job. I have it. Now here's my promise, good for a couple of days, anyway. If you decide to turn yourself in, I will give you the money to take with you. Earnest money, you might call it. That might win you some understanding from the FBI. What I want from you in return is an exclusive interview in which you tell all.

Call me. Come get the money. Try to get the FBI on your side.

Yours sincerely,
Brian Morrison

Writing a note like that had its risks, I knew. But why would Chen show my letter to anyone? Unless, of course, he got himself a lawyer. I wrote "personal and private" on the envelope and sent it on its way.

SIXTY-FIVE

"There's a bunch of emergency vehicles at the Wrights' place."

My 6 a.m. telephone caller was our publisher, Gradison Ritchie. Just out of the shower, I'd wrapped a towel around myself to answer the phone. I glanced out the window. Mist was rising over my scruffy grass. I had been considering taking the day off and maybe going fishing with Spike Rountree. He could sniff the air, test the wind, study the water, and predict the luck we'd have. He and his wife were not so young anymore. She put up with him.

It was Friday, August 14—four days after I posted my double-sealed "personal and private" letter to Chen. He hadn't yet tried to contact me.

"Thanks. I'll be right over," I said to my publisher.

Covering city news—mostly government and crime—for the Post-Times was now the responsibility of Mike Hutmier. But I got to the Wrights' house before Mike did because Grad had alerted the guard shack to my coming, leaving Mike to bluster his way through the gate, waving his press card. Grad wasn't being rude to Mike; he just wasn't clear on who did what.

I looked around for a WSTV truck but didn't see one.

As I watched from the Ritchies' yard, EMT's emerged from behind the Wrights' garage, pushing a gurney. A white sheet was draped over the body, head to toe.

I quit watching and walked over to Grad's house and tapped on the kitchen door. Mrs. Ritchie let me in and got coffee for me. This gesture signaled an advance in our relationship.

"Who's dead?" she said, her eyes fixed on the window.

"Don't know," I said.

Grad, acting like a CEO, waited for me to tell him something.

I told him I'd sent a letter to Lincoln Chen, and recapped what I'd written.

"You wrote that? You must be crazy."

"Look," I said. "We're talking murder, robbery, interference with state legislation, the bombing at the art center. They're all linked. We need to get to the bottom of it. Chen is involved somehow."

This got me a nervous little glance from Mrs. Ritchie.

"I thought this was really about your daughter," Grad said.

I waved my hand dismissively. "Grad, I admit the hit on Allison was like a motor to me. But, look at the whole picture. A little kid sees something falling in the forest. What, three months ago? I get curious and chase the story. Stuff like that is fun for my column. It turns out what the kid saw was a suitcase full of money—maybe three million dollars—stolen from Hamilton Beets' safe. Think about the killings. Beets. The janitor. Then the art center blows up. Lee Ann is killed. The watchman. My car gets blown up. The mechanic dies. The licensing bill gets tabled. That's the key, I think. The licensing bill. That's a hell of a story."

"So why aren't you out there covering it?"

"Hutmier covers the news here in Stanton. I'll help when and if I'm asked."

Mrs. Ritchie was listening, but watching out the window.

"So what's he up to?" Grad said.

I shrugged. "I don't know. Doing his job. We'll know what he's got pretty soon."

My mind was on Allison. I had a flashback of buttoning up the big black buttons on her little gray coat. She could just as easily be one of the dead.

"I'm calling Chief Connors," Grad said.

Grad had all the connections.

"Maybe you want to wait."

We learned soon enough from Hutmier that the ambulance had hauled off the body of Mr. Lincoln Chen. He had been shot dead—a bullet through his heart—in the Wrights' garage. I had a tremor of guilt. My letter got action, all right.

***

That night, having a drink at The Press Club, I ran into Melissa.

"I've been thinking about that woman," she said, "Helen Beaulieu? How did she get hired? Do you know?"

"What do you know about these activists blowing up university buildings?" I said.

"Are you still working on that?"

"Have you read *The Turner Diaries*?" I said.

"The what?"

"A novel, the bible of the white supremacists. The hero flies his plane into the Pentagon. At the end of the story the white patriots are nuking the inferior races."

"I think you're getting fixated on this white-supremacist stuff," she said.

"I don't know," I said. "I thought it was just about Americans having their say."

SIXTY-SIX

Our banner headline on Saturday said, "Lobbyist Slain in Oake Runne." Hutmier's story said Lincoln Chen, an independent lobbyist from Springfield, was shot dead with a handgun at the home of Jeffrey Wright, vice president of the Illinois and Southern Railroad, and that police were seeking "persons of interest."

Over lunch, Eric told me things were not going smoothly in the investigation. They had given up trying to question Wright's wife, Olivia, he said, because she was under the care of her doctor. "Wright's out of it, too. He keeps saying 'Not my fault. Not my fault.'"

"Sounds like a teenager," I said.

"They're an interesting couple," Eric said.

***

I was invited down to the police station for questioning. Apparently, I myself was a "person of interest." I waited a half hour in a metal chair bolted to the floor in a grim room painted industrial green. Lt. Whitt of Homicide sauntered in. With him was another officer I assumed to be the "good cop."

Whitt turned on a tape recorder. "You own a Smith and Wesson .459?" he asked.

"Yes."

"Where is it?" he said.

"Last I knew," I said, "it was in the trunk of my Ford that got bombed at my mechanic's place."

"Is that so? And you don't know where it is now?"

"How would I know?" I said.

"Answer the question."

"No. I don't know where it is. If the FBI hasn't got it, find whoever blew up my car and ask him." Ah, that's what's up. The gun Mrs. Foltz told me about. Somebody used it to kill Chen. The cops have it.

"What have you been carrying lately?" Whitt asked.

"A Baretta I took off a thug named Antony Biro," I said. Admitting to that was going to get me even deeper in the soup. On the other hand, maybe not. "In fact," I said, "I fired it into a mattress in the thugs's house. Before I got the Baretta, I was carrying Eric's ankle gun. I fired that into the mattress, too."

"What was that about?" Whitt looked astonished.

"It's a long story. Ask a guy named Henry Lockmann." I was giving Lockmann up, but we were down to that.

"Who?"

"He runs a detective agency in Springfield."

"Why was he on your case?"

"I think you should ask Mr. Lockmann."

***

My Smith & Wesson .459 was still a problem. But in due course they let me go. No doubt they'd found the two slugs in the mattress, and talked to Eric.

***

I was sure they were now leaning on various family members about the Smith & Wesson, and how it got from the back of my Ford to their garage. I figured sooner or later they'd widen the case to include the chauffeur and then the car bomb.

***

Because Henry Lockmann lived in Springfield and had his office there, the Springfield police interviewed him. According to Eric, Lockmann told them he'd been hired by Lincoln Chen to "investigate" me, and that I had "attacked" his two investigators, whom he identified as Otto Hirsch and Antony Biro.

The Stanton cops got a deposition—that is to say, an oral statement under oath—from Otto Hirsch, taken by Sheriff Tully down in Eagle County, his jurisdiction. In the deposition, Hirsch was quoted as telling Tully he didn't know why I beat him up. It appeared from the transcript that Hirsch managed to keep his mouth shut about kidnapping Abi and me. That was good, because if he'd talked about the kidnapping it would have led Tully to ask Hirsch what happened to the money. Hirsch would have said that I told him, while he was in the hospital recovering from snakebite, that I'd given it to the FBI. And that would have opened a new can of worms, because, in fact, the money was still in the pillowcases in my rental unit.

***

Sugar Beets called. She said Joy Chen had called her, crying her eyes out. "Her life is crumbling," Sugar said. "She's not a bad person, you know."

Like Sugar, I felt sorry for Joy. You fall into a grain-filled silo, there you go. I recalled Eric hammering me about the social imperative, that the whole point of society is helping people in need. "I'll see what I can do."

***

I learned from Eric that the FBI had matched Bert Long's prints to prints on the jacket, and thus were able to identify him as the man the Chinese were looking for.

***

Talk about a wild turn of events. The new director of the FBI, Mr. Wilbur M. Snyder, appeared at a press conference in Washington to hype this. Thus, our little southern Illinois story suddenly got frenzied national attention. The New York Times and The Washington Post wanted to know if Bert Long was to be turned over to the Chinese government, as it demanded.

First, somebody had to *find* Mr. Long.

No surprise to me, he had fled the coop.

SIXTY-SEVEN

The Chinese angle wasn't the only fresh focus in the case. It came to the attention of The Wall Street Journal, and then the Times and the Post, that a vast amount of Illinois state government money was missing.

National papers and the TV networks pressed the FBI director, and the head of the CIA as well, to tell them what was to be made of the Chinese connection. Was the Chinese government involved in a murder and a heist in the U.S.?

Hutmier was cranking out new leads every day. He was bedazzled. He'd become a reporter for a small daily newspaper in flyover country, and suddenly what he wrote was the focus of media attention all over the world. Would I help him? Sure. The angle I was to pursue was the whereabouts of Mr. Bert Long, "a person of interest" in the case.

***

I didn't think I'd have to look too hard to find Mr. Long. In fact, it was likely he'd come looking for *me*. As Lincoln Chen took a bullet and died he was probably waving my letter at Mr. Long. In the letter, I claimed to have three million dollars in my possession—money that Mr. Long would find useful in attempting to escape the clutches of two governments.

Mr. Long apparently had convinced Lincoln Chen that he was a Chinese agent. I doubted it, but that was not the point. Chen thought he was. Whether he was, or was not, was for the FBI or DOJ or whoever to figure out.

I wondered what Mr. Long's lover, Julie Wright, was doing to help him. I could approach her, I thought. Maybe she would somehow lead me to him.

I called her.

"Hi, Brian," she said. "I guess you know about the mess we're in."

"Yeah. I was wondering if you needed some cheering up."

"That's sweet of you, but I don't know what you can do."

"Well, I could soothe your fevered brow," I said. Lenny, my editor, who had taken my press card for getting mixed up with my news sources, would have had squinty eyes about *that*. I myself wasn't sure what I meant.

"I'm really too distracted for any kind of social engagement," she said.

"It was just a thought," I said. "If you need to get away from it all, you know where to find me."

About an hour later, she called me back. "My brothers have lured me out to the quarry to do some diving. I thought maybe you'd like to go."

"Dive at the quarry?

"Sure. It's fun. I've been diving since high school."

I imagined her diving.

"I used to go off ten-meter platforms," she said. "I get similar kinds of heights at the quarry."

"When are you going?" I said.

"We're heading out about two o'clock."

"I'll see you there."

Platform diving was not my idea of fun. But I'd get to see her. In my head I was hearing the reliable voice of my friend Eric: *"I'm afraid you've had a brain transplant. Or maybe you need one."*

I remembered jumping off an aircraft elevator of the Eisenhower. We were having what the navy termed "swim call." The drop was about forty feet. I didn't break my neck. I could do this.

I had to go by the house to get my stuff. Nobody was home. I ran in and grabbed a suit, a towel, and my sandals. Jumping instead of diving, I might look like a wimp to Julie's two brothers. But maybe not. Maybe they jumped. Maybe one of them was married. I'd meet a wife or two.

When I got to the quarry, suited up, Julie and the boys were already there. The boys were down in the water. A woman was swimming with them. Maybe a wife.

Julie was up top, sunning herself on a blanket. She was wearing a one-piece suit. I forget the movie star who made swimming look so wholesome. Esther somebody. She wore a one-piece suit. Julie was slimmer than whoever that was. Smiling at me, she was radiant.

"Hi."

I was in her net, like a tiny fish at Green Lake.

"This suit is not so glamorous," she said, displaying herself for me, "but it's better for diving. I guess it's my security blanket—the kind of suit I wore when I was a kid."

I imagined her as a teenager.

"You look great."

I went to the edge and saw the boys and the young woman clowning around down in the green water below. Pretty far below, in fact. Forty feet? I assumed Julie had graciously waited for me. I figured that in dropping down off that cliff I'd fall about as far as I did off the carrier. I noticed that about ten or fifteen feet down from the ledge the rock face bulged out maybe four or five feet. I could jump to the left. Green water. The way Green Lake ought to be.

Stepping away, I walked back to Julie's blanket and sat down close to her.

"What's going on with the investigation?" I said.

"Oh, boy. What isn't? It was your gun, you know," she said. She smiled. "You didn't shoot him, did you?" She touched my arm as she spoke.

I belched a surprised laugh. "No, no, whoever it was, it wasn't me. And how he got my gun, I haven't the foggiest. Last I knew, it was in the trunk of my car, the Ford. You know, the car that blew up? You didn't do that, did you, by any chance? Blow up my Ford?"

She laughed, touching my arm again. "You're funny. I have no idea how to blow up a car." She stood up. "Me first? You first?"

"Ladies first," I said.

She was slender, with legs that went up about to her ears, and she walked like a model, taking several steps on the sparse grass to the edge of the cliff. For a moment, she satisfied herself about her footing. Then, standing erect, the muscles in her back and butt and legs working a little, she put her arms forward and level and brought them back and pushed up, out, and off, disappearing gracefully, so quickly, under the bright sun.

I got up to look down at her. She had left a small trace in her entry into the water. She wasn't kidding; she could dive.

A single sound behind me, perhaps a footstep, whirled me around. There stood Bert Long, not dressed for water sport. In his right hand he gripped a hunting knife.

"You swim?" he said.

"I can."

He lunged on his left foot, bringing his right arm up and at me from his side, the blade slicing at my stomach. He was too far back. I didn't bite. I did not step back, either. His right leg, centering his power, moved forward, and he swung again—the blade sure to spill my guts. As he brought the leg forward I brought my left leg forward, and I slammed my crossed arms down hard on the lunging forearm, not breaking it, but wrapping my left hand around the wrist, and, still pushing downward, bending the wrist straight back with my right hand. He shrieked. I heard the wrist snap. By this time he was on his knees, head down, and I was straddling his back. I applied sharp and sudden pressure to his extended, twisted arm, breaking it at the elbow. He screamed again. Now he had two breaks, and he was defenseless.

I got off him. He clutched his arm to himself in the dirt, making grunting sounds.

I stepped to the edge, looking down into the green water, and called to Julie. She and the others were treading water, looking up. "You better come up and get Mr. Long," I said. I stepped back from the edge.

I picked up the knife by its blade, using my towel to avoid getting fingerprints on it.

I had been wrong about Mr. Long. I'd assumed he'd try to get the money and then attempt to kill me. Not so. Kill me, then get the money. The plan had been to frighten me off the edge. My falling body would strike the protruding rock. I'd be dead without a knife wound. Pretty neat. I should have been more cautious. Who said what you learn in the military can't be applied to civilian life?

Had the other swimmers been in the game? I doubted it. Cooperative planning would have been too complex in the time allotted, even if the others were complicit.

So, no. Just Mr. Long—and Julie. But, she hadn't been directly involved. In fact, she was never involved—in any of the mischief. Not ever. She was a student of Niccolo Machiavelli, who wrote the book on the management of evil. Our dinner conversation at Tony Spuds crossed my mind. Julie had conjured a madman with a gun suddenly confronting Eric. Eric's situation would be hopeless, she'd said. So she'd presumed I would be on the edge of this little cliff. I wondered if Mr. Long was her Pit Bull.

I got into my car and drove to the gate of Oake Runne Estates, got cleared to enter, and drove not to Grad's house but to the Wrights' place. First I had to pick a garage-door lock. That took a couple of minutes. I searched carefully, but I found neither the Rolodex nor the fliers. I wiped everything down and retreated to my car.

When I got back to my rental unit I called the Stanton police. "Bert Long, you know the name? A person of interest in the Lincoln Chen murder? You're looking for him, right? Look at the hospital. Ask for a man with a broken arm."

I called the FBI office and asked for Agent Walker. He called me back. "I've got about three million dollars for you," I said. I spent five minutes giving him an abridged version of how I came to have it. Then I changed into street clothes.

About an hour later an FBI truck showed up at my rental unit and two agents got out. One of them displayed a gun in a shoulder holster in a way that nobody could miss it. After looking at their badges I gave them the pillowcases.

"Give me a receipt," I said.

"For what?"

"I don't know. How about two pillowcases full of money?"

I called my attorney, Madrid Paris. He agreed to go with me to the police station.

"A classic case of self-defense," Mr. Paris said as we drove. "We give them the knife, I tell them what happened. That's me, not you, doing the talking, darling. If you're expected to say anything, I'll confer with you before you say a word. No way you're going to skip, so they'll release you. The fact that Mr. Long was a wanted man makes you a hero, not a suspect in a felonious assault."

I nodded.

"Remember, I do the talking."

I was in and out of the station and back at my rental unit by nine o'clock.

***

Monday I sat down in the conference room with my new employee, Sarah Albright, and talked with her about what was going on across all fronts.

She had a journalist's attentive eyes, that is to say, different from a cop's.

SIXTY-EIGHT

I went by the house and saw a yellow Toyota wagon in the driveway. Mark the Home Wrecker appeared to be moving in. I didn't want him glomming on to any of my stuff, so I pulled in behind his car to block him and went inside to see what I might want to take out of there. As I headed out the front door with an armload of stuff, I saw Allison standing in the driveway.

"Where you headed?" I asked, dumping my things in my car.

"Over to see Carla." She pointed across the street.

Carla was the little girl who knew the hit-and-run car was blue.

Allison and I stood together by the Chrysler, surveying the neighborhood.

"I've been reading your stories," she said. "Pretty good." She rested a hip against the car, squinting a little. She was watching Carla's driveway. "What were all those Cayce meetings about, really?"

I told her I didn't know. Maybe they were just a cover for strangers, such as the guy from Tintown, coming and going from the house. "You want to get out of the sun?" It was shining down on her.

If Allison had an aura I couldn't make it out.

" I have one piece of news," Allison said.

"What's that?"

"Randy got a date with Caitlin."

I smiled. "Good."

We gazed across the street. Carla was in her driveway.

Allison waved at her and lifted her hip from the fender. She seemed to move with ease. Maybe her little limp would fade in time.

"What about you, Dad? What are you up to? I mean, now that this is over."

"Well, let's see. Um. I have a date with Sugar Beets."

"You do?" She grinned.

I shrugged. "We can put a canoe in right off her dock. But, you know what galls me?"

"What?"

"I never figured out who hit your bike."

"Get past it, Dad." She hurried across the street.

As I watched her go, Carla's mom appeared.

I walked over.

The kitchen was invitingly open and bright.

" I hate to keep calling you Mr. Morrison," she said. "I'm Francie."

"Just Morrison will do."

"First name of?"

"Brian. But nobody uses it."

"I've been seeing that car," she said.

"Yeah."

We chatted, me avoiding that issue.

As I got up to leave I glanced at the refrigerator. Stuck on the door with a bunch of other stuff was a piece of construction paper. On it was a drawing of a blue car and a bike. The bike, behind the car, appeared to be broken. Or so I assumed. You don't know how a six-year-old might draw a bike, let alone a broken one.

The driver of the car had a pointy little black beard. Next to the driver—or in the back seat, maybe, Carla had drawn a person with long, white hair. A woman. Or that's what it looked like to me. I hadn't known they had white crayons.

"She keeps remembering more. I guess she's past the trauma," her mother said.

I lifted a magnet off the drawing, held it up close, and studied the images.

"Carla thinks two people? A man and a woman?"

"So she says."

"May I take this?"

"Certainly."

Drawing in hand, I went out into the sunlight. Allison was sitting on Carla's pink bicycle, walking it along with her feet.

I smiled at the kids, crossed the street, got into the Chrysler, and headed for my rental unit.

SIXTY-NINE

Getting the three million dollars from me got the FBI motivated. They assigned a Belgian Malinois named Spot, whom they employed to find bombs and such, to sniff out traces of explosives in the Wrights' garage. Straightaway she smelled something in the trunk of an old Packard, and then led agents to a wall in the utility room. They took an ax to the wall and discovered a storehouse of materials for the manufacture of homemade bombs. Good dog! Her work pinned the bombing of the art center pretty squarely on Bert Long.

The D.O.J. investigation had gone as our retired expert in the newsroom had said: First get clear on the cause, then try to nail the perpetrators. And they got him! And, given that they knew the bomb was identical to the one that destroyed my Ford, the cops figured he was almost certainly the person who took my gun out of the trunk and used it on Lincoln Chen. So, ipso facto, Mr. Long was charged with murder.

An Airworthiness Op with the FAA confirmed damage to the luggage-compartment door of Jeff Wright's Piper. That pretty well verified the FBI theory that something had fallen from the plane into the Shawnee. And of course they had the three million dollars to support their case.

Given FAA records, Julie Wright had to admit she flew the Piper that day, picking up her dad's friend, Lincoln Chen, and a friend of his, near Springfield, and taking them to Lincoln Chen's retreat. She'd flown that day because her dad had asked her to, she said.

But she had no idea what Mr. Chen and his friend were doing in Springfield, she said. Nor did she know what fell from the plane. She'd just been logging flight time, she said, ferrying them around for her dad. And she absolutely had not been in Senator Beets' office, she said. But was it possible, officers asked her, that she knew who was with Mr. Chen? Might it have been her father's chauffeur? Given her piloting obligations, she said, she paid no attention to who Mr. Chen brought on board.

Nor did she know anything about the art center bombing, she told interviewers. Nor had she been to Huston, where the mechanic died when the car blew up. Yes, she'd invited Mr. Morrison to go swimming, but she had no idea how Bert Long got involved. "He must have been following Mr. Morrison, and caught up with him there." Nor did she see Mr. Long try to kill Mr. Morrison, she told the investigators. As other swimmers would attest, she was in the water at the time.

As to her relationship with Mr. Long, she said she and her father had encountered him in Washington when they went to the Chinese embassy on whatever business her father was involved in. Then, Mr. Long had come to Stanton, for whatever reason, and her father had hired him on as his chauffeur. She didn't know the Chinese were looking for the guy, or what *that* was all about, she said.

Her father, feeling that his daughter's comments to law enforcement officers implied his own possible complicity in whatever was going on, conferred with his attorney, who apparently suggested he just keep his mouth shut. He complied, but was feeling more depressed, my friend Eric told me.

Eric said it appeared to him that Julie had an evil heart.

"What's that?" I said.

"Well," he said, "I heard about it at a workshop; evil hearts are experts at fooling people, crave control, play on the sympathies of good people, have no remorse, and believe they should face no consequences."

My friend Susan Mittleman, the retired psychiatrist, said something equally interesting about Julie. "There's something controlling about her, don't you think? Like this man, Mr. Long, is maybe her sex slave?"

Sex slave? I didn't know anything about that. I suspected something less dramatic—that Mr. Long hoped his lover could get out of the mess, and wasn't too angry—so far, anyway—about her denying their relationship to do it.

"That's part of the same syndrome," Susan said. "He's a sort of puppet for her."

I confess I knew from personal experience that Julie did have a certain power over men.

And I have to say the grocery store rags liked her. They liked stories filled with anxiety, helplessness, the likelihood of doom. Plus, of course, Julie had the looks—and the moral ambiguity. So they got lots of long-lens shots of her coming and going. One of Julie's brothers broke some paparazzo's nose for him. They got a shot of that, too.

70

SEVENTY

Frustrated that Julie was going to get away with it—not just the conspiracy but the deliberate hit on Allison—I told Agent Walker I had information for him. When I got to his office, I showed him Carla's crayon drawing of a blue car, with two occupants, crunching a bicycle.

"The little girl who drew that picture was traumatized for weeks," I said, "but maybe she's ready to talk about it."

"The kid would be traumatized even more in a courtroom," he advised gently.

"I have a letter," I said.

"Seen it," he said.

"Different letter," I said. "It was written by the woman who got killed in the trailer park. You remember the Tintown story—a woman died with her lover in a boudoir shooting? About six weeks ago? A double murder?" I hauled out the letter. "She wrote this letter to her sister the day before she got killed."

Walker looked sheepish. "Yeah. There was a lot going on. The sheriff handled it. They couldn't find a gun. So he was ruling out a lover's quarrel, thinking of maybe a jealous third party. Or, that's where it was when the Beets job went down."

"Yeah. Well, anyway, in this letter"—I handed it to him—"the woman says maybe her boyfriend is mixed up in the art center bombing. She names some outfit in Idaho he was connected with. Not good people, I suspect."

Walker began reading, and I waited.

"So?" he said.

"The guy was about to send out some fliers—mail them to people all over the country—suggesting they come to a meeting of that outfit the woman mentions in the letter.'"

"Yeah. We found the fliers in the garage." Walker looked bored. "We have people planning to put it to Hispanics every day."

"Were they addressed yet?"

"Nope."

"Wait," I said. "Here's the point, I think Julie Wright was behind those fliers. I think she and this guy who died in Tintown were in a 'joint venture,' as they say. She had the money and this 'Liberty League,' or whatever it is, had the connections."

"So?"

"So after the tornado, my colleague, Abi North, figured out what the guy in Tintown was up to. We just didn't know yet that Julie Wright and Bert Long were running things, but we had a bead on the guy. And all three of them knew it."

"Yeah." Walker held the letter but wasn't reading it.

"Okay, so after he screwed up, Julie sent Mr. Long to Tintown to take him out—before he spilled his guts. The timing is right, I think. He gets my gun from the trunk of the Ford. That night, he goes down there and uses it on the flier guy and the poor woman.

Then he uses it on Chen. My gun, both times. Check the ballistics."

I was a little nervous suggesting my gun was used to kill the Tintown people. But I was getting desperate to get Walker's attention. He looked up at me. "The guy screwed up how? Tell me again."

"The tornado blew his cover. Maybe it wasn't his fault, but he was exposed." I pulled out the papers that Abi had picked up after the tornado, and handed them over. "I guess he told Julie or Bert Long what happened, Abi picking up the papers, coming back looking for him. Big mistake. Julie figured the Post-Times would expose the operation, and was afraid she'd be implicated. So she sent Mr. Long down there. The woman happened to be in bed with the guy. So Mr. Long bumped her off, too. She wasn't involved. She was just unlucky, that's all."

"You think Julie Wright engineered it? How would we prove that?"

"What if we could prove they were all in it together?" I imagined the FBI showing the guy's picture to a bunch of Cayce people who came and went from the Wrights' house. Somebody had to have seen the trailer guy come and go.

"I don't care about the dumb mailing campaign," Walker said. "The murders might interest us, though. Why are *you* so interested in all this?"

"I'll tell you why. They were okay with killing my daughter."

"Take it easy."

***

I left Walker's office frustrated over what I assumed was my failure to convince him that the FBI should pursue a conspiracy led by Julie Wright. After a couple of weeks I couldn't resist checking one more time. I called the FBI office. It was my last shot, after which I was going to "get over it," as Allison had urged me to do.

But it turned out I'd lit a fire under Walker.

"We got with the sheriff down there," he said. "The ballistics match. We found out the guy burned a lot of trash behind the trailer, so we went through it. We found out he was burning packaging. We traced it to that outfit in Idaho. They were sending 'furniture' to the guy. It didn't take long to determine that the 'furniture' was things like dynamite, blasting caps, wicks, that kind of stuff. So, bottom line, we're going after the Idaho people. I appreciate the tip."

And there he left me. They were focusing on Our Liberty League, not on Julie Wright.

***

I stewed for a week, and decided one more time to confront Walker.

"You're wearing out your welcome," he said.

"Here's a thought," I said. "I'll give you just this one thought and then you won't see me anymore."

"Okay. One thought."

"Why not offer Bert Long political asylum?

"What are you talking about?"

"I'm talking about saving him from the wrath of the Chinese government. I think he'd love that idea, even if he knew he'd have to tell all and give up Julie Wright. I have a hunch he'd rather do that than go back to China."

"Why?"

"He's no more a Chinese agent than I am. He's caused them a lot of trouble. If they get him back they'll fry him like bacon."

"Sounds like he deserves what he'll get."

"Wait. We could use him. Think about it. He probably speaks Mandarin. Maybe even writes it. Maybe he speaks Mongolian,

Cantonese. I don't know. But here's the thing. Maybe your new FBI director—what's his name?—would like your idea. Offer asylum to the guy? It might make your director look good. And it might make *you* look good to your director."

"And you want?"

"You know what I want. I want Mr. Long to spill his guts about Julie Wright. He'll do it if that's the price of skirting Chinese justice."

***

Bert Long decided seeking asylum was a great idea. In the process, he threw in Julie Wright, just as I'd hoped. He had tried to help her, but now he had a chance to save his own skin. He was answering FBI questions, fully admitting what he knew, what he did, what *they* did, what they planned. He was no more a Chinese agent than I was. He was a rogue profiteer, and if the Chinese got him they were going to squeeze his— Well, you know. He could imagine what they planned for him. So, no, he'd stay in the U.S., thank you very much.

***

Based on Bert Long's testimony, Julie Wright was charged with conspiracy to subvert the Illinois legislative system, conspiracy to bomb the Stanton University art museum, and conspiracy in the murders of several people. They wanted to press for charges involving a terrorist conspiracy, but they needed the Rolodex as evidence and they didn't have it. No matter. She was going to prison for a very long time.

***

I called Henry Lockmann. I had to find him quickly because pretty soon the opportunity would be lost. "I need you to get a Rolodex for me."

"Hey, you threw me in," he said.

"But if I don't press charges, you walk."

"I'm in the middle of this," he said.

"No you're not. All they know is that you're the link between Chen and a couple of thugs that beat me up. If I don't press it, they won't go after you."

"So what do you want?"

"I want somebody to get a Rolodex out of Julie Wright's bedroom. I know a woman who used to be the Wrights' housekeeper. She can give us the layout, maybe even tell you where to look."

***

The Rolodex showed up on my desk. I had guessed right. My theory was, it had been handed like a hot potato to Julie by Mr. Long when he was confronted by the cops in the murder of Lincoln Chen. I didn't want the people who were named on the Rolodex to be bothered forever by either the federal government or the seditionists. After all, what harm had the people done? But I didn't want to be accused by the FBI of destroying evidence, either. I put the Rolodex in a plastic bucket filled with wet cement, allowed it to dry, and dropped the bucket from a canoe into the lake just off Sugar's dock. It would be the first building block of a brush-covered island where fish would congregate and be easier to catch. And of course if the FBI demanded that I hand it over, I'd know where to find it.

"You've saved a lot of people from grief," Sugar said, trolling a green jitterbug behind the canoe. She took a sip from a cold bottle of Genesee.

Some. Not everyone.

After we caught a couple of bass and a nice-sized bluegill, we had dinner at my little rental unit. I showed Sugar Carla's crayon drawing of a blue car crunching a bicycle. "I'm going to frame this and hang it here in the kitchen" I said.

She gave me that remarkable smile.

***

Madrid Paris called me. "You may be coming into money," he said.

"How's that again?"

"The federal government hands out monetary awards for special service. You not only found and turned over three million bucks to the FBI but, even more important, you gave them a heads-up on an anti-government conspiracy."

"Yeah? How much?"

"I don't know. Fifty grand? A hundred? Times three? But they don't just mail it to you. You have to go after it."

"So?"

"I could handle it for you."

"Let's go get it," I said.

ABOUT THE AUTHOR

I've been a journalist, and I've worked for a military intelligence outfit. As the editor of my college daily I covered panty raids, those parodies of the noble quest. I became a newspaper editor in downstate Illinois. I covered the first draft card burning in America as a stringer for the *New York Times*. I became a speech writer, and did that interesting work for 25 years. Along the way I got a PhD and taught clear writing and speaking to MBA candidates. Now, as a free-lance editor, I edit manuscripts—fiction and non-fiction. And I write: My first book, *Run For It!*, won a Royal Palm Award from the Florida Writers Association in 2010.

Cemetery Plot, my second novel, also won a Royal Palm, in 2013. It was the first book in the Morrison series. This book, Avenging Allison, is the second. As you might surmise, I am a slow writer.

You can get a look at me and my work at **www.tombenderbooks.com**

V1/ We dream ... x 3
about you

V2) we dream x 2
about you x 2

V3) Cos your not here
BM and if you were
we'd rest easy
through the night.

V3 we dream x 2
about you
and all the things we
used to do

V4 we dream x 2
about the things we did
when you were kids

M8) If you were here
we'd feel your joy
But you mom got cello's
~~so we dream~~ + love
~~so we dream~~ dream x2

V5) we dream x 2
about yet
Lead + all the things we used
to do